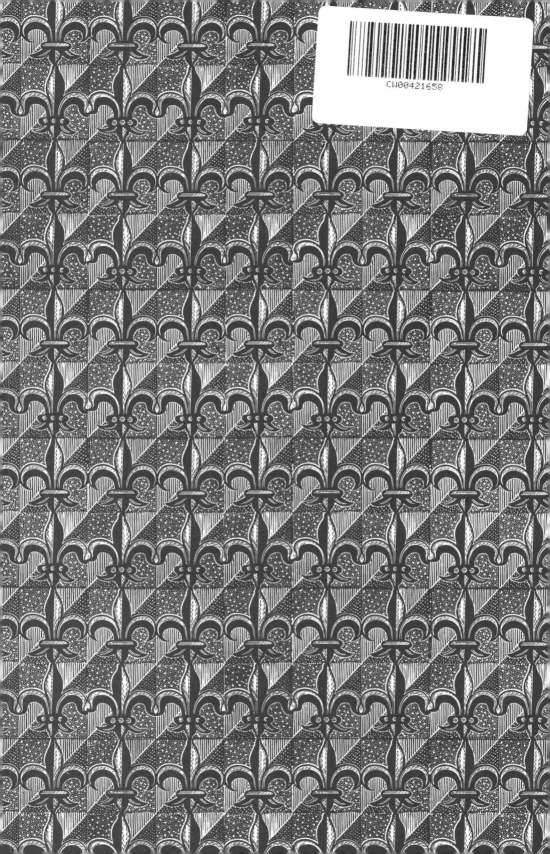

Freeland

FREELAND

J.D.F. JONES

SINCLAIR~STEVENSON

The author and publisher are grateful to
Secker & Warburg Ltd for permission to reproduce
the lines from *Henderson The Rain King* by Saul Bellow
as an epigraph to this book.

First published in Great Britain in 1994
by Sinclair-Stevenson
an imprint of Reed Consumer Books Ltd
Michelin House, 81 Fulham Road, London SW3 6RB
and Auckland, Melbourne, Singapore and Toronto

A CIP catalogue record for this book
is available at the British Library

ISBN 1 85619 492 2

Typeset by ROM-Data Corporation Ltd, Falmouth, Cornwall
Printed and bound in Great Britain
by Clays Ltd, St Ives PLC

To the memory of
James de Vere Allen
(1936–1990)
scholar of Swahili history and culture

'What made me take this trip to Africa?
There is no quick explanation.
Things got worse and worse and worse
and pretty soon they were too complicated.'

Saul Bellow: *Henderson The Rain King*

'A map of the world which does not include Utopia
is not worth glancing at, for it leaves out the one country
at which Humanity is always landing.'

Oscar Wilde: *The Soul Of Man Under Socialism*

'...all this is life, must be life,
because it is so much like a dream.'

Joseph Conrad: *Nostromo*

Author's Preface

On 1 April 1894, twenty-five Europeans of different nationalities, members of 'The Freeland Association', landed on the island of Lamu, on the northern Swahili coast of East Africa. Their intention was to travel into the African hinterland, using the Tana River, and to establish a Utopian 'Freeland' in the vicinity of Mount Kenya.

Their expedition is remembered today only as one of the smallest footnotes of African colonial history. We know that the Freeland movement prospered briefly in Europe under the inspiration of Dr Theodor Hertzka, a Viennese economist and visionary; we know that the Freelanders sent a pioneer party to Lamu; we also know that it turned out to be a disastrous failure.

The details are largely lost to us. In less than three months the expedition broke up in disorder and disunity. The Freelanders never carried their dream into Africa; they were forgotten by the chancelleries of Europe and the people of Lamu as though they had never lived.

One

A hitherto unappropriated large tract of land will have to be acquired
for the founding of an independent community. There remains only
Africa, the oldest yet the last-explored part of the world. Vast
highlands, which unite in themselves the advantages of the tropics
and our Alpine regions, there await settlement. Communication with
these hilly districts situated far in the interior of the Dark Continent
is certainly difficult; but it is a condition necessary to us at first. We
therefore propose that we should fix our new home in the interior
of Equatorial Africa.... We are thinking particularly of the mountain
district of Kenya, the territory to the east of the Victoria Nyanza,
between latitude 1 degree south and 1 degree north and longitude
34–38 degrees east.... It was unanimously agreed to fix the number
of pioneers at two hundred of the sturdiest members of the Society,
the best able to endure fatigue and privation and to face danger, and
every one of whom gave evidence of possessing that degree of
general intelligence which would qualify him to assume in case of
need the whole responsibility of the mission.

Theodor Hertzka: *Freeland: A Social Anticipation*

From the sea, they could not have understood that this strip of
sand and scrub was not the continent but only an offshore
island. From the perspective of the second-class deck of a German
steamship making its first African landfall, they might have assumed that they had arrived. You may say that they were deceived, or at least over-sanguine, or that they deceived themselves
from the beginning. And it is true that the channel between Lamu
and Africa is a narrow one: the bolder farmers used to make their
cattle swim the narrow passage in years when the island *shambas*
had pasture to spare, just as the occasional lion takes the same
route even today, and elephant have been known to see the
afternoon sun glinting on Lamu's mango plantations and have
taken to the water, only to arrive, splashing and bewildered in
the shadows of dusk, to discover that the green paradise has

mysteriously disappeared. But without that creek there would be no Lamu, no town, no ancient history, no rich and secret civilisation. An island, however minimally offshore, offers safety – or at least a comparative safety – from the raiding tribes, the bandits and the *shifta* of the continent. It is therefore not surprising that, since Lamu was – and is – the first port of call in Africa for the dhows which have for centuries been brought on the *kaskazi* monsoon from India and Arabia, it was – and is – behind the frail security of the island that the Swahili traders, since the heyday of the Pate kingdom, have been accustomed to gather their merchandise for export: copra and cashews and tamarind and dates; ebony and mangrove poles; ivory, rhino horn, turtleshell, mother-of-pearl; verdigris and sea-slugs; and, in particular, slaves. All of these they stored in the lower floors of the ornate and beautiful and secret houses which lined (as they still do) the dirty lanes of the unwalled town, until the dhows were ready and the monsoon had turned.

*

They gathered, in the dazzling dawn, on the deck of the *Reichstag*, chattering a little too vigorously, too cheerfully for the hour, perhaps to conceal an understandable apprehension. They squinted at the raw green line of coast that had arrived in the night and was fast accosting them, and their leader produced a chart (which he acknowledged to be his by courtesy of their captain) and offered to explain how they were a degree or two south of the Equator and approaching a jumble of islands set into a serrated coastline of deep, high-tide creeks. Dekker did not join the group as it peered over Dr Wilhelm's shoulder: he knew, without need of Wilhelm's crib, that they had come to an underwater delta belonging to the Tana, which is one of Africa's greater, and lesser-known, rivers. The town, he guessed, would still be hidden from them, behind its safe and shallow and ancient anchorage. There were low hills coming up to the north – it was impossible to tell at this distance and at this time of day if they were mainland or island – and, swinging into view now, dramatic against the dull green of the mangrove swamps, a long and brilliant cliff of high white sand dune. Dekker had memorised the chart while they were still in the Mediterranean. He thought he knew what to expect and yet, like a landlord who has studied his surveyor's sketches and only now

2

takes possession of the estate, its reality was all so strange to him that he admitted his bewilderment and rejoined the others and listened, polite as if he were still in a Bloomsbury tea-party, to Dr Wilhelm's even more approximate description of their landfall.

It was already very hot, even in the breeze of the open deck, and to the west, beyond and above the low and empty landscape, the blue sky was possessed with a great confusion of cumulus, a towering mass of black-bellied storm in waiting, a colossal cornu-copia of cloud which seemed to climb ever higher to demand their attention, their astonishment, even their momentary and untypical silence.

The Rains! thought Dekker in that brief pause. The Rains will soon be breaking, what else can those clouds mean? His compan-ions were suddenly full of exclamation and marvel and a chatter that was intended to restore their equanimity. Dekker said, to no-one in particular, 'You see – the Rains will soon be here! We must not stay on this island too long...'

*

A mile or two from Dekker's bewildered landfall, a dhow was racing north, charging into Lamu harbour from the direction of Shela. Major Rogers, at ease on the rooftop of Charter House in the heart of the town, reached for his telescope and watched the boy – an acrobat – balancing on the outrigger. He stood tall, suspended, triumphant in ragged shirt and scanty turban, hands held high as though posing for the photographers of a later generation. Another boy – the helmsman – was forcing the boat even tighter into the wind. The long plank tilted deep into the ocean, scraping the water like a plane cutting into fresh timber and throwing up thick shavings of spray. The dhow rocked – shuddered – in the tension between the thrust of the single sail and the balancing weight of the boy on his frail beam. It became a challenge between man and elements. It threatened disaster. The boy soared over the waters. He was laughing, Rogers could see through the glass, he was utterly confident: it was not possible for him to fall.

Major Rogers looked down on them from his terrace high above the creek. I love this place, he might have admitted, I cannot deny it. The island has devoured me. It has become my only life. I rule it, and yet I am in turn ruled by its magic, obsessed by its exotic mysteries, enchanted by its daily routines...

All of which may be to overstate a simpler truth. The Major was taking tiffin after a difficult interview with the His Excellency the Liwali (which had not disturbed him as it might once have done, because he had learned that all his interviews with the Liwali would be difficult, that was bound to be the essence of their relationship). Rogers was an Englishman of the tall, thin and angular type. His most striking physical characteristic (concealed beneath a variety of headgear which he alternated according to the time of day and the function of the moment) was that he was prematurely bald – not thinning, or receding, or sparse, or even tufted, but ostrich-egg, billiard-ball bald, his pate shining in a manner disconcerting for his years. He compounded this effect by wearing thick and bushy sideburns, beginning to grey, which – because he did not think of himself as having *hair* – he only occasionally remembered to trim, when he would summon Iqbal Ali who did it with the kitchen scissors. The moustache was similarly neglected and, again, he did not bother to shave carefully – and anyhow he invariably did it in the shadows of early dawn, with the result that his bony and deeply tanned face was often studded with tiny patches of stubble. To complete this tonsorial portrait, he seemed unaware that, as if to compensate for his baldness, his ears and nostrils sprouted vigorous sprigs of hair which he allowed to flourish unnoticed and uncontrolled.

Since Rogers manifestly had no sense of personal vanity – and he had no woman to advise or correct him – it is noteworthy that his kit, which he changed twice every day, was always scrupulously clean, starched and pressed. That was one of the functions of Iqbal Ali, the bearer he had brought from Bombay. The Major preferred to wear trousers, not shorts, not because his legs were thin and knobbled but because he so often needed protection from the thorns and insects of the bush. He chose also to go in shirtsleeves, except that when he approached a village he would feel obliged to don a linen jacket (on those occasions when he was not in his Indian Army uniform) and a thin and ancient necktie. In daytime he usually wore a solar topee, the General Wolseley model which had been so popular in the colonies for years. His bare arms were thin, but the muscles denied that he was an office wallah. His eyes were clear and cool-grey; their expression was also cool, and did not attract affection.

On this first day of April, as the island waited for the Big Rains, he turned his glass away from the creek and down the length of the quayside which lay directly at his feet. Lamu was in the full bustle of mid-morning, aggravated by the season. Two great *booms*, ocean-going, two-masted dhows, had arrived in the night to dominate the harbour, their scarlet and green pennants billowing in the breeze, great painted eyes staring from their prow to watch out for reefs; their cargoes were being loaded and unloaded by dozens of jabbering slaves watched over by haughty Omani captains and by the Company's Indian police. Their arrival suggested that the monsoon had 'turned round', which is to say that it would be raining on the mainland and the dhows were readying for the coming of the south-westerly wind which would drive them back to Arabia and India. With the monsoon winds would come the Rains and two months of near-intolerable humidity and heat.

There would have been another arrival, Rogers remembered, out in Mataoni Bay. The Durban steamer had been expected in the night, and would not risk the shallows of the creek: he remembered how he had stirred in the small hours, woken by a distant siren, to recall that his despatches to Hardinge had been handed to the launch the previous evening. He had no expectations of the mails that the steamer would be carrying from Europe. London would communicate with Zanzibar, and Arthur Hardinge would be so kind as to shield him from that nonsense. He rather hoped that the liner might have brought the saddles and bridles he had ordered eight months ago, but he did not allow himself to be over-sanguine. He had told Gopal Singh to ship out the renegade Swiss missionary on the same boat – Hardinge would deal with the fellow.

A line of prisoners, loosely chained together and supervised by two rifle-toting *askaris*, clattered down to the Customs post from the Fort, chattering with their guards. There were donkeys everywhere, bustling to and fro in a jumble of caravans, the placid creatures lurching under the weight of the double panniers of sand and coral that were destined for the new houses rising beyond the Friday Mosque. The rough earth of the waterfront was splattered with their droppings. One lone donkey camouflaged beneath great hands of green bananas trotted towards the *giriama* women who ran the market stalls beneath the whitewashed walls of the Fort. A dozen paces beyond the jetty an old man, who would never know that he was watched by the Englishman, was struggling to keep his balance in his rough dug-out canoe: it was a desperately unstable craft when the waves are choppy, and he was trying to hoist his goat onto the quay where a party of his friends, even older than he, cackled and mocked at his plight from the safety of dry land. As always, there were small boys splashing and swimming in the filthy water, and scores of yellow-billed kites and pied crows loitered overhead.

Rogers had been appalled, when he first arrived, by the stink of it all, the disorder, the chaos of limepits and mangrove poles and rotting *dafu* gourds, the steep alleys leading up into the town that doubled as open drains. As Hardinge always said, on his official visits from Zanzibar, the place was little better than a latrine and something must be done about it. Rogers agreed: he had not been impressed to be assured that Lamu was an ancient seat of Swahili civilisation, that its purdah women were the finest romantic poets in Araby, that behind the drab, stained walls there was exquisite architecture and plasterwork, that the town's medieval sewage system was the most hygienic in the Tropics, that the Rains always washed the town clean in good time and before the cholera took hold. After his years in manicured Indian cantonments and storm-swept Pathan mountains, he had been too conscious of the filth, the squalor, the smell. And now – a couple of years later – he scarcely noticed them. He responded instead to the people. There was something about the racial confusion of Lamu that delighted him – the jumble of Arab and African, the spectrum of tribes from Somali and Omani and Coast Swahili to Oromo and Pokomo and even Nyasa, the shift from pale to black, sleek to curl, beautiful to grotesque. These were the men whom he observed, of course: he knew nothing of the women, except that the bolder and younger (or perhaps they were the womenfolk of the less conservative men) came out after dusk like flocks of singing blackbirds in their flowing *bui-buis*, the veil held with right hand high across their face in the posture of an ancient Egyptian frieze so that you saw only the eyes, deep with kohl, mocking, glinting, enticing. Major Rogers was not permitted to meet a respectable woman in Lamu and knew he never would; the alternative, in the mud-wattle quarter to the south of the Ismaili Mosque, was unthinkable for a man in his position, and anyhow he had accepted that he was fated to live his life alone. He did not miss women, he sometimes told himself, he could cope with that, but he missed the babies. When he had first arrived on the Coast he could not pinpoint the peculiar difference with India – and then he realised that in Lamu you never see the babies, or the very young children: they are hidden away at home, in the secrecy of the lower storeys, behind the great wooden doors, until the young boys escape onto the waterfront. But the girls you never see.

The townspeople did not know how often, or how carefully, or indeed how affectionately, Rogers looked down on them from the rooftop of Charter House. A few of them understood that although he was technically only the Agent of the Imperial British East Africa Company – and they might well have wondered why a serving Indian Army officer was representing a London trading company – he also had some mysterious authority over the Liwali, who was the official representative of their sovereign, the Sultan in Zanzibar. It was too complicated for most people to grasp. The Sultan had granted the British company the right to 'administer' the ten-mile coastal strip to the south of Somalia some years before, and the British Government had signalled its 'protection' over the Sultan – and the strip – in 1890. But the Germans had claimed a separate protectorate over the 'Sultanate' of Witu, which was simply a stockaded village in the forests of the mainland directly opposite Lamu, until the British, or rather the Sultan's British-officered army, had come and expelled them. The diplomatists in London and Berlin had sorted it out in the end, and now Major Rogers exercised all the authority that mattered from Charter House, his newly built residence on the waterfront, while the Liwali grumbled among his friends over hookahs and halwa and the German traders also grumbled, and privately threatened to do something more than grumble, from the rooftop of their own mansion on the other side of the jetty which they had had the impertinence to name Imperial House. But Rogers controlled the Indian *askaris*. That was why a professional soldier had been sent by the British Government to an obscure tropical island to represent a trading house.

The sun was already so intense that the water that lapped the shoreline a dozen yards from Charter House was no longer twinkling but shuddering with an intensity of reflection and refraction. Across the creek, towards Shela, the low tide had revealed a long and yellow sandbank on which three mangrove trees somehow managed to maintain a purchase, so that even at high tide the dhows could steer by – and clear of – these incongruous bushes which seemingly grew out of the ocean. He saw that there was blue sky beyond Ras Kitau, which meant that the afternoon would be clear and hot, but here in the town it was still heavy and sweaty, the island shadowed by great black-bottomed clouds; there was scarcely a drop of wind to keep them moving on their course inland. Down at the Customs jetty the dhows were parked in a long and orderly line, their bows pointing out to sea so that their angled masts jutted forward like lancers raring for the charge. Major Rogers looked for the acrobat and his helmsman: he had it in mind to give the boy a word of praise, if and when he ever met him. He took up his glass again...

'And who – ' he asked aloud 'and who might *they* be?' and scowled like a country squire who has discovered intruders in the shrubbery.

Iqbal Ali, bearing fresh coffee flavoured with cardamom in the Swahili style, did not feel obliged to reply. Major Rogers, like many men who live solitary lives, and like so many of the European ruling class who lived and worked in exile from their own people, had developed the habit of addressing himself out loud in a muttered monotone; it was a habit that did him no harm in the Tropics, where eccentricity was expected of the lonely white man, but one day it was going to embarrass him in St James's. (He was developing other, less acceptable habits, though no-one in Lamu was going to warn him. A man who lives alone does not need to conceal the belch or the fart; he can slouch at table if he so chooses, or rest his head on his elbow, or read the magazine which has just arrived by steamer and is only six weeks old...)

Rogers said again, out loud, 'Who in God's name?' and gazed long and hard in the direction of the jetty. Then, to Iqbal Ali's surprise, he sighed heavily, rather as a man who discovers he is weary even before the day's work has properly begun. He was remembering again how he had been woken before first light by the siren of the steamer bound south for Zanzibar. Any passengers would by now have been brought ashore by dhow – and yes, there was commotion on the quay beyond the rusted cannon which he had found in the Fort and installed on the waterfront as a mock gateway to his territory (good for nothing but to be straddled by small boys; or else, for the old men, a reminder of Lamu's defiance of the fleets of Pate and Faza and Siyu and – who could remember the tale? – of the Omanis and the Hadhramautis in years long gone). But, he now realised, the commotion was excessive: extra donkeys were being trotted urgently down to the jetty; a small hubbub of drama reached up to the Englishman's hearing so that he scowled again and watched, from the shadow of the verandah, as a group, a throng – no, a *party*, they were laughing, exclaiming, at play – of Europeans emerged in twos and threes and gathered just across from the German store under the Denhardts' battlements. He could see, through his glass, a pale-faced man with long, sparse hair and a thin beard, who seemed to be the leader; there was a younger man, his jacket slung over one shoulder, a bottle in the other hand; a trio of older figures and another couple who were gesticulating at the dhow sailors. Then there was a tall, bearded man, with a shock of pepper-and-salt hair who was gazing about him with serious attention and was somehow apart from the others. Behind him there were a dozen other, anonymous figures, all in the creased and casual cotton of the white man in Africa. And, ye Gods, he could see two women, all smiles and dimples he'd be bound, their long skirts sweeping the filthy waterfront.

'*That*,' said Major Rogers, out loud and intending it, 'is all that I need.' And this time Iqbal Ali understood that he was being addressed and turned back to await his orders.

'Bring my hat!' declared his master. 'And send an *askari* to Gopal Singh – to be here on my return. I shan't be long.'

Later, Rogers was to remember the date.

All Fools Day, 1894.

*

When she looked back on their arrival, for the purpose of the daily journal which she intended to turn into a regular letter to her sisters in Hamburg, the first thing Martha Wilhelm remembered was that little Jimmy Dunn had broken his spectacles. But it was not to be a day when private disasters could compete with such an intensity of communal drama, and from that morning on it was rapidly accepted, without any great concern, that the Englishman was half-blind. Even Martha soon forgot about it, except when she noticed that he squeezed his eyelids into narrow slits because, paradoxically, by restricting his vision in this way he found he could tighten the focus and give a better and crisper shape to the world which had accidentally, catastrophically, become a blur of

9

meaningless colour.

The steamer had crept into the bay on the early morning tide as they gathered on deck, chattering over details of their hand luggage. It was a few minutes after six when the sun came up behind them; the whole arc of the morning sky was flecked, dense, with cloud which rapidly gathered into great masses of vapour. It was too soon for the Big Rains, said her husband; later this month, perhaps. But it is going to be hot, you must take care to protect yourself, my dear. Then there was much confusion. Small, clumsy-timbered dhows had appeared at the stern, manned by a rabble of half-naked boys screaming and shouting, manoeuvring furiously with poles and oars in their efforts to beat off their rivals and win the passengers' custom. Selling and Rabinek, it appeared, were to stay on board to supervise the cargo, twenty tons of it – that will take all day, said the purser, and seemed unhappy with the thought – but it was the good, stalwart Selling who insisted that the others disembark at once. 'Your priority,' he told Wilhelm, leader of the expedition and also Martha's husband 'is to take the vanguard. Lead us into Africa, sir! And who else has the authority to present our credentials to the authorities of the island?'

So over the side they all went, with hurried farewells to the skipper (a dour man who seemed bewildered, even red, when Louise threw her arms around his neck), tumbling down into a heaving, overcrowded vessel, a score of them, and there was much laughter as they balanced themselves between the gunwales and the crew hauled on an enormous, patched and battered canvas triangle that served as the only sail.

'Imagine!' wrote Martha in her first letter, 'There we were at last, sailing quite fast down a long cliff of deserted sand dunes and into a wide creek, past islands of dense green bushes (Mr Salner says they are mangroves), the sun so welcome in our faces, the sea spraying over us until we were all wet through though drying at once in the breeze. And then, after no more than three kilometres or so, there was a small town ahead of us – the first houses were simple things, almost mud and thatch, but then we came to stone houses, some of them several storeys high, climbing up the slope as far as a line of palm trees. There were donkeys on the shore – it was quite smelly, I noticed! – and people in white robes, looking at us as though in surprise and then running down to the big jetty to meet us, where we could see some men in

10

uniform, soldiers or policemen, it wasn't clear.

'Almost before I knew it we were standing on the quay – I was holding Julius's hand and we could hardly believe it, he was bubbling over with excitement and delight. The others too were so *happy*, they were like children arriving at a birthday party.... Perhaps Lieutenant Stokkebye need not have opened a bottle of champagne – he must have had it ready for the occasion, and I remembered that Julius had warned us that the natives do not approve of European drink, but it was such a natural way to celebrate and we all swigged from the bottle, even Julius who, I noticed, was wondering whether a speech would be appropriate. Some of the others seemed to be waiting for him, but I was shy for him so I said to him quietly, "Not now, Julius, let us wait a little and take possession of our land." That was when I noticed that we were being observed from the nearest balcony by a very large European gentleman, who looked *unmistakeably* German (but not at all out of place). When he saw me he bowed, very formally, directly to me, and said something to the companions who must have been in the shadow behind him. So at least we know there are other Europeans on the island – and of course there are the English, too, as we soon found out.

'We were strolling down the – what shall I call it? – the *corniche*! (That's hardly the word to describe so *scruffy* a seafront.) Scavenius, the young Dane, had removed his hat *and* his jacket and was jesting with the children, who had fallen in behind us and were making a merry din. There was a big fort on our left, with the gates closed tight, and a sort of market area, with little clusters of vegetables and some strange fruit arranged on the bare earth, and ahead of us a large new-looking building with a flag flying above the front porch. "That," said Salner to my husband, "will be the English – the IBEA Company. It would be wise to stop there and ask about Customs regulations and our stores..."

'But an Englishman was already coming towards us, from the house. You couldn't mistake him for anything but an Englishman. He was tall and thin and wearing a sort of tropical army uniform, though without a gun. He did not look at all welcoming, but I knew that we had permission from his government to be there, so what could he do to us? Nothing. He did not raise his solar hat, he did not even respond to our excitement and happiness with a smile or a welcome.

11

'We stopped, in a group, in front of him. We were all so *happy*, so triumphant, but I noticed that my colleagues had become a little less *noisy*. The man stared at us: at Julius, at me; at Stokkebye, who was still holding his bottle; at Scavenius, who was looking very hot, and Hans Salner, who was carrying all our documents; at Gleisering and Ducoffre and Schmidt and little Felix; at Goddfrey and Bosanquet, who had chosen to make a joke of it and dress up for the occasion; at Mr Dekker, very preoccupied; at Jimmy Dunn, who was too blind to recognise his own countryman; at Louise, who had her arms around me and her husband.

' "And who," said the Englishman, "might you be?"

'He did not sound hostile, but he didn't sound welcoming either. He sounded very English.

'Julius took a step forward and inclined his head with a proper formality. His English is really very good. "I have the honour, sir, to represent the International Freeland Association."

'The Englishman looked as blank as the walls of the grey stone houses that lined this part of the water front.

' "We are the Freelanders," called Scavenius, whose English is also very confident.

'And Louise smiled her sweet, wide grin – "Sir!" she cried, in her charming accent – "We have come to Freeland!" and she made a deep curtsey in the dust of the quayside...'

Two

The wealth of the civilised man is not the product of his own individual capabilities but is the result of the intellectual labour of numberless previous generations, whose bequest belongs as much to the weak and helpless as to the strong and capable.... All our brothers and sisters have a right to share in the common heritage... to claim a fraternal participation – not merely a charitable one, but one based upon their right of inheritance.

Theodor Hertzka: *Freeland: A Social Anticipation*

Major Rogers loved the town in the hour before dusk. The sun fell back behind the hill and, for the first time in the long day, the seafront rested in cool shadow; then the breeze would pick up again off the sea so that the dhows bobbed and balanced and jostled against the jetty as the people came out in their scores and took their regular places, the elders on their usual stone benches, fingering their beads as they shook the sleep from their dazed eyes, the young men preening and plotting (but with no danger to it), and Rogers would promenade up and down – once up and once down – exchanging formal greetings with the dignitaries, allowing his favour to be glimpsed when he paused to make time for an extended word, and ignoring the occasional wit or mischiefmaker.

Invariably he wore his topee, a reminder to all of his background in India and also, he did not doubt, of his imperial authority as representative of the old Queen, whose portrait, he had been gratified to discover, was displayed in many of the shops and rather more prominently than that of the Sultan: he had enjoyed pointing this out to the Liwali, who could do no better than rejoin that such representations were not encouraged by their religion. It was time, Rogers had decided, to introduce a little more of the Indian style into this African informality. He had a plan to start a modest daily ceremony here on the waterfront, when the flag would be lowered with a proper respect, as it was everywhere else in the Empire, at sunset every evening, just before the evening *muezzin* called the menfolk to prayer. It would be particularly appropriate in view of Hardinge's hint that HMG was about to take over administrative responsibility for the island as it had done for the Witu district nine months ago; Rogers had made it clear that he wished to stay on, assuming that that would simply mean changing his title from Company Agent to some degree of Consular Officer – the reality would not change, whatever the Liwali might hope.

Rogers did not think the natives would object to standing for a moment of silence and respect. He did not see why there need be any local disaffection for the principle of imperial authority, though he would always be prepared to listen to any complaint about the detail of the implementation of that authority by its human and therefore frail servants. He did not fear a contradiction in this: he sometimes flattered himself that he was not disliked for himself, though he was too experienced – too wise – a man to deceive himself that his authority was equally welcome, conceal it though the natives might with flattery and subservience.

Perhaps he also enjoyed that evening hour because he knew that Iqbal Ali would be preparing his bottle and his pipe. He was punctilious about total abstinence during the daylight hours; like many an Englishman in the Tropics, he would say that he had learned that discipline in this matter was as essential as drill to a platoon. When he had first arrived at the Company's new head-quarters building beyond the Customs gates and taken possession of the first-floor verandah which looked out over the channel, conscious that this strange place could be a home to him, knowing in his heart's instinct that it would do fine, he listened to the din of the evening *muezzin* from the Friday Mosque, just one street's width behind his chair, and resolved that he would not drink until that dusk call to prayer had sounded. That was his resolution. There were guests who had said, 'Look, the sun's behind the hill, surely that's all right now,' (though he never denied his guests beer or brandy at whatever hour), but Rogers had chosen another of the rules of his daily life. 'Where the hell is that man?' he would mutter after a bad day with the Liwali, when he could have sworn that the prayers were late, but Iqbal Ali knew that he must wait until the first quavering notes of *'Allah! Al akhbar...'*

14

That evening – it was a Thursday, when the call to prayer is particularly ornate and extended (one mosque on the hill had a man with a near-falsetto of extraordinary delicacy and feeling) – the Major lingered on the quay, down by the mangrove stacks. He was working out where best to place a new flagpole for his little ceremony. The tide was high and the water choppy. The boats were lurching and plunging, bumping into the mangrove poles – the *boriti* – that lay in loose and jumbled piles in the seawater, leaking a red-brown juice into the stream like a corpse draining blood from a hundred wounds. Later, after many months, they would be hauled ashore, sorted by size, and stacked, ready for the ocean dhows to take them away with the monsoon winds to the timberless wastes of Arabia.

Yes, there would be a nightly ceremony of the lowering of the flag. The sun does not set on the Empire, he should have thought of this before. The *askaris* must be trained. What to do for a bugler? He was satisfied with his Indian police. They had handled the latest Witu expedition with commendable energy and enthusiasm – so much so that Subedar-Major Gopal Singh had told him that his men had been reluctant to come back to Lamu before settling with Suleiman Kimenya. They had been bloody cross, said Gopal Singh, that the rogue had slipped out of their hands and into the Forest. Tell them we'll get him next time, Rogers had replied. Tell them we'll deal with Suleiman's new stockades at Safareh the same way we dealt with the nonsense of Avatula and Fumo Omani last year. Very soon now: as soon as my scouts report back...

The flagpole just this side of the gates, he decided. Everyone to be upstanding while the bugle sounds. One platoon, rotated each night, before they relieve the Fort. The chappie who hauls down the flag gets it as a commendation. And we must be careful to finish before the bloody *muezzin* starts up.

*

The day started with cloud in the east, soon to be blown inland from the ocean by the freshening monsoon. The clouds were busty, grey, with a promise of rain; they bundled together, the hot early sun went out, and the people of Lamu looked up and debated whether the Rains were about to arrive. That morning Dekker had spotted wet drops on the terrace floor, large as pennies but no more than a sovereign's worth in total. After a week on the island

15

he did not trust his judgment and called the servant. 'It's too soon for the Rains, bwana,' said Bakari. Later this month perhaps. But today will be hot. And so it was. The *kazi* had chased the cloud into Africa by mid-morning, where it piled high above the palm trees of the *shambas* behind the town, and the sky, now clear as a celadon plate, turned pale and beat down upon the island as the shadows in the narrow streets twisted into right angles and everyone retreated into the safety of the houses.

It was in that time of blaze and emptiness that a *jahazi* dhow arrived from the south and tied up, not at the main jetty but next to a rough infill of sand and stinking rubbish and steep piles of coral-rag (jagged as Neolithic flints, betraying that this was a stone not of the earth but of the water, wrested with crowbars from the ocean creeks at low tide, humped on the bleeding shoulders of Major Rogers's convicts from the Fort: the deeper the water the better the rag, it used to be said, and there may be a truth in that). Next to these symmetrical pyramids of rough rocks were bundles of *makuti* piled high on the wharf, freshly landed from Matandoni and the outer islands – rough-sewn strips of the leaves of the coconut palm, bisected and lashed together, ready either to be laid like thatch on the roofs of the mud-and-wattle houses that were always sprouting, and crumbling, on the southern edge of the town, or – the superior quality – destined to provide a rich man's shelter over his stone-and-rag mansion until the day he discarded tradition and bought a dozen sheets of the new-fangled corrugated iron.

The dhow touched land deftly and gently, the sail collapsed, and one of its occupants leaped ashore, looked around as though with the pleasure of a returning and familiar visitor, and strode off without hesitation and without apparent instruction to his crew. He was a white man and, on a rope, he hauled a dog to which he gave no sign of affection. The others, bare-chested and turbaned, promptly arranged themselves for slumber in the shadow of the mast.

The newcomer was dressed in the conventional African style of the day. His hat was floppy and broad-brimmed, his jacket was loose linen, creased and not of the cleanest, and his boots were high, soft and serviceable. He carried no weapon. He was tall and well-built, and he sported the reddish tan of up-country, not the darker tan of the Coast, and he would have been somewhere in the mid-thirties. If the Germans had observed his arrival from their

16

rooftop – and if they had not recognised him already – they might have guessed that he was a familiar of the island and that he was happy to be back.

Indeed, he paused to glance up at the Denhardts' mock-battlements, just as he stepped aside to look into the Customs Yard (whether to inspect its contents or to look for someone in particular). Once, he accosted a couple of local venerables and inquired of them in fluent Swahili. He mentioned Bwana Rajees, and they gestured in the direction of Charter House; when he thanked them, in the ornate courtesies of their language, they responded in kind and gazed after him benevolently as he strode down the waterfront, though they muttered darkly about the dog. He might have been whistling, quietly, a happy tune.

*

Major Rogers said, 'But it's Dugmore! My dear fellow, come in... make yourself *entirely* at home!'

The tone and idiom were intimate, though an authority on late-Victorian etiquette might not have been entirely convinced of the authenticity of the greeting.

Captain Dugmore (Retd.) produced an explosion of laughter and delight, pointing his right arm in the direction of Rogers's skull (though not seeming to think it necessary to shake his hand), tossed his hat onto a vividly-painted Swahili sofa, and deposited himself in a long and low cane chair with an exaggerated sigh of exhaustion and relief. He paused only to fiddle with the extendable arms of the East Indies chair so as to hoist his legs onto the wooden slats which served to expose his lower parts to any breeze, and lay back like a patient awaiting internal examination. He was tall and gangling and his limbs seemed uncoordinated: his every gesture was excessive, signalling energy, enthusiasm, goodwill. His face was chubby and jovial, his moustache worn in a walrus exuberance; his tangled crop of brown curls was beginning to recede. He was evidently strong and athletic, though the energy of his every movement suggested, misleadingly, that he was clumsy: in fact, as Rogers knew, he was a crack shot and a skilled and silent tracker. There was still a hint of the puppy in him, a reminder that the man had not yet arrived at his serious and effective maturity. Rogers remembered him as an enthusiast for everything; Dugmore was not a cautious man.

Major Rogers's office, though not on the top floor, was wisely left open to the elements; the French-style windows were rarely sealed and the inner doorway was never closed, not even on the rare occasion of the Liwali's visits. The furnishings were spartan in the British colonial style: a wide and elegant oak desk of the type beloved of provincial solicitors; a portrait of the old Queen on the wall behind the desk; a couple of dubious watercolours, whether of Lamu or Suffolk no visitor could be sure; a very ornate black ebony Swahili throne, encrusted with ivory embellishment, unuseable of course, and impossibly uncomfortable; a long table strewn with maps, chitties, glasses, bundles of tag-eared documents, a half-open box of cartridges, a litter of maps; in the corner a gun rack, conspicuously barred and padlocked; a teapot and a single cup on a small table; a good Indian carpet before a Swahili day bed strewn with red and silver cushions.

'You'll take lime juice? *Chai*? Or something stronger?'

'Something stronger,' said Dugmore, rather faster than he intended. 'I reckon it's over the yard-arm.'

Rogers called a phrase in some strange language, and an Indian servant appeared immediately. Beer was requested, as well as lime juice. Through the wide windows and beyond the balcony Dugmore could see the black bar of Manda Island and remembered that in Lamu you never see the open ocean, you are trapped between Manda and the mainland. He watched the creek turn grey as a cloud darted in front of the sun. There was no doubt that the Rains were building up: the sky was heavy with clouds which moved ever more slowly across the islands to stack themselves in the west.

'I hear that you've left the service,' Rogers was offering.

Dugmore nodded vigorously. 'I was bored to death – and then they offered me the choice of Aden or a posting back to Chittagong. Fair enough! I can't stand the Colonel, and his wife couldn't stand me. But I *like* Africa, Rogers – I don't know what you feel about this place but, hell's teeth, after the Punjab I *like* it, and what's the point of moving on when you've found a billet that suits you.'

Rogers offered no comment. It would have been hard to guess how well these two men knew each other.

'So I told the Colonel what I thought of him – not to mention his lady wife! – and I decided to claim my freedom. I thought I'd do a spot of shooting in these parts before I gave any serious thought to *what's next*, if you see what I mean. No hurry, don't you see...'

Was that a reminder, Rogers wondered, of their social difference? Dugmore, he vaguely remembered, came from a Sussex family, younger son etc., but no disaster in that, there'd be no shortage of the readies – wasn't there an uncle at Westminster? He could have been in the Guards but had chosen a more exotic world. An altogether different background from his, but no matter, no problem...

'No shooting worth having round here,' he offered. 'They all tell you *nyambo teli* – lots of game – and when you get there you'll find nothing but bushbuck and mosquitoes and a few warthog if you're lucky.'

Dugmore said, 'I'm not particular, Rogers, whether the specimen has four legs or two. So long as it's sport.'

There was a long hiatus. The Indian servant appeared, hovered, vanished. The habitual hubbub of the waterfront was distant, muted. Rogers smoked one of his Indian *bidis*. Dugmore lay back on the Dutch chair and allowed himself another exaggerated exhalation of relaxation and relief.

'God! I like this place. I don't even mind the stink. I envy you this job – d'you realise that?'

'You must be joking.'

'Not for a moment. I always say that it's the best posting on the Coast.'

'It has its compensations.'

Dugmore said, 'Busy enough, are you? Enough to keep you occupied? Haggard used to say the place was a bit of a graveyard.'

'Haggard liked to exaggerate. Like his brother, whose books I hear are all the rage these days. And he was here in rather different circumstances. We've had various developments on the mainland since his tour.'

Dugmore offered, very tentative, 'In that context, I had a word with Arthur Hardinge when I was in Zanzibar the other day...'

'He sent you here?'

'Now relax, my dear chap. *Of course* he didn't send me here. I told you, I'd just put in my commission and called in on Government House to make my farewells – offer my salaams, that sort of thing. We got talking about this and that, and he told me about the Witu business. Said some very positive things about you, if you must know – and about your chaps.'

'Witu is under control, Dugmore. I was there last week and you wouldn't recognise it. The stockade has been burned to the ground. Even that scoundrel Kimenya is in retreat, and I'll settle him for good on my next sortie.'

'But the Forest isn't – entirely – under control?'

'Hardinge told you that?'

Dugmore shrugged. 'Just permit me to ask. Is the Forest under our control?'

Rogers said, 'If you must know, and since you evidently do know, *of course* it isn't under control.'

'And the Germans? Our new friends, the *Wa-Germani* as the locals say?'

'Let's just say that they are on their best behaviour. They are very polite to me when we meet in the dirt track that passes for the main street in these parts. You must have walked in front of their house just now – the place with the ridiculous battlements, near the Post Office. Did you see any sign of revolution?'

'I wouldn't trust them an inch, any more than you do. Especially if it's the same Liwali as when I was here last.' (Major Rogers allowed himself to make a face; he nodded.) 'And his brother? *He* used to be a real shit.'

'Abdullah? Yes, the brother's still here. I won't disagree with you.'

'So,' said Dugmore, 'here I am, looking for a spot of sport, that sort of thing. Fancy-free, as some might say. Rogers, I'm bored! I need to forget the Colonel. I need an adventure or two, and you're the man to show it to me.'

'You flatter me, Dugmore. This is the end of the world, you must surely know that.'

Again a silence, though not unfriendly. Dugmore reached for his glass, found it empty, and gestured. Rogers muttered 'Iqbal Ali,' and the tall Indian was there at once, a new bottle foaming in his hand.

'I don't want to insist. Just thought I'd let you know I'm in your parish. I've got a small arsenal in the dhow if you want me to go – hunting.'

'This place is stiff with guns already. You wouldn't believe it, but another hundred rifles turned up this week.'

'For you? Or for the Liwali?'

'Of course not. I've got to manage on the Company muzzle-loaders and the Liwali isn't allowed a pea-shooter! No, they came in with our newest neighbours. One hundred brand new Werndls straight out of Hamburg if you please, with 5,000 cartridges.'

'Where are they now?'

'I confiscated them at once, what do you think? Slapped them into the Fort and gave their headman a chitty. He was flaming mad at first but I said to him, "What do you want with them on Lamu? I'll happily give them back to you when I see you sailing to the mainland." '

Captain Dugmore, perspiring gently in his Dutch rattan recliner chair, said, 'Rogers, forgive me – but what? – who? – are you talking about?'

The two Englishmen, having avoided all personal, let alone emotional, contact until that moment, for the first time glanced at each other, eye to eye. It was only a fleeting contact, but they were both entirely conscious of what had happened. Dugmore would say afterwards that that was the moment when the idea must have been born in the policeman's mind.

*

Julius Wilhelm was in his new home, drafting his weekly report to Dr Hertzka. He had explained the success of the voyage, the transfer of his Freelanders to various houses in Lamu Town, the difficulty of operating without a launch (which had not yet arrived from Europe), the imminence of the Rains, the existence of a sand bar across the Tana River. He assured Dr Hertzka that all was well within the Association, that morale was high, that everyone was eager to attack the mainland as soon as conditions permitted.

He did not propose to mention that the English authorities were unwelcoming, that Free House was still overcrowded, that Lieutenant Schindler had left them at Aden to return to Vienna after a disagreement with Hans Salner, that Reinhold Gleisering was showing signs of moral if not mental decay, that Felix Thomas must on no account be trusted, that Stokkebye seemed to be a drunk, that Emil Ducoffre was driving them all to total exasperation, that James Dunn had broken his spectacles. He did not intend to add that Sasse had just wasted an hour of his time demanding that he allow him and Hassemer – and of course Frau

21

Sasse – to take private accommodation, 'since, Julius, we seem to be resigned to an unfortunate delay in this absurd place...' He did not admit that he had been waking in the night, long before the island's cockerels and the first muezzin, in a seizure of panic: while Martha lay beside him under the mosquito net breathing gently in the sleep of the just, he sweated heavily, unnaturally, into the pillows, his heart pounding, a weight pressing high in his chest, his brain thundering with the clash of problems, apprehensions, indecision; he longed for the first light of dawn, the first rustle of the morning breeze off the sea, which would allow him to extract himself – oh, so carefully – from the net and the sheet and his sleeping wife, to climb up onto the roof and stare at Manda and rally himself for the day.

'All is well,' he assured the visionary in Vienna. 'We await the second shipment of stores with impatience and shall thereafter set off for the mainland – no, for Freeland! – without further delay...' He thirsted to report to Dr Hertzka the coming of the Rains. Until they arrived, he knew that they could do nothing. The Rains should have arrived earlier. Or later. It was a simple error of timing – how could they have known this as they made their plans in the gentle drizzle of the Viennese winter? That morning, as he had crept from Martha's side, he thought he could smell the moisture in the dawn air, and indeed there were dark storm clouds draped along the horizon, blotting out the rising sun; there was even a particularly black cloud sitting on top of Manda, but it did not rain, it refused to rain. Instead, despite the regular whiff of breeze from the south, it was hotter, more humid, than he had ever known it.

From the porch, two floors below, he heard the cry that signalled another visitor – 'Hodi!' – to which there was, he gathered, a formal response, designed to ensure a pause in which the womenfolk could be hustled into their own quarters. It reminded him that he must really find time to learn more Swahili, as his dear wife was always urging him: she had worked at her grammars so hard on the boat, and he was proud to see how she was already so fluent with the servants. It was not a difficult language, she had promised him, and Saidi was so patient with her mistakes that he would be the best of tutors for Julius while they sat out this enforced delay on the island...

It was the same Saidi who ushered in the visitor – a tall and well-built man in early middle age and, thought Wilhelm, most evidently self-assured. A stranger but apparently well-disposed: a white man, of course, casually dressed in rough cotton, sporting a heavy moustache, and – Julius had the wit to notice Saidi's distress – hauling behind him a villainous pale and plump dog on a leather leash. Julius, who did not share his wife's affection for dogs, found himself sympathising with Saidi's Mohammedan sensitivities.

'My name is Dugmore,' said the intruder in English.

'Yes,' replied Wilhelm, and bowed formally. 'Wilhelm!'

The stranger seemed to struggle to explain himself, as the dog snorted and sniffed at Wilhelm's trousers as though considering whether he might cock a leg.

'I wonder... I was hoping to find you.... Happened to be passing – you *are* the International Freeland Association? Of Vienna? And London – and Paris – and of course Berlin?'

'Yes, yes,' said Wilhelm with a touch of impatience. He was not a curious man by character, and did not bother to wonder who the stranger might be.

His visitor seemed to struggle with an extreme diffidence so that Wilhelm, notwithstanding his incuriosity, found himself tempted to reassure him, put him at ease, anything to dispel this English hesitation. 'You see, Professor Wilhelm – ' (Julius did not correct the error) 'I rather wondered if it was permitted – if it might be possible – you see, I've heard so much about your organisation, your founder, your *ideals*. It must be strange to you, but here I am, just a wanderer, a bit of an adventurer, you know, and fate has brought me to this island at the same time as you and – well, frankly, I wondered if there was any chance of *joining* your Association – or at least, if that sounds too presumptuous, *associating* myself with you and your colleagues. If you see what I mean...'

Wilhelm said, 'But I don't understand. We are a pioneer group of Freelanders, sent from Europe...'

'Yes, so I gather – all of you specially chosen, hand-picked, I'm sure. And I'm just a traveller. Always looking for a spot of sport – adventure, that sort of thing. Then I heard about your expedition – your *mission*, I should say. You're aiming for Mount Kenya, aren't you?'

Wilhelm, still bewildered, could only nod.

23

'Know that part of the world quite well. You see, I've been in the country for several years. Done a lot of hunting. Then I used to have a commission...'

'A British officer?' demanded Wilhelm in some alarm.

'No, no!' protested the stranger, and seemed distressed to hear it. 'Chucked it in long ago. Fell out of favour, if you see what I mean – *they* fell out of favour with me...' He chortled, abruptly, like a man surprised by his own memories, and Wilhelm found that he was grinning, inanely, in return.

'You see – ' said the tall Englishman, as though to begin a confidence – but then he seemed to change his mind. 'Who's in charge here?' he demanded, as though it might concern him considerably. 'Who's running the island these days? Who's the Company man?'

'He's an Englishman,' proffered Wilhelm idiotically, as he noticed at once. 'A thin man – dark, with a bald head. Not very friendly, I regret. His name, I think, is Major Rogers.'

'Ah, Rogers!' declared the visitor, in a tone of instant dismissal, as though the matter need concern him no more. 'Frightful stick! Knew him years ago in Ooty. Heard he'd been posted to Zanzibar. You'll get no change out of him...'

Wilhelm was still struggling to master the idiom. He was also wondering whether he had the power to co-opt members – in effect to open a Lamu chapter of the Association. Dr Hertzka had clearly intended this to be a pilot expedition, and there had been no thought of a larger party. On the other hand, the Doctor had always emphasised that Freeland would attract new adherents by the thousand – indeed, the million – once it was seen to exist, to have its territorial reality. Now they were in Africa, he and his vanguard team, on the very frontiers of Freeland, so to speak, and their first recruit was sitting before him, offering himself as a very omen of success.

Wilhelm became aware that he and his visitor had been interrupted without the benefit of the local courtesy of a *hodi*. Sasse was back, and no longer alone: with him he had the tedious Hassemer – Wilhelm's charitable heart sank as he saw the wrinkled Frankfurter forehead of the Sasses' intimate friend and, he suspected, their financial supporter – and the formidable Madame Sasse (he was never sure whether, with her Alsace origin, she saw herself as German or French – not that these petty things would

24

figure in Freeland). He had learned enough about Frau/Madame Sasse on the outward voyage, with the guidance of Martha, to guess that the wife was not one to urge patience on a normally patient (and older) husband. Another thought came to Wilhelm as he observed the undeniably vivid style of her garments that afternoon. She must be agreed to be an attractive woman, that he could acknowledge, and Martha had frequently offered him the thought. Therein might lie another problem. He did not wish to be uncharitable, and he did not consider himself to be burdened with the morality of the bourgeoisie – but was Madame Sasse going to be an entirely positive influence in a house occupied by a score of single men? He tried to banish the thought – Martha would not have sympathised – but he knew that he was right. Perhaps it would be a good idea if the Sasses did have a separate household, at least for the first weeks before they all set off for the mainland.

Sasse was in a flood of complaint and demanded the leader's attention. How – he asked – was he supposed to find a lodging? Free House was ridiculously overcrowded, that had been agreed between them. So how had the Wilhelms (there was surely some implied criticism here) managed to find this charming house for themselves – look at it! So cool and spacious, so full of *air*, so much more tolerable than the stifling cellar you have assigned to me and my friend Hassemer. Was he supposed to go cap in hand to Major Rogers? He did not speak the local dialect – perhaps Frau Wilhelm could help, he had heard that she was very fluent.

The tall Englishman coughed, murmured indistinctly, took – as he put it – the liberty of intervening. 'Allow me, gentlemen,' he proffered, and at the same time managed to suggest an exquisite embarrassment. 'I used to have some knowledge of this miserable town. Perhaps you would come with me and we shall investigate the matter. A house, you say? Not too large, I suggest, but as high as possible in order to maximise the wind at this time of year.'

Sasse looked dubiously at the stranger and then at his leader. Wilhelm nodded enthusiastically and saw that Louise Sasse was tickling the dog's furrowed brow, apparently to its ecstatic satisfaction. 'Most kind,' declared Wilhelm loudly, and led them to the door as though to brook no debate. 'Most kind of our new friend here!'

The Englishman stood back from the entrance and signalled to Louise Sasse to lead the way. He was looking at her with un-

25

disguised appreciation. She was slim, light as a dancer, always –
he guessed – in mid-gesture; her mouth was very wide, the lower
lip was thick and cracked, her brown eyes enormous, outlined in
kohl, her hair raven black, cropped short and curling onto a thin,
high neck; she wore gold rings on her hands, her arms, her ears,
her neck, so that they threatened to set up a clangour whenever
she moved.

'Allow me, madame – ' and he held out his hand. It was
tentatively judged and, she decided, done with undeniable charm.
She took it in her painted hand and allowed him to raise her fingers
to his lips while the dark eyes held hers and seemed to sound a
note of mockery, or at least of amusement.

'I have observed you on our local *corniche*,' he said. 'The name
is Dugmore. Captain Dugmore, Retired. I hope to be recruited to
your Freeland and have been lodging my application with your
distinguished leader.'

'You must allow me to propose you,' said the woman, and smiled
at him; full lips, white teeth, brown skin. 'I am sure that my
husband, and our dear friend Hassemer, will be happy to be your
seconds.'

*

The Major admitted that he was weary. It was later than he
normally allowed, the sky over Manda had turned mauve, even
violet, and the evening breeze had almost chilled him. He felt the
drinking man's deep need for his *burra peg*.

Dugmore, he saw, was already established in the shadows on
the far side of the verandah. The servant gave a worried glance at
his master, and Rogers spotted it and found himself wondering
whether he wanted this man to make himself a familiar – and his
brain flickered to ask whether he liked this man – but their
greetings were surprisingly warm, like subalterns who have once
served in the same regiment and have long since gone their
separate ways.

'Forgive me making myself at home like this,' said Dugmore,
who was not without sensitivity. 'It is wiser not to advertise that
I am on visiting terms with "Bwana Rajees", as you seem to be
known, and I had to seize my opportunity to escape from Free
House.'

'Does one escape from freedom?'

26

'They call it Freeland, and I would have fled post haste if I had not agreed to play your little game.'

'Only so long as it amuses you, Dugmore. I know that I have no right to impose on you.'

'Don't worry, I am adequately amused. I am being indoctrinated into the mysteries and shall take care to show myself a prize pupil.'

Yes, that would be necessary, Rogers was thinking; they might be innocents, these people, but they could hardly believe that the British authorities would not be keeping an eye on them, whatever permissions they had been given by the idiots in London.

'They have no suspicions?'

'Not so far as I can see. I shall have to be careful. You may find that my behaviour will become a touch extreme. Some of them can get pretty wild when they're in their cups – and that means most of the time – and I mustn't play the spoilsport.'

'Then I shall lock you up just like the others.'

'I could suggest some other candidates for the Fort – white men, too, but not as harmless as my new friends.'

'Are you sure they're harmless? As I told you, they were carrying a hundred rifles when they landed. When I confiscated them, they had the gumption to be annoyed.'

'So I gather. They're still talking about you.'

'Good God, man,' cried Rogers. 'Only last month I put down a full-blown revolt on the mainland. Everyone knows that that little affair at Witu was whipped up by the Germans. I don't trust the Liwali an inch, for all that he sits here as the creature of the Sultan, who's the one native I do trust. I have to get back onto the mainland as soon as I dare, or we'll have Kimenya up in arms again. And now two dozen of Europe's flotsam and jetsam – Anarchists or lunatics, whatever they are, I don't care – turn up on my doorstep, *from* Germany, spouting *German* nonsense, *led* by Germans – oh yes, very polite, I grant you – and hauling a hundred Werndls with some cock-and-bull story about sailing up the Tana to found Heaven-on-Earth in the sunshine. Am I supposed to take it seriously?'

'They take themselves entirely seriously.'

'All of them?'

'No, of course not. They have their share of fools and scoundrels. But I reckon that at least half of them are serious types. Even decent. A few of them I rather like. And they take their catechism

27

very seriously indeed – believe me, the daily prayer meeting is the worst of the trials you have inflicted on me.'

'Catechism?'

'There's a book by their founder and inspiration, some fellow in Vienna called Hertzka. Wilhelm and Salner are his first lieutenants, so to speak – the old boy must be too frail to come out and face the heat. They all carry this fat tome called *Freeland* – it's an absurd mixture of high romance and moral correctness. They presented me with my own copy, in English. Want to borrow it?'

'Certainly not,' said Rogers hastily.

'You'd enjoy bits of it. It's about this splendid bunch of noble white men – yes, that's right – who get fed up with the political system back home, particularly because they have to pay interest when they borrow money, so they decide to come out to equatorial Africa, which is apparently pretty empty, and anyway they make pals with the Masai and so on – no, don't look like that. It's full of adventures – they train the local elephants to work like our Indian variety and they harness zebra to their carriages and they persuade the Masai maidens to practise chastity (that's three miracles for you), and – not surprisingly – lots of people come out from Europe to join them, and – there you have it. "Freeland" is the answer to all our problems...'

'They must be barking.'

Dugmore said, 'That's the interesting thing. Most of them are no more barking than you or me.'

'So why are they here?'

'I haven't got as far as that. I guess that most of them, all of them, have their own private reasons for leaving Europe.'

'Failure? Poverty? No expectations?' Rogers was posing a serious question: this was a decade when millions of Europeans were departing the continent for America, Australia, South Africa, Brazil.

'Not necessarily. A good proportion of this lot aren't short of cash. Slingsby Goddfrey and his friend Henry Bosanquet are high society back home...'

'Yes, you mentioned them, they're the buggers. They're probably running away from some scandal.'

'You may be right. But Dekker – the big one with the prematurely white hair – used to have his own business and quite a reputation. I think my aunt used to use him for her curtains in

Chester Square, though she also said he was a bit wild politically. And Sasse – the younger girl's husband – looks well-lined to me. The Danes are both out of the top drawer, even if they're a sight too crazy for their own good, and Selling and Salner and most of the rest aren't exactly skin and bones. Remember, they all paid a hefty fee for the privilege of coming out here.'

'So how do they explain to you why they have turned up in this dead-end island? Are they some sort of political outcasts? Are they Anarchists? – Revolutionists on the run? Should I lock them up? Or ship them back home?'

Dugmore shook his head and scowled out of perplexity: he had never been a Political Officer, and these things came too slowly to him. 'No, I don't think it's as simple as that. I've been watching them, listening to them, and the best I can come up with is that they all have their separate reasons for leaving home. Different reasons. Some of these reasons may be better than others. Or wiser; more acceptable. But they're not the sort of people who wanted to emigrate to New York to make a fortune. They've come to Africa for some other reason. Some of them because they believe in Hertzka and his idiot book. Some of them because – oh, who knows, whatever damn reason. All I know so far is that some of them are shits and some of them are dangerous shits and some of them are perfectly decent folk. You'd be surprised, Rogers, you'd get on splendidly with some of them. Give me your permission to arrange a dinner party!'

'You'll do nothing of the sort. I won't give them any excuse to delay their departure.'

'They're not dangerous,' offered Dugmore. 'That's my tentative, preliminary, ill-considered report to you.' And he added, 'I may be wrong. But I don't see what damage they can do. Serious damage, I mean...'

'You mean these revolutionary friends of yours aren't planning to overthrow the Liwali.'

'Good luck to them!'

'Or hang me from my new flagpost?'

'They really aren't interested in Lamu. It's simply their staging post for Africa.'

'For "Freeland".'

'Yes. They have this ridiculous idea that they can somehow carve their own country out of the bush.'

29

'But *where*?'

'Somewhere near Mount Kenya, if I understand Wilhelm. Our own Foreign Office in London seems to have given them pretty near *carte blanche*. God knows why anyone in London ever took them seriously. Perhaps that's the problem – perhaps our masters didn't take them seriously enough! And now they're here.'

Rogers was hungry and tired and therefore easily exasperated.'So, you and I are to sit here meekly – yes, yes, help yourself, the soda's over there – and look the other way while this gang of maniacs and desperadoes (oh, all right, this group of noble idealists) charges off into Africa in all innocence and ignorance, and without anyone's say-so carves out a territory for itself. When Carl Peters tried it a couple of years ago, at least he claimed to be representing the German flag, and we soon put an end to his nonsense.'

'Aren't you putting this too strong? My guess is that they'll never get beyond Golbanti.'

'But good God, man, that's not the point. How dare they even *attempt* this. What right have they? – I insist you answer me, Dugmore – What *right* do they have to impose themselves on the wretched peoples of this continent? Good God, man, I sometimes ask myself what right *we* have – '

'Do you really?'

Major Rogers checked himself. 'There's all the difference in the world between our own imperial mission and a ragbag collection of European layabouts.'

Dugmore observed his host sardonically, as though surprised by this outburst, and not necessarily displeased.

'As I said, they're not all of them like that.'

'Are you so sure?'

'Positively. There are rogues, yes. Remember the names Gleisering, Ducoffre, Rabinek, just for starters. Felix Thomas is another, but I have my own plans for that young man; I'm going to need an ally at Free House. As for the Germans – remember, not to be confused with the Austrians – the Germans are in a minority and I wouldn't vouch for them either, they have too many recent grievances in this part of the world. Don't worry about the English contingent: you'll find Goddfrey and Bosanquet good company, but bear in mind Goddfrey plans to send back despatches to the *Pall Mall Gazette* and will enjoy making mischief. Some of the others

30

are genuine in their ridiculous way. Dekker, for instance, and Fallon – the younger Englishman. Wilhelm, the boss man, is a bit of a bore, but he's straight and his wife is far too good for him. Salner, the intense young Austrian, is still a mystery to me – there's your real revolutionist, I suspect. There are a couple of wild Danes and another couple of stupid old men, but there's no great harm in most of them. They spout a lot of nonsense but there's nothing *dangerous* about them.'

'So why are they here? Of all the out-of-the-way places in God's world, why have they turned up *here*? In my parish? Just precisely when I don't need them.'

Dugmore said, 'Do you mean that the situation is worse than I guessed?'

'What situation?'

When it was clear that Rogers was not going to answer, they fell silent. They smoked, and they gazed at the stars, and they reminisced a little about India and Dugmore's run-in with the Colonel's lady, and each had his own thoughts. There was no longer any tension between them. Each was happy enough with his circumstance, his location, his fate. The visitor had apparently forgotten the need for discretion and had begun to pace the terrace under the bright half-moon, still deep in reverie. He leaned on the parapet, gazing down on the shuttered town, across at the shadows of the Customs jetty, the flicker of lamplight behind the Denhardts' mock-crenellations. The moonlight had transformed the choppy waters of the creek into a bubbling cauldron of molten lead.

'It's splendidly cool up here after a scorching day like today,' offered Dugmore. 'It's never like this in Mombasa.'

Rogers used to sit there every night for hours, as though to cleanse himself of the humours of the town, the heat and the vexation of the sun-blasted hours. He would smoke, and drink, and eventually retire in a half-daze. A couple of hundred yards away the Germans – the Denhardt brothers and Toeppen and sometimes Bwana Pembe, when he was not conducting his mysterious business on the mainland – had their own retreat behind the tall battlements which Rogers always mocked for their military absurdity but which irritated him because he always felt overlooked, spied upon, when he took a turn in the town. They too, he realised, would be smoking, and drinking, and refreshing themselves after the wearying business of the tropical day. The difference was that he had no-one to talk to. It made a pleasant enough change to have Dugmore turn up on his doorstep like this. Pleasant enough fellow, too. He seemed to have lost that social thing which made him a bit of a pain in India. And come to think of it, it might be useful to have a sensible chap on seat when he next took the *askaris* back to Witu...

Rogers said, 'You must admit, there's some humour in it. Here we are, two white men in the heart of Africa, with a handful of nigger soldiers and a couple of Indian NCOs. We're hundreds of miles from reinforcements, administering a territory the size of Scotland and ruling a million savages, most of whom would cheerfully cut our throats. And just across that street – over there – the only other white men in the district, because they are Germans, are doing their damnedest to do us down.'

'Are you sure of that?'

'Increasingly sure. Give me a little more time. I'll tell you when I can prove it.'

'When you talked about fellow white men, you were leaving out my chums in Free House.'

'I find it so hard to take them seriously.'

'Then you needn't worry about them.'

Rogers said, 'So why did they come here? I mean, why *here*?'

'God only knows.'

*

Poste Restante
Lamu Island
Kenya, E Africa
15 April 1894

My dearest Sisters,

Now that Julius and I have settled into our new house – an elegant little place (not so little!) down on the waterfront, and next to a lovely mosque which wakes us every morning with the call to prayer (you'd love the house – it has strange and beautiful local furniture and *plaster* carvings on all the walls) – we are beginning to feel quite at home, here on the edge of Africa. Julius of course spends most of his time at 'Free House', as we have named the big building which is our headquarters and where many of our members are lodged. That leaves me a little time to explore this wonderful town, and also to persevere with my studies in the local language – Swahili – which occupied many of my hours on the voyage. I tell Julius that it will be important to be able to converse with the natives, and he agrees, of course, but he is so busy and he says (so kindly) that I have a better 'ear' for these things than he will ever have. Most of our colleagues do not want to bother either, except for Captain Dugmore – I must tell you about the Captain! – who seems to speak it as a second language, though in a peremptory tone of voice, and yesterday I heard Major Rogers (I shall *also* tell you about Major Rogers!) talking Swahili with the local Liwali so fast that it sounded really beautiful, almost like Italian...

It is very, very hot, and dear Julius finds the humidity very difficult. He carries a selection of cotton handkerchiefs which Saidi launders and irons every day, and he is always mopping his face, so that I am tempted to make fun of him because I do not seem to suffer to the same degree. It is a great help to have a bedroom at the level of the roof, where we can benefit from the breeze – some of the men in Free House have to sleep in the lower storeys, and when they emerge in the morning you can imagine how they complain. To which Captain Dugmore (who is in the Free House cellar) said at breakfast the other day, 'Why come to Africa if you don't like the heat?' No-one knew what to reply.

The Captain is a strange one, and I don't yet make any sense of him. He is English, of course, and has *enormous* knowledge of these parts – which, says Julius, will make him very valuable to us – and he has asked if he may join the Association. Julius confesses that he was a little surprised, but he does not think that Dr Hertzka would want us to discourage *local* recruits: on the contrary! So the English captain has been allowed a temporary 'provisional' membership, and Julius has written to Dr Hertzka to ask if that is in order. Captain Dugmore is very polite and courteous – indeed, *galant* – to me as well as (of course) to Louise Sasse, and it is evident that he respects Julius and is truly interested in the principles of Freeland, but he is not yet really one of us and there are, I think, some dangers ahead, particularly from some of our German members who were not enthusiastic when Julius (with Salner's agreement) said that the Captain might join us. These *political* disagreements are so ridiculous! As Julius said to me, what does it

33

matter that the English are the governors on the Coast, it means nothing to us, we are going to the hinterland where we will have our own system, free of all these petty rivalries? The bigger problem, in my opinion, is that Captain Dugmore has a dog – what is called an English bulldog which, he tells me, has never been seen in these parts before. Apart from the fact that the local people hate it (because, I think, Muslims do not respect dogs???), it is a very bad-tempered brute, fat and angry, which breathes loudly and smells and is *not* popular in Free House except with Louise, but Captain Dugmore insists it is his 'best and only friend'.

I was going to say that even his servant hates the dog, but that reminds me to tell you of our first *scandal* a few days ago.... Have I told you about Felix Thomas, a little man from Wales, or somewhere from the Celts, who did not conceal on the ship that he came from a modest family background and had joined Freeland to better himself and because he truly believed in Dr Hertzka's cause? He's a mysterious young man, and none of us quite trusted him as we are supposed to trust our fellow members.

Well, last Thursday there was a great to-do. Felix Thomas was caught *red-handed* in Salner's room, apparently searching his baggage. He couldn't possibly deny it. Salner came straight to Julius, as I suppose he had to, and after the briefest discussion – because while Freelanders may not believe in private property, *theft* is a different matter – Julius declared that Felix must be expelled from the Association. Such drama! What was he to do, asked the Welsh boy? He had paid his passage with his last savings – was he to work in the plantations like a native? That is no concern of ours, replied Julius, and I think I can say that everyone at the meeting agreed.

But, believe it or not, Captain Dugmore has intervened. Without even seeking our own opinion, he tells us he has – 'in these delicate circumstances' – hired Felix as his personal manservant. 'Think of it as my private act of charity, madame,' he said to me when I asked him whether the rumour was true. 'We surely do not wish to cast one of our own brethren into the gutter on account of a foolish misdemeanour. Do not concern yourself, I shall keep a close eye on the lad...'

And, when I think of it, I must say that I think there is something truly charitable in the Captain's action, though Julius does not agree with me. As for the Major, who rules all our lives, I shall write again when I am a little clearer in my thoughts about that

34

other Englishman.... I shall tell you, too, about the mysterious Mr Dekker, who is a very private man who has made a great impression on Julius. I like him too.

But the nice young Dane called Pier Scavenius has come to tell me the mails are being collected for tonight's steamer, so I must end for now, with many kisses from—

Your Big Sister
Martha

Three

Supply everyone to satiety, and no-one will covet what others
have.... When it is perceived that nothing but perfect equality of
rights is needed in order to create more than enough for all,
Communism disappears of itself like an evil, tormenting dream....
Civilisation is not merely compatible with, but is necessarily implied
in, the economic equality of rights. Hence Nihilism also must be
unknown among us...

Theodor Hertzka: *Freeland: A Social Anticipation*

Major Rogers strode the long roof terrace of Charter House,
welcomed the breeze that had sprung up from the east, and
discovered that he had made his decision. I'll go back to the
mainland at once, he thought – I don't need to consult Zanzibar
or London, my authority is enough for a renewed reconnaissance.
And then I'll march on Witu, I'll take every man I've got, and I'll
catch that bastard Suleiman red-handed and, so help me, I'll string
him up and end this business. Hardinge can like it or lump it. This
is the moment to seize my chance. They'll assume I'm sitting here
waiting for the Rains. The Liwali is preoccupied with his new
catamite. They haven't had time to repair the stockade. The
Germans have scarcely realised that I'm back. And the point is –
he thought, with an access of triumphant confidence – that they
will all assume I'm waiting for the Rains like everyone else. But I
can risk it. The clouds are here but the Rains are holding off. If I
risk it – yes, *risk* it – I'll get twenty miles beyond Witu before they
know what's hit them. Then we'll see if Hardinge objects. In the
old days I'd have sent him Suleiman's head in a sack. Or, best of
all, Toeppen's to go with it. But hold on, my dear friends down
the road – I could probably see their lamplight if I deigned to step
out onto the terrace – think they are in the clear. They've been
spreading mischief about me around this town, and they have the

cheek to give me *Grüss Gott* in the marketplace. Well, we'll see to their game, once I've razed Witu to the ground, and Safareh to go with it. Yes, I know the Germans have their grievances. Hardinge always tells me to remember they had a rough ride in '89. But whose fault is that? It was Carl Peters who signed up all the local chieftains on scraps of paper that were never going to be worth a brass farthing. Then Peters gets reined in, Bismarck does his swap with Heligoland (yes, a lump of rock in the North Sea but it was Bismarck who valued it, not me), and now the Denhardt household blames *me* for their reverses and plots with the Liwali to do me down. What do they expect next? The return of Carl Peters (who was a murdering adventurer if ever I've seen one)? The German flag flying over the Lamu Fort?

No, thought Major Rogers, who paced his twenty-metre rooftop with a steady stride, as he had done for two years and as he was to do for another eight – this is my moment. My masters have cleared the game plan with Berlin; they've given me the nod, the Germans are prepared to cede this Coast, and if that's a source of grief to the Denhardt household, then so be it, let them weep into their bottled beer. I'll allow them to hang on to their trading stores on the island but I'll rid them once and for all of their pretensions to Witu and the mainland. Then, and only then, Hardinge can incorporate the whole Coast – these islands as well as Witu and the hinterland; we all know it's time for the Company to step out of this business. And then I can get a serious grip on the Liwali and run this island properly.

He had heard a muttered *Hodi!* from below. Iqbal Ali clattered, in his deliberate way, on the stairs and Dugmore emerged against the skyline. Rogers, full of this new resolution, was pleased to see him, but they did not exchange greetings, as if to acknowledge that their relationship was a clandestine one. The visitor slumped full-length on the Swahili couch and muttered his needs to the Indian.

'I don't know what sort of day you've had,' offered Rogers, 'but I'm absolutely buggered. I'll be relieved to get back to Witu.'

'Hanging some poor beggar at the Fort?'

'Not so easy. It's the day for my weekly call on the Liwali and he expects me to keep up the formalities. That means dress uniform for me – yes, in this heat – and half a dozen *askaris* with drawn swords and red waistcoats to escort me through the town. They love it of course, but I feel a prize idiot parading through the

37

donkeys like the ringmaster in a circus, and all for the sake of exchanging chit-chat and compliments with a gang of senile old men and drinking that filthy pink sherbet.'

'You said his brother was still here.'

'Abdullah? I'm afraid so. He's the runt of the litter. Used to be Liwali before my time. We fired him because he was suspect on the slave trade. Vicious-looking fellow. If looks could kill I wouldn't be standing here now, but I'm damned if I'm going to make him the usual presents.'

'Why does Sud bin Hamed keep him around?'

'He probably doesn't trust him out of his sight.'

Dugmore said, 'You seem remarkably chipper in the circumstances.'

'Do I? That's probably because I've just decided to get back to the mainland. I'm a soldier, not a diplomatist.'

'You just prefer kicking their arses, not licking them.'

'You could be right. But in this case I simply want to finish the job. Witu has been a nightmare. D'you know the place?' Dugmore shook his head. 'You haven't missed anything, I promise. Back in the Seventies it was run by a chap called Fumo Omani and got itself a great reputation as a home for runaway slaves. What your friends would probably call a "Freeland"! But from what I've managed to discover, that's poppycock. Fair enough, all manner of escaping slaves turned up there – and still do, they call themselves *watoro* – but they still sound like slaves to me, they have to do a spell in the local army and hand over most of their crops to the chiefs.'

Dugmore said, 'You cleared out the Germans in '93. You've destroyed the Witu stockade and chased – what's his name? – Suleiman Kimenya into the Forest. Tell me – is there really a problem any more? Does it *matter* if an Arab villain pretends that his miserable village has any sort of significance? Does it even matter if a bunch of drunken German merchants, most of whom will be taken off by the blackwater in a year or two, think that a gaggle of grass huts called Witu deserves anyone's attention? It's no longer of the slightest interest in either Berlin or London – it's over, finished, no-one gives a damn...'

Rogers was still promenading; Dugmore was slumped beneath the parapet. Rogers therefore dominated. He had been drinking since the evening *muezzin*, he was aware of it, and he had not yet

38

eaten; he observed in himself a dangerous inclination to the overstatement or exaggeration which comes out of the bottle.

He scowled down on Dugmore and said, 'I'll take your point, and I'll answer you in a phrase. I don't give a damn about Witu, I agree that it's a shitty backwater. And if there's a chance of a German revival in these parts, that's a problem too big for the likes of you and me to handle. But you miss my meaning!' Dugmore looked up at him as though to protest. 'No, forgive me, Dugmore, we haven't had a proper chance to talk about these things. The reason I'm interested in Witu – and in Suleiman – and perhaps in my esteemed neighbour the Liwali, not to speak of his brother – is that Witu is being used as the hub of a new slave route.... That's right, I said a slave route!'

They paused, out of an unnecessary discretion, as Iqbal Ali brought more drink and murmured to Rogers about food. The sky over Mokowe seemed to gather the last glimmers of dusk. So many dhows were turning homeward into the creek, their sails white lacunae in the fading light, that Dugmore was reminded of the yachts that used to gather across the straits in front of his grandfather's summer place at Beaumaris. Rogers was wondering, should I be telling him these things? He's a colleague – a chum – one of us. But he quit. He no longer 'needs to know'. And do I need him to know?

Dugmore may have understood the silence that followed the servant's departure. He said, diffident as an undertaker, 'Look, I don't want to be a problem. As I told you, I came up here for a spot of sport. I'm very amused to play the Anarchist on your orders with these idiots up the road – it amuses me. And I understand about Witu and your problems there; I'd probably be doing the same in your shoes. I've tried to follow the German business, and I was as relieved as the next man when they were told to get off our patch and stick to their own bloodthirsty ambitions in Tanganyika. But I'm not with you on this slavery thing. I always heard that Witu was the place every runaway slave made for because they knew that the boss boy would give them a *shamba* and a hut and even a Pokomo wife, if you like that sort of thing – as well as their so-called freedom and his protection so long as they turned up when he needed them to join a raiding party or beat off the Somalis. As you've just said, Witu has a reputation as a sort of Freeland for slaves...'

Rogers interrupted: 'It's not like that at all. I'd better brief you.'

First, he called for more beer – 'Make sure it's cold!' – and Iqbal Ali's fish curry which, bachelors both, secure from the gentilities of the Victorian *memsahib*, they elected to eat without ceremony from the side tables on the rooftop, where the Indian served them bowls of steaming swordfish and marlin and gritty rice and trays of *maridadi* chutneys and grated coconut and cool papaya. It was a meal so sharply spiced that in Free House it would have earned a torrent of abuse and calls for gallons of water, but Rogers and Dugmore were old India hands and despised the sweetness and cloying sauces of Swahili cuisine: the point of food in a hot and dangerous climate, they would have told you, is to make you sweat. The last dhows had vanished and the moon was rising, colossal, over the dark bar of Manda Island, beaming directly into their eyes and onto their simple tables. A wisp of cirrus gashed it briefly, yielded, passed by. At that moment the glare was so dense, so *rich*, thought Rogers, that it could not be true that moonlight (as he had been taught) is without colour: it was yellow, honey, as it beat down on the rippled metal of the creek. But then the moon rose rapidly above the cloud and beyond the eastern haze and the landscape turned cold and pale, silver and then near-white.

Lamu had traded in slaves for centuries, Rogers explained. Most of these wretches came not from the local tribes on the mainland, the Oromo, the Pokomo, the Giriama, but had been passed on from the great markets in Zanzibar and Kilwa to the south. They were needed to work the plantations owned by Lamu's rich men on the mainland *bora*, that belt of fertile farmland which – with the exception of the heavily-cultivated flood valley of the Tana – extended just a few miles inland as far as the Forest belt, near-impenetrable, which barred the Coast from the inland plateau of flatland scrub and desert. These plantations had prospered for many years, with their crops of millet and rice and maize and cassava, tamarind and peppers and eggplant and plantain, and the life of the slaves may not have been as villainous as is portrayed in the novels of the American Deep South. If we look on the positive side of their lives, the slaves had their own smallholding on which to feed their families and which they paid for with a small rental or a share of the crop; they were at liberty on Fridays; they had their palm wine, fermented and distilled from the ubiquitous coconut palm, which also supplied them with *dafu* milk,

40

copra for oil, *makuti* for thatch, fibre and rope and a host of other miraculous benefits. (On the islands it was different: the soil was sand and the water table high and saline, so the farmers grew date palms and mango and tamarind, that sort of thing – but the landowners needed slaves for that, too. That was another part of the problem.) Of course, they were still slaves as you or I would understand the word, Rogers conceded. And a lot of them objected to their fate and – who would blame them? – ran away. That was why Witu – because it was in the first Forest belt as you move inland – got its reputation for sheltering fugitives behind the Forest stockades. Only ten or twenty years ago there must have been *thousands* of these *watoro* runaways in the Forest villages, protected by a rascal Sultan called Ahmed ('otherwise known as "Simba" – you probably heard of him. He died a few years ago of the finest case of elephantiasis I ever saw. He had a portrait of the Kaiser on the wall behind his bed, and his balls were so enormous that they had to be supported on a stool. He'd become very devout: he read the Koran all the time and groaned over his aforementioned balls...').

Rogers was smoking his favourite Indian *bidis* and had sunk into a deep string armchair. 'Simba was always partial to the Germans, presumably for the sensible reason that he was an enemy of the Zanzibar Omanis who were in bed with us Brits – my enemy's enemy, you know the phrase.... But he was nervous of the Somalis, who were beginning to be very active on the immediate mainland – that's why he insisted on his *watoro* building these remarkable stockades around the Forest villages. You need cannon to get into those places, as Haggard reported, and indeed recommended, when he visited the area ten years ago.'

But, said Rogers ('Tell me if I'm boring you...'), the arrival of the Somalis from the north wasn't entirely a bad thing for old Simba, because they wanted slaves both for themselves back home and for shipping on to Araby. They had cattle to pay for them. 'Now of course, you will tell me, the old-fashioned slave trade has been terminated by HMG and Parliament donkey's years ago – the sea trade in slaves was banned in 1873, if I've got my dates right – *but of course, it hasn't stopped at all.*' The Royal Navy had been patrolling these waters enthusiastically and effectively ever since. It was romantic and not too dangerous work for a young captain in his first command, and many a dhow master risking a huddle of stinking humanity in his hold had lost his vessel in consequence and finished up in Zanzibar Fort. 'But the trade, if truth be told, has simply moved onshore. And these grand and distinguished and oh-so-civilised Swahili merchants of Lamu are still up to their necks in it. *Or so I suspect*,' added Rogers in a punctilious and emphatic qualification.

It's all hypocrisy, he was thinking. 'From what I hear, Simba was selling slaves to the Somalis for twenty years and more – he used to steal them from this very island and, if their owners wouldn't pay a ransom, he'd sell them up north. It's all a damn nonsense about Witu being paradise for every disobliging poor bastard slave on the Coast, and I intend to prove it. Especially when Fumo Bakari took over from his father-in-law. That was an elegant young fop for you, in all his finery and his arrogance – they tell me Carl Peters made a beeline for him and declared that he was "a true German". We'll see about that. But he had the sense to take a long holiday in Aden before he met his maker. That left Suleiman Kimenya.'

Dugmore said, 'All this is splendid stuff for me, absolutely fascinating – I'm very grateful, Rogers, I promise – and now I think we've got on to your own sterling feats on the mainland. Not to speak of the unspeakable...'

'How d'you mean?'

'The *Wa-Germani*. I gather the locals have taken to calling them the *Wa-Schwaini* for some reason. Where do they come into all this?'

'Bear with me for a moment. Start with Avatula. He's a bad bastard. Avatula bin Bahero Somali, to give him his honorifics, is a renegade half-Somali chief in the Forest north of Witu. I gather that he took to the life because his father had been "broken" in prison here in Lamu by the Liwali's predecessors – you can imagine what that means, poor sod! Then we took his estates away, which must have been the last straw. Avatula was a useful ally for Simba because he had Somali connections. The slave trade through Lamu was picking up in leaps and bounds and Avatula was at the heart of it, but Simba had the wit to realise that he and Avatula couldn't hope to stand up against us and Zanzibar, so he was tickled pink when Carl Peters turned up five years ago and offered to turn him into their own German protectorate of Witu. Without a word to Hardinge in Zanzibar, of course. Mind you, I've never believed that Simba had much idea what he was signing away. He had a bunch

42

of German traders operating in his part of the Forest, spreading around some gold, and he may have wanted a quiet life now that he was taking to religion.'

'But there was some anti-German revolt on the mainland?'

'Not really a revolt, but yes, a spot of trouble. Eight or nine Germans were killed in Witu in 1890, so we – Freemantle from Zanzibar with a thousand men and a seven-pounder – went in and blew it up. Best thing we'd done for years. That disposed of Fumo Bakari, who ran off pretty quick and, I'm happy to say, died of a poisoned hookah – there's a way to go! And we took over Witu, or rather Zanzibar did, and Bismarck gave in, to the fury of Peters and his friends down the road here.'

'In return for Heligoland.'

'That's no great consolation for Toeppen and the Denhardt brothers.'

'I've never been quite sure where, or what, Heligoland is.'

'It's an empty, tiny island in the North Sea. Peters was sick as a dog.'

'What happened to him?'

'Peters? He was given a job as DC somewhere near Kilimanjaro. Last thing I heard, he was suspended – apparently he's still a bit too keen on rough justice. If you've seen his books, that won't surprise you.'

'Meanwhile, you've been going back to the mainland ever since.'

Major Rogers scowled at him. 'True, if you put it that way. I don't know what Hardinge has told you. I don't have enough men, of course, and the Forest is difficult terrain. I need to talk to the chap I mentioned called Suleiman Kimenya. *He*'s the ringleader these days, rather than Avatula. I nearly got him on my last trip. Once I've got my hands on that gentleman, we'll have Witu as snug as Somerset.'

'No Germans in Somerset.'

'No slaves either. That's where Suleiman comes into my calculations. This is where we come back to the wretched slaves. We've failed to halt the disease. Every week I get delegations of local grandees wringing their hands and protesting that their plantation slaves *here on this island* are vanishing. The Liwali has the cheek to put in his oar on the same theme, and I suppose he's complaining to Zanzibar at the same time – and when I ride out into the *shambas* I can't deny that they seem to be short of labour, they're not

43

looking as good as they ought.' Put it another way, he thought, someone has realised that, at a time when the flow of slaves from down south is faltering, the island of Lamu is a reservoir.

'So where are the slaves vanishing?'

'They're going to Witu. Someone is funnelling them out of this island and into the Forest. I swear to God they're being moved up beyond Witu, to Suleiman and his stockades, and then they vanish for ever...'

'Then you'll be taking Witu. Again.'

'I've already got Witu. I want the slave villages deeper in the Forest. This very month, if I dare leave this island to its own devices.'

'My dear chap,' said Dugmore. 'You must know that I am yours to command.'

*

Hans Salner, professional revolutionary, convicted arsonist, reformed and repentant manufacturer of bombs and associated items, convinced disciple of Dr Theodor Hertzka, advocate and passionate adherent of the Freeland movement, wrote to his mentor.

Confidential and Personal

> Free House
> Lamu
> 20 April 1894

My esteemed Dr Hertzka,

I hasten to report to you from the Freeland expedition on the basis agreed between us, to my great honour, before our departure – viz., that you would be willing to accept my private and personal communications from time to time, as distinct from the regular and official memoranda which you will no doubt be receiving from the leader of the project, Dr Wilhelm. I write, as I shall continue to do, in an individual, not to say confidential, capacity, as I understand to be your wish.

As you will have learned, we are established here in Free House, on Lamu Island, after an uneventful voyage. There has been an inevitable degree of dispersal of your members because there turns out to be no single house in this town which can accommodate the entire party, so, while the majority of us have been established here – in what we have proudly dubbed 'Free House' – in a spacious and pleasing mansion a small distance above the sea front, the Association has been forced to find additional lodgings elsewhere.

Your representative Julius Wilhelm, with his excellent wife Martha, has moved into a smaller and cooler house nearby – as I am sure we all agree is necessary – while the Sasse couple, with their friend Hassemer, have taken a place near the edge of town, though they emphasise, very properly, that they have done that at their own expense. The Association has been compelled to take various lodgings elsewhere in the town for other, junior members. I trust you will agree that this is a necessary and short-term burden on our funds, since we shall be moving to the mainland in the near future. I do not of course know whether Dr Wilhelm has reported to you his reasons for taking separate and private accommodation for himself, but I am happy to offer you the thought that, in the light of the undoubted overcrowding of Free House, and the occasionally jubilant mood of some of our members, it might be difficult to allocate suitable accommodation for a lady. In this context I must record that Frau Sasse continues to be *la fille du régiment*, loved by all, though I must allow myself to add that if it were not for the inspiring example set in all respects by Frau Wilhelm (whose enthusiasm, energy and charm know no bounds), I should continue to maintain the doubts I expressed privately to you some months ago about the wisdom of attaching females to what is certain to become a rigorous and perhaps dangerous expedition.

On a separate front, I need to report that Dr Wilhelm has taken it upon himself to admit to the Association – albeit as a 'provisional' member – an English adventurer whom we encountered here – formerly a military man (I suspect, without the slightest evidence, that he may have left his regiment under a cloud and therefore entertains some bitter feelings on the matter). He undoubtedy has charm and, more to the point, he has considerable experience of and expertise in this continent, features which could be most valuable to our project. It may appear unorthodox to recruit a new colleague at this late stage, but I must agree that the man, who is most civil and also manifestly persuaded by your own writings, has already proved a fund of resourcefulness and expertise as we make our preparations to depart for the mainland.

The English authorities have been formal and distant, not at all welcoming, but they have done nothing to obstruct us except to insist on temporary confiscation of our armoury, where they are probably within their rights. The representative of the IBEA Company, who is in effect the dictator of the region, has been abrupt but correct. Frau Wilhelm suggests, with her usual womanly intuition, that he dearly wishes we would leave the island at the earliest opportunity. I suspect that his principal concern is with the Anglo-German rivalry on this coast, which seems to have persisted, notwithstanding Chancellor Bismarck's best efforts and the withdrawal of the famous Carl Peters from the immediate vicinity.

Our German members, who have been cordially welcomed by the small group of German merchants on the island, tell me that their compatriots' relations with the English administrator are not at all good. These gentlemen, though commercial rivals among themselves, are an object lesson in national amity: their leaders are the two brothers Denhardt (much renowned in the region, having been here for a generation) and Herr Toeppen of the Witu Company, who has suffered the full displeasure of the British. They have been profuse in their hospitality to some of our party, though I confess that I personally find their attitudes a trifle xenophobic, an opinion with which I suspect my fellow Austrian, Dr Wilhelm, might agree. However, as Wilhelm Selling points out at every opportunity, the bruises that they and Carl Peters suffered at the hands of the English a mere couple of years ago – wounds reopened, you will recall, by the Chancellor's curious decision to exchange the Witu Sultanate for Heligoland – make it only natural that in their private conversations over schnapps and tobacco they should aspire to a larger German imperial role on the East African mainland. By that time 'Freeland' will be their flourishing neighbour in the interior, and I therefore urge that you recommend Dr Wilhelm to do his utmost to preserve good relations with the German interest.

To turn to a related theme: you will, I know, be interested to hear how our own members are progressing in the necessary eradication of national identity and petty rivalry. I regret to report that the residues of parochial 'little' nationalism have not yet entirely vanished, although these of course are early days. Bearing in mind the care you gave personally to the selection of the present party, you may be interested to know of the transformation that the venture has effected so far – or failed to effect, as the case may be. The French, by whom I refer to Ducoffre and Kaufman, with the Belgian Schmidt, continue to hold aloof from the communal spirit of the expedition. The English, who include (I exclude our new member) Fallon – an impressive enthusiast – and Dunn and that intimate couple Bosanquet and Goddfrey, have turned out to be less reserved than you feared, principally, I think, because of the example set by Dekker, who as his name suggests comes of classic European stock. We Austrians, who are in a slight majority, are of course deeply conscious of our personal relationship to yourself and are therefore inspired to act the very model of the true Freelander and Frau Wilhelm, though from Hamburg, is certainly 'one of us'. Our other German-speaking colleagues seem more hesitant, and I must report, as my earlier remarks may have indicated, that I am a little worried about the influence of the local Denhardts etc. on men like our own Austrian colleague Rabinek, and even Selling. Frau Sasse is of course excluded from all such comment: she is truly a citizen of the world. Her husband and their friend Hassemer are curiously remote from our party, perhaps because they live at the other end of town. The Danes – Stokkebye and Scavenius – are the truest, and I must add the wildest, of our enthusiasts.

In obedience to your instruction that I inform you in strict confidence about all such matters – and I remain most appreciative of the honour you have done me – I should add that your own doubts about the moral quality of our Dutch member Gleisering have been reinforced by his behaviour on the voyage. We do not have either the numbers, nor the quality of leadership on the ground, to be able to discount the damaging potential of just one rogue character. I also have private doubts about the character of the Celt, Felix Thomas. Finally, it is now evident that the Hollander, Riekh, does not possess the mental agility required of a true pioneer. It is regrettable that we felt obliged by the Dutch chapter to accept him, and I trust that Dr Wilhelm will be able to assign him to some appropriate and minor role.

I shall be relieved if you find it possible to send a medical man to join our party, as we originally planned, before we set off for the interior. This coast is an insalubrious place and our members are not all as fit as they might be, nor as conscious of their duty to the Association to do their utmost to safeguard their health.

I very much hope, Herr Doktor, that I have not overtaxed your patience in writing at such length. I can only plead that I do so at your specific instruction, and I repeat my impertinent protest that you should not have been allowed to cite your (comparatively!) advanced years as reason for not leading our expedition in person. I look forward to that happy day when you will be prevailed upon to visit 'Freeland' in its established reality, here in the heart of Africa...

Salner added the final courtesies, but paused before sealing the envelope.

I have not been candid, he thought. Not candid enough. We should have been more scrupulous in our selection processes. The only hope for us is to move to the mainland before this place destroys us. We cannot afford to sit here much longer. Can Wilhelm not see that simple truth? Am I the only one to understand?

*

Major Rogers had business in Matandoni. The headman of the village to the extreme west of the island – it is so close to the mainland that Africa seems within hailing distance – was reported to be sick; Rogers esteemed the man and thought to demonstrate his favour by making an official visit. He took the launch, flying the ensign, and steamed past the Mokowe jetty and through the narrow creek lined with mangrove swamp. He always relished the contrast between the urban bustle of Lamu Town and the sleepy peace of Matandoni; he allowed himself to stroll beneath the frothy leaves of the enormous old tamarinds and on into the deep shade of giant acacias which challenged the brilliant green of the mango trees. This was where Lamu built its dhows: scores of men, half-naked, were constantly hammering away on the waterfront under great canopies of palm frond. They greeted him cheerfully but saw no need to break from their task. Times were hard, the old Arab assured him, proffering a giant *dafu* which he sliced open with a swift slash of his panga. Rogers professed disbelief – did Matandoni always have five dhows under construction at the same time? – and they all heaved shoulders in an African hilarity.
The headman, he reckoned after his visit, was dying. He must discuss the succession with the Liwali. In the next hut he paused to watch a giant mat being woven out of coconut fibre in a pattern

48

of ornate geometrical abstraction; he commended the work – it was his job to boost morale. A boy came to offer another *dafu*, chopping out a mouthpiece with another vicious machete, and Rogers felt obliged to thank him and drink the cool milk to the dregs. I must pause at the old mosque, he thought – I cannot enter, that would not be permitted, but I want to see if the ostrich egg is still there.

He was startled, and then irritated, to find that another European was standing in the dirt in front of the mosque, also observing the courtesy of not entering, and also, it seemed, gazing at the glittering white sphere which was the only ornament inside the simple whitewashed structure. The man was tall and apparently vigorous, though not young, tanned and dusty, his hat held in one hand, a rough staff in the other. His jacket was stained with patches of sweat, and he had the air of a man who has recently indulged in vigorous exercise. Rogers saw the mane of prematurely silver hair and recognised him as one of the Freelanders whom Dugmore had mentioned more than once. But he paused and held back – thought to leave – except that the visitor had heard his arrival, the chattering of the small boys who attached themselves to any stranger, and turned to see who it was. They exchanged glances, nodded diffidently as two Englishmen would always prefer, and then, after a palpable delay, the visitor took the initiative and came across the sandy courtyard to Rogers and said, in a surprisingly deep voice, 'This is absurd. I know that you are Major Rogers. My name is Dekker. I am one of your temporary visitors, and no doubt a source of concern to you. But at very least let us introduce ourselves as fellow-countrymen...'

Rogers shook his hand and said, more abruptly than he intended, 'Why are you here?' and then, realising the ambiguity of the remark, added hastily, 'I mean to say, what brings you to Matandoni?'

The tall man seemed in high spirits. 'Oh, I explore the island while we are forced to wait here. This is not my first visit to this village. The children, you observe, are getting to know me. And I'm fascinated by this mosque.'

'Why?'

'By its utter simplicity. Can you imagine a simple ostrich egg as the sole ornament in an English parish church? Instead of all that jumble of stained glass and choir stalls? What does it signify, I wonder.'

Rogers said, 'I can't say I've given much thought to it.'

The stranger persisted. 'Fair enough. But I'm sure you are the man to settle an argument for me. Tell me, please, are there 42 mosques on this island or only 36?'

'At my last count,' said Rogers, 'there were only 29. But I was counting them from the early-morning call to prayer, and when I woke up again I'd forgotten the number.'

Dekker laughed. 'For me, it makes a change from church bells in Gloucestershire.'

'Which particular part?'

'Chipping Campden.'

'Good Lord,' said Rogers. 'I was born only ten miles from Chipping. Haven't been back for years. I was in India, you see...'

'Well, I packed my bags three months ago, and I promise you it's still as beautiful as you remember, but I've plumped for Matandoni. That is, until we can get ourselves out of your hair and up the Tana. God knows when that will be; my colleagues are less impatient that I am.'

'You have problems? If there's anything I can do to help...'

'No. Too kind of you to offer – but it's out of my hands, I'm just a footsoldier in this regiment. I gather we have to wait for the Rains before the Tana is navigable. In the interval there's nothing to be done but explore your splendid island, Major, and prepare ourselves for our expedition.'

Rogers said, to his surprise, 'Can I offer you a lift in the launch?'

The stranger protested, adamant. 'No, no! I shall walk across the island. I'll wait here a little – perhaps wander down to Kipangani – and exercise myself by strolling back through the *shambas* before dusk. I love that time of day.'

'Watch out for the lion,' said Rogers, and it would have been hard to tell from his tone whether he was serious. 'One of them swam across last week and is causing grief among the donkeys.' And then, to his even greater surprise, he invited Dekker to visit him in Charter House. 'Come tomorrow for a sundowner – if you're at a loose end, that is. You can tell me about the Cotswolds.'

To hell with the Cotswolds, thought Dekker an hour later as he struggled through a patch of the deep white sand which masqueraded as the main track across the island. The sand was curiously difficult to traverse; the locals stormed through it, their splayed flat feet pounding down the 'path' without apparent effort, but strangers strained and struggled, their calf muscles tightening, the soles of their sandals unable to make an adequate purchase on the shifting grains. He had discovered that it was wiser not to hurry but to seek the patches of green turf even when they threatened long diversions, when the protesting legs rejoiced and you could stride ahead at a European tempo until the inevitable next quicksand.

The *shambas* at the heart of the island were a rolling repetition of coconut palm, acacia scrub and mango orchard separated by brief stretches of thin grazing. There was a ripple of sand dunes to his right. Once he came upon dozens of baby donkeys in the shelter of a dune – a donkey ranch, he thought at once! In the distance a dozen mangy cattle were being brought in for the night. There were simple, frail fences around each *shamba*, and a simple, frail shelter with a *makuti* roof at its heart. The resident slaves, bare-chested, a faded *kikoi* around their waist, showed no interest in the stranger when he paused to watch them tending their plot, trimming and pruning, burning the dead branches, cocooning the new palms against the wind, spreading goat manure around their trunks. They seemed to work so slowly; their lives, it occurred to him, must seem – to them – to be a routine without end.

There had been no routine in the Cotswolds. On the contrary, it had been an unending drama. How odd that he and the notorious Major Rogers had something in common: that would amuse Tom Fallon and Martha Wilhelm when he told them. So he and I both know those secret valleys, those villages of golden stone, the purple hill beyond Evesham, the folly of Broadway Tower, the rolling plateau above Burford.... I wonder if he is often homesick for it. For such beauty, such simplicity, such tranquillity. I wonder why he left. I wonder why he came here....

I wonder – he allowed himself to think, as he sweated through the sand – whether they miss me. I wonder if the factory is running itself without me. Will Harold have mastered the boiler? Has Mrs Groves buried her father yet? Have Hamptons sold the house – my beautiful house? And Carrie? And all the rest of it. Did they ever clear the sluice? Has Bill found a tenant for Upper Farm? Did the Vicar mislay my cheque, or did he simply forget to thank me? Is Blacky happy with the Thomsons? Did they put down Duchess?

Enough! he declared. It was my deliberate doing. When I told them the firm was theirs, they didn't understand me for days and days until they had their letters and the Vicar called a parish meeting and Bingham did what I'd told him and took command. After that, how could I go back? But I wish I'd said goodbye to Mrs Feathers, and Wilson and his boy, and Duchess. I suppose I couldn't face them, I couldn't risk it. I might have been tempted to change my mind. Cornwell told me I was a bloody fool, though a solicitor doesn't use such words – 'You could disengage for a while,' he had said, obviously suspecting I was round the bend, 'and I can make an arrangement which would allow you to return one day. In the meantime, if you absolutely insist, your holding can be put into some variety of trust. In that way you would be able to make your intentions clear, without cutting off any hope of any change of mind in the future. Your employees would be the beneficiaries in the immediate term, but the future would be left open to a more considered decision.'

'But my point,' I said to him, 'is that I do not wish to be allowed the opportunity to change my mind.'

He looked at me as though he truly doubted for my sanity. 'Mr Dekker,' I remember him saying, 'you have spent twenty years building up a business – a business of the highest repute, known and respected throughout this land – and now you declare that you want to walk away from it.' 'Mr Cornwell,' I remember replying, and I'm happy to remember that reply, 'you're right. Let's do just that before people like you persuade me to change my mind.'

He's a sensible old bird when you reach beyond the bluster. He gave in at once. '*All* the firm distributed among all the *present* employees?' he asked. 'In equal measures?' 'Yes, but check that Ebenezer has turned up for work on the day you announce the share-out.' 'And nothing for your family?' 'I have no family. My sisters are well married, and their children do not need my charity.' 'And your friends? Your – friend?' 'I have separately made settlements for my staff.' I knew what he meant. But it wasn't his business.

I hope the man did his job, thought Dekker, as he approached the first outbuildings of Lamu Town. I honoured them. I owed so much to them. I loved them. I hope they do not think I deserted them.

But of course – why do I play games? – that's precisely what I

52

did. I deserted them, and so much else. Perhaps Cornwell was right. Perhaps I was – I am – a touch unhinged.

That night he dreamed again of his valley. It was his home in a fold of the Cotswolds, he guessed at first, and he groaned in his sleep because he feared the reproaches of its faithful inhabitants, rebuking him for his departure – but no, this was a different valley, it was wide and green and blessed with sunlight, and there were purple mountains in the distance. He was high above it all. He knew that it was only a dream, but he studied the landscape with an intense concentration. He recognised that he was weary. He felt in himself a deathly exhaustion. He was looking down from a great height on the valley, and he did not believe that he would ever find it.

*

There was a dark and discreet place on the south side of the town, near the Monument and just before the stone houses turned to rag and coral, where Slingsby Goddfrey and Henry Bosanquet found a natural home. It was called the Jambo Club and, although they did not know this, it was a haunt famous to the sailors of the Indian Ocean. Indeed, the same place, under one name or other, had been operating for three hundred years. The main attraction was the transvestites, who have long been a speciality of Lamu, as they still are today.

Neither Goddfrey nor Bosanquet was interested in that particular trade, and once they had made the point their preference was respected. A 300-year tradition produces a sophisticated and flex-ible management. They were given their usual table, and the cruisers in *bui-buis* let them alone. The manager, who was a handsome young man with exquisite Nilotic features and who seemed to do his job efficiently despite being constantly stoned, welcomed them with a hint of an embrace and took their hands to lead them to their corner.

'Don't you feel that Dr Hertzka would love this place?'

'Or Julius Wilhelm? I could have sworn I saw him over by the bar.'

'The good Dr von Liebe und Erde, as young Scavenius calls him after that *particularly* tedious lecture last night.'

'No, Martha wouldn't stand for it.'

'She's the best thing about him.'

53

'Too true. Poor Martha!'

'Quite seriously for a moment – our colleague Gleisering is over there – don't look now. He's with Ducoffre.'

'Do you think that tells us anything?'

'Only that Lamu is the whorehouse of the Indian Ocean. "Anything you want, sir, you can find it here" – or so Felix Thomas assured me only yesterday, and he sounded very shocked. I assured him that that was why the Freelanders had come here and seemed to be so reluctant to move on, and he was even more shocked. "Felix," said I, "this is simply another version of Freeland!", but it was a bit above the boy's head, so we left it at that.'

'You know, I have a craving for a dugong tonight.'

'A what?'

'Dugong. "Mermaid" in vulgar sailor talk. They come from this ocean, you know.'

'Come on, it's a myth.'

'Not at all, I promise you. It's an enormous great beast, weighs about a ton, but very shy. I'm told it has moustaches, which shows the sailors must have been getting desperate.'

'Or why they go for these transvestites.'

'It hides in the creeks near here. You sometimes find dugong steaks in the fish market.'

'What does it taste of?'

'Dugmore said it's like streaky bacon. Not at all bad, he said, but needs to be thoroughly cooked to get rid of the fat.'

'You think Ahmad will have any?'

'Doesn't really belong in an establishment like this. Can you imagine the *carte* – "Breast or thigh, sir?" – they wouldn't be amused.'

The floor show, as it would be called in Europe – the cabaret? – had started. A Somali woman, bulging in surprising places, was about to invade the private parts of an Omani sailor to the hideous accompaniment of an Italian violinist who had fallen on hard times and no longer even dreamed of seeing his homeland again.

'*A propos* of Somalis,' said Goddfrey, beckoning at the scene that was being played out in front of them, 'did I tell you that I was spat at in the town this morning?'

'What were you doing?'

'Nothing – oh, all right, I was with Stokkebye, who had the stupid idea of singing a descant to the midday call to prayer, which

54

I agree was tactless. But one of these Somali sailors came past and he actually held his nose and spat. Yes, real spittle! Handsome chap, I have to grant him.'

'You should have punched him on the nose.'

'You didn't see the size of the dagger he was wearing.'

They pretended to study the cabaret. They were drinking a local variety of brandy sours.

'Isn't this rather amusing?' asked Goddfrey after a while.

Bosanquet replied, 'Since you ask, dear boy, and if you absolutely insist on a reply, my answer is no.'

They looked at each other with the understanding of their seven years together. 'Then I agree. Why don't we go – shall we call it "home"?'

'Let's hope Dugmore isn't ranting on about his adventures up-country.'

'Rather Dugmore than Monsieur Ducoffre holding forth yet again about his Montenegran princess.'

'She wasn't Montenegran – that's another one – she was Belgian.'

'I've never understood what happened after her husband caught them *in flagrante*.'

'He came to Freeland, of course.'

'Come on, let's get out of here before Abdul takes his knickers off. Throw them a handful of gold – I never know why we come here in the first place.'

'Your treat, remember? Five rupees max., I suggest. And keep an eye on that pretty fellow in a sari, I think he's developing a passion for you.'

'You're welcome to him.'

'Do we mean "her"?'

'No, it's definitely a "him". This time I'm sure.'

'As opposed to last time?'

They smiled, laughed, looked into each other's eyes. Then, ignoring Ducoffre and Gleisering, and arm in arm, they wandered, not so steadily, out into the Lamu night.

*

Sisters, dearest!

In my last letter I promised to tell you about the stern Major Rogers, who represents the IBEA Company here on the island but is in fact our lord and master, which is not always easy for Julius because the Major has made it very clear that he is not a *sympathiser* with the Freeland movement. (Though I must say I can understand why he took away our guns and ammunition when we first arrived – Scavenius and Selling were *furious*.) I suppose that Major Rogers is afraid we are going to be a nuisance, and when I hear of some of the things our wilder members are getting up to you can understand his point of view.

Yesterday, for example, a dozen of the men – I don't know if Louise Sasse was with them – were fooling around on the roof of Free House waiting for the dusk, when they usually go to a sort of café down at the end of the town called Mabrukki's – Julius doesn't go there of course, but he tells me it is a disreputable place, not at all suitable for a serious group like ours.... Anyhow, in this case they were killing time on the roof, with nothing else to do, I suppose. There would have been Scavenius and Stokkebye and Rabinek and young Schmidt, who's a nice boy, and Captain Dugmore, whom I've told you about, and half a dozen others. The point is that they must have been drinking, and Mr Dekker tells me there was a lot of noise because he could hear them all the way from the Customs jetty, where he was checking our new cargo which has just arrived (also our steam-launch which we have christened the *Eden* – that's the best news for ages!). Anyhow, I suppose they were bored, and egging each other on – certainly no-one intended any *mischief*. But it was the time of day when the servant girls can be seen hurrying down the narrow lanes balancing enormous waterpots on their heads – even the youngest children can do it! – and, apparently, Stokkebye, who says he used to be an officer in the Danish Army, produced a rifle – no-one realised what he was doing until it was too late – and leaned over the parapet and *shot* the pot on the head of a poor girl a hundred metres down the road, so that the water poured all over her, and of course she was absolutely *terrified*, while all these silly, drunken men were roaring with laughter four floors above her. It makes me faint to think of what would have happened if Stokkebye had missed!

But that isn't the end of the story. Captain Dugmore, of all people – I'd have expected more sense of him – told them all that this was nothing, the girl had been an easy target, and when they protested he took the gun from Stokkebye and pointed to a big, black crow that was circling high overhead and – bang! – he shot

56

it out of the sky so that it plummeted down like a stone in the direction of the Fort, while all of them whistled and cheered.

Unfortunately, as fate would have it, Major Rogers was at that very moment inside the courtyard of the Fort (which is used as a prison) and was inspecting it with the Liwali. He heard the first shot, and then the second – and this *enormous* dead bird crashed down on them, only just missing the Liwali and giving him a terrible fright. Dekker says that the Major was absolutely furious – especially when he heard that it was Captain Dugmore's doing.

So you see why at today's Free House meeting Julius had to *implore* everyone to behave in an exemplary fashion, for the sake of the Association and its reputation. Dekker says, there isn't anything for most of our people to do except to get up to mischief. It will be better when we get to the mainland, he says. I must persuade Julius to organise more activities, not just the daily meetings (which, to tell you a secret, are sometimes just a little boring).

Our own house is lovely, it's down near the sea, next door to the Friday Mosque, where all the men of the town arrive in crowds at noon on Friday, which is their Sunday. It is good to have privacy after the noise in Free House, but the only snag is that we are woken long before dawn by the first call to prayer, the *muezzin*, just outside our bedroom window and a terrible shock when you first hear it. We have a charming young man called Saidi as our servant; he is very slim and handsome, like lots of the younger Swahili men here, short and slight, but well-proportioned and very kind and polite. Every night he puts a jasmine flower on my pillow! But I suspect that he smokes the drugged tobacco that is common here, which makes him a little vague in the afternoon. Captain Dugmore told me it is called *kif*, and asked me if I would like some. He said he wouldn't tell Julius!

I see that I haven't really told you about Major Rogers, but that can wait for next time.

> Lots of kisses (and hugs for my aunt)
> Martha

*

Dugmore said, 'Rather than get shirty with me, you might credit me with some pretty quick thinking...'

'Quick thinking? When you nearly killed the Liwali?'

'Bombed by one dead pie-crow!'

Major Rogers grimaced; it was the nearest he would allow himself to a grin. He detested the Liwali, and Dugmore knew it. 'I still don't see why you were encouraging those drunken fools to use this town for target practice.'

Dugmore protested indignantly. 'That is precisely my point. You didn't see Stokkebye – who's one of the villains of this little party – pick off the waterpot. I had the fright of my life. One drink more or less and he'd have had her between the eyes, and then we'd have had a lynching party at our doors. I knew I had to get the gun away from them, and the only way to do it was to make them think I was the wildest of them all. But I'm sorry about your friend the Liwali.'

Major Rogers said, 'His Excellency will survive. But one of these days there'll be real trouble. Do they realise how the town is losing patience with them? Apart from the shouting and screaming late at night, the locals don't like the way the younger of the women dresses – they say it's immodest, and I can see what they mean. And the other day, I'm told, someone was peeing into the street from three storeys up...'

'That was Gleisering. He thought it was funny. He said "They'll think the Rains have come".'

'But it's *not* funny, Dugmore, they're supposed to be grown men. Please God they keep their hands off the *bui-bui* women, and stay out of the mosques.'

'I had a word with Wilhelm, and he's read them the riot act about the mosques. As for women, those with the inclination have discovered that place behind Mabrukki's – d'you know the place I mean? No, of course you don't. The rest of us can fantasise about Frau Sasse.'

'Fantasise?'

'I'm told she's not entirely averse to spreading her favours.'

'She's the one with the black hair and the Socialistic dresses?'

'Yes, and the come-hither look. Bit of an Israelite, I imagine, but don't get me wrong, she's a real charmer, she makes a fellow feel it's good to be alive.'

Rogers said, '*Really*, Dugmore, I never guessed you had such a romantic streak in you. We're both supposed to be crusty old Coast bachelors.'

Strange how that hurts, thought Dugmore. Is there a moment when you resign yourself to these things? Did Rogers have his memories too? Would he understand me if I told him the true reason the Sasse woman disturbs me? How she reminds me of Edie and that summer in Hampshire? And then I found I was infected. By her, there was no-one else...

'You know how they are, these Anarchist ladies,' he said.

Major Rogers said, 'No, I don't. You're supposed to be the Anarchist, not me.'

*

In the hour before dusk the people of Lamu emerged from their dark and cavernous houses to sit or stroll in the breeze on the waterfront. The stranger would not have understood the degree of ritual in it. They emerged at the same time, like the chorus from the wings in an opera house, just as the sun began to topple behind the line of palm trees on the sand-hill horizon behind the town, and the old men took up their reserved seats on the stone benches in front of the Ismaili Mosque or on chairs under the *kungu* tree next door to the Denhardts. The younger men squatted on the ground in long-established groups, playing an ancient Swahili form of chequers. Even the children gathered at the same rendezvous, and if it was high tide the boys would hurl themselves, clothes and all, in somersaults and belly-flops into the waves. And the more daring young women, leaving their mothers in *harem*, would promenade in nervous and giggling groups along the stretch of open ground where the rope makers plaited their fibres throughout the day; the girls held their black robes high across their faces, their dark eyes devouring the forbidden, outside world, while their servants flocked to the lamplit shops in the alleyways inside the town. This was the moment when Major Rogers liked to make his appearance, but he was the only white man to be seen. The Germans invariably took to their hidden rooftop after their merchant ventures of the day, to smoke and drink and set the world to rights. The Freelanders had quickly learned to do the same.

Although they had been forced to disperse some of their members in various lodgings around the town, Free House was the formal headquarters, and everyone was supposed to gather there at least once a day, which in practice meant the sunset hour. Julius Wilhelm would have preferred them to dine there together, but the cooking of Bakari left much to be desired and, possibly more importantly, the post-prandial lectures which had been arranged by Wilhelm and Salner quickly proved (with the exception of what promised to be a more practical, less reverential series by Captain Dugmore) an added incentive to wander off into the mysterious, throbbing darkness of the town, either to their own quarters or, more often than not, to Mabrukki's, which could rustle up a fillet of cold kingfish, a bowl of rice and a plate of chappatis to soak up the raw spirit. So Free House was rarely crowded in the evening.

Louise Sasse sat on the roof terrace and pretended to pay close attention to the game of whist that was in progress between her husband, their dear friend Hassemer, Gustav Rabinek and the sober Selling. She had drawn up her chair at her husband's right hand and was allowed to spy on his cards. It was, she knew with passion, a stupid game, but it was the only way she could keep herself free of the attentions of – well, for a start, Lieutenant Stokkebye, whom she really shouldn't have encouraged on the voyage, he was going to be a bore, and Emil Ducoffre, who always wanted to twitter at her, and the sinister Gleisering (she certainly didn't like the way that one looked at her, he reminded her of one of those disgusting maribou storks on the road to the abattoir). She preferred the hawks, which hovered overhead each evening and seemed to sweep down closer and closer so that she could see their brown feathers etched clear as *makuti* strips on a rooftop, patterned like palm leaves, beautiful as the pleats in a banana tree. Her husband, who knew about such things, told her they were not hawks but African black kites – yes, he insisted, that was what they were called, although he agreed that they were definitely brown – but she always thought of them as hawks. They were scavengers, he said. They frightened her because they were so big, but they also fascinated her.

Why must her companions always be making such a *noise*, she wondered. At the table, thank goodness, there were only the familiar evening sounds – the shuffling of the pack, the slap of card on card, a mock groan of disappointment, a murmured post-mortem. Two of the Englishmen were sitting just beyond them, as though – she guessed – to get as far as possible from the hoarse laughter and tipsy braying of Stokkebye and Ducoffre and their party. Both of the Englishmen were reading, though the younger one, Louise had noticed, frequently drifted into meditation, seemingly oblivious of the din around him. Martha had told her that the older one – he had a shock of hair that would soon be silver and a beard cropped short – was famous in his own country, and not just for the courage of his political convictions. Louise had never heard of him, which did not worry her: the junior schools of Alsace do not concern themselves with the political scene in Great Britain, and by the time she had grown up and launched herself in the sophisticated radical circles of Berlin she had learned that she and her friends assuredly had nothing to learn from the English...

He was a big man, with broad shoulders and large hands (muscular, if that is a word that can be applied to hands), middle-aged but with a vigour in his deportment which her husband had never enjoyed. He did not look like a man who was often ill. He was always very courteous to her, though distant. She had asked him straight out on the *Reichstag*, in her direct way, and he had replied that he had never married, which was strange, she had thought, because he was evidently not a man of the other persuasion, though also he was not of her *'type'*. There was something dismissive in his eyes when she looked at him; she had the wit to suspect that he was not a man who would ever respect her. His loss! But what did he *do*, she wondered, since she guessed that he was not a man who would patronise the whorehouses on this island. He reminded her somehow of the Englishman who ruled this island like a Governor and was so hostile to them – the thin, ugly Major with a hard face, who had looked at her in the same dismissive way; she had caught him inspecting her when he did not think she would notice. He, too, had the same energy as Dekker, poor man, there was a vitality in them which she might be able to respond to, as she could see that he wasn't a *pédé* either, like most Englishmen – like those darling boys God and Bos.... Yes, he was almost *possible*, except that he frightened her a little, there was too much strength in him, she felt that there was a violence there which was strapped down by the conventions of his colonial role. She thought she would discuss this new instinct with Martha, then decided that Martha would disapprove, and anyhow Martha probably wouldn't understand what she was talking about. Martha sometimes got flustered when Louise wanted to talk about men, almost cross, if dear Martha could ever get cross – 'You're just a bourgeois housewife,' she'd teased her one day on the ship, and

61

Martha had snapped, 'And you're just a slave to your instincts!' and then hugged her quickly.

Martha's favourite Englishman, Louise knew, was the quiet one, Tom Fallon, the slim one who was reading his book next to Dekker. He had interesting eyes, she decided; they were horribly candid and understanding and – she wondered why she felt something so ridiculous and sentimental – so sad. When you looked at him, as she had done just now, and he looked back at her, briefly, scarcely recognising her, she felt a pang of sympathy: there was no reason why she should, she scarcely knew him and she had suspected on the steamer that he was avoiding her, but she couldn't deny herself, she suffered that stupid sympathy. At least his expression didn't dismiss her like Dekker. Or dismiss her in that other way, which she remembered from Europe – the expression she had spotted on the blunt features of Wilhelm Selling, or the more sinister sidelong glance of Reinhold Gleisering; she even thought she had seen it once or twice in the leer of Stokkebye after he had finished with her. She was only half-Jewish, but she would never deny that half, and it was enough to enrage her when she saw that expression on their faces. She first discovered it in Rykwert, in her father's shop. So when her father's honest business friend from Berlin pleaded with her to marry him and forget his age she said yes, but it was even worse in Berlin, and soon it was she who was pleading with him to join these wonderful new friends she had made, these idealists who spoke up for the perfectability of man, and set off on this adventure in the sunshine. What she wanted she always got, in the end. But she hadn't realised they would be taking the same disease with them.

She had definitely decided that she would not go to Mabrukki's this evening. Her husband had been so sweet about it. He had not attempted to 'forbid' her to go there, because when she agreed to marry him he had sworn that he understood that she must be a free woman, and he had always kept his word, even when she knew she had hurt him. But he had explained that Dr Wilhelm had very discreetly mentioned to him that her presence in Mabrukki's had been responsible for some incidents among their members – well, that was true, the silly men – and dear Hassemer, who hadn't been very well, had said to her how nice it would be to have a quiet supper like they used to do in Berlin. She couldn't have agreed more, she was sick to death of Stokkebye, not to speak

62

of Ducoffre, and even that Danish boy Pier Scavenius was getting ideas, she could tell. She would get Ahmadi to make a special meal, she had told the two men – you don't know how much Swahili I've been learning with Martha's encouragement. I'll explain what we want, and he can go to the market and spend all day cooking for us. What do you think? Let's start with that vermicelli wrapped around pounded cashew nuts, we all like that! Then I want fish for the main course – a big fresh fish stewed in coconut milk and served with rice and banana. And let's just drink lime juice for a change. We can invite Martha and Julius, we owe them for last Saturday. What a wonderful meal, thought Louise. What *bliss*! Then we'll finish with mango, the way they serve it here, sliced in deep hedgehog slivers of yellow flesh, reversed in its skin like an inside-out glove, with the juice running down our faces and staining the napkins, and that wonderful *pétillant* aftertaste on the tongue – really, I'd have come to Africa just for the mangoes of Lamu. I wonder if Julius Wilhelm can cope with a juicy mango!

You are silly, said Louise to herself. *Au fond*, you are not *sérieuse*. That's what my father used to say. That's why Dekker looks at me like that. But not his friend.

Lightning was rippling across the horizon to the north. A storm on the mainland, said somebody: another voice added, 'It can't be long now.' The lightning was miles away, playing behind a ridge of jagged raincloud so that they caught brief glimpses of a black frieze against the electric white. The younger Englishman had wearied of his book, she could feel him looking at her – the dark-haired, pale-skinned, clean-shaven one. She looked across at him suddenly and trapped his eyes in hers, and was gratified to see him flush as he turned away.

'I'm hungry,' said Louise to the card players. 'It's time to go home.'

Four

The order of the day was as follows. We rose about 4 a.m. and took a bath in Eden Lake.... After the toilet came the breakfast, which consisted, according to individual taste, of tea, chocolate, coffee – black or *au lait* – milk, or some kind of soup; to these might be added, according to choice, butter, cheese, honey, eggs, cold meat, with some kind of bread or cake. After this first breakfast came work until 8, followed by a second breakfast consisting of some kind of substantial hot food – omelettes, fish or roast meat – with bread, also cheese and fruits.... Work followed until 10 a.m. Then came the long midday rest, when most of us took a second bath in the lake, followed by private recreation, reading, conversation or games.... At 1 p.m. the principal meal was taken, consisting of soup, a course of meat or fish with vegetables, sweet pastry, and fruit of many kinds, with banana wine or, when our brewery had been set up, with beer. The meal over, some would sleep for half an hour, and the rest of the time would be filled with conversation, reading and games. When the fiercest heat was over, the two hours of afternoon work would be gone through. After this, a few indulged in a third bath. At 7 p.m. a third meal similar to the first breakfast was taken, out of doors if it did not rain, and in large companies.

Theodor Hertzka: *Freeland: A Social Anticipation*

C urious,' said Major Rogers, 'that we have a background in common.'

That evening Dekker was at ease with the world. It was one of those days which he valued so well, now that he had escaped from all social obligation and artifice.

'Let's be warned that there might not be much more than a common geography. I don't want to sound graceless, I promise...'

This is an unpromising start, thought Rogers. He said, 'I think I mentioned that I haven't been back for years. I came out to India ages ago, and I suppose I lost touch. None of the family is left, which I regret.'

'No need to regret a sentimentality,' answered Dekker, and found himself adding, 'I beg your pardon, that must have sounded too strong. I think I meant to say that I too have no family connections.'

The sky was wild with scatterings of white cloud silhouetted against the starlight. The cloud was scudding, fast, and the moon was coming up early.

'Though I was always enchanted by the area,' added Dekker, his voice still apologetic.

'Your family...?' proffered Rogers with extreme discretion.

That was the moment which broke the ice. 'Great heavens, *of course* not,' replied his guest. 'Now I see it! You've been trying to remember whether the Dekkers came from Moreton or Paxford. Not a bit of it! My father arrived in England in '48 – he was escaping a death sentence in Dresden. He was a species of revolutionary, and he had a friend from his varsity days who had a sentimental commitment to us European radicals on the Continent. So we came to Broadway – I ought to say that I wasn't actually born at the time, and when that event occurred, a few months later, it was the cause of my mother's death. So my father and my sisters and I found ourselves in Gloucestershire, or rather in Worcestershire, though our cottage was literally on the county boundary.'

And I was about to be born to a second son of a second son, not so many miles away, thought Rogers, but said nothing.

'Then – to complete my autobiography – my father managed to survive, precariously, as a writer and philosopher, and I in due course discovered an interest in the plastic arts and eventually built up a modest business in the same area.'

'So I understand,' said Major Rogers, 'and I accuse you of undue modesty. Your colleague Captain Dugmore tells me you are famous in your field. The equivalent of William Morris, I believe, and with rather similar opinions.' (Now that, thought Rogers, is a bloody silly thing to say. The man will conclude that I am in contact with Dugmore. But Dekker appeared not to have noticed.)

Dekker was smiling. 'Morris is a genius, and I am certainly not,' he said. 'He and I at one time shared certain opinions, and even used to meet on the same platforms, but to my regret we no longer have much in common except for a passion for medieval architecture.'

'I've lived my life overseas,' offered Rogers, 'and I know next to

65

nothing about your Anarchists and Syndicalists and Socialists and whatever...'

'Believe me, the words cover a host of sins. And we may not be the monsters that some of you – some of your friends – believe. I shall not name names, but I have left dear friends in England whom you – no, forgive me, I think I am merely saying that we may discover we have friends in common, even though you and I might disagree about many matters.'

'Who was your father?' My own, thought Rogers, was a nothing, a pranting parson who related only to his elder brother, the baronet, and to his grandfather, the squire.

'He was in his way a great man. He had the gift of inspiring other people – my mother had been one of his pupils – but in 1848 he overtaxed the patience of the then authorities. So he had the good sense to retreat to your own – our own! – country, where free speech was better tolerated. I suppose that he was a failure in the eyes of the world. He was certainly what we today call an idealist. I did not at first follow his political position. I was a Socialist, of course, and I was close to Carpenter and the others....' (Oh Lord, thought Rogers, recognising a name.) 'But my great passion was for my work. Bill Morris, you should remember, only embraced the political life ten years ago, long after he had made his reputation as a craftsman and artist, and I followed him shortly after. Yes, I suppose I was influenced by him. He and I then spent far too much time making speeches and writing pamphlets...'

'Too much time?' Rogers was reminded that in the Eighties he had been governing an Indian district the size of Yorkshire and Lancashire combined.

'Yes, too much. I lost interest in my business, though it seemed to carry on rather well without me. But I also came to lose interest in the day-to-day detail of my political activity...'

'The beginning of wisdom, you might agree?' Rogers was smiling, and he didn't notice that, from this moment, she was talking not with a stranger but with a new friend.

'Perhaps. At about this time I read the English translation of Dr Hertzka's book and found it interesting – the philosophy, I mean, not the rather romantic style of his exposition.'

'I confess I have not grasped the fundamentals of Freeland-ism, or whatever it's called. The debates of radical London seem very far away from Lamu.'

66

'The essence of Dr Hertzka's philosophy is very simple. He argues that if we abolish both interest rates and private ownership of land, and at the same time and – this is where he is at the opposite extreme from Karl Marx and Engels – introduce economic liberalism, absolute personal freedom and so on, then the innate goodness of man would enable everyone to enjoy the fruit of their labours unhindered by a capitalist and entrepreneurial class. He calls this happy state of affairs the free social order. He wrote his book to illustrate how this might work out in practice – and he chose East Africa. Parts of his tale are, I suspect, rather optimistic.'

'And this philosophy has been well received?'

'There are local Freeland Associations in many of Europe's cities. Of course this is an age when Utopianism has a widespread appeal. My old friend Morris had a great success a couple of years ago with his own version, *News From Nowhere* – you probably know it.'

'I have heard of it.'

'I assure you that I used to be sceptical of such things. But many entirely serious people have become disillusioned with the conventional business of political debate.'

'That reminds me – what has happened to your own business, if I may ask? I seem to remember you had a partner. My elderly cousins used to write to me about the news of the parish – the letters stopped some years ago – and they may have mentioned your firm. "Dekker and – something"? I can't remember.'

' "Dekker and Lomax".'

'That's it. Tables and chairs to go with William Morris textiles, wasn't it? What happened to Lomax?'

'He didn't exist. When I first set up shop I thought my *mittel-*European name sounded a bit abrupt, so I decided I needed something Anglo-Saxon to go with it – or, better still, something authentically Celtic. So I invented my partner Lomax. When he was feeling mischievous, Bill Morris used to introduce me as Mr Lomax.'

'You mean that you have closed down your operation? That must be sad for your Gloucestershire craftsmen.'

'No, no. I gave it to them.'

'*Gave* it?'

'Yes, I gave it back to the men who were – and I hope still are – the business. I did not want to be tied down and diminished by possessions.'

Major Rogers reminded himself that this amiable fellow was after all travelling with a party of Socialistic cranks. His guest was saying, 'I had been impressed by a young man called Ashbee, who has set up a Guild of Handicraft in the East End. He seemed to me to have a true sense of the importance of the craftsman.'

'That was very noble of you, I'm sure. But will your workmen be able to carry on your successful business without your own skills?'

'Perhaps not. I really don't know. All I knew was that it was time.'

'How do you mean?' asked Rogers. It flashed through his mind that it was good to talk, to take an interest for once in something beyond his small professional world: I've probably become an awful bore, he almost thought.

'It's hard to explain. Even to myself, believe me! You mentioned tables and chairs, for instance. Yes, I was – or rather, my workers were – making good, simple furniture. Beautiful furniture, if you insist. And I was charging an arm and a leg for it, so that the only people who could afford it were the very people I was attacking in my weekend speechifying. Morris had the same problem on a bigger scale. Do you know that wonderful sentence of his – "Have nothing in your house except what you know to be useful or believe to be beautiful"?' (Rogers grunted noncommittally and thought to look around the room at his own Swahili furniture as though to testify to the point.) 'Well, I woke up one morning and I thought, that's all very well, but you've got to be a rich man to practise what Morris is preaching. He and I had a real set-to about it, and I reckon I won the argument.' And now the dear man is writing his romantic novels, he thought. And I am sitting as near as dammit on the Equator and drinking whisky with our Imperial Proconsul, who turns out to be my old next-door neighbour – he probably remembers as a child overhearing grisly tales about my eccentric pater.

His host was struggling. 'I'm not sure I see what's wrong in making beautiful things,' he ventured. 'Couldn't do it myself, of course – by the way, you know they have wonderful things here on this island? Hidden inside these great houses. Tables and chairs, and your sort of stuff. I used to think, when I arrived here from Gujarat, that Africa was populated with savages, but when I started to be invited into the houses (just the ante-rooms, of course) I had

68

to change my mind. *Magnificent* stuff. Ebony and ivory and so on – very ornate, but simple at the same time. Look at that throne over there!' (Perhaps that's what Morris and this fellow are after, Rogers thought, with a moment of insight. They were on their fourth *peg* and he was beginning to think clearly, even to want to understand the strange life of this man across the table, this – what was it? – this 'Freelander'.)

'Have you had the opportunity to see what's inside these Lamu houses? I know they look pretty bleak from the street – all that's deliberate, of course, intended for security – but *inside* there are things that you in particular would find very striking.'

'I'm afraid that we are transients, we haven't been welcomed by the community.'

Nor by the rest of us, Rogers realised, and refused to accept it as a reproach.

'Believe me, it's a deeply traditional society. The women, as you have seen, are in purdah. Their religion dominates everything, although they don't appear to be particularly devout. The Liwali – notwithstanding my own presence – is an absolute ruler. On behalf of the Sultan in Zanzibar.'

'Forgive me,' said Dekker, 'but you jest. Every single person I have spoken with, in the remotest corners of this island, assures me that "Bwana Rajees" is the bossman, as they put it.'

'Do they really?'

*

By nine the next morning the sun had broken through and the day was hot, ferociously so, the brilliant light bouncing back off the twinkling water and persuading any casual pedestrian to return indoors. There was a breeze – or so the rustling palm leaves testified – but scarcely of a strength that a European would recognise. Only later would a proper wind spring up, after the morning clouds had been completely despatched, and then it would be fresh and scorching at the same time, and there would be no relief in it. Manda Island was already only a blur of scrub and bush through the haze: when the sun shifted, the detail of Manda's thorn trees and mangrove and the two baobabs would emerge to the naked eye.

Major Rogers, a monarch surveying his kingdom, sat in his office and looked down on the scale of the place: he could see, at one sweep, the entire scope of the town. On all three sides he could identify the outer perimeter, the silhouette of palm trees which confirmed that 5,000 people were crowded onto a small patch of sand and coral at the end of the world, close-packed together and surrounded by *shamba* and sea. He spotted his visitor a hundred yards away; the man was walking briskly towards Charter House, dressed more formally than he would have expected. Good, the chap was on time: let's get this over – he wasn't sure he was playing fair.

'I am grateful to you for agreeing to call on me,' he said to Julius Wilhelm, after the Freelander had been ushered into his office, a great corner room placed so that its high windows, curtained with muslin to deter the flies and filter the sunlight, commanded both Manda Bay and the Customs post behind the quay. No, he thought, no lime juice; not too many courtesies.

Wilhelm was slim, almost skinny. His hair was brushed back, thinning, and he wore a spare beard. He inclined his head slightly and replied, in impeccable English, 'It is my honour...'

'No, I insist. You must be a busy man – I know the problems and complications that are entailed in taking an expedition to the mainland.'

'Now that our own steam-launch has arrived, we hope to make better progress. We also have two barges, for our stores and for our porters. Even so, it will require several crossings.'

'You have hired porters?'

'Not yet. I am trying to arrange to recruit them on the mainland. Several of my colleagues – two young Englishmen, it so happens – are presently at Kau on that business.'

'You know how careful you have to be with the porters,' said Rogers, who discovered that he was entirely happy to give these people advice when it was designed to get them off the island in the shortest possible time. 'The beggars have a habit of accepting your rupees and then vanishing into the bush the first night of your safari.'

The Denhardts, it appeared, had mentioned this very point and had recommended a thoroughly reliable foreman. 'And we have also been joined by another Englishman with experience of the African mainland, who will be most valuable – he claims to have been a colleague of yours in India years ago.'

'Ah! Someone told me that Dugmore had turned up. He was

70

always interested in politics, that sort of thing, though I didn't realise he was of your persuasion.'

'We are – as I think you say in England – a remarkably broad church.'

'Well, I'm afraid,' said Major Rogers, seizing his opening, 'that that's what I wanted to talk to you about. Your church, as you put it, may be a bit broader than even you realised.' He was rummaging in a basket of documents. 'Yes, here it is. I'm afraid we have a small problem.'

'I beg your pardon?'

'To do with a fellow called Rabinek. Gustav Rabinek. Is he Austrian? Ex-officer in their Sappers, if that sounds familiar to you.'

'Of course,' said Wilhelm, looking as puzzled as a priest at a party. 'Lieutenant Rabinek is in fact one of my deputies, insofar as that means anything in an organisation with the principles of the Freeland Association.'

'Trouble is,' grunted Rogers, and pretended to read from a sheet of paper as though he had forgotten its contents, 'Rabinek's been less than candid about his background. It matters to me only because it means he perjured himself in his application to enter this territory with a view to settling up-country. I thought you would want to know privately.'

'But,' said Julius, 'there must be some mistake. He's an excellent man, one of our most enthusiastic members. I lean on him in many ways.'

'That of course is your affair, and this conversation is a private one. I merely felt you ought to know.'

'But know – *what*?'

'Well, according to my information from my chief, Sir Arthur Hardinge in Zanzibar, we have been notified – one, that Gustav Rabinek is no longer an officer in the Austrian armed forces, he was cashiered in 1891; two, that he was cashiered because he was found guilty of embezzlement – something to do with gambling debts – and sentenced; three, that he escaped serving a prison sentence because he evaded his jailers on being removed from the court house, and has not been seen since.'

'That's unbelievable.'

'I assure you that it is officially confirmed. I'm sorry it took so long for the papers relating to your expedition to be checked by

71

London.' Another sort of man, he was thinking, would have been protesting, blustering, refusing to accept, abusing the English for interference in areas which arguably fell outside their territory, jurisdiction or concern, but Wilhelm was no fighter. Rogers was almost sorry for him, his shock and distress were so patent.

'What do you intend to do?'

'Frankly, I don't know. I have more important things on my plate just at present, as you may have heard. I suppose I could put Mr Rabinek in the Fort until I get back from my own expedition. But no – it's not a place for a white man.'

He paused, tossed the Hardinge cable onto the desk, and took a turn across to the open window, pretending to deep indecision. Surely the man could see that he was offering him an escape.

'That is kind of you. I personally appreciate that, Major.... May I ask one more concession, in confidence between ourselves?' Rogers shrugged noncommittally. 'If my colleague were to – shall we say – to cease to be visible – indeed, he might not even be on Lamu Island – would that be helpful?'

'Perhaps,' said Rogers and decided to switch the mood. 'Best of all, if the whole Freeland mission had taken itself off to Mount Kenya by the time I got back...' and he guyed a laugh.

'That may be too much to hope for,' said Julius Wilhelm hastily. 'We are warned that we may have to stay here until June, and you appreciate that we have permissions from London to remain as long as we need. But I assure you that all of us, without exception, are deeply anxious to press on with our expedition at the earliest oppportunity.'

'Sooner the better,' observed the Company Agent, and his tone of voice was empty, almost bored, so that Wilhelm realised that the interview was over.

'I cannot believe it,' he said to his wife. 'Rabinek has always behaved impeccably. Even Dr Hertzka chose him to be second-in-command with Salner.'

Our founder's judgment has not been impeccable, she thought; I could mention a few more names where I imagine the English might find some similar tall stories if they were minded, but I don't want to upset Julius any more. He was slumped at their breakfast table, long since cleared by Saidi, with an expression of such dejection that her heart went out to him. She worried that he was looking quite ill these days – his skin was pale (because the poor dear never allowed himself a moment on the beach, like the rest of them), and those blazing grey eyes of the true and selfless idealist, which had first enlisted her devotion, were weary with indecision and dismay and betrayal. Julius was so modest, *too* modest, she thought; people did not understand the strain he had been under, only I know that the man who can entrance an audience without a single note, the man whose sincerity and integrity no-one has ever doubted, is burdened with this dreadful and secret diffidence.

'Could I send him to Kau with Riekh?'

'That would be to waste his energy entirely. Can you assign him to the *Eden* with Selling?'

'He and Selling don't get on.'

'So ignore it. Let him carry on here on the island. He's valuable, you know it.'

'I shall have to talk to him – that's going to be awful.'

'Why talk to him? The Major was speaking to you privately. He can't tell you what to do with your expedition. We'll have left before long.'

Wilhelm looked at her in horror. 'My dear, what can you be thinking? I must of course expel Gustav from the Association. Dr Hertzka would not expect me to do anything else! We Freelanders are men and women of honour: without that we would be no different from all the other Europeans we see around us.'

'Yes, my dear,' said Martha, though it would have been imposs-ible to judge whether she was agreeing with him or merely taking note of his opinion.

*

It was later in the same day that Martha heard the cry of '*Hodi*!', followed by the sound of Saidi scurrying to the porch. There was a murmur of voices, soft footsteps on the stairs – it is the universal convention in Lamu to remove one's shoes and leave them in the outer doorway – and Dekker entered, shuffling onto the terrace like an amiable and ingratiating bear.

'I was about to take my evening stroll in the *shambas* behind the town, and it occurred to me that you and your husband might like to join me. I don't know if you have explored them, but they are very beautiful at this time of day...'

Martha cried, 'What a lovely idea. But Julius is in a boring meeting with Hans Salner at Free House, they're doing the accounts to be sent to Dr Hertzka.'

'Then perhaps another day.'

'But why? I'll come with you happily.'

The man hesitated. 'That will be delightful. Will you leave a note for Dr Wilhelm?'

She laughed. 'Of course not. He is not my keeper. Just my husband. And he spends far too much time in committees and meetings. He always has done, and even here nothing has changed. So take me to your *shambas*, Mr Dekker. What do I call you? My name is Martha, as you must know.'

'People just call me Dekker.'

She was, he realised at that moment, very beautiful. Not sensationally, desirably and flamboyantly beautiful, like Louise Sasse, but – yes – beautiful. She was blonde, like so many women from the Baltic coast; her hair was drawn back, shining-smooth and held at the nape of her neck in a heavy wooden comb; her eyes were grey-blue like the morning light over the Malverns, her mouth chiselled and firm, her ears very small; she was shorter than Madame Sasse, and her neck seemed thin in contrast with the weight of her breasts. She wore no jewellery and no paint. Afterwards he realised, with a self-knowledge that is given us just a few times in our lives, that he would fall in love with her. There was nothing to be done about that.

Behind the town, the stone houses soon yielded to dusty lanes lined with mud and thatch hovels. That category covered a host of architectural varieties, since many of the 'mud' houses were made out of timber frames in which small chips of coral were embedded in the wattle. But all of them, even the poorest – he showed her – had a base perimeter of stone to prevent the seasonal rain from splashing back and undermining the house. Everywhere there were chickens and children. Boys were climbing up the notches of the palm trees, and the coconuts came down with a dangerous crash. Toddlers scuffled in the dust, stopping to gape at the strangers in their grand clothes: Martha tried to talk to them, but they only giggled and retreated into shy silence. '*Salaam'a, bwana*,' said Dekker to an old, old man reclining outside the mosque on the outer perimeter, and then noticed that she was laughing at him for his lack of the language; he tried to compliment

74

her, and she brushed him aside. They came to a score of donkeys hobbled together behind a stable – apathetic, weary, docile, eyes blinking, undisturbed by the arrival of strangers. A woman hobbled past, limping and leaning on a heavy stick, ignoring them. 'I hate the cats in this place,' said Martha. 'In Europe I love cats. Here they are somehow so mean, so vicious...'

They were emerging from the town into the fields and suddenly Lamu was no longer an urban society. The mango trees were majestic, great groves of luminous green stretching as far as the distant dunes. They could see cattle being brought in for the evening by obedient small boys, and everywhere they could glimpse the oblivious, bare-chested, black-skinned slaves, preoccupied and silent in their unceasing labours. He tried to explain to her the pruning and the lopping and the fertilising. She said, 'How do you know all this?' 'I come to walk here most days. I think we must learn all we can before we go inland.' 'So you have explored the island?' 'Of course. I tried to circumnavigate it a few days ago. I calculated it wouldn't take me more than twenty miles – but I got stuck in a mangrove swamp the far side of Kipungani.' 'And?' 'I was lucky. I begged a lift from a passing dhow. But my legs were covered with leeches, and I'll bear the scars for years to come.' She said, 'Is this deliberate? Are you exploring the island for a purpose?' 'I suppose so. We must discover this place and then move on. It's only our first foothold in Africa, and we have so much to learn. You must understand that – Martha.' She said, 'Yes, I understand.' I shall have the language, she thought. And I have the conviction. Then we shall see.

Dekker said, 'Allow me to arrange an excursion – for you and your husband – to Matandoni. We could take a dhow and then return across the island on foot, if it wouldn't be too exhausting for you. Matandoni is a village that oversees the mainland, I go there often. They build dhows there. And there is an interesting mosque with an ostrich egg.'

'An ostrich egg?'

'Yes, an enormous egg hanging by a string in the *mirhab* – that's the niche that shows the direction of Mecca. But of course we are not allowed to go into the mosque...'

'I've been hoping to visit the Women's Mosque here in town. I need special permission.'

'Matandoni is only a village, it's probably more conservative.'

She said, 'I'd like that. Is it far?'

'Just an hour or so. It means walking back across the sand and through the mango orchards, which is more tiring than it looks.'

'Dekker, you have explored this island while the rest of us have been lazing in Lamu Town.'

'As your husband knows, we did not set out on this expedition to twiddle our thumbs on a decadent offshore island.'

She understood him so well that it hurt her deeply, and she was angry with him for a moment. She could not have brought herself to speak for that instant. They had retraced their steps towards the evening bustle of black-robed women flitting through dark and shadowy alleyways.

'It's curious,' he observed – and she guessed that he knew that he had offended her, and so he changed the subject – 'that you and I, and all our colleagues, cherish the upper storeys of our houses – we positively seek out a breeze in these latitudes – whereas the locals are terrified of a draught. They huddle in the lower floors and have a crisis if they feel a suspicion of a wind. I wonder if they suffer particularly from consumption. Does that interest you?'

'Yes,' she said. 'That interests me.'

She paused and allowed him to stroll ahead of her into the deeper shade of the street; she looked at him for the first time with careful attention, *attending* with care to what she saw, studying as if to begin again this tall, intense, bearded, white-haired man.

'Dekker!' she called, when he stopped, realising that she was lingering behind.

'Why did you come? Why did you join us?'

How do I count the ways, he thought. Do I explain that I wearied of Morris and the disciples in Hammersmith? Would this sophisticated citizen of Vienna – or is it Hamburg? – understand the smallness of life in rural Gloucestershire? Would she have heard of my father? Can I ever tell her of Carrie? Is it possible to explain in a sentence that I had come to the end of my life?

He said, 'I saw myself one day in an amateur portrait. My godson had been fooling with a camera.'

'And?'

He remembered the moment. He had always assumed that he was young; that was what made him respectful of those around

76

him, shy and unassertive in company, more eager to agree than he sometimes wished in retrospect.

'On that shiny card I saw a middle-aged man.'

She did not protest as convention might have suggested.

'So you came to Africa. To be young again? You make it sound so easy.'

'It turned out to be much easier than I expected.'

'But you know perfectly well that it was easy for none of us.'

'I wonder. The better I get to know some of our companions the more I wonder about our various motivations.'

'You do not believe that many of us share the same political inspiration? An authentic ideology, as my husband puts it. "Integrity" is another word he uses.'

'Madame, you know perfectly well that some of our colleagues know nothing of Freeland and care even less.'

'And you are a true devotee, Mr Dekker?'

He made himself pause. He hated this sudden retreat into formality. He would have stammered if he had grasped at too quick, too easy, a reply.

'I have an admiration for many of Dr Hertzka's theories. I have studied his writings with attention. You will not expect me to agree with everything, Martha.'

She said nothing.

'And besides,' he offered, after a pause, 'I have long experience of similar writings – the same debate – in England. For a time I was active in such things. I am my father's son. Perhaps I was too much my father's son. I have lived through disappointing times. I have learned that none of these theories is ever perfect. Some are less perfect than others....'

He was thinking, perhaps I was too much my father's son to be temperamentally suited to the hesitations and timidities of English politics. I was always more at home with our Continental comrades than I could be in Stepney or Sheffield. When I went with Eleanor Marx and Aveling to the Second International in Brussels in '89, I had the feeling that I had come home. I said to her, 'Don't you feel the same? You're as much a European as I am, yet you pretend you're here to represent the Gasworkers.' She wasn't particularly amused. Nice woman, but missing an English sense of humour. More seriously, I remember saying to her, what's wrong with us in Britain that we're stumbling along in the rear of the movement

77

– there were no less than thirty-five Social Democrat deputies in the Reichstag at the time, and we had one single Socialist in the House of Commons. Eleanor tried to argue that there had been ruthless repression in Britain – Bloody Sunday, Black Saturday and so on, that the Revolution was just round the corner – but that was nonsense. The fact of the matter was that the great British working class wasn't sufficiently interested in our Bloomsbury dialectics and our 'Men and Women's Club' and our obsession with prostitutes and sandals and homogenic love and our endless squabbling – and I had to confess that I agreed with them! The Fabians were recruiting all my friends, who were tickled pink to be persuaded that reform would take a very long time, and last year everyone was cheering the formation of the Independent Labour Party, which makes a positive virtue of turning its back on the Revolution. All the zest had gone out of it by then. Carpenter had vanished long ago with his boyfriends into Leicestershire, and now spends his time writing naughty pamphlets about sex. Morris gave up too soon, and now he's writing his Gothic romances in Hammersmith and getting old before his time. I could have struggled on, I suppose, but I lost the energy. The firm was a success, I could have lived the life of a rich man, and to hell with my conscience – there's nothing so satisfying as a revolutionary speech in an evening rally when you've spent the day overcharging the aristocracy for its interior decoration. So what was I to do next? Refurbish a medieval castle? Commission a landscape garden? Compete with Bill Morris's fictions? Grow old disgracefully? I was born in '48, I can never forget it, and my father brought me in my mother's belly to his London exile out of the riots of Dresden. I have failed his memory; I have become a successful businessman; I am an honorary Englishman; I have made a few speeches, but I have achieved nothing; I designed some pretty buildings and built a lot of decent furniture, but I cannot claim my father's respect.

She said, 'Dekker!' and he noted her signal. 'This is a new beginning for all of us. That thought moves me – moves me greatly. It excites me, and of course it frightens me too. *Don't you see?* Yes, I know you do – how this journey must transform us all. Look!' and she turned and with elaborate drama, laughing openly at him, with him, pointed to the far horizon – to the east, towards the sea.

'Look at what?'

'*There* is the past! *Our* past, all of us. It's over. It's behind us. For

78

my part, I promise I shall not mourn it, not in the slightest. *Now* do you see why I'm so happy?'

Dekker gazed at her but said nothing.

Dekker dreamed that night of a small and mischievous and persistent monkey. It seemed to be the pet of Martha Wilhelm, who was always playing with it, and he paid it no attention and certainly had no interest in the creature, until one day it suddenly started to take a great fancy to him, jumping onto his shoulders, into his hair, hugging him, pushing its tiny fingers into his beard. He was not amused by this, but tried to treat it as a mere nuisance. When the monkey tried to kiss him, Dekker got annoyed – and when the little brute *bit* him on the lip he recoiled (although the bite wasn't sharp, more of a nibble which didn't draw blood), fearing a wound, thinking of rabies and what have you. He wondered if Mrs Wilhelm had noticed this new, unwanted attachment. One day he discovered that his mouth was full of something hard and sharp and peculiar: he tried to spit it out and found that his mouth was stuffed full of large nuts – acorns, hazel, Brazil, almonds – which the monkey must have been hiding there...

*

Charter House
Lamu
May 3...

Dear Sir Arthur,
1. I write in order to confirm that I plan to return to the mainland as soon as I can, taking as large a force as I can muster. As I reported in my last communiqué, I took steps to deal with the Witu insurrection on my recent visit to the Coast, but it occurs to me to return before the Rains settle in (they have not arrived here at the moment of writing: I gather that Zanzibar has been more fortunate), in order to ensure that Suleiman Kimenya does not have the impertinence to rebuild the stockades. If he does, I shall give myself the pleasure of dealing most firmly with his unacceptable impertinence.

2. An additional reason for my decision to absent myself from Lamu Island so soon is that I am developing grave suspicions, based on information to hand, about the role of Witu in what appears

79

to me to suggest a resurrection of the human trade. As I have reported to you in the past, the Somali *shifta* have this year become a growing problem in the northern mainland territory, and it is known and understood that they are usually to be found behind any revival of trafficking in slaves. I have for several months been concerned, and baffled, about the growing number of 'escapees' from Lamu's *shambas*; the Liwali has been most eloquent on the subject, as he has no doubt informed you. I cannot any longer believe that these wretches are all – and coincidentally – setting off for freedom in the villages around Witu. I have begun to suspect that some sort of organisation lies behind the phenomenon, and I believe that the answer may yet be found in Witu – as well as, I venture, on this island.

3. I take the liberty of assuming that you will have no objection to my proposed course of action.

4. I leave the island, on what I intend to be only a brief *safari*, with the consolation that, in emergency, we have a former colleague 'on seat' (as our colleagues in the west of this continent would put it), whom I assume you would be happy to act for us. I gather that you saw Captain Dugmore before he moved into these parts, and I understand that, while he may have resigned his commission, he remains a colleague deserving of our confidence.

5. In this context I confess that I have not been best amused by the recent arrival in town of a bunch of Anarchists and suchlike from Europe, who rejoice in the name 'Freelanders'. You will be aware that HMG – I assume Sir Philip Anderson in London was particularly involved – appears to have authorised them to proceed up-country, in the direction of the slopes of Mount Kenya, where they propose to establish some sort of Socialistic community. It would be wrong of me to comment on the matter any further – I do not begin to understand why our superiors thought fit to encourage them – except to say that I shall be thoroughly relieved when they depart my parish.

Some of their number turn out to be surprisingly respectable characters, but the presence of their brotherhood in the town at present is provocative of the traditions of the island, and I fear that an incident could easily arise. The situation here is not so equitable that I do not need to take account of such apparently minor factors. I trust that Nairobi is aware of the imminent arrival of the State of Freeland somewhere – does anyone know where? – up-country.

I have made polite inquiries, and they appear not to have the faintest idea where they are going. That is not my, nor, I hope, your problem.

6. I confiscated their armoury, but shall of course return it the moment they make their (much-postponed) departure. I very much hope that their departure will take place before I am compelled to assign one or more of their party to the Fort. Their organisation seems to have its headquarters in Prussia (or perhaps Austria), and the contacts they have thereby made with the German merchant community here should not, I feel, be ignored.

7. I trust you will not feel that I am exaggerating this factor. I frankly admit that I am apprehensive, though I have no good reason for my fears. Their leaders seem respectable to a fault, although their party evidently contains some unruly members whose reasons for quitting Europe may not, I suspect, be entirely ideological. But the wider situation here is such that I cannot afford to have two dozen renegade white men indefinitely on my territory, not to speak of the additional and delicate presence of two ladies.

This brings me again to Dugmore, whose arrival, I have decided, was well timed. He was fishing for a role in the Forest (as you may have guessed), but that is out of the question. He has no standing here, and I am able to contain any threats from the direction of Suleiman. I thereupon had the happy inspiration of persuading him to help me by 'keeping an eye' on the Freelanders, who have settled into one of the larger (and less ventilated) of our Swahili mansions and re-named it 'Free House'. I am delighted to report that Dugmore fell in with the spirit of my proposal and is currently playing the Anarchist to the manner born, to the extent of moving himself and his baggage into the aforesaid Free House and – I am told – of losing no opportunity to take my name in vain. I shall also feel happier in my next absence in the knowledge that an Englishman is minding this part of the shop...

8. H.E.the Liwali yesterday asked me to be particular in conveying to you his *salaams* and respects. This I hereby do.

9. I shall communicate again on my return from Witu.

I have the honour to remain yr. most obedient servant,

A.S.Rogers (Major)

Oh, Arthur! thought Rogers, as he scrawled his signature. Why do we have to pen these ridiculous memoranda to each other, when we ought to be talking it through over a *peg* or two. Yes I know, London always needs to see the file, so we dare not mention that evening in Cairo when the C-in-C's wife farted and you propositioned the belly dancer. And there was that night when you managed to hang your boots on your prick and went roaring down the corridor looking for action. But now you're a Great Man – God Almighty on Zanzibar Island, with the Sultan in terror of you and HMG happy to leave you a free hand the length of the Coast. And I suppose I'm a sort of Little Great Man, or so they must think in this ridiculous island. Here I'm Bwana Rajees, and all I ever wanted was my own Indian regiment. Instead I sit here on a stinking waterfront in the middle of Africa penning hypocritical letters whose whole point, as you can see, is to conceal my intentions. I have no friends, because even a Little Great Man doesn't have friends; I reckon on malaria twice a year, and my only prayer is that I won't be taken off too soon with the blackwater; I have home leave coming up and haven't the faintest idea what to do with it; and – you silly bugger! said Rogers to himself, you love this place, don't you understand that you're that rarest of creatures on God's earth, you're a Happy Man.

No, that's too easy. I know that I love the progress of the working day. I love the moment when Iqbal Ali brings my tea at first light – I love that first light, the brief cool on the rooftop. I love the cold shower and the rasp of the razor, the clean starched shirt, the mango and pawpaw on the plate to go with the Swahili coffee, the bustle in the street below. Even the bloody *muezzin* at eight. And then the brief chill of the office as the big fan gets going and Gopal Singh brings me the schedule for the day. That's the moment when the island belongs to me, when I love it.

Nothing is so good after that. I resent the cables from Zanzibar and London. I dislike the chiefs and the *sharifs* and all their selfish persuasion. I detest the Liwali and all his works, I don't even like my *askaris*, though I've trained them since they were boys – murderous buggers, I reckon – I've seen it in their eyes, and I suppose I put it there. Sometimes they frighten even me; sometimes I see why they must frighten the Liwali; sometimes I might agree with what the Germans say about me over their schnapps.

I'm not so sure that I like the man I have become, thought

Rogers. (He checked himself: no, it wasn't that late and he had not been drinking, so why this interrogation?) I might have waited, plotted, for my own regiment in the Punjab, but instead I was persuaded to come out here. The Viceroy called me in and was very kind – your sort of chap needed, that sort of thing. And I responded to Africa from the first. I can take the climate and I had Iqbal Ali to look after me; Arthur Hardinge had expressly asked for me, and is always making hints about moving me down to Zanzibar. I can't really complain about the job, there isn't too much pen-pushing, and Hardinge has the wit not to interfere. And there's still the element of soldiering which I enjoy – yes, I'll take Witu again and for good, if I have to raze it to the ground, by God I will...

So why do I sit here in this 'tropical paradise', as my sister always says in her letters, and feel the need to resist the call for a pre-*muezzin* drink?

Because, thought Rogers, in a moment of terrible understanding, I do not adequately believe in my authority to do what I am doing. This was a thought so catastrophic that he sat back, dropped his pen, rose, paced the room, visited the *choo*, considered (again) summoning the servant, although the *muezzin* was at least half an hour away, kicked off his slippers, shuffled up the stairway to the roof and hurled himself onto a day bed.

He forced himself to take it closely. I am, he told himself, a fairly senior officer in Britain's imperial establishment. I am responsible for the security and the welfare of the population of this Coast from Kiwaiyu to Kau. I don't know how many people that means, no-one does. I report to no-one except, in theory, to Arthur in Zanzibar, and he, in theory, to Lord Ripon in Westminster. Which means that I am the master of this land...

He had rolled off the couch again, was pacing the terrace in his socks, unaware of the sun drifting down behind the hill, the shadows deepening on the waterfront.

He said – not quite aloud, though the question seemed to burst from out of his deepest being – 'Why me?'

By which he can only have meant, 'What is my authority? Why should I, in this Year of our Lord 1894, have the power of life and death over these hundreds of thousands of savages on this remote coast of East Africa?' Rogers did not doubt his ability to carry out that function, he did not defer to, nor even greatly respect, the culture of the peoples amongst whom he lived, he did not for a moment doubt that his own English civilisation epitomised the highest point to which mankind had thus far evolved.

But these stray and dangerous moments when the voice spoke to him – he did not encourage them, and his career was to be successful because he learned to cope with them – marked him out and distinguished him. As now, when he had written a dishonest letter to Arthur Hardinge, his friend and notional boss, who lived in some splendour and in even higher humidity a dhow-ride to the south. Who *are* you, Tony Rogers, younger son of the vicar of Lower Slaughter in the county of Gloucestershire, to convince yourself that you are also the King of Lamu Island? You sit here in lonely state, and everyone assumes that you're a terrible tyrant sent here expressly by the Queen Empress, and all the time you know that you're a barrel of shit...

Rogers was a very untypical colonial servant of that decade and also a very good one, as historians would now tell us. He was a very early harbinger of a later generation of British colonial administrators. Dugmore might have understood this: Wilhelm, and Dekker, and Fallon, would never know it.

*

Lamu, Monday

My dears,

We are still here on the island, waiting impatiently to launch our great expedition on the River Tana, but for all sorts of reasons we do not seem to be able to get under way. Julius tells me the Tana is blocked by a sand bar – I think that's the latest story! – until the Rains come, which we are expecting very soon. (It is getting hotter every day, and everyone in the town is looking up at the sky and praying for the big clouds to break.) Julius says that there is also a problem with our new boat, which is a pretty little steam-launch called the *Eden*. I don't understand why there should be a problem, because Selling and the others take it out almost every day for trials, but I admit that most of our members do not seem to share my impatience. Dekker, who is a sweet man (have I told you about him?), certainly agrees with me, and threatened to have 'a few firm words', as he put it, with Julius (I persuaded him to be patient a little longer), and another Englishman called

Tom Fallon spoke up rather violently on the subject at yesterday's Free House meeting. But I mustn't gossip because I have such *interesting* news of myself...

As you know, I have been working hard at my Swahili, which turns out to be not so very difficult after all. I have been studying the grammars and every day I insist that our cook-boy Saidi spend an hour in the garden with me so that I practise and extend my vocabulary, with the result that I can now talk quite easily in the little shops and with all the friendly people who have started to recognise me, and who come up to me in the street to say hello. Even Major Rogers congratulated me the other day on my efforts with what he calls 'the lingo'. Julius was cross because he thought the Major was saying this as a way of criticising him.

Perhaps it was the Major's doing, but – try to imagine how extraordinarily unusual this is – last week I received a letter, an *invitation*, all in very ornate Swahili (but I could understand almost all of it!) to me to pay a call on the Liwali's mother, none less. I showed it to Dekker and he said to ask Captain Dugmore, who got very excited and positively goggled at it, and said that this was a most unusual *honour* and I was very lucky, etc., because (as of course I am well aware by now) the women in Lamu are kept in ridiculously strict purdah – you only ever see them after dusk, and then they are covered up to the eyes in black sheets called *bui-buis*, and the superior women of the ruling families scarcely ever go out of their *harem*. It must be terrible beyond words! Yet here I was being asked to meet the head wife of the most important man on the island! Why me?

That's what I said to Captain Dugmore, and he made a few of his usual compliments but also pointed out that I was no doubt invited as Julius's wife, i.e. the wife of the Freeland leader, and everyone knows the Liwali and Major Rogers are enemies, so.... But when I asked whether I should decline he got very agitated and said *of course* not, she would be terribly insulted, this is like a summons from Queen Victoria (he always exaggerates!), and anyhow – though of course no white man has ever met her – Ma Fatima, as she is called, is apparently a remarkable person.

So yesterday I went to the Liwali's house, accompanied by Saidi as my servant (who was very impressed and wore his best *kikoi*). Saidi called '*Hodi!*' and at once servants came down and ushered me (not Saidi) through a whole series of porches and rooms until we came to a small, *lovely* room, narrow but very long (all the houses in Lamu are not wider than a couple of metres, says Dekker, because the mangrove beams cannot take a wider span), full of wonderful ebony furniture and mats and carpets, and also some surprising things (I noticed a couple of cuckoo clocks!) and extra-special plasterwork on the walls, which I have only recently begun to study – and there was an Old Lady waiting for me.

She was very small – shrunk, a bit wizened – and she wore heavy silk robes in pale colours and lots of jewels, most of which looked like old gold, and her eyes were bright as diamonds. She seemed to be laughing at me as well as with me, if you see what I mean, and at first she spoke very slowly, to see if I could understand her, but soon we were at ease and – it seemed so natural – I sat on the low stool below the couch she was lying on, and a pretty maid brought cardamom coffee and sweet *halwa* – and she welcomed me to Lamu and, yes, we had a wonderful talk!

Ma Fatima will be a friend, I know it. She is also a poet and tells me the Lamu ladies really are 'the best Swahili poets in the world'. I told her I looked forward to reading them, as my studies progressed. Then we began to talk of the differences in our lives – she has a ferocious curiosity, and too often her questions were beyond my comprehension and my vocabulary. She says that she only leaves her quarters on rare occasions, when she has to be fully veiled and walk under a canopy held by a dozen slaves. We did not talk of the Liwali, or of Julius and Freeland. She made me promise to return, which I shall do, with impatience. *At last* I feel I have come to Africa. If only we could set off for the mainland. But I'd miss Ma Fatima – my new friend...

More, dear sisters, with the next mails –

Martha Wilhelm

Five

Their costume is very similar to that of the ancient Greeks; even the sandals instead of shoes are not wanting, only they are worn not on the naked feet but over stockings.... The impression the Freelanders made upon me was quite a dazzling one. Full of vigour and health, they moved about with cheerful grace in the shade of the trees; they showed such an aristocratic, self-possessed bearing that I thought at first that this was the rendezvous of the best society of the leaders of the place, yet these were but ordinary country people – agriculturists and gardeners, with their wives, sons and daughters. Not less astonishing was the respectability of the negroes scattered among and freely mingling with the whites. Their dress was still lighter and airier than that of the whites – mainly cotton garments, instead of the woollen clothes worn by the latter; for the rest, these natives had the appearance of thoroughly civilised men.

Theodor Hertzka: *Freeland: A Social Anticipation*

Tom Fallon lay prostrate, stretched dangerously along the top of the low wall that fenced the rooftop terrace of Free House from the street far below. The midday heat, so long as he lay absolutely still, could be tolerated, but once he moved, even to exert himself in the slightest way, the sweat burst from his face, neck and chest, temples, lips, small of back, like summer berries and tumbled down so that his arms and shirtsleeves were instantly soaked by the reflex gesture of brushing a hand across his brow.

'We must accustom ourselves to this heat.'

It was Dekker who had joined him, unheard, and proffered a cigarette.

The *kudu* skin of a stool across the way stretched and tightened in the sunlight with a sharp cracking noise like fingers being popped out of double-jointed knuckles.

'It won't be as humid as this when we get to the mainland.'

'And when will that be, I wonder.'

'All in good time, say our leaders. They claim that the Tana is in flood.'

'Does that mean we are marooned in this place for the season?'

Fallon wondered whether to query the older man's urgency, then thought better of it. The two Englishmen – if Dekker was truly English, Tom wasn't clear – had steered away from any intimacy on the journey out. There was, to Fallon, something intimidating about the other man's manner; something withdrawn, though admittedly there seemed no discourtesy in it.

'The island has its pleasures,' he offered.

Dekker actually laughed, so abruptly that Fallon was startled. 'I imagine that neither of us shares the tastes of some of our colleagues.'

'I'll take that as a compliment.'

They were looking down from their high roof on the house across a street so narrow that it was the merest lane, only wide enough for a donkey to traverse. Gaudy banners of *kangas* and *kikois* were looped to dry on ropes stretched across the opppposite rooftop. Immediately below they could see down into a courtyard where the women, liberated from their billowing robes, padded about their chores, cuffed small children, and swapped shrill gossip. Just at that moment an old crone looked up and shrieked to see the two *wazungu* in silhouette above her. Tom waved, gay but uneasy, and they both instinctively stepped back, uncertain of the gravity of their intrusion.

Dekker said, 'Captain Dugmore was telling me that he had joined us for the adventure. "Solely for the purposes of adventure" was his actual phrase. And he said that he was hoping for "a spot of sport".' There was no hint of mimicry, nor for that matter of criticism, in his tone. Tom Fallon understood that there was a question implicit in it. Why did you come? Why are you here?

That was the beginning of their alliance. It was never really a friendship.

*

The clouds seemed to hang even lower over the town the next morning; they dragged themselves over Manda Island and the Creek, weighted down by their bulging black bottoms, drifting like overloaded galleons which could catch scarcely a whiff of breeze and so must depend on the sluggish current to despatch them, hours later, over the African horizon to the west. The sea was still high and the waterfront jagged with pools of foul water from last night's high tide. The bigger of the two *booms* from Somalia had sailed at dawn. The shaded streets were near empty of people. The old men gathered in the mosques and chattered, with neither urgency nor conviction, in the shadows of the pillars; then, as if in universal accord, they turned to the wall, stretched out, and slept the morning away.

Inside Free House, Tom Fallon attempted to sponge from his naked body the sweat of the night and made at once for the roof. To his relief, Captain Dugmore and his bulldog were not in evidence. Stokkebye was slumped on a day bed, reading an ancient newspaper; he looked up, raised a finger in silent salutation, and resumed his reading. On the adjacent terrace, in the comparative shelter of *makuti* shade next to the kitchen, Ducoffre and Gleisering were playing cards. They had not seen him.

Tom Fallon thought, Sweet Jesus, why am I here? What am I doing in this arsehole of the Empire? Fucking around, what else, and – he allowed himself the cheap crack and even grinned, briefly – it's not the proper place to be, if you see what I mean, squire. So the sun is shining, by God it is, and I'd give my fortune for a real, dirty, rainy day and an honest-to-goodness fog to go with it. But this is April. It must be Spring back home, windy and wet and always disappointing, but Spring all the same. Easter was early this year, wasn't it, so term will be beginning next week. I always liked the summer term. The kids used to work harder because of the exams, but I could switch from rugger to cricket, which was an improvement. (I wonder if they've managed to improve the cricket square this winter; it would be good to have a proper pitch to teach the boys the point of a leg break.)

Oh shit, thought Tom Fallon, I'm getting sentimental for the place. Remember – yes, remember, you idiot! – that you hated it. Remember how they used to ape the manners, the despicable aspirations, of their betters. I should have seen through it from the start. 'A grammar school of ancient foundation,' said that prize prick Ambrose, the Head, when I was desperate enough to apply, 'may not have the privilege of educating the scions of our upper classes, but we have the rather better good fortune of attracting the younger members of our own local community.' The old fart was right, he now admitted; we had a host of bright lads, and I taught them everything I knew. Which was my problem. Ambrose got to hear of it. 'Mr Fallon,' he declaimed one afternoon, 'I do not think it is a part of our pedagogical function to instruct our boys in the principles of Monsieur Proudhon. You are, I suspect, a truly gifted teacher. I respect you for that. But I will not – I *cannot*, good God man, you must see this – I cannot allow you to convert the Remove to Anarchism! There are already parents threatening to withdraw their sons. And I say nothing of your extra-mural activities. Grant me, please, that I do not interfere in those, whatever my private opinion of *your* opinions... '

That had left too little room for manoeuvre. That was sad. He was a good teacher, he sometimes thought, though he would deny it. After the preaching had come to its end – when he had to realise that he had somehow lost the faith – he had gone through his week-long crisis and had said, so be it, there are other things. On earth if not in heaven, and first I'll catch up on all the things I passed up at the theological college.

He met Meg at the first school, the dubious one where he had to exaggerate his Classics (which he did not now regret: he had made it a matter of honour to catch up, so that he soon became a Latinist, and even his Greek came to give him pleasure). Dearest Meg, she had struggled so valiantly to travel, to *grow*, with him. Then there were the children. He stood today on this equatorial rooftop in a temperature of give-or-take one hundred degrees, and he writhed – he literally, physically *writhed* – when he thought of what he had done in abandoning his children. Not Meg, but the children. Meg would survive; she had told him she would. Even as she cursed him. He did not want to wonder what she had said to the children.

The morning was so hot, so empty. He might have been sleeping. Yes, he must have allowed himself to sleep after all. Now he was awake. He had been woken. He must force himself to concentrate. Sasse's wife was standing over him. She said, 'There is a crisis. I cannot find Julius Wilhelm or Salner. There is an *askari* at the door. Tell me what to do, please...'

She had come to him, not to the French card players on the roof across the way.

Tom Fallon, still stupefied by the sun, said 'What is it?'

'I think they are saying they have a body. There is a dead man, Mr Fallon. Please help me.'

90

*

Dunn was the first to die. Jimmy Dunn, whose spectacles had been shattered on the day of their arrival. He was blind; only he understood the scale of that disaster, but none of them paid him much attention, and he understood that he would have to live with this. Dr Wilhelm had promised to send for a duplicate set of his lenses; Jimmy Dunn was sure that Dr Wilhelm would do that, and he knew that that would take several months.

So he practised an alternative solution. He found at once that if he squeezed his eyes into tight slits he could focus surprisingly well on objects in the middle distance. He quickly got used to that, and managed to move around so that his colleagues sometimes forgot that he was blind. They were not unsympathetic, but they forgot.

He was in a limbo. He no longer understood what had happened to their plans. He did his best to be helpful – to pull his weight, as he thought of it – but it is hard to be helpful when you are blind, and they were all very considerate, when they thought of him. He spent a lot of time at Mabrukki's. He had no particular friend. He had no particular regret.

That night Jimmy Dunn had drunk, slowly but steadily, at Mabrukki's. The French had been there earlier, not so civil. Then Stokkebye and Scavenius turned up and insisted on treating him to a round. All very convivial. Then the English arrived, Goddfrey and Bosanquet, just back from the mainland where, they said, they'd been looking for porters. They had a couple of local friends with them; when they saw him they came over to chat and called for a beer, but they went back to their own cubicle.

'I'm on my own,' thought Jimmy Dunn, 'since that nice Dutch guy Riekh volunteered to stay on the mainland with the stores. I was sorry about that, he and I got on fine.'

After an hour there was no fun in it, so he went for a stroll along the waterfront; he knew that the stars out here were enormous, but to him they were no better than floppy chrysanthemum buds, however tight he forced the muscles of his poor eyes. He realised that he was not too steady on his pins. Perhaps he was a bit pissed. Perhaps he also needed to piss. Jimmy Dunn had been educated to do these things discreetly. He looked for a shadowy corner and wandered – staggered? – in that direction. He sprayed his member into and over the high tide, which was rattling the *boriti* poles where they were stacked by the quayside to be seasoned in the shallows. He squeezed his pupils to try to make sense of it all, gazed down on the reflection of the moon as it lay shattered in the water, looked deeper, started to button his trousers, and tripped on a length of rope.

Jimmy Dunn, half-drunk, unseen by anyone, dived over the jetty, hit his head on a lump of mangrove tree, and drowned at once. They found him in the morning, unbuttoned still, his limp organ protruding, shrunk like a seaweed pod. There were confusions and delays, and when they eventually came to Free House, hours later, they found Louise Sasse.

Later still, after they had coped with the *askaris* and sent messages to Wilhelm, she said to Fallon, 'This is terrible. Your countryman was alone. Do you think he was attacked?'

He was startled. 'Why was he attacked? He was half-blind. Fact is, Jimmy was pretty plastered most of the time. Surely he fell off the jetty and was too smashed to swim for it. If he could swim, which I doubt. But it sounds as if he landed head-first on those bloody great mangrove beams.'

'Are you sure he wasn't attacked?'

'Louise!' said Tom Fallon, 'these people aren't interested in us. They have their own lives to lead – haven't you noticed? We've arrived, and we rent a couple of houses, but we don't *matter* to them. Jimmy Dunn didn't enter their calculations. Nor do you or I. We arrive, we leave – Lamu will forget us.'

She protested, 'Perhaps Jimmy had rupees in his pocket. Perhaps they wanted his money.'

He laughed at her. 'You're an innocent. These people are twenty times richer than you or I. They tolerate us because they know that we are in transit. That's one of the traditions in Lamu. This place may not look much, but it's been an international port since long before Liverpool – or La Rochelle or Hamburg. That's why you can buy anything you want here. *Anything*! They simply tolerate us, and make a respectable profit out of us, like any other travellers who arrive from the sea. But they will not allow us to stay here very long.'

'My husband said, too, that they would not let us stay.'

'He's right. And they're right too.'

She's too beautiful, thought Tom Fallon. It's not fair, I came on this crazy expedition to escape. I had the right to assume that I'd be setting off for Africa with a gang of madmen, and no temptations except for the occasional dusty maiden. Instead, I find that I'm holed up in a medieval village which positively reeks of every sort of sex and perversion I've ever heard of and a woman in my discussion group who has a mouth to charm the angels and is looking at me at this moment as if she had carnal ambitions for us. Louise, he pleaded with her silently, can't you content yourself with that Danish officer – yes, we all saw what was happening on the steamer, he's daft about you, God knows why your husband puts up with it, he may be old enough to be your father but he can't be blind as well. I know the Danish boyfriend is as thick as two short planks, but I don't imagine you were in his cabin to debate Dr Hertzka's theories of negative interest rates. I *know* we are all at a loose end, but there must be other things to do. You could learn Swahili, for example, like Martha Wilhelm – have you heard her lately, she's getting to sound pretty impressive? Or you could explore the island like Dekker, who charges off every day and comes back at dusk looking shagged out. Fair enough – I suppose it isn't possible for you to wander around by yourself. So why doesn't the handsome Stokkebye escort you? Your husband could hardly object, he probably wouldn't notice, he spends his time with that dismal crony of his.... As Dekker was saying the other night, we might be stuck here but we don't have to waste our time, there are plenty of worthwhile experiences to hand here on this very island...

Tom Fallon said, 'Young Schmidt was enthusing last night about the beach beyond Shela. It's only an easy stroll from here, and he said there are shells and things...'

Robert Schmidt had also said that the Shela dunes were thick with the bones of warriors who had fallen in the great battle between Shela and Pate in 1813; that was why Schmidt spent so much time there, he liked to think he was an amateur archaeologist, and he gloated over every skull he disinterred, his room at Free House was stacked with them, but Tom thought that this was not a suitable, or enticing, prospect to offer a lady. Instead he said, 'I haven't yet been out there. Have you? I wonder if you'd like to explore. Schmidt tells me we can always hail a dhow if you feel too fagged out to walk back...'

'Yes, of course. But not today. Surely they will want us to bury Jimmy Dunn at once?'

93

There was no Christian cemetery on the island, but there was a strip of sandy soil near the first outcrop of bush on the path to Shela where the islanders tacitly agreed that these things might be done. There had been a Tutsi soldier a couple of years ago (he needed an extra-long grave), and more recently one of the Goan clerks with the Customs treasury had been knifed in the bazaar and his colleagues had insisted he have appropriate burial, so he was here too.

Wilhelm approached Major Rogers for guidance, who suggested that they send for Fundi George. Bakari was with them and, when he heard of it, said in Swahili, 'He's a crazy man,' and Rogers said, in English, 'He's a missionary. Eccentric – perhaps a bit dotty. He lives out at Shela. He was a member of the Methodist mission at Golbanti, up-stream on the Tana, when it was massacred a few years ago. He survived, and has been a bit strange ever since. By the way, he's black – he hails from Liberia or somewhere on the west coast. But he's qualified to bury a Christian corpse if we can find him in time.'

'Can your men find him?'

'He's usually in a shack out behind the beach. He has a suicidal habit of standing outside the mosque there – have you seen its pillar minaret, by the way, it would interest you – preaching the Gospel after the Friday prayer. Anywhere else in Islam he'd be dead. Here they simply laugh at him.'

He called for Gopal Singh and gave orders. 'If my *askaris* can't find him, I'll do the job myself. I am empowered to do so under certain circumstances. I can do weddings too.'

'I don't think we need you for that,' replied Wilhelm innocently, and was surprised to see the Major struggling to stifle his laughter.

'By the way – this wretched Dunn fellow. I never met him. Would he have wanted a *Christian* service? I always imagined a lot of you people had given up on that sort of thing...'

'He would certainly have *expected* it,' said Wilhelm with dignity, as he later explained to his wife.

They found Fundi George, and Jimmy Dunn was buried at sunset. These things have to be done fast in the Tropics. The preacher turned out to be a dishevelled giant with a broad American accent: Fallon guessed that he had been educated at a

Methodist bible college in the United States. He wore a parson's collar and a threadbare black frock coat, though his hair and beard were a tangle of curls and his feet were bare. He spoke, acceptably enough, of Christ and the Resurrection, and then launched into a sermon on the evils that were apparently riding unbridled on the island. At one point he seemed to be suggesting that Jimmy Dunn had fallen victim to these same evils, which even the most impassioned of the revolutionaries around the grave might have demurred at. Julius (said Martha later to Louise) was at his best, she so admired his diplomatic skills; just at the point where the preacher paused for breath Wilhelm intervened – as though he had supposed that the man was finished – and offered a short homily, in English, on the nobility of Dunn's sacrifice. Louise confessed to weeping a tear, or even two.

The other mourners were Fallon and Dekker, Slingsby Goddfrey and Henry Bosanquet, Hans Salner and Dugmore (without the dog), young Robert Schmidt and Gustav Rabinek. To general surprise and – said Martha to Louise, to our very real appreciation – Major Rogers arrived at the last moment, in uniform: he stood slightly to one side, as was perfectly appropriate, and left as soon as the sand began to tinkle onto the top of the thin coffin. The sky over Manda Island turned purple, the stars came out. A dhow was hastening, on tide and wind, from Shela Bay, a white feather quill scratching on the ink-dark sea.

*

As from Free House, Lamu

Strictly Personal

Dear Dr Hertzka,

I trust you will shortly be receiving the long letter I took the liberty of sending you a week ago. I mention this because the postal arrangements on this island appear to be erratic and, I suspect, unreliable. Dr Wilhelm told us at last night's Free House meeting that he had received a generous and heartwarming message of encouragement from your own hand. It might be diplomatic if you did not correspond directly with me since it is better that our communication should remain utterly confidential...

First, it is my sad duty to confirm the news – which Dr Wilhelm may have already conveyed – of the tragic and accidental death by drowning of one of our older members, James Dunn. His body was discovered yesterday morning, here in the heart of the town. While the precise circumstances of his death will never be known, I do not think we need suspect foul play. 'Jimmy' was one of the simpler of our members, but his virtues were stalwart, as was his dedication to our cause, and we all mourn him. I trust that you will record the sad news in the next issue of the Association newsletter. Dr Wilhelm has no doubt arranged for 'next of kin' to be informed.

Sad news of a different nature – Dr Wilhelm, with my strong endorsement, has been compelled to suspend the membership of young Felix Thomas (we are uncertain as to whether expulsion is within our powers or should be referred to Vienna). You may remember that in my last report I made mention of my doubts about Thomas's moral fibre. It is now clear that I was correct. Thomas was caught red-handed, rifling the contents of my own chest, no doubt looking for money. He did not attempt to deny the offence, but we have been in something of a dilemma to know what to do with him: as Frau Wilhelm pointed out, in her charitable manner, it would hardly be appropriate to hand over a Freelander to languish in the Fort (which the English employ as a particularly unsavoury prison), nor even to turn him out on the streets. The problem has been temporarily resolved by Captain Dugmore's rather surprising offer to employ the lad as his servant. Thomas has been warned by Dr Wilhelm that any further 'episode' will certainly take him into the Fort.

These two episodes have, you will appreciate, cast something of a blight on the mood of our more serious members, but I have to report that the greater danger to the morale of our party threatens to be the continuing delay. We have now been on Lamu Island for a month and it sometimes seems – I am in this matter relaying many private conversations in Free House – that we are likely to be confined here for many more weeks. Some of our members continue to make laudable efforts to develop new skills in preparation for the mainland, and the recent arrival of our splendid steam-launch, the *Eden*, has kept its newly appointed crew more than busy. But the weather is particularly trying at this time of year, and – I believe I referred to this in my last letter – a few of our colleagues suffer from the (no doubt natural and good-hearted) wildness of youth and are finding the inactivity trying. Only

96

yesterday we had an absurd but nonetheless alarming incident when Lieutenant Stokkebye and Emil Ducoffre attempted to fight a 'duel' over the 'honour' of Madame Sasse. The situation was saved by the quick thinking of Dekker and Goddfrey, who substituted blanks in the two weapons – though not before giving both of the combatants the fright of their lives, I am happy to add – but you will no doubt sympathise with my concern. I am not usually an enthusiast for 'discipline', as you can imagine, but I confess that I feel we could do with a dash of that commodity here at present. We have instituted evening lectures at Free House, but by no means all of our members bother to attend.

Dr Wilhelm will have informed you of the various and technical reasons for our delay. I find myself not always convinced that they are insuperable; that private and inexpert opinion is not only mine but is shared by several of our colleagues, notably the English contingent. We are assured that the 'Big Rains' are very close, which will – according to Captain Dugmore – change the contours of the Tana Valley.

The English authorities continue to ignore us. I am told that they are preoccupied with tribal tensions on the immediate hinterland. Our German neighbours continue – I am told! – to offer daily hospitality to their compatriots. That is probably just as well – the temptations of this town are exotic (or so I am given to understand) – yet another reason why I shall be heartily pleased when we set foot on Africa proper...

Salner signed his name with sincerely affectionate greetings. I cannot worry our founder, he thought. I cannot bring myself to tell him the true state of affairs. I cannot tell him that at this rate we'll still be here next year.

*

Dekker, naked to the waist, lay on the hard floor of the rooftop terrace. It was mid-afternoon. He had an idea in his head which he needed to test out – was it Tom Fallon who had put it there? – that the body must be compelled to acclimatise. The natives do not suffer in this way, he had said, so why should we? It must therefore be a matter of training, and Dekker had ponderously explained this theory to Salner at dinner last night, to that worthy's obvious incomprehension.

So he lay there, slightly self-conscious (though he was alone), and composed himself to rest, even to sleep. Small hope of that. The sun smote down. His sweat splattered onto the cement. Every thirty seconds he was forced to comb a finger through his eyebrows, briskly, so as to splay the perspiration to one side before it poured through his useless brows to sting his eyes. Even so, the sweat poured out onto the ground in great dollops, thick as blood from a slaughtered goat. He lay flat, face down, his eyes only inches above the ground, and watched the drops splash onto the cement – first it was a black patch, then it was grey, then just a shadow, shrinking so fast into nothing under the burning impact of the sun until it was gone, vanished, a merest memory – and then the next spray of salt water.... He remembered that he had been dreaming of cats. He was being pestered by them. They were small and wild and kittens, and there were dozens of them. He grabbed at one of the most persistent, intending to throw it out of the way, as far as he could, but she bit his finger and fastened her tiny teeth into his flesh so he couldn't shake her free, while the others jumped and snapped at him, un-rebuffed and unafraid.

Fallon had arrived silently and Dekker was startled, though he tried to conceal it. He guessed that the younger man must have been examining his thicker, sodden and inflamed body. Tom burst out at once, 'Let me interrupt – please – and ask you something. Tell me, am I unfair? Am I right to declare that I am getting bored? Is it a fair point?'

'You have a perfect right to be bored. We did not travel all this way to sit on an offshore island. Perfectly pleasant though it may be.'

'Most of our colleagues seem entirely happy to do just that. They seem to adore this place.'

'I agree with you. I suspect they'd be delighted to stay on here for ever.'

'Rather than brave the interior.'

'Odysseus and his friends sat outside Troy for ten years.'

'And how long did Achilles sulk in his tent?'

'Which one of us is Achilles? Surely not Dr Wilhelm.'

'Then for Christ's sake, what do we have to *do* to get off this bloody island?'

'Wilhelm may be right about the Tana and the sand bar.

98

Dugmore ought to know, and he admits that the river is dicey right now. We need the Rains, I can see that.'

'Did our friends from Vienna realise that it might not be sensible to arrive here in April?'

'The more I see of Africa, the less faith I have in our Viennese mentors. Perhaps I shouldn't say that. But have you read *Freeland* lately?'

'No, but I remember it all too well. I think I take your point.'

'The detail – as opposed to the theory, which I exempt – is obvious and total bullshit.'

'So why are we here? You and I? Should we turn round and go home?'

'You know we can't do that.'

Later, after Dekker had sluiced himself with water and found a new shirt, when Bakari had brought fresh lime juice, unrequested, and when the sun was beginning to descend, Fallon said, 'Speaking for myself, I do not wish to go home. But I discover that I cannot tolerate this *inaction* which seems to afflict us.'

'A friend of mine once told me that the only way he kept depression at bay was to live his life so that every day his *work* was the justification for that day. He was arguing that idleness, vacation, call it what you like, was too dangerous. He maintained that only if he achieved something in a day could he rest content.'

'You have it there precisely.... No wonder you and I are in this state.' Tom Fallon's voice was urgent.

'Oh, I hope not. I have been trying to move beyond my friend's position. I would not want my "work" to be the definition of my life. I have increasingly wondered whether our "work" can be utterly satisfying, and yet at the same time – if you understand me – not enough...'

'You must be talking about yourself,' said Fallon. 'Look, I was just a teacher. I enjoyed it, but I was just a teacher. They tell me you were some sort of successful businessman. You were with Morris, weren't you?'

'No, I wasn't "with" him. Our companies co-operated on a small number of contracts. At one time he was a friend, yes, but we must have disagreed about more things than not.'

'I think I heard you speak once, at a public meeting.'

'Oh Lord! That's possible, I went through a period – it must have

99

been in the late Eighties, when I was too easily persuaded to get up on my hind legs. I only slowly discovered that I had very little to say.'

'If I don't offend you,' said Fallon, 'that is the way I now remember your speech.'

Dekker blinked. 'You're candid, I'll say that. But those evenings in London seem ridiculously far away.'

Fallon grinned. 'Mr Dekker – Dekker! – here we are in this jungle. By the way, Dugmore insists that we call it the Bush, he says the Jungle is only in India. And you and I both know that that is an exaggeration, since we've got nowhere near the jungle, or even the bush, as yet. Let's let bygones be bygones. In those days I was still with the Socialist League. I realised that it was increasingly dominated by the Anarchists and that the nobs like you and Morris were quitting, but that didn't worry me then. My job left me time to spare, and I enjoyed the street politics. I used to go out to the Bryant and May strike, and then there were the London dockers.... Heady days! Do you remember? I suppose you don't see it like that – it was a bit too close to a real revolution for you and your friends.'

Dekker made a gesture of silent protest.

'Don't get me wrong. I always respected Morris for his honesty. I still do today. I still agree with his argument that you can't use parliamentary reform to transform capitalism into socialism – I'll assume that you and I still agree on that. But Morris – (and you? Forgive me, I ought to know) – was over-sensitive to the presence of a handful of self-styled Anarchists amongst us. I still believe that Morris needn't have withdrawn his money from "Commonweal", there were enough of us left to fight the idiots.'

'Idiots?'

'Yes, the bomb throwers. The worshippers of "The Great God Dynamite" as someone put it. The "Propaganda of the Deed" – do you remember that frightful phrase? *Of course* it was a nonsense – all but a tiny minority of us knew that.'

'But the tiny minority, as you describe them – and I'm sure that you are right – set back the Revolution in Britain for many years.'

'And where's the Revolution now?'

'In the hands of the Fabians and the ILP.'

'Which – I imagine – is why you and I are here in this fucking jungle today.'

100

'You were just saying that we hadn't even got as far as the jungle!'

'Never mind the Revolution, we can't even find the Jungle, is that what you're telling me?'

'Tom,' he attempted, and sensed that the younger man was responding to his voice. 'Let's not make it simple. I promise you, I'm not here because I lost faith, or whatever cliché we may be accused of by Slingsby Goddfrey in the *Pall Mall Gazette*. Why are *you* here?'

Fallon wanted to reply, I was to be a minister – a priest, you would say. The career had been prepared for me, but one day I had the God-given grace to realise that I had no vocation. No faith. No religious feeling. No feeling at all, for God or for man – nor for woman either, but that's a different point. I discovered in myself a *non*-need to worship. So, resigning myself to the *non*-existence of the God I had been brought up to serve, and the *non*-demands of faith, and the *non*-need of feeling, I threw myself and all those frustrated energies of youth into the affairs of this world as opposed to the next. The body, you might say, as opposed to the soul. The body-politic as well.

That led, after a wild few years, back to the same emptiness. Here was a hollow man, untempted to return to religion, gregarious but without the capacity to allow himself to love; so he became, first, a teacher, and at the same time he moved into radical politics. He was good at the politics (he had inherited the rhetorical gift from his lost vocation: a speech from a soapbox is no great distance from a sermon). He was said to be a good teacher, though he suspected that that was not true, he did not have the teacher's selfless concern to urge his pupils to excel the teacher. So he used the teaching as an adjunct to the politics. The radical women came with the radical politics. And then, one day, he discovered that he wasn't really interested in the politics any more, just the women.

He tried to say just a small part of this to Dekker as the day wore on. He talked and he talked, and Dekker seemed willing to listen to him. Somehow it took up a good part of the evening. They finished up at Mabrukki's, which neither he nor Dekker normally patronised, and he found he was still talking, as he hadn't allowed himself to talk for longer than he could remember. At one point he wanted to proclaim, 'I am a half-dead man', but he stopped himself because he knew that that would be a nonsense, a lie. He was thinking, as he drank, that Dekker was too good a listener, he gave away nothing in return. We must have something in common, he thought, that we can spend the day like this. If we were happy and fulfilled in our previous lives, neither of us would be here today. QED. Our circumstances may seem so different, but we surely share certain things. He is rich, I am poor; he is known in the world, and I am a nonentity; yet we have both come here out of some solitary shared impulse. We must in some mysterious way share the same knowledge of ourselves – which can only be that we are empty, unfulfilled. Maybe it was a negative impulse that brought us here together – the need to get away from an unsatisfactory life – and not the positive inspiration of a convinced and ecstatic ideology. But an impulse is surely, by definition, positive not negative. Or is it? Are we all in flight, in rejection, in rebound from our European lives?

I am in flight, yes, from the emptiness of my earlier life, from the boredom of my profession, from a desert of the emotions, from a disillusion with the political movement which has sustained my vitality for ten years. I have come to Freeland to attach myself to a new and vigorous purpose and commitment; to refresh and revitalise myself in this new world. And now, already, I find that we are drifting into pettiness and waste. The months roll by, and we do not even summon our resources to get off the fucking island.

Dekker must understand this. I know he does. He will be my saviour.

*

Major Rogers was felled by a fever. He cursed its timing, but was not unduly put out. On the Coast these things happened from time to time, there was nothing you could do about it, and he sensed that he was not in for a bad bout. But no point in denying it. So he took to his bed and called Iqbal Ali. 'Bring my pills – yes, the medicine from Bombay – and a pint of champagne. Very cold. Then, Iqbal Ali, watch over me. Until the fever breaks.'

The servant rolled his eyes because he understood that his master had decided on the dramatic treatment. He was frightened of these magic pills from the bazaar, he knew what they did to a man; at the end of it, the Major's thin body would have lost another half-stone. Rogers noted the hesitation. 'Don't hang around,' he snapped, and his teeth were beginning to chatter as he reached for a blanket to cover himself. 'I know what I'm doing. So do you, dammit! I can't waste time with fever just now, I'm needed on the mainland. Tell Captain Dugmore that I have to have two days of peace. Make my apologies, that sort of thing. And warn Gopal Singh.'

He was thinking of the Sasse woman. She had looked him in the eyes. She always looked at him in a way that no-one else on the island would dream of doing – she looked at him as a man, not as the Company Agent. The first time she did it he felt the blood rise in his face, and still she did not have the modesty to look away, and he had felt embarrassed, then moved, and eventually *invaded* by her, so he had decided to feel angry – with himself, and therefore against her. He thereafter took pains to avoid her, but there were moments of reverie when he would catch himself thinking of her mocking eyes, her wide mouth, her candid, lewd grin, and he would reprimand himself. For he knew that he had chosen a certain life: he accepted that he had agreed to live his life without certain things. He missed music, for instance. On home leave he would seek out London's concert halls. One evening, only this week, he had been passing Free House in the secrecy of evening and had heard a woman singing; the words, he guessed, were French, and he could make nothing of them, but the melody floated down from the distant rooftop like the feather of some fabled bird, and he stood there in the shadows unable to move away; he knew that it was Louise Sasse.

It was good of her to understand. She must have been told of his fever, and she had come to nurse him. She was sponging his face. She was murmuring to him, soothing him in a language he could not understand, leaning low over him so that her breasts brushed against his blanket, and he could almost – no! This was impossible, this intimacy was unspeakable, how dare she? He half rose and tried to push her away, crying her name in outrage and reproof – and in a fleeting moment of consciousness he saw that it was his faithful servant Iqbal Ali who was leaning over him, sponging his bald head, muttering comfort to him, gazing in perplexity at him. He felt the water bottle rattle against his teeth, the lime juice splashing down his chin, and then he slept.

He dreamed that he was back in India. His beloved India. He was travelling on horseback with Dugmore, and they were searching for something. It was hard to pick the right track over the high

103

mountain, but eventually they doubled round behind a deserted village and came out on a plateau of stone-desert, with a panorama of snow-covered peaks in the distance. There was a church. They rode straight *through* it. Then there was a pigtailed Chinese man talking with the priest. He asked, did we have a map? Rogers found that he was able to peel back the skin of his bald scalp, from the crown to the brow, and he demonstrated this to the Chinaman and showed him there was a simple map underneath. The terrain was very steep as they crossed a sequence of valleys. The horses were floundering through a volcanic dust, beneath which they could see ancient brick terracing. At one point they glimpsed a freshwater lake far below, with a single boat like a Spanish galleon which, said the Chinaman, belonged to him. He puzzled how to press on across the deep valley up into the distant mountains. A young girl with a Botticelli face walked towards them from the lake and warned them not to go on. 'There is no more water,' she said. 'You will all die.'

Six

The civilisation of the Masai, as well as other tribes in alliance with us, made rapid progress.... We offerd to every Masai girl who made a solemn promise of chastity until marriage admission into a Freeland family for a year, and instruction into our manners, customs and various forms of skilled labour. Even those who could not be immediately received were decorated with the insignia of their new honour – a complete dress after the Freeland pattern, their barbarian wire neckbands, leg chains and ear stretchers, as well as the coating of grease, being discarded – and they solemnly promised to be 'friends of the white women'.... The ultimate result was that in a very short time the once so licentious Masailand was changed into a model country of good morals...

Theodor Hertzka: *Freeland: A Social Anticipation*

Martha Wilhelm sat in an inner room of the Liwali's house. It was very long and also narrow. There were no windows, only a profusion of lamps to augment the daylight that beamed through the open doorway from which she had been ushered. It was suddenly blessedly cool. She observed that the long wall was an extravaganza of ornately sculpted plasterwork, of gleaming white, deeply recessed mini-archways set inches deep into the surface. It was a masterpiece of deliberate invention. The slots were filled with objects – Korans, candles, porcelain ornaments, books, metalwork – but the basic proportions were undisturbed.

Ma Fatima said, 'I see you are looking at the plasterwork. Sometimes I spend many hours in here, with my daughters, when my grandsons have visitors in the outer room. When we have to retreat into *harem* we find that we can gaze at that wall and our confinement is relieved, so we are happy again.'

Martha stared at the plaster and began to understand. There was a trick of perspective in it. You could sit in this cell and – because of some obscure mathematical formula – your world became larger, you might almost be looking out on an urban landscape. She could not applaud the ploy, but she began to understand that its beauty, which came out of its subtle proportions, had an extra purpose: to keep Ma Fatima and her womenfolk in sound mind!

But why, she wondered, were these rooms so crowded? Everywhere there was furniture – she had to pick here way around it with particular care – and she had also noticed something strange, which was that there were chairs, beds, sofas and stools in profusion, but no *tables*, as she would have expected. Later, she discovered that meals were eaten sitting on the woven mats on the floor, though her coffee and sweetmeats, perhaps in deference to her European status, were placed by the slave girls on the nearest string bed. And there were mysteries in these rooms, because everywhere there seemed to be niches and recesses hidden behind heavy curtains that hung from brilliantly enamelled poles: the *arras*, thought Martha, must be important in this society, and she imagined that she could never be certain that she was alone in this room with her hostess. She guessed that people – children, slaves, even Ma Fatima – *slept* behind these curtains; she guessed, correctly, that Swahili architecture does not share the European concept of the bedroom.

Today, she was sitting on a couch and Ma Fatima's servant girls were painting a pattern on the soles of her feet in purple henna. Julius would be furious, she realised – but why should he be furious? She knew that what she was doing was an idiocy, but why not? The designs were so simple and so pleasing to her, it seemed such an innocent way of identifying with the island where she was living, and Ma Fatima had been so delighted when she asked. That was the best reason. 'It will last for six to eight weeks,' she had warned her, 'depending on whether you go barefoot. Your husband will approve?'

'No,' said Martha, 'I don't think so.'

The old woman said, 'You prefer we do not do this?'

'No, you do it. Please.'

'Good!' said Ma Fatima, and ordered the girls to carry on with their brushwork.

*

The sun came up over Manda a few minutes after six, beaming low and irresistible into the rooftop bedroom and through the

cheesecloth mosquito net. Enormous clouds, fluffy, dark-bot-
tomed, filled the rest of the sky and wandered over their heads on
the way to Africa. Dekker had heard the rumours that the rains
at Garsen were heavy. He staggered to his feet and looked out onto
Manda. The island, flat and without feature except for two silhouetted baobab trees, covered the full length of the horizon, hemming
them in; there was no sight of the open ocean, and yet it was
impossible to doubt that the sea lay just over this accidental strip
of barren bush. To the far left, if you knew what to look for, you
could trace the entrance to the Mkanda, the high-tide creek which
separates the mangroves of Manda from the mangroves of the
mainland. Only to the far right, seen from the communal dormi-
tory, could he spot a hint of open water beyond Shela, but perhaps
it was his imagination, inspired by the fresh breeze blowing up the
harbour roads.

He could hear how the house was stirring: a voice calling out in
the basement kitchen; a muffled curse as Dugmore reached for his
boots; a chattering from the room Ducoffre shared with Schmidt;
the unmistakeable whine of an early mosquito. Below, in the
narrow streets where the sun had not arrived, there was the clatter
of a string of donkeys hastening down to the quay, the thwack of
a stick on a rump, and, as if to welcome them two blocks away,
the hideous braying of a donkey stallion, like the sound of a
blunted saw on corrugated iron. Dekker sat on a reed stool and
waited for the *choo* to be vacant. He was confused because he had
been dreaming heavily. He had been back in his Cotswold valley,
the one with the village in the distance and the spire and the gentle
sweep of the beechwood that protected a steep field, with a hint
of a stream beyond, signalled by a line of willow trees. He had been
looking down on it from the hill, planning – no, he had been
talking with the Vicar: he had been telling the Vicar how he had
a passionate desire to be buried in this churchyard. 'I don't know
if that's possible,' he had volunteered, 'I'm not a local, I'm not even
an Englishman – though I live only a few miles away, but not in
this parish – and I can't pretend I'm much of churchgoer, on the
contrary...' What had the Vicar been saying? He had a good face,
he remembered, a little like Cornwell's, but what exactly had he
been saying?

The *choo*, when he got there – succeeding a grumpy and recently
disgraced Rabinek – was occupied by an army of cockroaches.

Dekker was willing to grant that the Lamu deep-drop system was clean and did not stink and was no doubt entirely sanitary, all of which he had been told by Dugmore, but he was convinced that for some reason it was a breeder of cockroaches. He hated them in the way that women are supposed to hate spiders; he had a horrid sense of them climbing out of the depths to grope at his naked parts. All in a panic, he splashed himself in a gourd of water, drawn modestly from the cistern which Bakari had to fill by hand. The skin of his feet, he saw, hardened by weeks of walking in sandals in the *shambas* and by the convention of going barefoot indoors, was peeling in great healthy strips of rubbery flesh, like a snake sloughing its skin, and he discovered that the soles beneath were already hard and clean and unscarred again.

He did not linger there, which was as well because Tom Fallon was jogging up and down outside with the expression of a man who regrets the night before. 'Cockroaches again,' said Dekker. 'Can we have a campaign? After breakfast?'

'Ask Dugmore,' replied Fallon. 'He's in charge of bloodsports.'

'Report them to Rogers,' called Dugmore, who had been observing this exchange, unnoticed, from the balcony above their heads.

Dekker regretted the cockroaches because he admired the Swahili bathrooms. Not just the deep-drop but the plasterwork, so ornate and geometrical and yet so simple (he would send a sketch to Morris), and the cistern of water with one swimming goldfish (to eat the mosquito larvae, Dugmore had explained a dozen times) from which you sluiced your body, never soaked it in the European style. He also admired the breakfasts: the pawpaw and the mango, both drenched in the juice of lemons picked that morning in their own garden; the strange coffee, thin and gritty, thick with cardamom, no milk; the tiny eggs, boiled or scrambled; the rough, raw bread (no butter, but bowls of thick and aromatic honey).

Fallon had joined him at the long table. 'It's Friday, isn't it? Do I detect that the town is quieter than usual?'

'Like an English Sunday?'

'Yes. Do you think people are "sleeping in", as we used to say?'

'Wait for midday.'

Dekker remembered how on their first Friday he had been startled to encounter a multitude of men, young and old, all in freshly laundered *kanzus*, pouring down the lanes on their way to the noon prayers.

'Did you hear the rain in the night?'

'No. You must have been dreaming.'

Fallon shrugged. There was certainly a lot of water suspended above them at that moment. The whole arc of the morning sky was flecked, densely, with waves of light cloud; towards the horizon it became heavier; the sun was beginning to burn through but it would take time...

They had been joined by Selling and Schmidt, who greeted them with reserve. Stokkebye and Scavenius were at the far end of the table. The Freelanders, Dekker appreciated, employed at least one of the conventions of the Oxford college or the London club: you did not make conversation over breakfast – though here you did not have the morning newspapers to hide behind.

'What's planned for the day? Another route march around the island?'

Dekker replied, 'You flatter me. I still haven't found a track to take me beyond Kipungani. And you?'

'I may go out to Shela again. I must say it's a wonderful beach.'

'Have you been exploring the dunes? Young Schmidt is raving about the archaeology of the place – I think he means the bones. And he says the shells are very special too.'

'I'll keep an eye out,' said Fallon.

*

Later that morning, a number of them met by accident on the foreshore. Dekker was looking for his favourite dhow captain because he planned to explore the rock pools on the seaward side of Manda; Fallon, who had declined to accompany him, had advised him to take plenty of water. Martha Wilhelm had it in mind to follow after Ma Fatima's heavily-veiled progress to the Women's Mosque, though of course she would not be allowed to enter, even with the old lady's authority. Louise Sasse, in a gaily embroidered white skirt that hugged her slim waist, professed to be fancy-free and entirely happy with whatever the day might bring. Captain Dugmore arrived in the company of his new manservant, Felix Thomas, and paused to pass a compliment in his most mocking and insincere style which, he suspected, disconcerted her.

The town was suddenly crowded, and in the distance they heard the sound of drumming – not the frantic improvisation of party-goers, but a slow, measured, not quite rhythmic beat. 'We should

109

stand back a little,' murmured Dugmore. 'The Liwali is coming to the Friday Mosque for the noon prayers.'

The retinue was preceded by a rabble of soldiery armed with canes and staffs, who roughly and with much unnecessary shouting pushed aside the donkeys and small boys who were too lazy or too curious to follow Dugmore's advice. Then came a more dignified squad of *askaris*, in white robes and turbans, bearing heavy Omani daggers at their belts and ancient muskets shouldered in approximate fashion; next, the elders, the *wazi*, shuffling along with the benevolent self-importance of any group of prosperous aldermen in any corner of the world. At the heart of the procession, four slaves carried a palanquin of red silk over the head of a vigorous-looking, middle-aged man who wore a thick black beard and an expression of ill-disguised arrogance. 'The Liwali himself!' muttered the Captain, and appeared to sketch a minimal bow, the merest flicker of respectful greeting, which earned him a sharp stare and a belated wave of recognition and, perhaps, greeting. The Sultan's representative wore a turban of white silk wrapped loosely around a *kofia* cap densely embroidered in gold thread, a white *kanzu* of the same material which billowed extravagantly in the light breeze, and at his side he held a great curved sabre with an ivory handle that appeared to be inlaid with gold and ebony. He looked about him now with lively interest, and from time to time acknowledged an *hommage* from the crowd. Dugmore whispered something in Louise's ear, and she looked up at him with a frown of interrogation, then shrugged and pulled a scarf loosely, nonchalantly, over her hair, her neck and her bare shoulders. The Liwali slowed his pace and addressed a remark to the younger man who was immediately behind him. He had none of the Liwali's handsome looks. His beard was thin, his pallid complexion deeply pockmarked, his eyes were shifty and evasive, and he suffered from a thick and drooping lower lip, almost a deformation, which failed to hide a set of over-perfect teeth.

'Who was he?' asked Louise, when the procession had passed and the crowds had moved on.

'Abdullah bin Hamed. One of the Liwali's brothers, by a different mother. He used to be Liwali here until we fired him. Best thing we ever did.'

'*We*, Captain Dugmore? You are in Freeland now, please remember...'

*

Major Rogers, recovered from his fever, sat with his pipe on the familiar rooftop and looked out over Manda. He could hear, as he could every night, the discreet sounds of his servant clearing his solitary dinner table. Rogers and Iqbal Ali had been together since Ahmedabad in '87. It was not a word that could be used then, or even today, but each loved the other, though neither could have admitted it to himself, let alone to the other. They were master and servant. Either would have given his life for the other – though neither of them knew that, nor ever would have considered the possibility.

The Rains, Rogers was thinking, could no longer be far away: today he had had the sense that a storm was holding off only by a minor miracle. This evening the sky to the west had been heavy again, but Lamu seemed to be slipping past the threat and preparing for an unsettled night. Still, the Rains were coming, as they came every year with a remarkable punctuality when you checked the records, and the Tana would soon flood and for weeks the clear turquoise of the seas around Lamu Island would be stained with red silt. By then he would have resolved the unfinished business at Witu. And by then his Freelanders would have no further excuse to delay their departure. And a good journey to them, promised the Major, who had drunk a bottle of warm claret and knew that he was in benevolent mood. He wondered if Dugmore would feel obliged to accompany the party – it was amusing, he noticed, that neither he nor Dugmore had thought to discuss that prospect. The sooner they go, the better, he reminded himself, and paused and allowed himself to qualify the thought. Some of them I'll almost miss, he granted. The Wilhelms are a sympathetic pair, and at least they're an improvement on the Denhardt brothers. And Dekker – he'll be going up-country like a shot; I could have had time for that man...

'Iqbal Ali!' he called. 'Leave that for a moment and go up to Free House – you know where I mean? Ask for Bwana Dekker, and see if he wishes to be my guest for a nightcap. But speak to no-one else, you hear, only Bwana Dekker. Do you understand?'

He could see below him, newly arrived in the creek, the outline of another great ocean-going dhow from Somalia; it was enormous in comparison with the coastal vessels that were moored

111

around it, its proportions broad yet not clumsy, its great beak of a prow painted with the traditional black and white snout to defy the storms, and two latrine boxes protruding to port and starboard. This was further proof that the monsoon was turning; the dhow would be loading in the morning – he made a mental note to have the cargo checked. There was still no adequate system of supervision of the outgoing cargoes, which worried his bureaucratic mind. The Customs office at the main jetty was inefficient, he knew it, and he knew it because the Customs men had no idea that he spied upon them for so many hours of the day. Never mind a Somali *boom*, the Germans hardly bothered to deny that they brought in, and sent out, their merchandise with only the most cursory reference to the rules. He fancied he could see a light glowing over the balcony beyond the post office; no doubt they were playing *skat* with Toeppen – whom he knew for a fact to have arrived from Kipini that afternoon – and were plotting God knows what mischief. It was becoming an effort to be civil to them when they met in the street. I am so alone, thought Rogers, with a sharp and sudden access of self-knowledge, like a reminder from a rotting tooth. I have no friend; I am the worse for it.

Dekker, who had arrived unannounced, said, 'This is very civil of you. I was dreading the prospect of an evening in the company of Stokkebye and Gleisering – they are two of my less congenial companions.'

'Mr Dekker! I hope I haven't tempted you away from – what's her name? – Frau Sasse, or for that matter the charming Frau Wilhelm.'

I'm being crass, thought Rogers, but the visitor did not seem to take offence.

'The delicious Louise is never short of company, I promise you, and Martha has already retreated to the little house which they were so wise to take for themselves, just down the jetty from here. "God" and "Bos", as they're known – do you know our countrymen Goddfrey and Bosanquet? They're excellent value – have taken themselves off to their usual haunts – *not* my sort of thing! – and I was left with, as I say, Stokkebye, who's a drunken Dane, and Gleisering, who is a Dutchman and, I suspect, a criminal.'

'You need a brandy,' said Rogers, and Iqbal Ali was at his side instantly.

112

Much later, Rogers said, 'Look, from what you've been saying, this "Freeland" idea is admitting that you don't have a hope of estab-lishing your own preferred society in Europe, so you aim to transfer it lock, stock and barrel to – in this case – Africa. Where you'll have a chance of seeing whether it works, and where there's nobody around to object. An experiment, you could say.'

'I wouldn't put it quite like that, but yes, I take your point.'

Rogers said, 'But you can't *do* that. It's not as simple as that. There are people here already. On this island, for instance, there is a civilisation – yes, a civilisation – which I wager is more sophisticated than most of what we can offer in Europe, and I doubt if any of you have caught a glimpse of it. (I exempt yourself, of course, forgive me...)'

Dekker did not seem disposed to disagree. 'Did you know,' he asked inconsequentially, 'that Martha Wilhelm is very deep with someone called Ma Fatima? She tells me that there is a depth, a richness of culture, here which no outsider ever understands. From what she says, Ma Fatima is a woman of great quality. Do you know her?'

'Of course not. I would never be allowed to meet her. She is the Liwali's mother. One of the various wives of the Liwali's father, of course – the brothers have different mothers, it's very confusing.'

'I did not know that. Martha did not mention it.'

'Mrs Wilhelm is fortunate to have made the acquaintance.'

'The point I suppose I'm addressing is your perfectly correct indictment that we are imposing ourselves, intruding on an au-thentic local culture – and for essentially selfish reasons, our critics might add. But that, surely, is precisely what *you* – the forces you represent, whether the IBEA Company or the imperial presence in Zanzibar – are doing. Forgive me if I seem blunt. We can, I think, talk as friends. But it is you, Rogers, who is intruding on Africa as much as we Freelanders.'

'Precisely! Your organisation indicts us for imperialism, and yet claims the same right to inflict yourselves on this continent.'

Dekker was visibly taken aback. 'That implies that neither of us should be here.'

'Oh hell!' said Rogers. 'It's late. I've had a glass too many. We are talking in confidence, are we not? I am about to take my *askaris* onto the mainland and I shall have to string up various scoundrels – which I don't enjoy, I promise you – and *of course* I ask myself late at night what I'm doing. Do you and your friends think that we are oblivious to these questions? I am the effective ruler of a territory the size of Wales. Can you imagine that I don't occasionally ask myself, "By what right?" No, don't worry – I have an adequate answer to my own question. I won't bore you with the detail...' He added, abruptly, 'Look around you! That's the detail.'

'The Liwali might not agree.'

'Of course he wouldn't. The Liwali is an evil and corrupt petty chieftain. You happen to have mentioned the best justification for my presence here.'

'What I query,' said Dekker, with the courtesy of a wise man who liked his host and did not want to offend, 'is why we English – and the Germans and the French, for that matter – have taken it upon ourselves to come out here and interfere with people like the Liwali. It's not as if we didn't have other things to do. *You*, Rogers – I take you as one instance, if I may – are manifestly a person of energy and integrity (yes! yes!), and your energies and integrity should surely be employed at home. You probably don't know it but there are horrors in Hackney, in East London, as bad as anything in Lamu Town.'

'You surely grant that we have an imperial mission.'

'I don't think that I do. That's the nub of it. I suspect that it's the easier option – it's easy, too easy, for you and Sir Arthur Hardinge (forgive me, I'm not really being personal) to order these black savages around, easier than staying at home doing something effective about the evils in the East End.'

Rogers liked the man more and more. He said, and poured more brandy, 'Don't concern yourself. I welcome a debate in this back-water.... I think you are saying we're in the same boat, you and I.'

'How d'you mean?'

'We have both retreated from our homeland. Perhaps because it's easier out here. I govern my natives. You build your new society.'

'You miss the central point, if I may say so,' said Dekker, and they were friends again now, they were enjoying themselves. '*We* – we Freelanders – are in transit. We are going inland. We are going to attempt to found a new society in which we shall not appoint ourselves as masters...'

'Do you really believe that?' Rogers interrupted. 'Don't you realise that over there' – he pointed west – 'it's swarming with a brutish rabble? Tribes which will massacre you for the sake of your tobacco? Ask Dugmore! The Masai will get you all before you pitch camp – except that you're actually prepared for them, that's why you were carrying the armoury which I had to confiscate, because you secretly know you will have to fight for territory. Just as we and the Germans have had to fight for it.'

'I'm assured that things are different inland.'

'You're expecting the Garden of Eden? And an empty one at that? Look, believe me, I go over to that mainland every month, and when I go I take a hundred *askaris* and a couple of cannon because I know what I'll find there. Anarchy! Somali raiders, slave traders, tribes who've been at war with each other for generations, villagers who are scared to sleep at night, chiefs pleading with me for a garrison I cannot possibly provide. Why do you think that Lamu is so rich, so quiet, so *civilised*, as I keep promising you? Because it's an island! The *shifta* can't raid us at night, much as they'd love to. From Witu across to the Tana there's rich farming land – you'll see – and there are good crops growing, or will be after the Rains. But the owners take care to live in this town, on this island, and under my protection.'

'And our glorious Empire could not protect them on their own estates on the mainland?'

Rogers replied, with a new degree of vehemence, 'I tell you, it's anarchy on the mainland. Or something very close to it. Until I am given the men and the guns I need. But that's what your friends are in favour of, isn't it?'

'I have never been an Anarchist, if that's what you are suggesting,' answered Dekker. 'I see its attraction as a philosophy, of course, but I am too much of a realist – perhaps I am a pessimist – to believe that it could ever be implemented.'

'And your colleagues in Free House?'

'Some of them, I agree. But probably fewer than you imagine.'

'Then why did you come?' asked Rogers. 'Why you, of all people?'

Of all people, thought Dekker, I was the one who had to come, though he did not say it out loud. I was possessed with the sense that the days, months, years, my very life, were rolling by at a speed which beggared my understanding, like a train departing

115

from the platform and picking up speed so fast that it is impossible to leap on board. Carrie used to see this, this daily defeat, this desperation growing into panic. 'You're not just a man in a hurry,' she once said, 'anyone would think you'd been vouchsafed the term of your days.' I'm a not unintelligent man, but my intelligence benefited me not at all.

'Believe me,' Rogers was saying, 'I find I am genuinely curious. Not about some of those drunken children who accompany you, but about people like yourself – and Fallon, is that his name? – and the Wilhelms, they seem to be pleasant, respectable people.'

'It must be difficult for someone like yourself who has a career, a professional life planned out ahead. I suppose that you have a concept of your future – promotion, advancement, retirement, that sort of thing. And you would not be in your present post, I imagine, if you were not secure in a conviction that you are doing the right thing. Not merely that this is what you want to do, but also that it is something that you – or someone – *ought* to be doing. It is a morally satisfying life that you lead.'

'Someone has to do these things,' said Rogers, and put elaborate irony into his voice while he thought, privately, why should this man assume these things of me, how little we understand our fellow men...

Dekker missed the inflexion. He was remembering the evening last year in Gatti's in the Strand after the monthly meeting of SPAB, the Society for Protecting Ancient Buildings, which Morris had founded fifteen years previously. There had been the usual group of amiable, dedicated friends, and the usual agenda of rural churches where energetic young clergymen had persuaded their squire, with the enthusiastic support of the local builder, to pull down the twelfth-century tower and 'restore' by the simple procedure of starting again. The Society had been one of William Morris's happiest inspirations, and the diners had the right to be cheerful, if only because they knew themselves to be steadily winning the sympathy of the nation.

After the brandy and port they were dispersing in search of their carriage or, in Dekker's case, a hansom, when Morris had beckoned at him and mimed that he should stay behind. The old man – as they all thought of him, but he wasn't really that old – was in a sweaty pallor behind the whiskers, and his normal ebullience

116

had faltered as the evening progressed. Dekker urged him, with the familiarity of long acquaintance, to take himself back to Hammersmith. 'No, I have a proposal for you,' Morris had said. He wanted Dekker to take over from him as Hon.Sec. of the society – 'Anti-Scrape', as it was dubbed.

Dekker, at that moment when he should have been suffused with the honour, the compliment, had been seized by a giddying rage. He had controlled himself with a great effort by reminding himself that there was no man in the world whom he loved and respected as he did Morris. He had told himself, furiously, that this was a token of esteem and trust and acceptance, and he should be grateful. But he had been irrationally angered. 'There is no-one I'd rather see succeed me,' the old man had said. 'I'd ask you to take it on for, say, five years, because we of all people have a proper concern for continuity, ha? But you'd be the perfect man to handle the Academy and all those crusty types who are trying to destroy the true glory of this land.'

Had it already come to this? Dekker had wondered. They'll be giving me a knighthood next. I am scarcely into middle age, and I discover that my dearest friend expects me to spend the rest of my life in the politics of medieval manor houses. And they all assume I shall be content with that. Is that how they reckon my ambition for myself? Is that the best they expect of me? And he wondered if he might be hearing the bitter laughter of his father, who had brought him to be born in this absurd country.

He realised with a start that the Major might be perplexed by his silence. 'Forgive me,' he offered, 'I was dreaming of something.... You see, I am increasingly conscious of my father's example. There is no reason for you to know it, but in his own country he was a famous man. He had to go into exile in '48, and of course he came to Britain. I sometimes feel that our generation has not been worthy of the example of our immediate forebears. But you may not agree. Was your father a similar influence on you?'

'Certainly not,' replied Rogers with a sardonic grin. 'I escaped to India with great relief, and discovered that I had found myself.'

'You are, it's evident, a man who enjoys command. I have never felt that ambition, though I do not deplore it...'

'Like some of your Freelanders, to whom I must be Lucifer.'

Dekker smiled. 'Some of them would be surprised to see where I am this evening.'

'And they do not see that, even as they are drinking at Mabrukki's – or enjoying those Oroma whores in less respectable surroundings – their very lives are guaranteed by me and by the civil order that I represent? This used to be a dangerous town, especially down beyond the Monument, and the Sultan's writ was pretty frail. But your only casualty has been the old fellow who tripped into the *boriti* poles.'

'I'll propose a vote of thanks to you at the next Free House meeting,' said Dekker. 'I'm sure Captain Dugmore will second it.'

Now what did that mean, wondered Rogers, but his guest had reverted to an earlier topic.

'If it really interests you, I think that our generation of *Englishmen* – for that is how I think of myself – has somehow missed out on the mainstream of political, and therefore philosophical and moral, European thinking. Perhaps I only feel that because of my father's background. When I was comparatively active in political debate a few years ago, I used to think that so many of my fellows were – how shall I put it? – such innocents, such amateurs. They had nothing of the Commune in them. Perhaps they had no need. Perhaps their more gifted and energetic members have – like you, Major! – been distracted by the imperial mission.'

'It keeps us out of mischief.'

'It does more than that. It fulfils a man somehow. I grant that, even while I am dubious about the mission. I was talking to young Goddfrey at breakfast, and I couldn't help myself thinking that he'd make a splendid colonial officer – he'd have been appalled to hear that, but instead he's just drifting – and *that* he knows. Some of the Germans in our party are in the same boat, though it may not be so feasible for them. Julius Wilhelm is no revolutionary or Utopianist – not he! – he has the soul of the conscientious bureaucrat. Or Wilhelm Selling (you won't have met him) would be the perfect up-country administrator, tough but fair-minded and wholly lacking in self-doubt.'

'I never thought to hear a Freelander extolling the virtues of a career in the Colonial Service.'

Dekker said, 'I'm trying to explain why I wearied of making furniture for the aristocracy. For Captain Dugmore's aunts, as he tells me.'

'The years go by...' said Rogers with a moment of insight.

'The French talk of *le cafard*. That I have never suffered. But I confess I was in danger of getting bored.'

'With making furniture for Dugmore's people?'

'With the rest of it, too.' He didn't want to itemise the rest of it – the radical philosophies, the Socialist conferences, the Syndicalist weekends, the Saturday afternoon rallies, the petty and perpetual politicking – to an interlocutor to whom the detail would be meaningless. Never mind the village; the house; the firm; dear Carrie. 'As I think I told you, I had been reading Hertzka, pretty well by accident, and I found I responded to something – not the nonsense bits. Then I heard of this expedition, and it suddenly seemed to me that it made sense.'

'*Make sense*! To carve out a new colony on the slopes of Mount Kenya? Most of you will be dead by Christmas!'

Rogers realised that he was speaking too strongly, and felt he should apologise. Dekker was silent. 'I beg your pardon,' said the Major, in a tone not often heard in Lamu, and he pushed the decanter across the table. 'I exaggerate, of course. But I know this country, and I feel obliged to warn you of the difficulties of your project. Dugmore knows the interior much better than I do, and he can explain the detail if you need it.'

Dekker muttered some courtesy, and Rogers realised at that moment that the conversation had no purpose, because for Dekker there was no alternative, the die had been cast, in London, in Gloucestershire, in Dresden, wherever, and he would not be persuaded, ever. This was a man, supposed Rogers, who had well and truly burned his bridges.

*

That night Rogers dreamed of the Sasse woman. She was slim and loving, and her eyes were strangely bright as though she had a fever. He woke in the darkest hours, disturbed and hard, and knew what he had to do: he went to the *choo* and masturbated, quickly, refusing all thought, and went back to his bed and slept at once, undisturbed by dreams.

That same night Dekker dreamed of Matandoni. His sister was with him, and he was showing her the island. They went down to the jetty where, instead of the usual *jahazi* dhow, a magnificent *mtepe* with a prow shaped like the head of the Prophet's favourite camel was awaiting them, its great sail of matting about to be

119

raised and a handsome Zanzibari in attendance. It was a very good boat and Dekker decided that he would take the helm, which the captain was happy to permit. Soon they were racing down the creek at great speed, overtaking even the big *booms*, and for a moment Dekker wondered how he would stop the boat if he needed to. Then they were on land again, and wandering through great meadows of tall and golden grass in which fat Hereford cattle grazed in the middle of herds of elephant and antelope. There were lion all around them, and Dekker was not frightened although he had no gun, he could see that they intended no harm, even though they were racing across fields and jumping over five-barred gates. There was one lion who wanted to make friends. He nuzzled at Dekker and licked his hand with a great rough tongue, but Dekker lost his nerve and cried out for help and the lion walked away.

He was on a magical journey now, travelling by a sequence of dhows whose captains transferred him from one to the other with much conspiracy and use of passwords and, always, hidden laughter; they all refused to accept money, however much he protested his ability to pay. Then there was a woman – she was black and very beautiful, and her legs were bare so he could see the henna patterns on the soles of her feet – and she welcomed him back to Matandoni village (where he recognised the mango trees), and she took his hand and led him to the simple whitewashed mosque (which he also recognised) and she showed him that he should go in. He explained that he, as a white man, was not permitted to enter, but she did not seem to understand him and insisted that he go in, so he took off his shoes and stepped respectfully from the dust of the street onto the stone floor and there, on the far wall, was the ostrich egg. It hung by a thread from a beam above the *mirhab*, he now saw, and it turned, slowly, gently, in the breeze from the doorway. He knew that he must not cross the floor of the mosque. He turned back and recovered his shoes. The woman had gone. He woke, drank water, looked up at the storm-scudding, star-strewn sky, and went back to sleep.

Martha Wilhelm was woken in the same night by the braying of an insomniac donkey (and heard the same sound of a rusty hacksaw urgently attacking an iron sheet). She sensed at once that Julius was suffering one of his sleepless nights. He never complained about them, but she had learned to tell, from the absolute

120

silence of his breathing and the tension of his body – he always lay on his back, his arms thrown back in crucified misery on these occasions. She knew from experience that his heart would be pounding, he would be sweating profusely into the bolsters, and he would be too proud to ask her help.

She said, 'My dear, you must sleep...' and leaned over and stretched herself along his naked thigh. She cuddled her head against his shoulder, as she had learned to do when they first became lovers, and she murmured, 'You worry too much, you silly man.' His whole body was drenched with sweat. She recoiled, and then she deliberately pressed herself against him again, to dry him in the cotton of her nightdress. She felt him shudder, and almost moan, and then his arm tightened around her and the breath went out of him and his pulse began to ease; she knew that he would not be able to speak of his private terrors, so she did not ask him. Through the folds of the mosquito net she could see a thin silver moon far above, and all she could hear was the rustle of the wind in the thatch; it must be the very middle of the night. The town was utterly quiet, and she was so wide awake that she could not believe that she would ever sleep again.

He began to make love to her very cautiously, as though he feared she might be either asleep or angry. His hands were soft and tentative. He had always been a skilled and considerate lover, she had always appreciated that in him. When they arrived at the point in their familar ritual where she hoisted her nightdress above her hips and arranged her limbs beneath him, she realised that it was not all right at all, that her body was refusing her, that she was dry and tight. He was urgent now, his mouth on her nipples, his hand inside her thighs, and still she could not respond. So – to her later astonishment – she thought of Dekker, allowed herself to run her fingers through his shock of white hair, wondered how the strong hands she had noticed that morning would caress her, fantasised about the stranger's tall, burly body, and when her husband entered her she did not recognise his familiar gasp of delight but imagined that she felt Dekker become her lover, and she thrust against him with a passion she had not felt for years. When she woke again in the bright light of dawn she was still naked, and she searched for her discarded nightdress, feeling ashamed and also apprehensive.

121

'I don't know how much longer I can take this. All your fault of course, you talked me into it.'

'Dugmore, you positively longed to be an Anarchist.'

'Then I've learned my lesson. They are all, almost without exception – yes, I grant there are a few exceptions – a wretched bunch of humankind. My patience is at an end, I warn you.'

'No stamina?'

'No more time for a bunch of shits.'

'Some of them – you'll be surprised to hear this, coming from me of all people – appear to be perfectly decent types.'

'Fingers of one hand!' pronounced Dugmore, and gestured in illustration.

Major Rogers said, 'Believe me, I'm grateful to you. Can you last out a little longer? Just think of Madame Sasse.'

'No point. She's screwing Tom Fallon, and they don't manage to conceal it.' He intercepted Rogers's raised eyebrows. 'The husband doesn't notice, he's probably used to it, and he's also too concerned for their friend Hassemer, who has a bad dose of malaria.'

'Is that why you're in a bate?'

'I'm not in a bate, as you put it. I'm at my usual point after a month on the Coast – I wish I were back up-country, d'you grant me that? This place – this island – is so bloody corrupt. Admit it, Rogers, Lamu is a cesspool! It's the most depraved place I've ever known.'

Rogers said, 'No, I protest. It has its debaucheries, I admit. But the longer I live here, the more I respect its qualities. No point in shaking your finger at me, Dugmore – I shall repeat, I *respect* its qualities...'

'Is that why you and the Liwali ignore the child brothels down behind the Monument?'

'Oh come on, don't play the Puritan with me. These things have been going on in Lamu for a thousand years. Do you of all people want me to close down the bordellos?'

Dugmore laughed with the bitter triumph of a man who has had his worst suspicions confirmed. 'You're a man of principle, I've always believed, yet you happily preside over an island which ranks higher in the lechery stakes than any of the deep-sea ports of the world – opium, bhang, liquor, small boys, sodomy, transvestism, underage girls, donkeys even, there's no end to the menu. And some of this is perfectly respectable! Did you know there's even a *school* here, endorsed by the mosques – the *unyago* school no less – which actually trains the young girls of Lamu in sex? Yes, it's official! And you can sit here on your terrace high above these things and pretend to ignore it all.'

'What else should I do?'

'You could try to reform the place, as Gladstone would have told you. Close down the whorehouses. Assign the transvestites to hard labour. Kick the Liwali in the arse. And deliver a stern warning to some of the inhabitants of Free House.'

'I take it that you're jesting.'

'Rogers, if you were a Justice of the Peace in Chipping Camden you'd be a stickler for the rules. Why are you so wonderfully tolerant here?'

Because I have learned to respect the authentic character of the place, thought Rogers. I understand your point: and I'm not a hypocrite. This place is unique. It isn't Africa, it's not savage and bestial and primitive and all those awful things that horrified me when I arrived here from India; this Swahili world has the redeeming Arab side, its Oriental manners and customs, its literature and crafts and arts and architecture. It's not really 'Africa', and yet it's hardly 'Arabia' either. It is certainly cosmopolitan, and yet it is also remote and isolated. It is Islamic and also pagan. It is sophisticated at the same time as being ignorant. It is self-confident despite being so extremely obscure. It is black but not African, *of* Africa while it lives *off* Africa. It is parasitic: it contributes very little to Africa while funnelling so much away. It is the middleman, the agent, the procurer, the pimp. Who can be surprised that it has no interest in the moral values that Dugmore suddenly wants to embrace?

He said not this but, 'You know the answer yourself, my dear fellow. This place is the best of both worlds. It's the mix, the hybrid. You respond to the native Africans up-country more than I do. Fair enough. I happen to prefer this meeting of the intelligence, the wit, the refinement, of the Arab world and the vigour, the brutality of your Africans. That frightens me – it's *dangerous* up-country, I never lose that sense, even when I'm only twenty miles inland. You love it, I know.'

123

'You really believe that we should stick to the Coast? Hold back from the interior?'

'I don't believe that we can withdraw at this stage from the Coast, now that we have put the Germans in their place, but I see no need to move inland.'

'You don't agree that we have a civilising role? Quite apart from the special pleading of the missionaries...'

'And the clarion call of "Trade"?'

'The African has no need of us,' said Dugmore. 'He has so much room. Space to move, to graze, to plant for a season and move on next year. He doesn't need us. He doesn't need our *rules*. He's better off without us.'

'So we agree that there's no mission to civilise?'

'What do we really have to teach them? Where's our contribution to this continent?'

They were both thinking of the Freelanders and the impertinence of their arrival: on that the two Englishmen agreed.

'Our best contribution, I've come to believe, is to leave them alone.'

'Insofar as that is possible.'

'Keep the trading companies away, you mean?'

'And the fucking missionaries.'

'I agree. Your kaffir has no need of conversion.'

'But you'd interfere if one tribe decided to slaughter another?'

'Yes, I would.'

'I wonder if you're right,' said Dugmore. 'Who are we to interfere in their petty wars? They never kill too many of the other side, and the young warriors need to be blooded if they are to become men.'

'But then they start selling their defeated enemies into slavery. To some handsome Somali trader with his caravan and his bag of gold.'

'That's the point where we interfere, you think?'

'Yes. Wouldn't you?'

'But you would interfere before that. You and your friends would be there long before the war parties set off. You'd be bossing them around and telling them what to grow and levying taxes and teaching them all sorts of ludicrous and unnecessary things. You'd be as bad as the missionaries – but I grant that, unlike the Denhardts, you wouldn't be making a fortune out of them. Though I have to observe, Rogers, that you continue to be officially employed by the IBEA Company which, whatever Sir William Mackinnon may claim, is no charitable institution.'

'That is a blow below the belt, and you know it. You know perfectly well that in reality I represent HMG. Hardinge assures me that all that is being sorted out.'

'My dear chap, I can say it because I suspect we agree. *Let's not interfere* with these splendid savages amongst whom we have elected to spend our lives. The savage, I truly believe, is better left "uncivilised", and happier, too.'

'Unless he's dead,' said Rogers. 'Or starving. Or tortured by villainous rulers. Or carried off into slavery.'

'Come on, we're each of us as cynical as the other when we come down to brass tacks,' said Dugmore. 'You don't believe in our God-given authority – or ability! – to uplift these people any more than I do. Our enemies would say that we are both humbug.'

'That would be unfair. We do our best, notwithstanding. In our different ways.'

'You're going to argue that, even if we are neither of us convinced, at least at this time of night, that we are doing any good out here, at least our intentions are good. Yours and mine, I mean, not the Denhardts'. Or the Freelanders', I might add.'

'So what are you claiming for the sum of human happiness – I'm sorry, it's a phrase that suddenly came back to me from my dim and distant education.'

'With respect to these people in the bush, I suspect the answer is zero.'

'There I disagree,' said Rogers. 'I *have* to disagree, of course, but I do believe it. I ask myself that question every night. Fact is, I really do have a restraining influence on that prize bastard, the Liwali. Fact! And fact! – when I cleared the Witu stockade last month I found a hundred wretches who were in leg-irons on their way to Yemen, and I returned half of them to their villages, where, you may say, they will die of starvation when the Rains next fail. But I sleep better for that deed. Don't ask me whether or not I have the *right* to do these things, I don't need that question. As for the other half, I returned them to Lamu, because here is where they came from, and they wanted nothing better than to come home to the *shambas* on this island which you see as no more than a pit of debauchery. Some people seem to like it here.'

'They'd been kidnapped from here?'

'Yes, they were kept in chains for a few days and then were taken off from "a big, big beach, *bwana*".'

'There aren't many big beaches round here. It's mostly mangrove.'

'Yes, they must have meant Shela. If I can catch up with Suleiman Kimenya on the mainland I'll follow the thread back to here, and I shan't be surprised when I find where the thread leads. But I have to do it that way – I have to start at the other end of the chain.'

'Good luck to you,' said Dugmore. Interesting reference to a beach. Sometimes he envied this man his job. He sometimes wondered whether he would do it better. That wasn't a thought to put to a friend.

'Let me get this clear.... Since we are here in Africa; since we need to be here in Africa; since we have to be here in Africa – let our motto be, "With as little harm as possible!" Do we agree? I'm sure that would sound better in Latin. We could put it up over your door!'

'There's bound to be someone in Free House who could translate it for us. Shall we ask your friend Dekker?'

'No, Tom Fallon's the man. He's the classicist.'

*

Dugmore was tickled by the jest, and the next afternoon at Free House he actually looked for the man. But Tom Fallon was at that precise moment being fellated by Louise Sasse and observed in the act through Felix Thomas's telescope, which happened to be the property of Captain Dugmore. So, in a remote sense, Dugmore found Fallon. Louise and Fallon were on Shela beach and had taken an understandable care to seek privacy. Shela beach is wide and open, very long and entirely empty, and behind the deep white sand of the high-water line, through a belt of ground creeper and thin grass and a species of low bushes whose tiny leaves are the silver-green colour of olive trees, they had found a dwarf-palm set in a soft hollow of sand, its fronds a curtain to shield them from the sun and from the occasional fishing dhow. They came here every day.

Felix Thomas was visiting Shela for the first time, sent here on Captain Dugmore's orders. There are high sand dunes behind the beach – not so very high, perhaps 200 feet at most, but they survey

126

the eight-mile sweep of the beach and command any approach, by land or by sea. The Captain had given Felix a spyglass together with his orders, though Felix had already defied his specific instruction to approach the dune from the rear, through a landscape of rough bush and thorn and coconut palm and not to expose himself on the beach; this was not possible for a first visit, Felix had the sense to decide, he would have to take the risk, at least on the first day, if he were to find his bearings and understand where he was.

Less than a mile beyond the promontory, on the highest cliff of dune, he saw a look-out tree; it was a lonely, branching acacia. He took his risk, dashed across the blazing white sand and toiled, sweating and panting, up the steep hill, which was ridged and contoured by the constant breeze. The thick grains of the slope slipped under his bare feet like a granite scree on the slopes of one of his Welsh mountains. Five minutes – ten? – and he had done it, the wind was drying his thin body and he was looking down across the saddle at Lamu Town to the north and the creek and a corner of Manda island; in front of him, steep below his feet, lay the full sweep of Shela's matchless beach. It was a belvedere, a spy nest, and, best of all, he had his shelter: the thorn tree, the only one for miles, was bigger than he had guessed, it was a great green parasol, twenty yards in diameter, clipped tidy by the breeze, and under it the shade was deep and blessedly cool after the blinding white of the screes of the dune. He would clear an embrasure in the sand ridge, arrange a branch or two, and so long as he did not move, no-one would ever know that he was surveying the beach – or, for that matter, the dark shadows beneath the palm trees below him, hidden from the sea and visible only from above.

It was, thought Felix, as he removed his shirt and his trousers, a wonderfully undemanding assignment. The Captain had been vague that morning. 'You are to keep watch over the beach. You will have this glass to help you. But you are on no account to be observed or to intervene. Whatever you see, you report to me alone.'

'What am I looking for, sir?'

'Anything. Everything. You are going to be a lover of nature, Mr Thomas. You may be required to spend many days of your brief life out there. And take care not to go to sleep.'

But of course, Felix Thomas did go to sleep. The circumstances

127

were so idyllic, the heat so intense, the shade of the acacia tree so soothing, that he was only woken by a bursting bladder. When he stood up and glanced casually down to the bottom of the dune, he was – to his astonishment and terror – looking straight down onto two white and naked bodies, and he did not need the telescope to see who they were. She was devouring him like a greedy child a lollipop, and Felix Thomas, who was young and more innocent – near virginal – than he would have admitted at Mabrukki's, actually blushed, and looked away hastily, bent down behind his parapet. 'Oh Jesus,' he muttered, though he had been taught in childhood never to blaspheme, 'what are they doing? Is this what Captain Dugmore was looking for?'

Seven

Even among the so-called cultured nations of the present day, woman remained without legal rights, and what is worse, she was left in order to obtain sustenance to sell herself to the first man she met who would undertake to provide and 'care for' her for the sake of her attractions. This prostitution, sanctioned by law and custom, is in its effects more disastrous than that other, which stands forth undisguised and is distinguished from the former only in the fact that here the shameful bargain is made not for life but only for years, weeks, hours.... Worse than the prostitution of the streets is that of the marriage for a livelihood sanctioned by law and custom...

Theodor Hertzka: *Freeland: A Social Anticipation*

Still it did not rain. There were huge clouds everywhere, heavy with water, so that the town was more often than not in shadow, but they would gather only to disperse again. Even the light seems wet, thought Martha, there's a new sheen rising from the sea: she felt the breeze falter and – was that a raindrop? – no. Even she was perspiring now, and Julius was having to change his shirt four times a day. 'It was raining on Manda this morning, *memsahib*, very early,' said Saidi, his eyes gleaming with excitement. 'But here? No, not today. Perhaps tomorrow. Or next week.' She looked out on Manda, which today seemed very close and absurdly clear – she imagined she could make out one mangrove root from another, but beyond the line of tide, where sand and soil met to breed mosquitoes amidst the *boriti* poles, she could see no evidence of rain having actually fallen, no puddle, no gleam of greasy mud. The Rains, rather, had moved onto the mainland behind her. To the west, beyond the minaret and the massed houses and the jagged horizon of date palms, there was a great wall of cloud which seemed to join earth to sky in a dense purple and black smoke.

How long, how long? asked Martha Wilhelm. Saidi had been

told by Bakari that the mainland tracks were 'very bad'. But what did that mean for them? Julius explained that they were delayed by the sandbar which had been built up across the mouth of the Tana by the *kaskazi*, so that they were unable to take the steam launch into the river. But if the Rains had broken, the Tana must be in flood: wouldn't that clear the sandbar?

Her husband was very patient. 'My dear,' he said, 'the problem in *any* exploration of Africa is the first few miles. The continent resists – you understand me? – that first penetration. We cannot attempt, and for that matter we cannot afford, to travel to Mount Kenya and to Freeland by a great overland expedition. We are not travelling like Carl Peters for exploration, we are engaged on an entirely different business – we have come to create a new society, not just to subdue a few chiefs and shoot lion and then go home. We need to use the river. Now that the launch is here and the barges to carry the stores, we merely have to be patient until the Tana is ready for us.'

She said, 'Your members are impatient, Julius. Do you realise that the mood in Free House is not good? Some of them are more foolish than you will admit. And the more sensible ones are the most impatient of all.'

'It would be madness to leave before we are ready,' he protested.

'Then can we try to keep them better occupied? Dekker thinks they should have more exercise. More training in the skills we shall need. He suggested target practice, until Captain Dugmore pointed out that our weapons are locked in the Fort. *Anything* to keep them out of Mabrukki's.'

'Is it not a respectable place? I have not been there.'

'Nor of course have I. But Dekker says that most of them now have their own whisky bottle sitting in a line above the bar each with a name on the label. That cannot be good. It is not what we came here for.'

'Martha, we must face facts. Wilhelm Selling has been taking out the *Eden* every day with Scavenius and Frans Buschel as his crew, and he tells me that the approach to the Tana is still too dangerous. Please – there is no great harm in waiting on this island. It is a pleasant enough ante-room, if that is how we must see it.'

He is not impatient enough, Martha thought. He is accepting this too easily. And, with a moment of intuition, she understood that he was cautious because he too was apprehensive of the future.

130

She tested that discovery again, alone on her rooftop under the marbled afternoon sky, and she could not deny that her loving husband Julius – to evade it no longer! – was too timid. In a word, he was afraid. His intellectual convictions had brought him to this point and to this equatorial island, but he lacked the will, and the boldness, and perhaps the madness, to press on – to insist that they storm the mainland and defy the sandbar and the Rains and the unpredictable and unplannable and everything else that Africa would no doubt throw at them. He is a fine man, she told herself, but he is not the leader that we need.

She stood on her high terrace and suffered a premonition. It made her feel disloyal, and guilty too, but she could not suppress it. Julius will be happy – she knew it – to lead us back to Europe. He will explain that we have made the effort; he will then be able to describe the technical difficulties that frustrated us. He will give many speeches on the subject, and Dr Hertzka will endorse his wise and prudent decision. Then they'll start talking about the next expedition. So we will all be home again, which will be a relief for some of them, and we shall have so many adventures to tell to our families and to our friends, and Julius will believe that he did his best. But a few of us – Dekker, and Tom Fallon, and Salner, and Selling, and a couple more – will know, with me, that we did not do our best at all. Major Rogers will laugh and the Denhardts will be contemptuous of us, and everyone will forget about Free-land. And when we are safely home again, people will ask, 'How was it in Africa?' and *I* shall say, 'We never got to Africa. *Did we, Julius?* We simply had a holiday on an exotic little island where it was much too hot but rather interesting, and nobody took us seriously.'

That is not for me, thought Martha Wilhelm. That would be to run away. I did not bid farewell to my sisters in Hamburg with the intention that I should be with them again next Christmas.

She said some of this to her husband that evening. He was harassed, he protested that he was preparing his next report for Dr Hertzka, which had to be ready for tomorrow's mails, but she stood her ground. She said, 'I do not understand some of the problems. I have not spoken with Selling about this business of the sandbank, though Captain Dugmore mentioned that he expected it would soon clear. But I hear a note of resignation in some of these things.

Surely, Julius, we can be too easily tempted to exaggerate the difficulties. Yes, I know that this is a strange and alarming place, and Dr Hertzka's book gave us no warning of the frustrations we would have to face, but between us all we are surely strong enough to overcome and press on.'

'We have to be realistic, Martha. They tell me we must be willing to wait here until August.'

'Why *August*?'

'Because they say the Tana may still be impassable. Even if the boat can cross the bar, the river is likely to be too dangerous when it is in flood.'

'Who says that?' She was thinking, before the Rains the Tana is impassable because of the sandbar, and after the Rains it's impassable as a result of the Rains. So why did we ever think that this was our route into Africa?

'Selling has been out there again, he spoke to me only this evening. And Dugmore doesn't deny that the river in flood is difficult to navigate.'

'But we *can't* sit here till August. Free House will become uncontrollable.' And the town won't tolerate us, she knew. And Major Rogers would certainly find an excuse to send them packing.

Her husband shrugged and made to turn back to his letter.

'Julius, you are too willing to accept defeat.'

'Martha! I resent that.'

'You may resent it if you wish,' she said. 'But I tell you, we cannot – must not – accept defeat, because we have not yet been defeated. Worse than that, we haven't even tried. Remember who we are!' she cried, 'We are the missionaries of a new society. That's how we used to talk of ourselves in Vienna. But, my dear, a missionary commits himself, up to and including his life, to his mission. He doesn't get as far as the railway station – yes, that's Lamu – and then change his mind because he can't yet see the train. We are turning tail because we have had a couple of problems and the odd spot of rain.'

'How dare you say that? After all that I have done for you!'

'You have been looking for an excuse to go home ever since we arrived!'

She stormed out.

As usual, after an hour or so they blundered back together, and muttered apologies and endearments, and hugged each other.

Later that night, after he had written his report, they made love, but she lay awake a long time because she could not forget the truth of what she had said.

*

I don't have your patience, Dugmore was thinking. I couldn't stand it, sitting in an office for year after year in this steaming heat, telling these devious bastards what they can or can't do and, to make things worse, having to pretend that you're not really the ruler anyway. The whole set-up on this Coast is grand hypocrisy. I used to get bored out of my skull whenever I was posted to a garrison town, and this life is worse, it would infallibly drive me into the ocean. He's a decent fellow is Rogers, and I'd trust him with my life, but I can see now that at heart he's as dull as ditchwater. No sense of adventure. Nothing of the Speke or Burton about him – he probably wouldn't understand me if I said we'd arrived here twenty years too late. *That* was the time to come to Africa, when a fellow could put his name on the map and have all the sport and adventure he could ask for. Now the place is filling up with missionaries and traders and Germans, and pen-pushers like Rogers. I might not have made old bones in those days, but I'd certainly have had a tale to tell them back home.... God damn it, I knew it, I'm getting bored again.

Rogers was being officious about the bulldog. 'Do you really have to keep that creature?' he asked, and gestured at the slumbering beast that was at this moment snoring inoffensively in the corner. 'He serves no purpose that I can see, and is causing great offence in the town. The Liwali mentioned it this morning.'

'Shall I tell you what the Liwali can do?'

'Perhaps not,' said Rogers. 'Just forget I mentioned it.'

Throughout the day yet another host of giant black cloud had been massing over Lamu, approaching from a couple of miles out to sea as slowly as a becalmed dhow whose crew does not have the energy to bring out the oars. In the town, on the waterfront and in the alleys, everyone kept looking up. The air was suddenly absolutely still, the heat unmitigated by a breath of breeze – and then there was a clean shaft of cool *cold* air from the north, and then another, and another. It *must* be the Rains! But the doors clanged tight again and Lamu waited, gasping, sweating, for either the rain or the night, whichever would fall the first.

133

'Are you eating?' asked Rogers of his visitor.

'No, I promised to join them at Mabrukki's. It's best for me to be seen to be around, if you see what I mean.'

'Do the Germans use Mabrukki's at all? The Denhardts? Or Toeppen?'

'I haven't spotted them there. But you don't see Selling or Buschel or Scavenius either.'

'How do you mean?'

'Some of our keener German members aren't seen much at Free House either, more likely to be at the Denhardts' place. Sitting up there behind those silly walls, eating sauerkraut and tinned sausage and weeping into their beer for the good old days when Peters was signing up every tinpot sultan on the Coast.'

'We stopped that little game,' said Rogers, in tones that combined nostalgia with the greatest satisfaction.

'They'll try again.'

'I assume that that's what they talk about every night.'

'Just as you and I might talk about how to stop them.'

'But you and I are alone up here, and we talk privately as old friends and companions in arms. We don't invite a gang of Anarchists to join us. You say there's a bunch of your Freelanders up there with my German neighbours every night?'

'The German chapter is often there. Remember to exclude the Austrians – they wouldn't dream of it, their view of the Germans would knock yours into a cocked hat. There's no danger in Wilhelm – nor Salner for that matter. They're not interested in Germany's imperial destiny, as Goddfrey put it at breakfast the other morning. They know as well as we do that Carl Peters was a murdering swine and should have been strung up by us.'

'Steady on! In the eyes of the world he was a great explorer who may have got a bit carried away from time to time, but he saw it as his patriotic duty to accept the freely offered allegiance to the Kaiser of those chiefs who were disaffected with the oppressive rule of Zanzibar.' The Major had to stop for breath.

'Sometimes, Rogers, you talk the most frightful balderdash.'

'I was just trying it out. Perhaps you ought to hold a debate at Free House one evening – "Carl Peters: Murderer or Maniac?" That sort of thing.'

'And the next week they can have "Rogers: Reactionary or Revolutionary?". '

'How about "Dugmore: Sportsman or Scoundrel?".'

They fell silent for a moment, but were still caught in the silly game. '"Louise Sasse: Goddess or Whore?"' – that was Rogers.

'That's very cruel. How about "Wilhelm: is he Radical or just Ridiculous?".' They chortled like schoolboys.

'I must go,' said Dugmore. 'Your tame Anarchist has to join his gang. Be warned, I shall be extraordinarily rude about you tonight – as your spies will no doubt report.'

'I can take it.'

He called Iqbal Ali and dined alone. The sea was grey metal, and the evening light had the dark-grained clarity of an engraving. A group of late-returning dhows scratched their wakes across the empty surface of the steel plate.

*

Felix Thomas had broken his trust and said nothing of Fallon and Louise to Captain Dugmore. He had told him of the acacia tree and its excellence. He thought to ask whether he should carry a weapon – 'since I've been thinking, sir, that you're half-expecting, like, that there's some sort of mischief going on...' 'Now, Mr Thomas, why should you be promenading in the dunes with a pistol in your pocket? How would you explain that to Major Rogers and his *askaris*? Be careful, by the way, not to be found with my spyglass. Hide it in the sand if anyone approaches you.'

'There's no-one there, Captain. I haven't seen a soul for three days, just a couple of small dhows. The launch went past again this afternoon. And I think I saw the Belgian Mr Schmidt in the distance.'

'The Freeland launch?'

'The very one, Captain. It's called the *Eden*. It kept out to sea and went round the far dunes towards the mainland.'

He had been watching Tom and the Sasse woman when he heard the engine; he was no longer embarrassed by their couplings – he reckoned it very interesting and instructive – and he giggled to himself when he saw them roll apart hastily and listen when they heard the boat. To make things even funnier, she was scrambling to cover herself in her discarded shift. He could see that they were speaking to each other, and Fallon made as if to kneel and look out to sea but she pulled him down. The little steamer bustled across the bay and its puffing engine faded steadily into the

135

afternoon. They were at it again, observed Felix, and groaned when he felt the throb of his own erection.

He said, 'Shall I write these things down, Captain? A sort of ship's log, if you get my meaning? I'm anxious to please, you see...'

'No, no. You mustn't be found keeping a record like that. If you meet anyone, they must think you're there for – for the exercise...'

'As you say, sir. And just one more thing, sir. Is there the possibility of a guinea on account?'

'Good heavens, Mr Thomas, why do you want a guinea?'

'We all have our *needs*, Captain, don't we now?'

'Then try to contain yours a little longer.'

'You've been very kind, sir, as everyone tells me. But it was because I was doing a little job for you that I was caught and *disgraced*, like.'

'What can you be meaning?'

'You haven't forgotten, sir, that you asked me to see if Mr Salner had his accounts books in his room.'

'You were perfectly happy to do that little job, as you put it, and an idiot to be caught. And you were extremely well rewarded, as you granted at the time.'

'I'm not complaining, Captain.'

'I rather thought you were, Mr Thomas.'

*

'There are times when I weary of this place,' said Fallon. He was strolling on the quay with Dekker at the moment of late-afternoon when the swifts gathered over the town. Every afternoon they arrived without fail, thousand upon thousand of them, swooping high and low, tossed in noisy squawls over the rooftops against the pale blue of the evening sky. 'Behind all the romance of this exotic island on the Equator, what does it come down to? – Squalor and dirt and smells – and *more* smells – and fish and fish and fish, and this *constant* sun and this unceasing wind from the sea, and flies and mosquitoes, these bloody birds, the *muezzin* five times a day until eternity, the donkeys and these lanes lined with drab blank walls. Everyone tells me there are treasures behind them, but I've not crossed a single doorstep and I know I won't if I stay here for the rest of my lifetime – which we're presumably fated to do anyway...'

136

'I know what you mean,' said Dekker. 'There's a feeling that life has been like this for centuries and will continue like this, because no-one finds that prospect unsatisfactory or less than fulfilling. It's difficult for our generation, from our society, to adjust to that.'

'Are you implying that they could be teaching us something?'

'I don't know if there is a Swahili word for "progress", but I rather doubt it. I can't see any Gadarene rush for a new order, can you?'

'So this is it. Never mind whether or not it's the life we ought to have, or whether we like this life or not, because it's the life we've been given, so let's do our best to enjoy our brief span.'

'I find that a rather attractive philosophy.'

'Our friends back home would be appalled to hear you say it.'

'I've started to think that some of our friends could do worse than come to Lamu and accept that the play is written, the performance has begun, and this is what it's all about, for day after day, generation after generation.'

'That's blasphemy from a Freelander. It's pretty blasphemous even to me.'

'Bear with me one last moment. I'm saying to you – just to see how it sounds out loud, don't be alarmed, I'm not entirely serious – let's accept the sun and the breeze and the fish and the flies, because that's all there ever has been and all there ever will be!'

'The sooner we get you off this island the better.'

'You're right on that.'

'Well, you're certainly giving us all a lesson on getting ready to leave.'

'You're not fair to yourself. You laugh at me for all the little ways I try to prepare myself, but I see that you're the one who goes to Shela every day. I deliberately stopped going to Shela weeks ago.'

'Why?'

'It's too easy. Too delightful. I was saying to – someone – that I tried to walk around the island the other day and failed ignominiously.'

'You remind me of my Chapel background. They tried to teach me to embrace suffering and denial. You sound a likely convert.'

'And what happened?'

'I objected. I escaped by the skin of my teeth. I was on the brink of training for the ministry. Calvinism, that sort of thing. I must have had a premonition that my character was going to lead me in the opposite direction.'

'It's a vocation that never tempted me. What next?'

'I became a teacher. But that couldn't be enough for a failed priest. So I discovered I was a Socialist. Preaching heaven on earth, you might say!'

They walked easily away from the town, past the long bundles of orange mangrove poles that were in process of being hoisted onto the great dhows. Fallon found that he wished for the Rains to come with a desperation that was more than any natural weariness with the heat and the humidity: if only all this *water* that hovered overhead from one horizon to the other would gather itself together and concentrate itself and *settle* the matter once and for all...

I hated the teaching, Fallon remembered. Funny, because I was supposed to be good at it. It wasn't so much the idiot kids, they were all right, it was the pompous colleagues. The foreboding that I'd be trapped in this grey and gloomy city until my retirement presentation on Speech Day. I was getting my drama out of the politics. At the beginning I used to love those evening committee meetings, the scribbled agendas, the endless cups of tea, the bold promises. And the Thursday lectures in the Union Hall. We had Eleanor Marx once, and Olive Schreiner, and Aveling, of course, and even Paul Lafargue. He's forgotten, and I don't intend to remind him, but Dekker came three years ago: he wasn't the best, but he filled the hall.

Strange. Now we're both out of it. Abandoned the cause, most of them would say. If they say it of me they'll be saying it of him, with knobs on. And he had more to lose, that's true, that business of his must have been turning over a pretty penny. Me, I quit the school, and the kids managed a tea party, and a copy of *Oliver Twist*, which was nice of them. He says he gave away his firm to his workers. I had nothing to give away. Except that I gave away Meg and the boys; Dekker never mentions anything like that. Fallon's guilt when he thought of his family was always qualified by a rushing need of self-justification. He had left them in order to save his life, he would tell himself, for he had discovered something perverse in himself. He loved them dearly, and yet his hand would fall back when he reached to caress his own children; he would make passionate love to Meg and then, minutes later, could not touch the vibrant, warm female being (not just body) lying next

138

to him, but would want to leave, to walk the streets, to escape from this intimacy.

'You have left behind no family, Dekker?'

'No, I managed to preserve my freedom.... I'm sorry, that is a stupidity, a remark worthy of the drawing rooms which we are so happy to have left. To answer you more sensibly, I have neither wife nor children. I suppose those of our members in a happier situation, like yourself, must find this delay in Lamu even more wearisome than it is for us bachelors.'

'I don't hear much talk of children. Selling plans to bring his family to join him when the time is appropriate, he told me so. The Wilhelms have no child. Louise Sasse scarcely looks like a mother. Most of the rest of us are – let's face it – either bachelors or debauchees!'

'Do you share my concern about the calibre of our colleagues?'

'I do indeed.'

'What can be done about it?'

'Nothing.'

'Not so. We can identify the quality, and the potential quality, and work with that.'

'Scavenius.'

'Selling.'

'Schmidt.'

'Salner. Of course.'

'Rabinek – yes, I mean it.'

'Goddfrey and Bosanquet, if they take themselves seriously.'

'Well, that's not too bad. Add Wilhelm and ourselves, and the two ladies and a bunch of what Goddfrey calls the "rude mechanicals", and we have ourselves an expedition.'

'No we don't,' said Fallon. 'We don't have leadership. We don't have a realistic picture of the interior – I've been talking a lot with Dugmore. We don't have an appetite for a hard struggle. We probably don't have enough funds. Frankly, we don't have the faintest idea what we've taken on.'

'Would it help if we divested ourselves of – say – one half of our present membership?'

'Of course it would. But how do we do that and keep the *Eden* and the supplies?'

'Hang on long enough,' said Dekker, 'and natural wastage will do the job for us.'

It was an appallingly prescient remark, and he would shudder for it in the weeks ahead.

*

Lamu

Most Confidential

Dear Dr Hertzka,

I take the opportunity of a passing steamer to remind you of the continuing presence of your most dedicated disciples on this tedious offshore island. You will no doubt be relieved to hear that I shall have to be brief...

It gives me no pleasure to convey bad news, but we have lost another of our members – not, I hasten to add, another death. You will remember how Lieutenant Rabinek made an excellent impression on our selection committee. Sadly, we have received evidence that the 'Lieutenant' is in fact a convicted criminal. Dr Wilhelm took an unusually strong position, and insisted that on this occasion he would not merely suspend but actually 'expel' a member from the Association. I did not feel able to disagree with this, but a number of our colleagues are unhappy about this decision by our leader. They seem to believe that Rabinek's misdemeanours in Europe are irrelevant to the needs of the expedition in Africa (I grant that he has been one of the more active and effective of our party). They also point out that, in practice, as with Felix Thomas, he will have to remain with us, though evidently feeling most acutely the pain of his public disgrace.

A more serious question was raised by Selling. Dr Wilhelm, he has been telling everyone, can only have received his information from the English governor here on the island. There may be no need to challenge (adds Selling) that Rabinek has a chequered past, but why should the English be so happy to seek out and disseminate this sort of mischief? The affair has inevitably cast a shadow, aside from its effect on Rabinek's feelings and of course on his enthusiasm for the cause. My own, unspoken, conclusion is that this underlines the imperative need that *everyone* on these pioneer projects be truly 'Caesar's wife'.

We continue, as I indicated above, to be marooned on this island. The frustration of the expedition grows with every day that passes, yet nothing seems to be done. At least the Rains have reached the mainland and are expected here every day, which can only be good news.

Wilhelm Selling and his two companions are gratifyingly active in their exercises with the *Eden*. They take her out almost every day, and promise that the boat will be in perfect condition when the moment comes to enter the river. My only concern is that they must be incurring expenses which our modest budget cannot easily afford – but that is no responsibility of mine.

To end on a positive note, you will be gratified to hear that our new recruit, Captain Dugmore, has turned out to be a splendid acquisition. He has been studying your writings avidly and with frequently professed admiration, and he has a gift for rallying our members' morale when we are feeling low. It also occurs to me to promise you that I happily withdraw my earlier apprehension about the inclusion of ladies in the party. Madame Sasse is adored by all, full of fun and energy, and Frau Wilhelm, as I have always granted, is an excellent person. I do not know how her husband would cope with his tasks without her loyal support.

I must break off, as I have just heard the siren in the Bay.

I have the honour, etc...
Your respectful disciple,

Hans Salner

*

Felix Thomas, installed once more in his spy-tree on the Shela dune, twiddled the brass ring and focused the glass on a new arrival on the edge of the sea. It was a great turtle, evidently dead, the reptilian head slumped in a tide pool, the flippers floating languidly in the water. He could see no sign of an injury. He supposed that turtles, too, died of natural causes.

The place had become familiar to him: he would never forget it, that he knew, and he stored away its images, its sensations, as if he guessed that in his difficult, successful life he would sometimes want to remember how he, Felix Thomas, in his youth had sat for day after day high above an empty beach on the African Equator. To his right – it must be at least eight miles – he could make out the high dunes of Kipungani, and beyond that, almost beyond the range of the glass, the distant hills behind Ras Biongwe on the mainland. Directly in front of him there was the translucent coral reef and the English gun battery (never completed let alone manned or used, Robert Schmidt had told him) of Ras Takwa. And behind him, by a quirk of geography, he could peer down on Lamu port, a couple of miles distant, where he used to see the *Eden* set out on its daily exercises and know that it would come chugging into Shela Bay thirty minutes later. He no longer felt in any danger of discovery now that he had discovered a route from the town which did not expose him to view on the beach. He would struggle through the sand-bush from behind Shela's tiny collection of huts, sweating and cursing because he was sheltered from the sea breeze, and – the Captain would be proud of him – dragging a palm frond behind him so as to rub out his footprints. But once he was at his post, and the wind was in his face and he had stripped to his drawers, he was happy again. Then he would peep over the ridge to see if they were there. He felt a friendly complicity with them. They could never know that they had no secrets from him; he had to make quite an effort to recognise Madame Sasse when he saw her in her clothes in Free House. Once, at the evening meeting, he was gazing incautiously at Fallon, admiring how he and Louise managed to pay no attention to each other in public, when the man looked up at him and – out of some instinct? – scowled at him, and was brusque with him when Felix served drinks at the Captain's table.

At that meeting (Felix was allowed to attend, but not to contribute since the disgrace of his suspension from the Association) there had been much grumbling about the delay. The English were polite and irritated, especially Fallon (Felix, privy to his private life, found himself wondering why the man was so keen to move on). The French and Belgians were more disposed to accept Dr Wilhelm's explanations about the sand-bar at the mouth of the Tana, but complained nonetheless. Dugmore, apologising exquisitely for his impudence, urged that everyone prepare himself to move on, and added some remarks about the distressing prevalence of the mosquito in the Lower Tana valley. The Germans seemed to have little to say. Hans Salner spoke up and said how vital it was to be certain that the *Eden* was in good shape. Selling said, grudgingly, that the trials were going well, and he would very soon be confident of the vessel's mechanical reliability; allow him, please, just a few more days – as they knew, he and his colleagues were using the opportunity of their daily excursion to transfer various non-perishable stores to Riekh at his lonely ('indeed, his heroic!') forward base at Kipani. Applause for the absent and lonely Riekh, a monosyllabic Dutch peasant who Felix happened to know was getting through a bottle of brandy a day. Wilhelm minuted the Association's gratitude to Mr Selling and his friends for their sterling work on the launch.

The *Eden*, as Felix observed it the next day, butting through a low swell in Shela Bay and proceeding in a westerly direction, was a pretty little thing, its single funnel belching steam like a picture in a child's story book. It would be less jaunty, he imagined, when it was hauling the two steel barges which would carry the stores and, once on the river, their porters. Felix focused his glass on Selling, who sat at the helm and appeared to be issuing instructions to – was it young Scavenius? – who was standing midships and gazing at the shore, shading his eyes as though searching for something. The Welshman panicked for a moment – were they looking for him? had the sun's reflection on the telescope betrayed him? – and instinctively ducked down and away, but when he next looked through the thorn branches the boat had moved a hundred yards across the bay and Scavenius was still scouring the land. Felix followed them with his glass: idly, unthinking, he swung it across the line of shore and, seeing nothing more noteworthy than drift-wood and reed, he tracked across the line of dune and horizon. Then he saw it. There was a great tuft of coconut frond sitting high on a solitary palm half a mile from where he lay. If he had not spent so many hours and days sitting in this eyrie, scanning the landscape to keep himself awake, he would not have noticed.

The tuft had not been there before. He could almost swear to it.

And then he saw something else. On the launch, Selling was fumbling at his feet in a locker. Felix could not see, or work out, what he was doing, except that he was bent over something, connecting something. Then – Felix saw him call out to Scavenius – he seemed to pull, hand over hand, and suddenly there was a pennant streaming in the wind. Felix squinted desperately through his master's modest eyepiece and saw that the *Eden* was flying the Freeland insignia – the same bunch of heavily-stylised flowers which adorned Dr Wilhelm's notepaper and the frontispiece of Dr Hertzka's famous book.

This was a mystery, thought Felix Thomas, and one he might

143

mention to his patron. Captain Dugmore was becoming impatient with his negative reports, and today of all days he could not even tell himself that he was protecting his lovers from the Captain, because today their nest under the tree was empty. So why was Selling testing out the flag? Why indeed was the *Eden* turning sharply into shore? Why had the Captain never told him what he was to look *for*?

Oh Lord! thought Felix, who was an intelligent man; there's a signal in this, in the pennant – and in the coconut leaves on the high pine tree, that must be it.

At that moment twelve human beings crossed the beach making for the sea. They were blacks; three of them were women. They emerged from out of the thick scrub above the line of sand, and the man in the lead seemed to be in charge and was carrying a tall spear. He looked to either side along the beach as though to check that it was empty, and beckoned, and the others followed. It was too far to be sure, but Felix guessed they were roped together. They stumbled, and hesitated, and the leader gestured angrily at them. The last man carried a *panga* and was also looking intently to either side. Felix thought, 'Captain, my Captain, you were bloody right...' and watched as the *Eden* swung into the shallows, the cargo was forced to wade out, waist-deep, and Selling – Felix faintly heard him shouting – hauled them savagely over the side, onto the narrow deck, and kicked them in the direction of the hold.

It had taken three minutes. The *Eden* swung out into the bay, pitching in the first waves of the open sea. Selling and Scavenius were chatting, or so anyone would have imagined. The two guards had vanished, back into the bush. Mark that pine tree, Felix told himself, and was focusing on the very spot as the bundle of frond toppled away, as though hauled down by an unseen hand.

Captain! thought Felix, as he pulled on his trousers. This is worth another guinea. And then I'll take myself to Mabrukki's and see if the pretty Scavenius has the nerve to turn up to celebrate his little day's outing.

*

'I want you to know,' declared Captain Dugmore to Major Rogers, 'that I've gone overboard for you on this ridiculous charade. Have you told Hardinge that he needs to appreciate the things I do for Queen and Country?'

144

'Her Majesty is very grateful.'

'D'you realise that last night I actually gave a lecture in Free House – God! what a mouthful, that is – on "Flora and Fauna of the East African Interior"?'

'You mean, how to spot it and how to kill it?'

'Precisely. They lap up everything I say. You'll be interested to hear that my subject next week is "Personal Hygiene Up-country".'

'You are an expert, I'm sure,' said Rogers, and ducked.

'This is no laughing matter. I've promised Wilhelm to keep the troops amused. Why don't you come across to Free House and give us a talk one evening?'

'I might stretch to a few words about the steamer connections between Lamu and Europe.'

It was, Dugmore realised, the nearest Rogers would ever get to a joke. So he laughed, extravagantly and generously.

Then they talked again about Witu and Suleiman and the Liwali's brother.

Later, when Dugmore and his brute had slipped discreetly away, Major Rogers took a final turn on his terrace. He gazed out on the black bar of Manda Island, which forever denied him his sense of the open sea, and realised – it had not occurred to him so clearly before – how Lamu Town attempts to turn its back on Africa: yet we cannot escape it, he thought, because we are denied the ocean by Manda and Pate and Kiwaiyu and all these hopeless, ancient islands that are jammed together in Formosa Bay, splashed like cowpats across the chart. And as I see every morning from the wall chart in my office, this coastline is just a nibbling at the African coast, an erosion, which is to say a decay, a rottenness, a corruption.... No wonder we are neither one thing nor another, neither Africa nor Arabia; we are one of the world's famous landfalls, and yet no-one has heard of us. So why am I happy here? Why don't I despair for Gujarat and the regiment and that Indian world I fell in love with fifteen years ago?

He was still wide awake; perhaps it was the brandy, or rather, he remembered, it was because he had broken his rule and had slept after lunch, slumped in his damp shirt on the Swahili day bed next to the clutter of plates and crumbs and an empty beer bottle, until he had been woken by the three o'clock breeze.

'We sleep too much in these latitudes,' he muttered aloud, and determined to take a last, unusual stroll down his waterfront. No need for the topee, but he chose a linen hat to shield his baldness. He let himself out, alarming the *askari* who was half-dozing at his box, and wandered past the rusty cannon he had had cemented to the steps. The small boys had deserted them by now, and the seafront was deserted. Why does it stink less at night, he wondered, as he navigated the salt puddles left behind by the high tide: was it that the wind was brisker, or simply that the sun had temporarily ceased its corruption? Why was there a cargo of copra dumped in front of the lower wharf? He would mention it to Ranjit Singh, his chief clerk, in the morning. His dhows were swinging in the ebb tide like gondolas from a half-forgotten holiday of his youth. He paused, listened to the gentle plop of the water on the stone steps of the jetty, breathed deep of the damp, warm air, and entirely failed to notice that, even at this hour, it was putrid and foul.

Time to turn in. Across the way he saw a light flicker on the roof of the Denhardts' house. He ventured on, careful to walk quietly, though not wishing to seem to spy. There was a murmur of voices high above his head; he could not help hearing a couple of words in a tenor, even falsetto German that could not be confused with the gruff bass of Toeppen.

Enough! They did him no harm. He turned to search the sky for the moon. Even the cats were asleep; even the donkeys had vanished. He was right, the moon was coming up now and it struck him that the whitewash of his own Charter House was garish, almost blinding. The Friday Mosque next door was somehow in shadow, and the older mansions beyond had a less vulgar patina. He could see a lamp burning in the smaller building which had been taken by Wilhelm and his wife: Dr Julius at his despatches, thought Rogers; does he guess how I'll celebrate his departure, poor man?

The memory of the man's conscientious hard work must have stayed with him a little longer because, when he had returned the *askari*'s salute, and climbed the empty, unlit house to the roof, his feet remembering every stone step in the darkness, he thought to glance over the parapet to see if the lamp still burned. The moon had risen with unusual speed and had opened a new perspective on the waterfront and on the lanes that led back into the town. Rogers saw a flicker of movement down in the street and paused, curious. Then he turned aside at once, and sank back into the shelter of a screen. He had seen a man and a woman, embracing, in the corner formed between the mosque and the Omani porch. He discovered that he was not so much embarrassed as appalled and shaken. It was not just the man's passion that was imprinted on his brain – the woman forced backwards in his arms, his hands grasping at her hair, her neck, but the woman's response: not merely the mouth frantic against his but, unmistakeably, the thrusting of her hips against him, seeking, demanding – Rogers had seen it in that second – as his hands descended to strain her thighs against his. Rogers was trembling with the shock of what he had seen. He forced himself to move away on tiptoe, a spy in the night. He slumped into a chair and realised he was in a cold, muck sweat.

He knew then that he was frightened. He could not have been mistaken, they were European, and they were Dekker and Martha Wilhelm.

*

Fallon said to Dekker, 'So all of these men have left their lives behind?'

They were sitting together in Free House, slightly to one side of their companions, waiting for the evening meeting to begin. Wilhelm and Salner had taken their places at the table and were sorting out their documents: another sermon had arrived from Dr Hertzka, Goddfrey had assured them mischievously. Ducoffre came in late, and Fallon noticed how he gave a wide berth to Captain Dugmore and his dog.

'Their wives? I suppose so.'

'No! Their *lives*.'

'They don't sound as though they regret it. Or their wives either, if you insist.' Dekker chuckled.

'But it can't have been easy even for the less serious of our members.'

'I can't honestly say. I suspect that secretly many of them must be lamenting their previous lives and wondering if they made a mistake.'

'Is that good or bad?'

'You're playing games with me,' said Dekker, and his tone was affectionate. 'For some of us it's probably just as well to say goodbye to the past.'

'I suppose everyone has his own reasons for leaving – coming here or going wherever. So there are as many reasons for the Freelanders being here tonight as there are members. Two dozen, is it?'

'You might be able to group some of them into categories, like sorting diamonds,' said Dekker. 'There are some of us, for instance, who are here to get away from our past lives and to escape – a negative reason. And there are some who are here to move on, to improve our lives, to aspire – that is a positive reason.'

'It must be more complicated than that. Look – Wilhelm Selling, over there in the corner, is an able man, he has thought through his ambitions for his journey and then, when he's achieved them, he will send for his family. Whereas the Austrian next to him, Gustav Rabinek, whose appearance is equally sincere and deter-mined, we now know to have come here to escape from his miserable little crimes. Then there's Emil Ducoffre, our preening little friend over there – I can easily believe that he's in flight from some dangerous passion.'

'The Montenegran princess?'

'No, the Belgian beauty. Her husband has sworn to have Ducoffre murdered. Not that I believe a word of it, the man lives for fantasy. As for Gleisering (he's not here, I suppose he's off in some whorehouse) – whenever I see him I wonder why he was *allowed* to join us; he worries me.'

'Martha Wilhelm assures me that everyone was very carefully selected.'

Tom Fallon snorted. 'Then the distinguished Dr Hertzka must be too innocent for this world. And Wilhelm and Salner with him, since they were on the same committee. I would never have signed up to go into Darkest Africa if I had seen the companions I was going to have.'

'Are you saying, then, that the majority of us are here for a negative reason? To escape, as I think you put it?'

'Can I exempt from your question the criminals on the run and the lechers and the simply stupid? We have our share of all three.'

'Yes, it's a serious question. Why have we come here, rather than to the Americas or the Antipodes?'

'Because those are lands of opportunity – lands where you intend to get rich. That's the reason for a European to emigrate. But it's not really the point for most of these people.'

'So why have they come here, and not to Patagonia or the South Seas or somewhere like that?'

'I'm not sure. Because we have been told that Africa is the last truly empty land which can support Europeans?'

'But you and I must have suspected that it wasn't empty. Check with Dugmore – we're not aiming for an empty Eden, he tells me we'll need every rifle we've got.'

Dekker said, 'I take your point. I am conscious of the fantasy in Hertzka's book. But I still believe that East Africa could be the last place on earth where it might be possible for society to start again.'

'So you believe in Utopia, Mr Dekker. Your friend Morris would be proud of you.'

'The sooner we test it out, the better. We'd agree on that.'

'Then why this delay, now that the launch is operating?'

'I suspect that takes us back to the motives that drive us – leaders as well as footsoldiers. We both have our doubts about our leaders...'

'And us footsoldiers. Where do you and I fit into your diamond sorting?'

'You're surely not lumping us in with those rough diamonds over there.'

'Fair enough. So – you?'

'I've forgotten the question.'

'No, you haven't. I began by asking – do we regret leaving our lives behind?'

Dekker said, 'I promise you that *I* do not.'

He had the courtesy not to return the question. I remember, Tom Fallon was thinking, how I used to share the bathtub with my elder boy. Meg didn't approve. We used to play with boats – they'd lurch, undirected, under the man's hairy knees, round the back, past the heavy sex, the child very serious amidst the soap suds, then laughing all of a sudden. I wonder if the boy remembers. That and things like that. Shall I write to him tomorrow? He'll be five – no, six – by now. What can I say to him?

He volunteered to the older man, 'Yes, I miss it. I miss my family, though it was I who chose to leave. I do not miss my job at the school, but I miss the affection and the response of the children – and I chose to leave them too. I miss a few friends in London. But there you have it. I was abandoning very little in comparison with you.'

149

'You must be jesting,' protested Dekker, and for a moment Fallon sensed his anger. 'I had no family. Isn't that the fundamental difference?'

Is that a reproach, wondered Fallon, and understood that it wasn't, that it was instead a revelation of a sadness.

'Believe me,' he offered, 'the accidental acquisition of a family is no certain path to happiness. If it were, then the whole world would be happy. You may be a luckier man than you know.'

Dekker said, so quietly that he might have been talking to himself, 'It would have been easy enough to settle down, as the English phrase puts it...'

'A comfortable life? The village squire in Gloucestershire? Fame and fortune in Mayfair?'

'There you understand me perfectly. Now you also understand that I had to get out.'

Julius Wilhelm called them to order. There was indeed the honour of a communication from Dr Hertzka in Vienna. It occurred to various of those present that the old boy did not know what he was talking about, but they suppressed any comment for later discussion at Mabrukki's. Captain Dugmore listened with particular concentration to Wilhelm's recital, and at the end actually applauded, though he had the grace to look abashed when no-one followed his example.

The two Englishmen had nothing to do but continue their conversation, and Fallon was eager to exploit Dekker's unusual volubility and *understand*.

'If I understand correctly, you'd moved out of the Socialist League. You didn't have much time for the Fabians, you were never an Anarchist, you certainly have doubts about the ILP and – I'm guessing! – you'd still turn up at Morris's meetings in Hammersmith, but mainly for old time's sake.'

'You read me very well,' said Dekker. 'You are in fact telling me once more why I am here.'

'Not there.'

'Precisely. There seemed no alternative. I may have been wrong. But you? You owe me an explanation of your own journey – your Calvary, as one might put it. Not that Calvary always seems to me the best of destinations...'

Fallon allowed himself to wince, in theatrical protest, and heard the other man laugh.

'I've been tempted by all of it, over the years, including, I admit, some varieties of Anarchism. Kropotkin, not Bakunin, you appreciate the distinction. I've always had a respect for Carpenter, though I see why he exasperates everybody – remember those ridiculous sandals he wears? But in the end I couldn't stand the Anarchists' fucking stupidity.'

'Or was it innocence?'

'In people prepared to murder their own class? *Innocence*? Of course not. Fine, exterminate everything – palaces, convents, barracks, banks, churches, Pall Mall clubs, prisons, the usual list. I agree with everything.'

'But not with bombs. Not you. That's your point, isn't it?'

'That's it, I regret. So I was blocked. Shit! I even thought of joining the Fabians.'

'They wouldn't have had you, if that makes you feel better.'

Fallon hadn't finished. 'There was the Walsall business a couple of years ago. *The bloody fools...*'

Walsall, as Dekker well knew, had been a classic example of the role of the *agent provocateur*. A Frenchman called Coulon had turned up in 1890 in the West End and joined the Socialist League where, without apology or discretion,he peddled textbooks for the manufacture of bombs and went so far as to run chemistry classes in the use of dynamite. The Walsall Socialists were to be the victim of a police stratagem. Four of their members were sent down, and Coulon vanished; the Anarchists' willingness to embrace violence had been demonstrated. Carpenter declared in his evidence that he believed that violence might sometimes be justified; Morris refused to agree to this essentially Continental extremism.

'Who were the fools?'

'My comrades. Those stupid innocents. They could not understand that the police would lay such a trap. I warned them.'

'Surely we all need to draw a careful distinction between rhetoric and action. I have mixed in these circles, grant me that, and I soon learned that it was necessary to separate the words of the preacher from the deeds of the rare activist. Though a plainclothes police inspector might find that distinction difficult to grasp.'

'Precisely. There is an intoxication in words. Deeds are more difficult.'

'But you yourself weren't an Anarchist.'

'I don't know what I was. By then, I knew I wasn't anything.'

151

'So now we find ourselves out here, of all places. In the same boat for the first time...'

He smote Dekker on the shoulder in evidence of solidarity.

Neither man thought till later that what they had just been been saying might be applied to their present project.

*

'Mr Thomas,' said Captain Dugmore – Felix had to admit that the Captain was invariably courteous to his servants, though he had once seen him kick one of his Swahilis most viciously in the backside: 'Thank God I'm a white man' was his spontaneous reaction – 'Mr Thomas, I think it is the moment for a conference. I am going to be candid with you. Yes, sit down, let us talk man to man...'

'I'm very obliged to you, Captain, you rescued me from a very tricky situation...'

'Never mind that Welsh bullshit,' ordered Dugmore, with the natural authority of the Hampshire squire. 'You don't have to remind me that you were performing an errand on my behalf when you were caught. As I told you, you were a damn fool to be caught, but I acknowledge that you were discreet. And I rewarded you for it, did I not?'

'You were very generous, Captain. I really don't know how I'd be coping on this island with all these heathen if it weren't for you.'

'Oh stow it, Felix!' said Dugmore, and Felix noted a real exasperation in his voice, so he adjusted his manner and his accent, and prepared to be whoever, whatever, this idiot aristocrat desired. One day, thought Felix, we'll all stop playing games. But I'm not there yet.

'I am going to take you into my confidence, Felix.'

Are you, hell! thought the Welsh boy as he said, 'I'm very honoured, Captain. You can rely on me entirely.'

'This conversation does not exist,' barked Dugmore.

'I'm sorry, sir?'

'I mean that everything I shall now say is strictly confidential! I emphasise that, Felix. I shall even tell you that it concerns affairs of state. You must never mention this conversation to any living soul. Do you understand me?'

Jesus Christ, thought Felix Thomas, but instead he said, 'Word of honour, Captain. On the Bible.'

152

The Captain glared at him – perhaps deep down in his suppressed intuition something was telling him never to trust a working-class Welshman on the make – but he ignored the warning and carried on, in the tone of the District Commissioner that he would one day become. 'Felix, you may have wondered why I have sent you to sit in the sunshine on Shela beach...'

Not to watch your mate Tom Fallon screwing Mrs Sasse, thought Felix, but sadly put the retort behind him; he would try a diversion. 'Well, Captain, I naturally wondered why you told me to have a shifty at Mr Salner's room – those were your very words, I remember – but it wasn't my place to ask...'

'That is a totally different matter,' declared Dugmore. 'Nothing whatsoever to do with this business on Shela, though I can hint to you that it might also have had to do with official affairs.... But you can put that businesss out of your mind.'

'As you wish, sir. It's an easy berth, sitting on the beach all day and coming home in the sunset to report that nothing's happened.'

'But something did happen, Felix, as you well know. You have spotted something which confirms the hunch I had when I sent you out to Shela. I was right all the time, even though I won't pretend I ever dreamed of the detail. So it was simply a matter of sitting it out. And it was worth every minute of your long wait. You are the hero of the hour, Felix!'

'Not in Free House.'

'You don't mean you've mentioned anything in Free House? After the orders I gave you last night?'

Do I really look such a fool, thought Felix, wearily. 'Of course not, sir.'

'Your report has been – I should say, will be – of great interest *elsewhere.*'

'You mean, sir...' said Felix, and he forced himself to drag it out slowly (how stupid am I supposed to be?). 'You mean that you aren't really a Freelander, Captain?'

'No more than you are *really* a Freelander, Felix. It's all very interesting, of course, but – would you understand me if I suggested that this expedition doesn't seem to me entirely "serious"? Not the business of grown men?'

'I would understand you, Captain,' said Felix Thomas, and a more intelligent man would have listened to the tone of that reply more carefully.

'So tell me, Felix, what do you make of that scene you described to me? The scene you observed yesterday.'

Oh to hell with it, thought Felix Thomas, let him have it between the eyes. 'With respect, Captain, I think I saw our own Freeland steamboat, crewed by three of our colleagues, pause and put into shore according to an agreed code of signals, in order to evacuate ten black slaves and probably convey them to the mainland.'

'Well done, Felix!' said Dugmore with a change to his tone, and the youth accepted that he had given himself the satisfaction of that one reply and would now have to give up the play-acting. 'Next, Felix, since you are so fucking clever, what do you suggest we do next?'

Oh shit, thought Felix, I've gone too far.

'We, sir?'

'Yes, Felix, we and my friend Major Rogers – don't pretend to look so surprised – we and every *askari* we can raise on this island. You're a clever lad, now I see it. Put yourself in my shoes. What do we do next?'

It was a not unimportant moment in Felix Thomas's life. He was a disadvantaged, disgraced, ambitious, greedy, intelligent and im-aginative young man. He understood that, beneath the Englishman's hard-voiced abuse, the question was genuinely in-tended. For the first time, he was being solicited for his opinion – his judgment, his recommendation, his intuition – on a matter of import.

He said, 'Captain, you have to tell me first – has this happened before? I don't know any of the history.'

'Slaves have been abducted from this island in alarming numbers this year, particularly over the past month.' He did not add Rogers's analysis of this situation, nor the Liwali's fury. 'You and I might agree in our opinion of slave trading, Mr Thomas?'

'We certainly do, sir.'

'So – I repeat – and while you prepare to return to your vigil tomorrow – what do you suggest?'

Felix paused long enough for Dugmore to wonder if the boy had the temerity to reply. Eventually he said, 'The natives came out of the bush pretty quick. They were tied together. I reckon they must be keeping them somewhere, waiting for the boat to arrive. And only when the *Eden* thinks it's safe – that's the reason for the signals. So they never know till the last minute.'

'That must mean they keep them in some sort of compound behind the beach.'

'I suppose it has to be like that.'

'Splendid. Once we're ready, all we have to do is sweep the area between beach and dunes, and we'll catch the buggers at it.'

Felix thought, you idiot, Captain, it's not as simple as that. Next he thought, I used to be a Freelander and now I'm working for the bloody police. Third he thought – so be it, I hate this slave thing. And fourth, he thought, we'll see what the Captain says when he catches Tom Fallon with his pants down.

'Do I have to go back tomorrow?'

'Of course you do. I want a detailed report on the activities of the *Eden* – every journey up and down that coast, fully documented.'

'You mean, sir, that you and Major Rogers aren't going to put in the *askaris* at once?'

'No, Mr Thomas, we are going to wait. I intend to collect a full file of evidence before we strike. I am so confident of that policy that we shall keep this information to ourselves, you and I – d'you understand me? – until the moment is appropriate to tell Major Rogers and ask for his support.'

Oh dear, thought Felix. That's pretty obvious. My Captain wants all the glory for this one. Lord knows what Major Rogers would say if he knew he was being kept in the dark.

'Don't you think we should tell the Major, sir?'

'Dammit, Mr Thomas, I said no! My colleague has the next Witu job on his mind, and doesn't need to be bothered for the moment. You will keep this to yourself, and that is an order if you wish to remain in my employ.'

'Beg pardon, sir.'

*

Lamu

Dear Sisters,

This will have to be just a note because there is much going on here which worries me, and I do not have the time to explain properly...

The Freeland expedition, I cannot deny it, is showing signs of a crisis. Julius sometimes seems near-overwhelmed with indecision and apprehension. He finds it hard to talk to me – or rather, he finds it hard to have patience with any questions or comments I may have, and as you can guess, my questions are much less searching than those of our members. Also, there has been too much bad behaviour among some of these same members. Why must these men spend their time drinking and shouting, when a few good souls like Salner and Dekker (and Julius of course) spend their every hour struggling to get the expedition en route at last?

Major Rogers, our Ruler – whom I have decided I like, though he'd probably be furious to know it – is about to go off to the mainland on an expedition against the poor natives in Witu. Captain Dugmore (with his smelly dog) is very courteous, but I begin to suspect he is up to something. Dekker, whom I have mentioned before, has become a good friend: one day I will tell you about his strange life. Ma Fatima – whom I know I described to you in my last letter – has become my other special friend.

The Freeland members seem to be dividing, sadly, into national groups. The Germans spend more and more time at the Denhardts' (at least so Captain Dugmore tells me, and it's true that we see less and less of them at Free House). I classify myself, you observe, sisters, with the Austrian party! The French are chattering amongst themselves, planning who knows what, and the Scandinavians are still very wild. The English are as taciturn as ever, while Tom Fallon (I mustn't gossip) is generally assumed to be madly in love with Louise. (Dear old Sasse appears not to notice and is preoccupied with nursing their friend Hassemer, who has a chronic fever, in their own house some distance away.)

There are rumours of trouble on the mainland – that may explain Major Rogers's imminent departure (says Dekker) with the better part of the local garrison. Dugmore urges us not to worry, but I can see that he, too, has thoughts he does not divulge, perhaps because he does not want to alarm us.

Dekker said to me again last night, let us *please* get ourselves free of this island. We are, he said, like Odysseus's crew entranced on the island of Calypso. 'Look!' he cried – and he was pointing towards the moon, which at that moment was rising *enormous* over the mainland of Africa – '*There* is where we are supposed to be! In Africa!' And I'm afraid he added, 'What is your husband waiting for?'

I could not answer him. I could only tell him that I share his longing...

In haste, and with kisses –

M

*

Dekker and Martha lay together on the beach beyond the Forestry Office, beyond the shore where the maribou storks used to gather in daytime. They had the shelter of a rotting, beached dhow and the confidence that they were safely beyond the town and any intruder; they did not realise that they were also far beyond Major Rogers's reluctant gaze. They strained together, *at* each other, they took every liberty with each other's clothing, his hand was inside her, her hand was on his cock, but she still refused him. 'What is the *difference*?' he demanded, as she cried out again under his mouth and his hand. She pushed him away. The sky was not just dark, but black; even the stars had abdicated. She said, 'Because the rest is what we both want so much. But I cannot do it to *him*.'

Dekker did not challenge her. Her words reminded him of another woman, another place, and he shuddered at the memory of a distant past.

Foolishly, he said, 'Please forgive me.'

'You idiot! My dear, it is not for me to forgive you...'

'Yes, I did not understand your – your loyalty. I have taken an appalling liberty. I had not understood...'

'You are an idiot, and I think you know it. Dekker, please do not talk nonsense, or I shall think you are a slave to convention.'

He protested: '*You* can say that? As we lie here in this stupid sand? No, take your hand away! Stop laughing, damn you – no, tell me the truth, who's the real slave to convention?'

'Give me a little time,' she said. 'Try to believe that I love him. These are difficult days for him.'

'So I shall deliver you back to your elegant porch,' said Dekker, and for a brief moment his voice was thick with anger, 'and you will no doubt be greeted by the man with a loving kiss – as he wrestles with his indecision over yet another telegram to Vienna. And I dare say, in due course you will take him into your bed and, dear God, into your body...'

157

'That is possible. Not probable. But possible and, Dekker, I insist you accept that.'

'While I have to lie in a corridor with Gleisering tittering and snoring next to me.'

She said, 'I love you. I have never said that before to anyone other than my husband. Does that help?'

'It will help.'

*

The early morning was clear and bright and promised great heat. There was no wind, save for a breath from the wrong direction, the north. There were white clouds in the south, over Shela, but not even ignorant visitors could believe that rain was imminent. By eight it was sweat-hot. The sea was flat, except for the under-lying ripple of the incoming tide. Ma Fatima's garden was all a crystal-bright green, as though the leaves had been polished one by one by her household slaves. The banana trees were a clash of great green blades – an armoury of sabres, cutlasses, *pangas*; in the sunlight their leaves were a brilliant pale green, in shadow they were like enormous ebony combs, and the two were set against each other like bundles of shears. Between the banana trees were the frangipani, the bougainvillaea, the jasmine – a jungle of colour and confusion and tropical luxuriance. Martha listened to the sounds of Lamu – the unchanging accompaniment to the day which she had come to recognise and to love: the occasional cockcrow in the distance; the far-carrying voices of men passing in the street, of women gossiping and cackling inside a house, of a squawling baby; a twitter of starlings; a sudden rush of water released into the tiny *shamba* next door; a clatter of plates from a distant rooftop kitchen; the rattle of donkeys in a narrow lane and the thwash of a cane on their patient rumps.

Ma Fatima had been angry, Martha acknowledged. It had been rude of her to suggest that the women of the island were not 'free' like European women – her Swahili was so approximate she may have confused the distinction between 'free' and 'bound' and 'tied' and 'slave', which was the point she had wanted to make.

'Permit me, Ma,' she had said – tried to say – 'you and your friends are restrained. In *harem*. In *purdah*. To us, that would be impossible to suffer.'

'Why do you think that?'

Martha struggled with the self-evident. 'You are – well, you are hidden away. *You have no freedom.* You are not permitted, Ma, to live your life as you wish.'

'Why should I wish?'

'But you *must* wish to be free.'

'I am as free as I choose.' The old woman was looking her straight in the eye. 'I promise you that I do not feel that I am not free, as you put it. Perhaps I do not go out into the street and expose myself before the strange men without a *bui-bui*. But is that freedom? Perhaps I do not ask my husband to make me drink coffee with all his friends whenever they call *hodi* at the porch. Perhaps I do not – or did not, when I was younger – meet my lovers on the street at night outside the Friday Mosque.'

Martha flinched, looked away, coloured.

'No, do not escape me. I want you to understand this. As you see, I know that you meet your lover. I may be in *harem*, but I know everything that happens in this town. Many years ago I met my lovers too, but not in a public place and not on the road beyond the Forestry *boma*. Do you really think that in Lamu a woman does not feel free to take a lover?'

'But it is surely forbidden...'

'Ah! Forbidden, yes of course. But everyone knows that it is not possible to deny love. That we all understand, wherever we come from. Our husbands have many wives in Islam; do you think the wives do not have many "husbands"?'

'In Lamu, that is permitted?'

'It is not "permitted", but it is understood.'

'And is that truly wise?'

The old woman nodded, and said, after a long silence, as though she was consulting her wisdom as well as her memories, 'How other? Is it so hard to understand, so surprising? From cradle to grave is a long journey. We all change many times. The henna has to be painted again. That is not always a bad thing.'

Then she leaned across and, for the first time Martha could remember, she seized her hand in her tiny claw and said, with a passion that contained a note of something close to venom: '*You* tell me that I have lived my life in *harem*. You tell me that you and your sisters are free, and that I and my sisters have been slaves. *Are you so sure*? How much do you know of us? How little do you know of yourselves?'

159

'Ma Fatima, what shall I do?'

'I shall not answer you.'

'Why?'

'Bcause you know what to do. Only you know.'

'It frightens me. Yesterday I discovered that I was making up a story – a day-dream – in which Julius was dying. Because of the climate here, or some fever, like Hassemer. I knew I didn't want him to die, but I couldn't help thinking how much *simpler* things would be if he died. It's so silly. I'm just as likely to die as he is.'

'That will also end your problem.' The old woman cackled.

'Tell me one thing more, I beg you.'

The old lady, Swahili poet and mother of the Liwali, but not of the Liwali's brother, shook her head. 'Only you can decide which one of us is free. Where is your *harem*? Work that out before you ask me more questions.'

'Ma, I do not want this to happen.'

Ma Fatima said, 'Why did you come here?'

Martha said, in her simple Swahili, 'To find you, Mama.'

'I know it. And why else?'

Martha shook her head. 'Tell me just that. Please.'

'To find the man. You know it.'

'I did not know it.'

'And he to find you?'

'Yes, I think so.'

'You are sure?'

'Yes, I am sure.'

'Then the fates will be good to both of you. Because you have discovered that which is true. You have arrived at the truth.'

Eight

Social life here is very bright and animated. Families that are intimate with each other meet together without ceremony almost every evening; and there is conversation, music, and, among the young people, not a little dancing.... I arrived at the conviction that what made social intercourse here so richly enjoyable must be mainly the genuine human affection which characterises life in Freeland...

Theodor Hertzka: *Freeland: A Social Anticipation*

The Rains came at ten in the morning. The sun had risen to promise a day of stifling heat. There was not a breath of wind, and the atmosphere was so heavy that Martha Wilhelm, after her breakfast, did what she had never done before and went back to her bed and slept. She was woken by a din of gleeful children and a noise like a Pentecostal wind rushing through the town, slamming windows and rattling utensils. The entire sky was a dense, smoke black. To the west Manda Island had completely vanished as the grey of the sea merged seamlessly into the sky; to the south the light was brighter but nevertheless grey – a dove-grey hinting at blue where the far horizon ought to have been.

The rain started gently, soaking, dense, then poured down with steadily increasing force. And with it came the unique, blessed odour of the earth of Africa exploding with the very smell of creation, a dense and dark and glowing aroma of fetid growth and fertility. Martha stood transfixed, and then remembered her husband; she thought to call to him, but remembered he would be at Free House. Let it go. The water was pouring off the *makuti* roof in sheets – and it was brown! Brown as liquid manure from her Austrian rainbutt, as it rushed down the layered gradients of the rooftops and spouted out into the centre of the alleys and lanes – far out, so as to protect the foundations of the houses, she noted – and so in streams many inches deep, torrents, pouring downhill to the sea. Heavier and heavier the rain fell, and the children rushed out onto the rooftops and into the courtyards to be instantly soaked and ecstatic.

Martha knew that it had grown cool and magically fresh. A breeze had blown up again, but this time it came from the north, not the monsoon south, and this time the rain fell more gently, a fine haze of spray that gusted under the low eaves, drenching her nightdress so that the cotton clung to her body like a healing poultice. Afterwards, she realised that she had stood there for near a full hour, as the northern sky lightened imperceptibly and the grey wall moved down towards Shela and the rain slackened and died. She saw blue sky break through on the horizon, though the cloud was still large and heavy, slow to disband. Two pie-crows flew strenuously over the house, heavily bedraggled, their feathers waterlogged; they called urgently, either to each other or to missing companions, in a harsh quack. The water stopped spouting from the thatch and immediately the streets were empty, unpuddled, almost dry again. It began to get humid almost at once. A few flies ventured out from wherever they had been hiding, and clung to her bare feet. She saw that she had begun to sweat again.

Martha dressed, hurrying as though she regretted her morning idleness. The servant boy came in from the porch, grinning wet; there was a dark shadow emerging on his shaven head like a birthmark; in another week he would have a stubble of black curl. She gave him orders, stumbling a little in the language, but he understood: these days they always did. And after you have been to the baker, she told him, take this letter to Bwana Dekker at Free House.

*

Martha went to call on Ma Fatima on this day, as she did every afternoon. The old lady demanded her with the authority of the mother of the ruling family, and the German woman obeyed without ever thinking to query the command. Each afternoon she took her instruction, and in the quiet evenings, after supper, she meditated on what had been so artlessly offered. She knew that she needed this surprising and unexpected guide because she had rapidly discovered that the movement to which she was attached, this European intellectual and theoretical construct, when once located in this real world of African experience had become foolish

162

and ignorant. She understood this from the very first day on the stinking jetty, and the speed of her discovery horrified her. That did not mean that she regretted the impulse which had brought her to this place. There was a deep and acknowledged need in her to come to the new and to explore its possibilities, a craving to awake to a selfhood which she did not believe was yet available to a woman in Europe. She knew, in the depths of her being, that she was in search of a new life, an emancipation which was denied her at home – and she was thinking not of the freedoms of politics or economics, which did not interest her particularly, but of the spirit, of an awakened self.

She had looked to Louise Sasse to accompany her on this journey, but Louise was a worry, even as she loved her as another young sister. The Alsace girl took a delight in asserting her emancipation, as she insisted on recounting to Martha in entirely unnecessary detail, but she seemed to be unaware of a wider dimension. She was content to be supported by her amiable husband (with the subventions, she had volunteered, of their friend Hassemer), but understood none of Martha's confusion about her own, similar dependence on Julius. She candidly enjoyed her liberation from the anti-Semitic disadvantages she said she had suffered in her European youth. She embraced the wildest ideologies, speaking up for the assassination of whoever and alarming even the Free House evening meetings with the extremity of her prescriptions, yet she seemed to make no attempt to find a direction, a purpose, for her freedom. Martha would have loved to discuss all this with someone, but Julius did not take Louise seriously, and Ma Fatima could not possibly understand.

When she slipped through the familiar lanes this afternoon of the Rains, hugging the shadows, she found that the sun had cleared the greater part of the sky and the stones were too hot for her feet. It would take longer to clear the puddles on the seafront. The sun was hot and very bright, but all around the horizon there were banks of solid raincloud.

She stood obediently in front of the long, white-plastered wall in Ma Fatima's inner room which, as she had noted before, was heavily indented with a complex design of symmetrical shelves and nooks and crannies. The screen was not much more than two metres away from where she had been put to stand – the total width of the room – yet it extended more than twice that distance.

163

Ma Fatima for some reason had called a slave girl to remove the Korans and the baubles and the candles and the beads which normally occupied the deep stucco recesses.

'Stand there!' commanded the old lady, and grasped at Martha's sleeve to bring her to a position central to the screen.

'Yes?'

'What do you see?'

Martha did not understand. She saw a sequence of whitewashed plaster holes in the wall, surrounded by some crudely incised ornamentation; she remembered how she had discovered why the *harem* needed this device, but Ma Fatima would not be telling her this again. She shook her head in apology.

The old woman's grip tightened, guided. 'Then explore,' she said softly. 'Try this way! Just a little. Or that? Stand here – and now *here*. Is that different?'

And in a heart-stopping moment Martha, in that last position, saw the perspectives come together into a mysterious, geometrical perfection, the fractional variations in the stucco sculpture make sense, the slim wall open into a mighty landscape...

She struggled to ask – as she wavered, and clung to that one and precise point of vision – 'Why here?' It was neither central nor symmetrical, she could have proved that with her sewing tape, there was no reason for it to work, and yet.... And all Ma Fatima would say from the doorway was, 'It is here. The point is here.' I would not have known it, thought Martha. The true perspective comes out of the search, not from the calculation. We can never know it until we reject calculation and go out and search for it. That is what she is telling me.

*

Robert Schmidt had fallen in love with the Shela beach and its dunes. He went there as often as he could, striding eagerly the two miles down the shore from Lamu Town, clutching his water bottle and his knapsack. The fishermen on the outskirts of the port had got used to him; they knew he did not need their boats. '*Jambo*!' he would shout, '*Habari*,' and race on his way in the illusion that he was almost a local since he was talking their language.

First he made for the dunes. He had found the precise site, he promised himself, of the famous battle of 1813 between the armies of Lamu and Pate. He had been exploring a couple of weeks ago, remembering something Dugmore had said about the island's history, not hoping for anything (his previous archaeological experience had been conducted in the dank and muddy trenches of the Orkneys) when, lo and behold, he had immediately discovered human bones. Hundreds of them. Skulls and tibias and pelvises and thousands of the minutiae of fingers and toes, all perfectly preserved and polished in the silver sand, enough to assemble armies of skeletons for medical schools; they were everywhere in the dune, lying wherever he scraped away a few inches of sand. He brought the skulls back to Free House in sackfulls, until Dr Wilhelm asked him to desist.

He hadn't been out here for almost a week and, after the excitement of checking that his bones were still there, he decided he would ski down the dunes and race for the sea and the shells. His second passion was shells, and on Shela beach he found himself – to quote the English phrase – as happy as a sandboy. He charged at the crabs, who scrambled, always sidewards, into the suds of the sea, only to be sent sprawling in a panic back onto his toes and vanish, frantic, under the wet sand, their claws windmilling in terror. A small dhow swooped past him only yards from the shore: the two boys shouted at him 'Lamu? Lamu?' and he laughed and waved back at them and called 'Hapana, hapana!' because he thought it was the Swahili for no, and they cheered and one of them lifted a great conch shell to his lips and blew him that most spine-tingling of all notes, the ancient siren call with which a dhow captain signals that he is entering port. He stood and watched them for a mile and more until the simple craft veered towards the shore again and let down its sail. From this distance it looked like a butterfly alighting on a flower and folding its wings – or no, not quite (thought Schmidt), the sail fluttered too wildly at a certain moment, it was moı ' of an uncontrolled and spontaneous collapse, like a piece of paper in a bonfire caving in above the flame. On board, as he knew well, there was nothing fragile about it: the boy let go the rope so that gravity brought down the great tattered sheet with a crash. But from a distance the sound of the crash is concealed behind the image of the crumpling of the sheet.

The sand at this part of the beach, he discovered today, was squeaking under his feet. No again! A poet would be more precise – the sound it made under his bare footsteps was stronger than a whisper, softer than a squeak, it was a mewing; he was pleased with

165

that. And it was bloody hot. He stepped back into the shallows to cool his feet. Today he would look for sand-dollar shells. Louise Sasse had said she was collecting them for a necklace, and he had promised he would find her the largest, most perfect specimens, in which the cinquefoil pattern on the frail disc would be un-smudged by wind and water but precise and delicate as a blue engraving – 'Much better than the ones you're wearing,' he promised, noticing that she had a rough string of them around her brown neck. 'Who gave you those?'

'Never you mind,' she had said, and smiled privately into his eyes so that he was discomfited. Perhaps she'll let me paint her portrait in her sand-dollar necklace, he wondered – for Robert Schmidt was also a painter.

Now he stood ankle-deep and gazed back at the battlefield dune where he had made his discovery. Would he have time to work up a paper on the Shela-Pate burial ground before they left for the Tana? These dunes were so wonderfully dramatic, he thought, a blazing white, powder-talc, with the splash of green undergrowth of cactus and thorn and dwarf-pine at the base of their steep slope; when he screwed up his eyes – like poor Jimmy Dunn used to do – the dunes became a great mountain range of snow and pumice but first, in the plains below, there was a forest of dense jungle....
He knew of course that he could cross that forest and climb those mountains in ten minutes. That was what he would do next. There was a dramatic and lonely tree, a sort of look-out pine, about half a mile to the east, which he hadn't noticed before. It might have had a strategic function in the battle. He set off across the hot sand and into the scrub.

*

They met on the outskirts of the town, on the path to Matandoni. He had been waiting for her, and after a quarter-mile drew her aside into an orchard of great mango trees. There was a small *boma* and a whiff of goat, and beyond it there was a secret place. They lay down together. They were confident in the privacy of this place under the great gnarled mango branches. They were soon naked.

She said, 'Be gentle... we have all the time in the world...' by which he understood that she was pledging herself for life, for ever, and his body understood it too and lost its frantic, bursting urgency so that he could wait. And instead he preferred to touch her, and she touched him, and to caress her, and she caressed him, the two of them so slow, almost thoughtful, always silent. Sometimes they paused and lay apart for whole minutes, just their fingers linked, and through the high branches they could see the stars coming out behind the scudding whisps of cloud.

And then they touched again, and held each other tight, and still it was true, the violent, wasteful urgency had gone, it was not needed, so he could savour the length of the moment just as she relished the discovery of her certainty, and he tasted her lips and her ears and her eyes and the gentle fold of her neck, and then – much later – her breasts (with hand, mouth, tongue) and then her soft belly and her smooth thighs, the sour-sweet inside of her, the rough bush of her (his hands on her hard nipples) and still, he found, he was able to wait because he was remembering her words even as he heard her sigh and shift under him. Until she called his name, loud in the silence of the *shamba*, and pulled at him and took him into her, and for a little while they were still again, tentative, almost shy of each other, overwhelmed – they later agreed, when they talked of it – with the enormity of the moment, and for a long second they paused, they gazed, she grinned, he sighed, he said 'Sorry' (for no good reason, and they both laughed aloud, the two of them) and she pulled him down and whispered in his ear, 'Listen to the wind in these trees...'

Later, much later, she said again – he remembered it all his life – 'All the time in the world...' But he had no words, no reply, he could only hold her, tucked into his shoulder as the moisture slowly dried on their bodies. He would have said, 'My love – my soul desires you,' but he knew that words had nothing more to add, and he had the new wisdom to be silent.

It rained again the next afternoon. The black clouds built up in the north, amid rumbles of thunder, and moved slowly and inexorably towards the island. At the same time it got hotter and hotter until the entire population retreated, the Europeans to their rooftops, the Swahilis to their lower-floor dungeons; each were convinced that the others were insane. There was a period of dead calm. Then – from the south again – there came a rustle of fierce breeze, almost cool, and soon afterwards the rain, but this time the centre of the storm seemed to by-pass the heart of the town. The rest of the afternoon was heavy and overcast, but it was endurable, and at

167

sunset the cloud relented and began to break away, leaving a sky sprayed with pastel cirrus – orange, peach and lavender – while the sea, still dead calm, turned a strange and silvery palest green. But the mainland was still heavy and dark with storm.

*

The beach at Shela was always empty except for the crabs, digging and vanishing with a speed extraordinary to behold. The sea was clean – this was before the Rains brought the Tana silt from out of the heart of Africa – and the fine white sand was stained only by a thin, high-tide line of weed and rotting coconut husks; sometimes a great hunk of driftwood or a palm branch; once a chair and a porcelain doll from some steamer passing through a storm and bound for Durban. When a seagull lay dead, the crabs in their dozens tore at its flesh so avidly that they forgot to run away when he approached them: they shifted sideways, eyes swivelling, claws marking a bird-like perforation on the wet sand, waiting, wisely, for him to move on – as he did with a shudder.

Once – worse – there was a dead goat, horribly distended with stinking gases; once a great turtle, up-ended, tragic, swarming with ants; and once, the body of a man.

It lay on the very edge of the waves, and Pier Scavenius at first thought that it was a man resting or sleeping. He never doubted that it was a man. The clothes were obviously sodden, which surprised him. He had the impression, from these clothes, that it must be a white man. He wandered across the sand to see if he was awake, or sunbathing, or – as he had first thought – sleeping. Or whether he knew him. But from five metres' distance he understood that this was not a man but a corpse. The flesh was swelling, putrefying, stinking, and the crabs, poised for a reluctant departure, were chewing at the eyeballs. Scavenius hesitated for the shortest possible moment, recognised the long blond hair and the thin moustache and – he remembered later, but was never absolutely sure – he screamed. At the horror of young Robert Schmidt dead on this idyllic beach, sprawled on the sand like the limp carcasses he had once seen outside the abattoir, where they were guarded by maribou storks.

Pier Scavenius retreated, tripping and stumbling in the sand, then stopped himself and forced himself to return to cast a second glance. He was pouring with sweat, and panting; it occurred to

168

him that he had never seen a dead body before. So he stared, from a careful distance, and saw that the eyes were empty sockets, eaten by the voracious crabs, and the mouth, too, was open, as though crying out to his friends for help, because around the puffy flesh of the neck there was unmistakeably, even to Scavenius's amateur eye, a thick hemp cord that cut deep into the Belgian's throat and would certainly not be there if the man had merely capsized in the shallows.

Scavenius wondered whether to scream again, and at that moment realised that he was alone under God's heaven. So he kept his silence. He edged closer to the body, but his own body failed him when it was assailed by the hot, sweet stench. He stepped back and vomited violently. When he had stopped shuddering, he cleaned his face in the sea and, without another glance at Schmidt, began to run down the beach towards Lamu, gasping loudly. Once he plunged knee-deep into the sea and sluiced his face again and again in the salt. Then he ran, ever faster, down the hard low-tide sand in the direction of the town.

His brain was in a fury. After a mile he stopped and actually sat down on an ancient stone bench set under the branches of a casuarina just above the water. He remembered that he had spotted the tree from the deck of the *Eden* and had wondered who had installed the seat, and when. He struggled to control himself. What shall a man do, he demanded, when he has seen his friend dead – not dead, murdered? Who can have done it? Who *needed* to do it? Whom had poor Robert offended? No native – impossible to believe. So *who*? *Why*?

This is a desperate land, decided the young, young Scavenius. We are on the fringe of a savage continent. Schmidt must have been meddling in some mysteries. I do not understand these things. I want none of this. He remembered how the crabs had eaten the eyeballs of his friend. At the same time he was studying the creek in front of him, where at low tide a great sandbank extends by five hundred metres the skirts of Manda Island's mangrove flats, their dark roots like crippled and naked limbs beneath their vivid greenery. Scavenius, even in his terror, found that out on that sandbank he was watching two small boys marching confidently into the middle of the ocean as though walking on water.

Would the high tide recover him? And – if he told no-one – where would tomorrow's tide deposit him? And where would the crabs devour him next? He had seen him only that morning. You must come to the dunes with me one day, he'd said, we can find some more skulls.... I am not worthy, thought Scavenius. I must leave this awful place.

He got to his feet and began to run, to scuttle, along the beach. He wondered where he might find Martha Wilhelm.

Martha said, 'Julius is not here. He's at Free House. Sit down. I'll get you some tea. Now *rest*! Lie down if you can. Compose yourself – please try!'

'It was the crabs,' he said. 'They had eaten his eyes.'

'My dear, he had died long before that...'

'No, he had been murdered.'

Martha said, 'Be very careful. How can you say that?'

'There was a rope round his neck.'

'You are sure?'

'Of course I'm sure. I saw him, I tell you!'

'But *why*?'

'I want to leave this place. Ever since we arrived I have known it was awful.'

Martha was thinking, we have to report the death, someone must recover the body, that sort of thing: whom do I tell?

She said, 'In Julius's absence, I'll send a message to Major Rogers. He'll have to send his men...'

'Don't mention me!'

'But I have to.'

'Why? There's a body on the beach. That's all they need to know.'

'But you say someone has murdered him. You found him. You have to testify.'

'I can't. I can't face it.'

'Why not? He was your friend.'

'I can't. Believe me, I can't.'

Martha said to the weeping man, 'Look, you tell me you found the dead body of your friend – your colleague – on Shela beach. You can't refuse to tell the police what you saw.'

'I couldn't go through with it.' He was shaking with great, gulping sobs.

Martha, thinking very fast and at the same time delving into unknown resources of intuition, said, 'You mean you might know why he was killed?'

170

'Of course not! That's nonsense.'

'I don't believe you.'

'Why should I know why Schmidt was killed on Shela beach?'

'Because he had to be killed. To silence him. There's no other reason. Because he had seen something. I've no idea what.'

'What are you saying?' he gasped.

Martha said, *'Why else* would anyone bother to kill the boy? He didn't have money to rob. It must have been because he *knew* something. He'd *seen* something. No-one in the world wished him ill – did they?'

Scavenius hid his face in his hands in acknowledgement of what she had said.

'So – ' said Martha, and laid her hand onto his. 'We need to know what he had discovered out at Shela. My dear, do you know? – Can you guess? – Can you help?' It would be good to understand these things, she thought, before the policemen discovered a body and set up their own procedures.

Scavenius said, and his voice was still thick and cluttered with sobs, 'I might have some idea. But I'm a dead man – like Robert – if I talk.'

'That's ridiculous.'

'No, I'll be a dead man. Like him.'

'What is this?' she demanded, in innocent outrage. This is an ordered world, murder is murder, why should a young Dane be terrified to tell the truth?

She said, 'Do I get the impression that something is going on which you cannot speak of?'

'Schmidt is dead with a rope round his neck.'

'And he knew something – which *you* also know.'

'I might.'

'My dear,' (she said it as though to the son she did not have) 'you must let me help you.'

'I need your help. I know too much.'

'What does that mean?'

'I have to leave this place. No-one must know.'

'What is it that you know?'

'I can't say.'

'Now stop!' cried Martha. 'That is too easy! If you know of things that are evil, you must tell us.'

'Us?' She saw that he was recovering his wits, beginning to think.

She started again. 'Your friend has just been murdered – I don't know why. You know why. You know what he knew – or so I think. You ask my help. You wish to leave this island – to escape your friend's fate...'

He was blubbing again, as if his earlier exchange had been a brief bravado. 'I can't carry on with the trips, Martha, believe me, I simply couldn't go on with them. I'd prefer to jump overboard...'

'What on earth are you talking about?'

'If I tell you – can you get me out of this island? Can you and your friends arrange it? Can you get me onto a ship back home? Without me having to go back to Free House? I'll feel an awful fool, but otherwise I'm dead – I mean it, they're serious!'

Martha said, 'My dear, you'd better tell me the story.'

*

Louise was making love with Tom Fallon. They were under their tree, and she was cursing the sand. When the breeze came from the west, they had discovered, it did not matter so long as you were standing up, because it did not blow the sand higher than your ankles, but if you were lying down, and if you were naked, your sweating skin was instantly coated in fine but sharp yellow talc. At this same ground level she could see the highwater debris rustling in the same breeze: brown and brittle mangrove leaves, whisps of clinging seaweed, some ancient coconut husks, a collection of cuttle shells, all of them within ten metres of her private den. They were surrounded by a circle of tiny crabs, gazing at them, suspicious and entranced; when she raised an arm they would scurry away and vanish, with furious activity, under the sand.

He was making love to her to the rhythm of the waves, as they pounded – but gently – onto the hard sand. There was a distant crash – a pause – a retreat and the slush of the undertow – then the next soft crash.... He said into her ear, 'I can keep this up if you like, until – until the tide turns!' and they both collapsed in helpless giggles.

She said, 'Not so loud, or Fundi George will find us again.'

'Then we'd better get dressed.'

'He's not exactly dressed himself – at least, not dressed like a parson. He only had a *kanga* round his waist. How were we to know that he was a priest and not a bandit?'

'We knew when he started preaching!'

172

'Why is a priest called a *Fundi*? I thought that meant a craftsman.'

Tom Fallon couldn't begin to guess. They had been walking in the shallows, a mile or so beyond their tree, when they had seen a figure striding towards them from Shela, which gave them time to compose themselves, drop hands, fix a button or two. It was a giant of a man and he was singing loudly – and to Tom's astonishment it brought a memory from years back, it was a Sankey hymn from the Baptist chapels of Southwark. In a splendid bass the black man with a tangled beard cascading over his bare chest was singing, 'We thank thee Lord / that all our joy / is tinged with pain...' Tom couldn't resist: he responded, in his light tenor, 'That shadows fall on brightest hours / that tears remain...' And, to Louise's stupefaction, the two men bellowed, in approximate harmony, 'So that earth's joys / may be our guide / and *not – our – aim*!' They hugged each other, brothers in that simple faith (how Fallon used to detest the sentiments of that ditty!), and the African chortled happily. Tom said, 'You remember, Louise, it's Fundi George. He buried Jimmy Dunn, but we were all of us better dressed on that occasion.'

Fundi George, Louise observed at once, was taking pains not to look in her direction. 'Oh heavens,' she thought, 'I must shock him the way I'm looking. He'll think I'm a Magdalene.'

But she may have been wrong. The crazy missionary had other things on his mind that afternoon, and he launched into a torrent of protestation at Tom.

'Brother! Friend in the Lord! I tell you that Satan is abroad on this strand today...'

He was not, it emerged, referring to them and to their activities under the tree. Satan had been up to something else. Fundi George ranted and raved and quoted the Scriptures at furious speed (which Tom was far better qualified to follow than she), and neither of them quite grasped what troubled him so.

He left them suddenly, without a blessing, sprinting through the sand in the direction of a dune where, he insisted, he had just observed the Devil – 'At this very moment, I saw his tail! – Did you see him too, brother?'

Tom had thought, I ought to mention this in Lamu. He's not as crazy as all that. Something has troubled him; something may be happening which we should report. But I can't say anything, because I can never admit that Louise and I have been here. I shall have to pass by on the other side (the metaphors of his youth were coming back to him).

He didn't want to alarm her. 'He's running away from you, did you see? He thinks you're a Jezebel.'

'Who?'

'Old Testament temptress. One of your lot!'

'What are you talking about?'

Later – as he was holding himself high over her, his arms extended, shuddering with the strain, and they were gazing at each other, eyes wide, rapt, appalled – she cried, 'I could die – yes! I die, I die! – I pray to God that this is the way I shall die!'

And later he said, 'This is our Freeland! Here – and here – and here...'

Felix Thomas was absent that day. He was scouting in the thickets behind the dunes, and he dearly wished that Captain Dugmore had allowed him a gun.

*

At a certain moment in the evening, just before sunset, the light in Lamu becomes two-dimensional and the townscape becomes a stage set, frail and unconvincing. Only an hour before, the shadows deepen suddenly so that the town's architecture becomes a crazy dissymmetry of cubes plonked down with the abandon of a child building a nursery city. Then the sun shifts, the sharp edge of the coral brick softens, the *makuti* of the rooftops becomes smooth as carpet, and the town achieves an order, and also a beauty, which no single householder can have planned or even imagined when he called in the *fundis* to add a room to his house, an extra floor for the married daughter, or a bathroom for a guest.

Dekker said, 'Martha, look...' and she rose obediently and looked out of the window at the first clouds of evening: they were beige and orange, with an underweight of dove-grey, and had appeared from nowhere. In the garden below their room the banana leaves rose and fell in a sudden breeze like great fans at an Oriental court. The birds were noisy at this time of day. One small creature, the like of which he had never seen before, pink as the inner flesh of a conch shell, zoomed in front of them and looped the line where three gaudy *kikois* had been hung out to dry. Martha lay back again on the couch, all modesty gone for ever. The wound of her sex

174

was vividly clear to him, and his cock rose yet again. (How ridiculous, he thought, I had convinced myself only months ago that my sexual life was ended – and I'd been happy enough to accept it.) She saw him and gurgled with laughter and said, 'No, Dekker, enough!' and reached for a cotton robe.

'Come back to the window,' he said, and drew her to his side. A papaya tree was thrusting its splayed leaves from out of the lush courtyard high towards the narrow sky. Its trunk was frail and fleshy, just as its fruits were frail and fleshy: Dekker had discovered that papaya needs the edge of lime juice to make it sublime, and now he thought of the breakfast taste of rough sugar against the pawpaw flesh with the gnash of the lime still to come, and then he was reminded of the tastes and textures of her body through the long afternoon, and he wanted her again.

They were in one of the many rooms of the house of Ma Fatima. Ask no questions, Martha had ordered. The room had been simple and shaded and scented with jasmine, after she first led him through doorways and up stairs as though she were at home in this strange mansion. There was no sign of servant or slave to confuse him. 'She is my friend,' was all that Martha would say. 'We are safe here. No, you will never meet her. That would not be proper.' 'Not *proper*?' She had giggled like a schoolgirl on a secret tryst, and they had grasped at each other.

*

Two brown cows were being butchered on the patch of wasteland next to the Women's Mosque. There was to be a grand Lamu wedding the next day, Bakari had explained at breakfast in Free House: there would be an *ngoma* and the *kirumbizi* stick-dancing and a great feast. The *ngoma* drums could be heard rehearsing in far-spread corners of the town. Soon the old ladies will arrive at the bride's house, over there behind the Fort, Bakari added mysteriously.

Dekker had already seen how the cows' blood had stained the sandy soil the black of pitch. The two heads, still crowned with horns, sat on the adjoining wall and surveyed their own dismemberment. The butcher wore a stained red *kanga* and enjoyed a swarm of young helpers, slitting and slicing and sawing and chopping. But when Martha hurried past on her errand an hour later, she had no need to avert her eyes from the reproachful heads,

175

because all that remained to be seen was a mountain of chops and a dense cloud of flies. Nobody seemed to mind the flies.

*

Martha said, 'Ma Fatima, I need you.'

'What is it, child?'

They sat as usual in the inner of the inner rooms. The only light was filtered from the central courtyard through a sequence of open doorways, all elaborately incised and decorated. None of these entrances seemed to match – be opposite to – another, so that there was never an uninterrupted view through the heart of the house.

Martha said, 'There are bad things in the *shambas*.'

'So?'

'It is to do with the slaves.'

'And?'

'They are being stolen. Taken away. You will know that.'

'Ah!'

'That is not my concern. I do not want to interfere in the matters of the island. I am a guest. I shall soon go away.'

'So why are you distressed?'

'Because, Ma, I think that *we* have become involved.'

Ma Fatima's expression changed. She had been offering ignorance and indifference, but now she admitted interest. She said, 'What do you mean, "we"?'

'Some of the Freelanders.'

'Explain!' said Ma Fatima, with the authority of her contemporary, Victoria, addressing one of her later prime ministers.

Martha said, 'One of our young men came to me yesterday. He was in a terrible state. He had just found the body of one of his friends on Shela beach. Murdered...'

'*Another* death?' interrupted Ma Fatima, which revealed that Lamu society had not yet generally heard of Schmidt's demise.

'Yes, a boy called Robert Schmidt. He used to go there to dig for bones. And look for shells. Someone killed him.'

'But why?'

'Scavenius thinks it is because Schmidt discovered the slaves.'

'But which slaves? There are slaves on every *shamba*, that is perfectly legal. We have them ourselves.'

'No, Ma Fatima, someone is stealing them. Taking them away to the mainland and selling them to the Somalis.'

'I know of course that slaves are vanishing. Are you telling me that you know who is doing this?'

'Pier Scavenius knows. He has come to me.'

'And he told you?'

'He told me some of it. He is terrified. He thinks he is the next to be killed. Like his friend.'

Ma Fatima said, 'Where is he now?' and spotted Martha's hesitation. 'You do not trust me? You think I will tell the people who do these things? You think I have always known of this and will warn them so they can kill your boy?'

'Forgive me, Ma.'

'I forgive you. Of course I forgive you, child. But where is he? He is in danger? If he is willing to talk, he will be killed.'

Martha gazed on the old woman who seemed to make so little of this simple truth. Ma Fatima glanced at her and made the briefest gesture with finger and thumb – open, closed: alive, dead.

'We hid him last night in a secret place we know in the mango trees. He cannot be safe there. But what can be done?'

'Nothing. If the young man intends to talk, then somehow – in the street, in the Fort, in my son's office even – he will die.'

'That's why he wants to leave,' Martha stumbled. 'He made me promise that I would get him out of here. He would never dare to give evidence – he simply wants to go away. For ever.'

'And not to reveal anything to Bwana Rajees?'

'No, he is frightened. He only wants to leave the island.'

'And the other people will not know?'

'No-one will know except you and me. And my friend.'

Ma Fatima extended her hand for only the second time to lay it on Martha's arm. 'I think it is better,' she said – Martha realised, incongruously, that her Swahili was getting very good – 'if the young man leaves this island. You will tell him to be discreet?'

'He'll do anything we say if we get him home. And then, you see, he won't talk because he won't want to incriminate himself. Because he has been part of the plot.'

The old lady did not seem too worried about what Scavenius might or might not do in Denmark. 'So, it is agreed. You must bring him here tonight. He must go into the *nyumba ya kati*.'

'Where?'

'It is the room where we lay out our dead bodies.'

Martha's expression would have betrayed her.

177

'Don't be silly, it is the one safe room in this house. No-one will ever go there and – listen to me – there is a separate doorway, because in our Swahili world it is bad luck to take a corpse out of the front door. So we have a separate, secret entrance for the dead. He will be safe in that room, and when you have found the next dhow for Zanzibar, he can leave privately.'

Martha said, 'Ma, you are saving his life. How can I thank you?'

Ma Fatima said, 'Promise me he does not talk. If he leaves, he will not talk...'

Martha tried to look into the wise old eyes. 'So you do know about this?'

'I know everything. Did you not realise it? I know everything.'

*

Fundi George buried Robert Schmidt in the plot next to Jimmy Dunn. There was a larger turnout this time because the Germans were there, led by Wilhelm Selling, though Pier Scavenius was absent, which seemed strange. Major Rogers did not attend, presumably because Schmidt was not one of his nationals. Felix Thomas stood behind Captain Dugmore and (said Louise to Martha) seemed to be distressed – had they been friends? Julius Wilhelm again succeeded in interrupting the preacher, though with considerable difficulty, so much so that Dugmore had to seize Fundi George by the collar and instruct him to leave off ranting about the Antichrist on the island. Dr Wilhelm spoke briefly but movingly about the frustrated promise of this young archaeologist, artist and Socialist. Louise wept. Martha was composed and withdrawn.

*

Dear Sir Arthur,

1. I have decided to return again to the mainland forthwith, having received word from my most reliable agent in Witu that Suleiman Kimenya has arrived in the vicinity from the north, accompanied by a large party and also substantial numbers of cattle. This suggests that he is planning a major trade to coincide with the Big Rains. I expect to find evidence that he will be trading cattle for slaves. If the numbers who have vanished from Lamu and the immediate inland territory in recent weeks are being held near Witu in readiness for him, it is imperative that I act at once.

178

2. I am conscious that I am spending too much time on the mainland and – you may be thinking – neglecting the governance of these islands. I hope and intend to show, with this present sortie, that we are very close to resolving the Witu problem once and for all. I shall take the opportunity to ensure that no stockades have been re-erected since my last visit, and to complete my subjection of the Forest villages.

3. As you are aware, Captain Dugmore is still on the Island and will be able to act in emergency.

4. He continues to masquerade as a 'Freelander'. I regret to say that these people are still with us, having found a thousand excuses to postpone their departure in the direction of Mount Kenya. (I assume that the permits they hold from you still hold good.)

5. Their behaviour continues to cause offence to the local community. I am grateful to you for London's documentation on 'Lieutenant' Rabinek, which I was able to use to embarrass their leadership and perhaps sow a little discord among the Brotherhood. I am told that Rabinek has in consequence been 'expelled', though he continues to live in 'Free House', as they call their lodgings.

6. Almost as I write, one of their members has been found murdered at Shela. I suspect that his death may be connected with the larger affairs that I am investigating. I also understand that a friend of his is also absent, though no second body has been found. I shall keep you informed.

7. The German residents of the island have protested to me about my refusal last week to permit them to import a quantity of elephant shot. I have rejected their complaint, and they will no doubt be writing to you.

8. The Liwali is most insistent that I convey to you his *salaams*. This I do.

I beg to remain.yr.mst.obed.servant,

A. S. Rogers (Major)

Rogers said, 'Sorry to drag you away from your pleasures, but I've had word from my people on the mainland. They reckon they know where Suleiman has holed up, so I'll have to go at once – this is our chance to settle his nonsense.'

'Then off you go,' said Captain Dugmore. 'I wish I were allowed to go with you, but I know that's off-limits.'

'Don't be an idiot. You know that I'm leaving this place in your safe hands. Unofficially, that is.'

'I promise that I shan't be rude to the Liwali.'

'That reminds me, there's a particular job to be done.'

'Give me strength!'

'The elephants are back on the island. A couple of them swam over last week, and the Liwali expects me to handle it. Now *there's* a task I can surely leave with you. You were looking for sport, I remember – go out and shoot them for me.'

Dugmore made obliging noises, while thinking to himself, to hell with that, the condescending bugger, he had other game in mind.

'More important – please, Dugmore – just keep things quiet. My people will do what you say, of course, but let's have no dramas. I've messaged Hardinge that I'm off and you're on seat, but he might object to that, he's a conventional old bird in some ways.'

'He'll never have cause to remember my name. I'm just a new recruit to Freeland, have you forgotten?'

'Oh Christ, keep an eye on them, too. I can't see them leaving before August, even if we're lucky. Just use your charm, Dugmore – keep them out of mischief, I don't care how you do it.'

'I'll concentrate on the ladies.'

'That's more like it. And no more shooting pie-crows, right?'

'I shall immerse myself in the profound philosophies of Dr Hertzka.'

'Who's he?'

Dugmore began to ask, 'What about the slaves...?' and skidded to a halt. It was his last chance to mention Shela beach.

'If you get more complaints from the Liwali about runaways, point out to him that that's precisely the reason I'm on the mainland. Promise him we're going to put a stop to it.'

'I know you'll do just that,' said Dugmore. 'How can the Liwali doubt it?'

And his heart gave a little leap of delight when he thought of the surprise he was planning for Rogers's return.

Nine

A Freelander incapably drunk is one of the rarest phenomena.... In Freeland there are no persons who are compelled to seek forgetfulness of their misery in intoxication, and the examples of such persons cannot therefore serve to accustom the public to the sight of this most degrading of all vices.

Theodor Hertzka: *Freeland: A Social Anticipation*

Afterwards, Dugmore was able to admit that it had been a catastrophe. 'No point in my denying it!' he would proclaim to all and sundry from a recumbent position on the verandah of the Mombasa Club. 'A God-almighty cock-up! I'm not surprised that Rogers will never speak to me again.'

His companions would invariably urge him on, for Dugmore had become one of the 'characters' of the Coast, and his indiscretions were legion and cherished. If they had not heard the tale before – if they were newcomers to the steamy delights of Mombasa, perhaps secretly apprehensive of the perils of the continent, or else thirsting for sport and adventure rather as Dugmore had explained himself to Major Rogers those few years before – they would sometimes become confused. Dugmore had told the tale so many times that he tended to skip over necessary details. Who exactly was 'Felix', for example? Why was the Liwali of Lamu always described as 'that bastard'? Was 'the luscious Madame Sasse' to be identified as Louise or Martha? Was it Rabinek or Ducoffre who had betrayed the whole operation? What happened to the young Danish lad who exposed the slave racket?

Captain Dugmore was contemptuous of such nitpicking: his decision to admit his own responsibility for the disaster had something heroic in it and entitled him to brush aside tedious interruptions. 'You will miss my point,' he would say, and extend a toe to scratch his slobbering bulldog in the gut. 'I tell you, all this

– yes, a minor episode that occurred a couple of years ago in a remote part of the Coast – minor but tragic, you will grant me – deserves its place in the archives because it did for the ambitions of our friends the *Wa-Germani* in this part of the world, closed them down, once and for all, if you see what I mean. You don't? Look – let's start with boring old history. When Carl Peters – and there's a *real* villain for you – was charging around the mainland back in the late '80s signing up every renegade headman he could find to join the Holy German Empire, little did he realise that he was doing deadly damage to his patriotic cause. Why? Because *that* was what put the fear of God up our own distinguished masters in Westminster. For the first time they began to listen to Hardinge's warnings from Zanzibar about German ambitions on our part of the Coast. So the direct result of Carl Peters's *safari*-ing was to send us into Witu, with Fremantle in '90, and then again in '93 when Rogers had taken over on the Island.

'But – remember – our masters still hadn't committed themselves. The Company was still the governing agency, whatever the influence of Hardinge on the Sultan – or Rogers and his Indian police, for that matter. It was a *peculiar* style of empire, I used to think. As though we weren't quite sure what we wanted...

'*That's* where the Lamu business in '94 – the Freelanders and all that – came in damn handy. I didn't see it then, I admit, but now I see it clear as a pikestaff. Remember, we were still dragging our heels, and nothing Hardinge said could induce London to get off the pot. Hardinge and Rogers were in an impossible position, I grant you. Was Rogers supposed to be working for the bloody Charter company or for Her Majesty? And were they allowed to put the boot into the Liwali or what? *That's* why the Freeland affair helped us, in the end, though God knows after a wretched tragedy – I promise you, I'll never entirely forgive myself. I tell myself that my own modest involvement made no difference to the end result, but sometimes I wake up at night and wonder if we could have got them out of there in one piece...

'But don't lose my point – it was the *consequences* of the Freeland business which, in the last resort, when all is said and done, resolved not just Rogers but also HMG to take a firm grip – at last – on the northern Coast. Rogers, of course, was like a man possessed. God help them in Witu, I remember thinking at the time. But after he had blasted the Forest stockades to kingdom come, and hanged a batch of them pretty damn quick, he was able to give Hardinge the evidence they both needed. Which was? – *Here* we see, the Huns are *still* meddling in our parish, even after Heligoland and all the solemn assurances of Chancellor Bismarck. Put up or shut up, we told them. And of course, we had to give up the nonsense of the Charter company pretending to run things. So now we rule the roost all the way up the Coast. A pity it took so long...

'Yes, thank you, dear boy, I'll have the same again...'

*

Dugmore did not of course attend the departure of Major Rogers and his *askaris* in person: that would have been indiscreet. After the steam-launch and its accompanying tugs and dhows had cast off from the jetty to the cheers – hypocritical? ironical? or just mischievous? – of a crowd of young boys and old men, the Captain paused, briefly and discreetly, at the ground floor of Charter House and said to a young, immaculately groomed Sikh in uniform, 'You are informed, I trust, that I am to act for Bwana Rajees in any emergency?'

'That is understood, Sahib. But I must not know you except in a very major crisis. So the Major ordered me.'

'Too bloody right, Sergeant,' said Dugmore, and returned to his Anarchist companions in Free House, where the departure of the military expedition was being discussed among the more sober members.

'What d'you reckon is up, Dugmore?' asked Bosanquet.

'Can't stand us any longer,' suggested Goddfrey. 'Needs to get a breath of fresh air on the mainland.'

Tom Fallon said in his dour way, 'Maybe he's decided we're not worthy of his attention.'

'Then he is right,' said Hans Salner. 'He has his business, we have ours.'

None of them, Dugmore observed, had any idea of the precise reason for Rogers's mission. Good. Their ignorance of the situation in Witu was just as well. They seemed to be settling to the prospect of several more months of enforced idleness, however they might complain about the weather and the island and the authorities and, yes, the delay. That, thought Dugmore, meant that he could get cracking on the slave business. He deserved his moment: if he hadn't picked up Rogers's casual reference to the slaves coming off a big beach, and gambled on putting in his servant as look-out, they would still be chasing around after the usual smelly dhows. He meant to astonish Rogers. By the time the man got back – and no doubt he would be bearing the head of Suleiman on a platter, Dugmore did not doubt that – he would find that the Lamu slave chain had been snapped. He might even find the culprits under lock and key in his Fort. The Captain grabbed his chance and got to work.

*

Bosanquet was trying to hurry through the usual morning crowd of servants and porters milling around the market trays that were laid out on the brushed brown earth in front of the Fort. Someone grasped at his sleeve, to hold his hand. 'You will come to my wedding. I invite you. And your friend.' It was the manager of the nightclub where the transvestites gathered. In the daylight he looked more nervous, ill at ease, but he greeted Bosanquet urgently.

'So it's *your* wedding? I hadn't realised.'

'It will be a very special wedding. Dhows are coming from Pate and Faza.'

Bosanquet offered congratulations. It was a bit odd, but this was Lamu.

'You must come and you will dance with me. Tonight I must take her virginity. I must make myself excited. You will dance with me, please, and your friend, too...'

'Lucky man!' Bosanquet brayed, as though he were back at Brompton Oratory in a grey topper with his frightful cousins, and allowed himself to be carried away on the crowd.

*

From his solitary acacia tree, Felix scanned the island through his spyglass (an appropriate name, he thought). Behind him there was a corner of Shela's tiny village, huddled around the ancient pillar minaret of the local, near-derelict mosque (Felix had taken the dangerous liberty of glancing inside, rather as Major Rogers usually succumbed to the temptation of inspecting Matandoni's ostrich egg. He had always been interested in the chapels of his Welsh valleys – Beulah, Temple, Sion, Emmanuel and the rest, he was a

184

bit of a connoisseur, he liked to think. These mosques weren't a patch on his chapels. They were empty, even the posh ones in the Town, they didn't even have a harmonium, simply a lot of threadbare carpets and mats...). Beyond, he could focus on Manda, with its line of old white navigation pillars set in the low dunes; he had never managed to work out how the dhow captains related to them and to the bigger, black Shela pillar not far to his foreshortened left. The channel was empty. And to the right he could survey the eight-mile length of Shela beach, as far as the end of the high dunes and so across to the dusky line of scrub-covered hills of the mainland on the southern horizon.

He enjoyed this moment because his victims were at more innocent play, and Felix could relax. They had ventured out from their palm-hollow – they had even thrown on a few clothes for the sake of any passing dhow, or for Fundi George, whom Felix had spotted a couple of times – and were frolicking on the beach like Felix remembered once at Porthcawl on a single Sunday School outing the year he was in love with Rhiannon. That is to say, Tom Fallon and Louise Sasse wandered hand in hand, heads down looking for sand-dollars; chased the crabs who were fleeing the fast-inflowing tide; and then he wrote a message on the smooth sand with a branch of bamboo cane. Felix fiddled the knob but could not read it. He was as curious as if he were still in Porthcawl. Was it a joke? A declaration of love? An affirmation, surely. It must have spread across twenty yards, and Fallon was reading it with pantomimed deliberation while she stood back, laughing at their private play. Felix wanted to read it too, he wanted to understand; they had no secrets from him, for goodness sake, only yesterday he'd watched them making love chest-deep in the water, but the waves were rushing in. Louise had retreated – he heard her laughter float up at him – as the scratches on the sand were eroded, covered, but the sea retreated and again he tried to read the bleeding, crumbling message, and with a rush the tide returned for good.

The two of them were in no hurry today, Felix acknowledged. They had wandered away to the south, paddling in the foam and fooling, still, with the fucking crabs. Then the beach was empty, as if the Englishman and the French girl had never existed.

He had work to do, and for the next hour he did it, cursing Captain Dugmore's insistence, reproaching himself for his timid,

185

beating heart, wishing that he had a gun (though his intelligence admitted that he did not really know what to do with one). Although it was mid-afternoon by now and the sun was falling, Felix was for most of the time protected from the sea breeze, and he was therefore very soon in a lather like an over-extended racehorse. But the Captain had been adamant: we'll come in with all the men I can find, he had said, but someone has to be the guide, someone has to know where they are. That has to be you, Mr Thomas, I can't risk frightening them off by putting in the *askaris*, so make sure you take the lie of the land – after all, you've spent enough time snoozing in those dunes.

Felix groaned but accepted his fate. He knew that between the deep white dunes, running directly inland from the sea, there was a system of narrow valleys – the word was too strong, they were crevices, mini-gorges – filled with a dense shelter of palm, thorn and an unknown shrub the colour and size of an azalea. The bush was so thick as to be jungle. But out of that same jungle, he and the Captain agreed, the slaves had emerged in single file; they must have been kept within quick reach of the shore, and there must be some system of stockades.

'It's a needle in a haystack, sir.'

'That may be. But you saw them, Mr Thomas. That's why we're going to find them. Take care now!'

He was right and Felix, to his horror, found them. He had been stumbling around in a jumble of thorn and dead leaves when, in a particular angle of the afternoon sun, he thought he saw a scuffle of tracks, no more than faint disturbances of the sand, at the foot of an overhang of cliff. He had no enthusiasm for this, but he had to prepare a story for the Captain to explain his failure (because he could hardly tell the man about Louise and Tom Fallon writing love letters in the sand), so he pushed through a tangle of creeper and past a stack of decaying *makuti* fronds, cut from the tree many seasons ago and forgotten by the farmer. He could smell something bad. It was like the bend in the Taff where the sewer overflowed; it was also a bit like the Lamu waterfront. He became extraordinarily cautious, and braver than he had ever been in his life. His heart was beating so hard he involuntarily pressed his hand to his chest to hold it in. Another three yards, moving inch by inch, and he took one glimpse through a barrier of thorn branch and rough stakes and gazed very briefly at two half-naked savages manacled back-to-back to a rough triangle of iron. He began to run. He ran for his life, although he later admitted that he had no reason to believe that he was being pursued. He needed company, the protection of his fellows. He needed a witness. At one level of experience, he was triumphant – the Captain would applaud him and surely reward him – but the more urgent emotion was to find help. He needed Tom Fallon.

Felix emerged from the top of the dune and, for the first time since he had started visiting Shela, wanted to proclaim his presence to the others. He stared up and down the beach and – yes – they had come back, they were strolling away from him in the direction of the village. Thank God they're decent, he thought, and started shouting and screaming as he launched himself over the sheer edge of the dune, skiing, stumbling, tumbling through the thick white dust and all the time hailing, 'Mr Fallon! Mr Fallon!', trusting that the urgency of his demands and the hubbub of his sudden arrival would dismiss any suspicions on their part that he might have known they were there – wait! Thank God he had remembered it: he skidded to a halt and jammed Captain Dugmore's spyglass into the sand; he doubted he would find it again. They had heard him, paused, looked back as he waved frantically – 'Thank goodness I saw you, Mr Fallon! There's luck for you – I was thinking I'd have to run all the way to town.... There's something I've got to show you, something I just stumbled on in the dunes back here. No, sir, I promise sir, it's life and death, sir.'

Fallon said, 'For Christ's sake, stop this row. You sound as if you'd found a dead body...'

'Oh my God,' blurted Louise, 'another one?' She had managed to arrange her shift so that she did not look entirely naked. To Felix, she was in comparative terms dressed as if for the Governor's Ball.

He said, 'No, not quite. But there's something bad. Mr Fallon, I need your help.'

Fallon frowned as if he were thinking, what's it to do with a servant? – except that Felix understood that Fallon wouldn't be thinking like that at all, he'd be worrying about something else. Like how to explain Louise and what to do about Louise.

'I'm sorry to interrupt your walk, sir, but I'll be able to explain later.'

'You want me to come with you to see something in those dunes?'

'That's it, sir. We must be careful, sir. Could be dangerous.'

Fallon said, 'Well, Mrs Sasse was planning to make her way back anyway. Weren't you, Louise? Pity we couldn't find more shells. Would you forgive me if I humour Felix? You'll be able to pick up a dhow at the headland...'

Louise said, 'What if I come too?'

'Not safe, Madame,' said Felix very urgently, and glared at Fallon, who saw him.

'Please, Louise,' said Fallon. 'Better to be *discreet* when danger is about. Don't you think?'

Pull the other one, thought Felix, she surely understands what he's saying: now bugger off, lovely lady, and leave us to get on with it.

'In fact,' Fallon was saying, and there was a degree of eye-to-eye contact going on, 'I insist. Please, Louise.'

'So you insist,' she said, in a voice higher than her normal alto, and swung on her heel and stalked off down the beach. She made no farewell except that after twenty yards she shouted back at them, with the volume of a fishwife, 'Remember to pick up our things from the tree. If you can be bothered.'

Felix briefly wondered how Madame Sasse planned to walk into Lamu in her shift, hatless and in bare feet.

When they arrived at the stockade – Felix had insisted they take it yard by yard, he was shaking with delayed shock and Fallon was angry about Louise, unconvinced of the Welsh boy's insistence, he couldn't imagine what he was on about – it was empty. Felix shuddered, uncontrollably: he guessed – he knew – that they were being observed from a dozen shadows. He awaited, for an eternity, the deluge of spears and arrows. To his later embarrassment, he wet himself. But nothing happened. Even as he waited for his end, he could see that the stockade was empty, except for the telltale iron triangle. Fallon whispered, 'So what is all this?' – at least the man had seen the stockade and smelt the stench: he had the wit to whisper, he must have the instinct to understand.

Felix whispered back, 'Mr Tom, sir, we're almost goners, we must get out of this. Sir, *quickly*, sir – back the way we came. Back to the sea!'

188

When they were standing on the beach, their sweat drying in the wind, he said, 'Not for me to explain, sir. We need to take you to Captain Dugmore.'

'*Dugmore?*'

'You'll see, sir.'

*

The deep hubbub of drums was suddenly everywhere in the town, and the narrow streets were crammed with men. The rumble of their deep voices echoed through the lanes in the unique male timbre of Africa, which is a buck bass flicking into falsetto giggle. The dancing will start before the wedding, Bakari had promised in Free House that morning: it is always the oldest slave woman who starts the dancing of the married women. Then, he said, the transvestites will entertain the women while the young men hold their stick-fighting games with the bridegroom. Only then is he taken in to the bride. Bakari allowed himself a leer.

As Felix and Fallon trotted, gasping and sweating, onto the quay, the wedding procession burst out of one of the narrow roads like the floodwater on the morning of the Rains. The drumming was deafening now, wild and excited and unsophisticated. Hundreds of men were prancing down the waterfront, shouting and singing – it was the men who were ululating, not the women as Felix had supposed. The whole town was overwhelmed by the frenzy, there was danger in it; this was a mob, you would have thought that some of them were drunk if it were not impossible in this Islamic society. And as if to emphasise that point, their ears were suddenly assailed by a separate din as all the *muezzins* from the town's multiplicity of mosques suddenly started up together with (thought Felix) the vigour and the harmony of a Welsh male voice choir. It was a cacophony that drowned even the drummers for a moment, as if a mighty orchestra was tuning up: each *muezzin* was determined to hold to his own pitch, his distinct key – Felix had seen them holding their hands over their ears to shut out their rivals and help them hold onto their particular version of the truth. There are as many mosques on this island, Felix always reckoned, as there are chapels in a Welsh valley, but the biggest difference with this place is that the chapels are ten thousand times quieter.

*

Dugmore said, 'You were damned lucky, the pair of you. I apologise, Tom – Felix should never have taken you back into the bush,
he's an idiot – do you hear me, Mr Thomas? – so let's thank your
stars that you didn't both get a spear in the back. I suppose the
guards must have been taking their patients back to another corral
for safety's sake at the very moment the two of you turned up.'
Felix was secretly unconvinced. Maybe they didn't want to account
for two more white men.

But who could ever be sure? He found himself sitting in a deep
chair in, of all places, Major Rogers's headquarters. He had of course
already been given to understand that his master enjoyed the
Major's confidence, but Tom Fallon was still betraying his bewilderment. There were refreshments, too, and Mr Dekker had arrived
and was in deepest confabulation with Captain Dugmore and Mr
Fallon, and the two Freelanders both wore the expression of men
who are thinking very fast indeed. Twice Fallon looked across at
Felix, who avoided him. Dekker seemed less surprised; he appeared
almost at home here, and Iqbal Ali had nodded at him as though
to a regular guest. But Dugmore was a transformed man. He was
talking urgently and quietly from the desk, and Felix could only
hear him mention a sequence of names – Bosanquet, Goddfrey,
Salner and, after a pause, Wilhelm.

Felix sat very quiet, calming his nerves and sipping the lime juice
which the Indian had brought him unasked. He had no interest in
their conversation. He neither wanted nor expected them to seek
his particular wisdom, the wisdom he knew he had always possessed. He was relieved when Dekker said, 'Felix, you look done
in. Off you go – we'll see you back here in the morning. But don't
say anything to anybody. We're going to need you.'

He did as he was told, slept for ten hours, and returned discreetly
to Charter House where he was admitted reluctantly by the Indian
servant. 'I'll have a nice cup of tea,' said Felix. 'Lots of sugar, mind,'
and scurried up the stairs and slipped into his old chair. Dugmore
and Dekker and Fallon were already in their places and acknowledged him, but did not invite him to join them. He did not expect
to be part of their conference; he was not of their totem. He sat
there, lookng out at the big minaret, sipping sweet tea, relaxed in
his own knowledge which had come to him in the night. A crow
flew past no more than twenty yards from his head, its wings
making the sound of a strap that is lashed rapidly, to and fro, in

the air. He dozed and he daydreamed and descended into his own world.

Later, he saw that Martha Wilhelm had just joined them. He was fuddled and exhausted and wanted the Indian to bring him more tea. She was dishevelled and wild-eyed – things that were alien to her. He heard her say, in a voice that trembled on the edge of panic, 'I have to interrupt you. I have terrible news. Louise Sasse has disappeared...'

After Dekker had stilled the hubbub and forced Fallon back into his chair with a firm hand, Martha said, 'Her husband came to see me just now. He was very shy about it. He's very worried. Hassemer is ill, as we all know, and Sasse has been nursing him at their house. But Louise did not come back last evening and – well, he said he'd wait until this morning – but still no sign of her, so he called in at Free House where he says he received no sensible answers, so he came to our house, but Julius is out. I thought I'd better come here to ask the sergeant of the *askaris,* and they told me you were all up here.' So, observed Felix Thomas, Herr Sasse was not so innocent about his wife as she and everyone chose to believe.

Dugmore called across the room, 'Felix, you and Tom saw her at Shela yesterday afternoon. What can have happened to her?'

Fallon intervened, 'She was going to make her way back to Lamu. You remember, Felix, I suggested a dhow?'

'Begging your pardon, sir, she might have changed her mind.'

'And if she did, what else would she do?' asked Dekker.

'That I can't tell, sir.'

Captain Dugmore asserted himself. 'Let's not get carried away too soon. There may be a simple explanation. Staying with someone else... twisted her ankle... that sort of thing...'

'Don't play the fool,' said Fallon. 'You know as well as I do that something's afoot. There's Robert Schmidt murdered and young Scavenius missing, presumed murdered too, and now Louise...' He was tearing at his cheek, staring at the ground. 'And between the four of us' (he didn't include Felix) 'you'll guess what I feel about this.'

'I'm the discreetest man on earth, Tom,' said Dugmore, 'but we're going to have to get every man we can lay hands on to search Shela. Sooner the better.'

Felix found himself suddenly bold enough to speak up. 'Please,

Captain, if you take the *askaris* to Shela with Mr Dekker and Mr Fallon, I can make inquiries in the town. Mrs Wilhelm – if you please, ma'am – will want to go back to Free House and arrange for the Freelanders to join you. With Dr Wilhelm's help, of course.'

Dugmore was gazing at Felix as though tempted to reprimand him for forgetting himself. 'Beg pardon, sir,' said Felix automatically. He refused to tell them that he knew that Louise Sasse would never be found.

'How do you mean, Felix, that you'll make inquiries in this town?' It was Dekker who asked.

Felix declined to look up at him. He preferred to mumble, 'You see, sir, I've made a few friends since we got here. We don't always speak much of the same language, but they trust me. Lord knows why. They might tell me things they wouldn't tell Major Rogers – or Captain Dugmore either, if you don't mind me saying so, sir.'

'Then good luck to you, Mr Thomas,' declared the Captain magnanimously, and turned back to the others as though to signal that the Welsh boy had exhausted his contribution. They began to talk about rifles and launches and platoons, but as Martha Wilhelm made her excuses and slipped out of the door on her way to Free House, she cast him a quick, searching gaze.

*

There was no help to be got from the town. Lamu was taken over by the drama of the wedding and, if Bakari could be believed, it was a fast-unfolding tragedy. The groom had not distinguished himself in the stick-fighting; he had stayed for only two minutes, when someone broke a finger and a fistfight took over, to the outrage of the old men, who declaimed the debasement of the island's ancient sport. Three musical traditions had gathered outside the bride's house: the *madrasseh* boys, swaying, singing and intoning the Koranic texts; a dozen transvestites dressed in *bui-buis*, who entertained the womenfolk with the foulest innuendo; and the professional drummers, who had earlier led the procession of the bridegroom, solemn and apprehensive in heavy Arab dress, under escort to his young bride.

Earlier – according to Bakari, who evidently relished these customs – she had gone through the traditional ritual of her 'revelation' in which she was seated, alone, on a decorated bed in the *harem* room of the house, set below a newly completed surround of stucco wall niches, in order to be viewed – that is, inspected – by all the women guests. First she sat in profile, veiled in a fine silk cloth; then she changed into other finery and took up various poses (perhaps rather as a bride is photographed from different angles in the society weddings of Europe). This ceremony, even more than the imminent consummation, was the greatest event of a virgin Swahili girl's life, and also of her family. Not so surprisingly, the townspeople had little interest in the mislaying of a *mzungu* woman whose deportment and dress had become notorious even in a few short weeks.

*

Felix started at Mabrukki's, though he knew better than to expect any information there. He had thought to carry the news of Louise's disappearance, and so to urge them, in Martha's name, to join her at Free House, but he soon discovered that they were more disposed to gossip than to act. The exceptions were Goddfrey and Bosanquet, whom he bumped into at the narrow doorway. They must have seen something in his expression because they did not brush him aside as they normally did ('that little thief', or however they saw him) but hesitated and gave him the time of day. He told them, very precisely, that the rumour was true; then he said to them not to go to Free House but to join Dugmore and the others at Charter House. Goddfrey said 'Why on earth – ?' and Felix said, 'Sir, believe me for this once, that is where you two gentlemen are needed,' and was gratified to see them run down the quay at his command.

The rest of the company at Mabrukki's was less encouraging. Riekh was sleeping on his fists in his usual corner, and could be ignored. Stokkebye was standing at the bar, haranguing Ducoffre. Felix approached him nervous as a schoolboy. 'What the hell can I do for you?' inquired the Dane, after ignoring him for thirty precious seconds. 'Beg pardon, Lieutenant, but Mrs Wilhelm asks you to join her for an emergency meeting in Free House.' 'And why, at this time of the day?' 'Madame Sasse has vanished,' Felix told her former lover, and allowed himself a second blow – 'She's thought to be dead. Or something.' 'Dear God!' cried the gallant officer, and abandoned his bottle and set off for the door, pausing only to seize Gleisering by the collar and drag him behind him, gabbling an explanation into his protesting face.

193

Emil Ducoffre had been observing all this while making no move. 'Sir!' began Felix again, 'Madame Sasse has been...' 'Yes, yes, I am desolated. But what is to be done? We are still searching for the charming Monsieur Scavenius.'

'They want you all to go to a meeting in Free House, sir.'

'Not *another* meeting.'

'Then they will organise a search for her, sir.'

'That will surely be too late.'

Felix agreed, but could not let it be at that. 'We have to do what we can. You must see that, sir.'

'Has anyone told Tom Fallon? Perhaps he can advise us where to search first.'

Felix said, 'Mr Fallon is already with Captain Dugmore and the *askaris*.'

'So the plot thickens,' said the Frenchman, and smiled to himself as he called for another glass. 'Don't wait for me – I shall be with you all as soon as my friend Rabinek has joined me.... Come to think of it, he may have heard the terrible news already. Tell me, Felix, do we fear that Madame Sasse has been abducted? Or merely killed?'

Felix Thomas said, 'Which would you rather, sir? If you take my point,' and turned on his heel and walked away from it all and out into the noonday glare, away from the *wa-ungwana* districts of stone houses and on into the simpler, poorer structures on the southern fringe of the town, beyond the old Monument and the Hadhramauti Mosque and the space where the *maulidis* were celebrated, to an area of simple shacks where he had friends. They were people whose existence would not be known to Major Rogers, nor even to the Liwali, nor perhaps to the *sharifs*, and many of them were black-skinned and came from far to the south of the continent, and some of them had once been slaves but had freed themselves; their priests had powers of divination and prophecy of which Felix had need, and he spent the next hours with them, engrossed in their mysteries.

*

When he emerged, he discovered that the wedding was in difficulty and the town was subdued and weary. It was late afternoon and the bride and groom had not emerged, as was required, with the blooded sheet which the old women were waiting to examine, as

194

was their traditional role. The women had come and gone three times, and still they waited. Until the sheet was produced, no food could be sent in to the bridal chamber, none of the mountain of presents could be exchanged, the bride price could not be handed over, and the music could not resume. All these things were remote and incomprehensible to Felix. He had always understood that this island and its culture were beyond his comprehending – hence his gravitation to the mysteries of the southern shanties. But he had the wit to know that the island was going through a drama, and perhaps a tragedy, which he and his Freelanders would never begin to grasp.

Felix never doubted that Louise was lost. His inquiries had done no more, no less, than to confirm that. He allowed himself just once that afternoon to remember her as he had seen her so often, spreadeagled and naked under the shade of her very own tree, and he had the wisdom to understand what the memory would do to him if he did not forbid himself to think of it ever again – a promise he kept for thirty years until he astonished a New York analyst with this suppressed and catastrophic experience.

He therefore saw no need to attempt to join the searchers at Shela, and so defied Captain Dugmore's unspoken assumption that his own familiarity with the beach required his attendance. Instead, he sat for an hour or more in the late-afternoon shade of the Customs post, thinking his own young man's thoughts, planning the life he was to lead, until he looked up and saw Dekker, stained with sweat and begrimed with sand and mud.

Dekker had no reproach for him. 'I assume, Felix, your friends in this town know nothing.'

'Nothing which would be good news, Mr Dekker.'

'You mean they know Louise is dead?'

'No, sir. They don't say that. They simply do not encourage us.'

'She could be anywhere on this island. We could search for weeks and miss her...'

'If she's still on the island, sir.'

'Of course. I take your point. But I fear our colleagues are not in rational mood.'

'Sir?'

Dekker explained that a dozen of them, with two score *askaris*, had ransacked Shela all afternoon. They had toiled over sand dunes, they had raked through groves of cactus and ravines of thorn – Felix nodded with truest sympathy – and had found nothing more than three or four stinking and deserted cattle pens. The party, said Dekker, had become exasperated as well as exhausted. Some of their members had been particularly so. There may have been liquor in certain hipflasks. When they returned to Lamu there had been an unhelpful demonstration outside Imperial House. Mr Denhardt, to the hilarity of the locals, had been ordered to appear on his balcony – and to give him credit (said Dekker) he had done so, the very image of a respectable businessman. He did not intend to go into the detail of what ensued (said Dekker), and he and Dugmore had agreed it would best be forgotten, but various remarks had been exchanged, principally coming from Lieutenant Stokkebye and, he regretted, from Mr Fallon. Of course, everyone was in a state of high emotion, as well as fatigue, as it had been an afternoon of ferocious heat. Mr Denhardt, and then his brother, had behaved with propriety and restraint in a difficult situation, as he, Dekker, would be happy to assure Major Rogers if any complaint were to be made. But a third person had then appeared on the balcony – he believed he was a certain Herr Toeppen – and the situation had thereupon deteriorated to a degree embarrassing for a group of Europeans who were now surrounded by an even larger number of Swahilis. The Germans had, quite properly, insisted from their balcony that they were horrified to hear of the fate of Frau Sasse, who, as they pointed out, was one of their own kith and kin. But the third one – Toeppen? – Was he sometimes called 'Bwana Pembe' by the others? Or is that someone else? – at one point observed *in German* (which most of us understand perfectly well) that our dear Louise was no doubt taking her pleasures elsewhere – yes, it was as crude and unforgivable as that.

'Tom Fallon, thank God, doesn't speak a word of German and Dugmore hadn't understood more than the general point, but Goddfrey and Bosanquet, for the first time I've ever known them, became very dangerous indeed. I understood every word, of course, and refused to listen. But Stokkebye had heard him, and was already in a particular bate, and the next thing I knew was that he'd put a bullet into those rafters – I reckon he missed Toeppen by an inch or two – before I could knock up his rifle and Dugmore was able to assert himself. God knows what the locals made of it.'

Felix said, 'Do you think Major Rogers will hear of it, sir?'

'I rather hope he does, Felix. But I think he has other things on his mind.'

The marriage, Felix soon discovered, was disaster, tragedy. The bride emerged into the moonlight looking haggard and desperate. No sheet was produced, and the word therefore sped through the town that she was not a virgin. The groom sent messages that he did not intend to emerge, and the old women began to discuss the renegotiation of the bride price. The musicians had been hired and were still there, waiting. Most of the guests had gone home. Friends of the bride's family were letting it be known that it was the groom's 'fault'.

Then the groom came out and, as even Bakari admitted, behaved well in that he was attentive to his bride, supported her in her embarrassment, put the ring on her finger, and so on. But the old women refused to sanction the handing over of the presents.

'So both of them are humiliated in public,' said Martha to Dekker when he explained the strange atmosphere of the town. 'Will they ever live it down? Or will they have to go away? I must ask Ma Fatima. Are traditional societies as competent in these things as we like to believe? This is much worse than a shotgun wedding in Europe, with all the village giggling.' And then she began to weep for Louise.

Ten

The departments of justice, police, military and finance, which in other countries swallow up nine-tenths of the total budget, cost nothing in Freeland. We had no judges, no police organisation, our tax flowed in spontaneously, and soldiers we knew not. Yet there was no theft, no robbery, no murders among us; the payment of tax was never in arrears, and we were by no means defenceless...

Theodor Hertzka: *Freeland: A Social Anticipation*

When Louise Sasse was dismissed (as she saw it) by Tom Fallon (who had that same hour been groaning in her arms) and by Felix Thomas (a nasty little thief who looked at her in Free House in a most unpleasant way), she stormed off in a fury which refused to go away. It was, she told herself, so typical that a man could remove his interest in you within, literally, seconds. Tom had been mad for her all day. Even after he had had her, and not just once, he had been the perfect admirer. She adored the way he had written his love in the sand and had wept mock tears when the tide took it away. They might have gone back to their tree. Yes, they certainly were on the way back to their tree when that Welsh boy came flailing down the sand dunes shouting fit to bust, and Tom had taken him seriously. Seriously enough to dismiss her.

So what if it was 'dangerous', though she very much doubted it. Come to think of it, they had never once seen anyone else on this beach, except for a passing dhow and, once, the Freeland boat, and then they had been protected by their tree. Felix Thomas must be hysterical: perhaps he was taking drugs like a few of the others.

She would have to make her way back to Lamu. Her husband and Hassemer always worried if she had not returned before sunset. That meant a two-mile walk unless she hailed a dhow – and then she noticed not only that she had no money but that she was certainly not dressed appropriately for a journey in an open boat with a trio of giggling, randy Swahili boys. If she walked she might be able to sneak into the house before the locals came out onto the waterfront for sunset. Better, of course, to go back to the tree and recover her clothes. Yes, if she was careful – assuming Tom and the Welsh boy had gone into the dunes – she would dash back very quickly and make herself decent...

When she met him on the shore she was not at all afraid because she recognised him at once and felt that she knew him, since she had been introduced to him twice in recent weeks when he had officiated at the funeral services, apart from the time she and Tom had talked with him. It was the reverend minister, Fundi George, and he recognised her too and this time, far from refusing to look at her, he shook her hand rather formally and said, 'I am so happy to meet you, lady.'

'How nice to see you again,' attempted Louise, conscious of her state of undress. She hoped he would not launch into a hymn, because she would not be able to accompany him like Tom.

He was looking at her with what she remembered as a half-crazed intensity, though there was nothing remotely 'sexual' in it; she had long ago learned to spot *that* sort of thing in a man's eyes. He said, in his incongruous Yankee accent, 'Ma'am, I need your husband – where is he?'

She began to say, 'He's in Lamu with our friend...' and stopped herself when she realised he must be referring to Tom, so the lie came very easily. 'He went for a walk down the beach,' she said and pointed, vaguely, to the dunes.

Fundi George groaned like a man afflicted with sorrow. He said, 'Ma'am, I need him *oh* so urgently! I need to show him the works of the devil on this accursed strand.'

'Can I help?' asked Louise politely, who still had half a mind on her belongings a mere hundred metres from where they were standing.

'No, no! I need your husband. I have fallen upon abominations which must be published in the land.'

Louise saw red. This was as bad as Felix Thomas descending out of the sky and insisting on Tom's private attendance. Now here was this crazy priest demanding the man, rejecting the woman. She seized him by the bare arm – Louise had an instinct to touch, to grasp, when she wanted to communicate – and did not notice that he recoiled from the shock of her white flesh.

199

'Fundi George,' she commanded, and was challenging the absent Tom Fallon as she spoke. 'If there are abominations to show, then show them to me!'

In the Golbanti Mission seven years ago, the late Mrs Houghton had been the equal, and more so, of her reverend husband Cedric, and Fundi George, having marvelled at this unnatural sight, had learned that this might sometimes be the way of the white man. His addled brain was therefore disposed to believe that 'Mrs Tom' had the authority, and the powers, of her absent husband. So he obeyed her and led her inland, into the dense bush that nudged the very edge of the sand and which Felix Thomas knew to contain such perilous secrets.

Louise had no fear. All of a sudden her mood had swung, and she was exultant, almost triumphant, now that she had been granted by this (admittedly black and lunatic) man a participation in these male dramas. The fact that he was black and lunatic could not take that away from her. It may also be relevant that she was confident, fulfilled, in the afterglow of sex – but, it must be noted, so was Fallon, and he had recently entered these same thickets with Felix with none of Louise's careless nonchalance. Perhaps the man had the experience to understand that he was on the brink of dangerous matters; perhaps it helped him that he was led by a canny and frightened boy, not a manic and renegade priest.

She let him lead her boldly into the scrub until the thorns began to tear at her naked legs and she called out to him, with a first apprehension, 'Fundi George, wait! Where are we going?'

He turned on her and admonished her and ordered silence. 'Now we shall crawl!' he hissed at her, 'As the serpent crawled on his belly in the presence of the Lord!'

That was the moment when her instincts signalled to her that she had overstepped a sensible caution. She thought to say to him that they should go to find Tom and Felix, who couldn't be so far away, but he prohibited speech, and she found in herself a passionate desire to be able to match and then out-match the menfolk – to be able (she fantasised quickly, as she disentangled a particularly large thorn branch) to sit demurely in Mabrukki's as Tom recounted his abortive adventures in the Shela dunes and then to say, at precisely the right moment, 'Well, Tom, *I* was there with Fundi George and *we* had no problem, we found...' – and then she realised she had no idea what she was seeking; the thought was disconcerting, which should of course have revived her apprehension, but she was still full of anger and boldness and the warm confidence in her body, and Fundi George was a half-man who had no hope of authority over her, so she ignored her scruples and insisted they press on, away from the sea which she could still hear behind her, sighing on the shore. Also, she was incurably curious; always had been.

Felix Thomas would have understood entirely how she was being led, by a roundabout route, to the slave-pen he had discovered earlier. Fundi George was no less cautious in insisting that their approach be slow and tentative. To crawl through thick bush is always wearying and dirty, and for a woman clad only in a simple shift it was doubly so, but the man of God refused to move faster. After twenty minutes of this – though it seemed like hours – at last her anger with Tom started to slip away and, thereupon, she began to lose her nerve. She was terribly hot and utterly uncomfortable, and she knew she was beginning to be frightened. She wanted to go back to the beach, though she could no longer hear the waves, and hail a dhow, and never mind the lewd remarks of the crew. But she followed Fundi George to the end, out of a wild and perverse courage, because she refused to admit that this was something a woman should not do.

He brought her to a sunken cage, invisible under a tangle of brushwood and thorn, and she saw that it contained a dozen wretched, soiled, huddled and chained human creatures. She gazed on them, unthinking whether they saw her too, as they surely must, though none of them acknowledged her appearance. Only a young girl, with a baby at her breast, seemed even to be aware of her, and after a minute of silent mutual scrutiny the girl began to stand up, presumably to move towards the white woman, but her shackles held her back and their heavy clatter broke the silence which had been blanketed under the drone of a million flies. At that moment, Louise heard a shrill scream of unholy alarm as Fundi George – insofar as she saw him – catapulted himself into and through a wall of thorn, followed by a frantic crashing and stumbling and sobbing as he receded into the bush.

When she looked round, she saw that she was surrounded by half-naked black men, all of whom carried broad-bladed spears. One of them held a gun, not a spear, and he directed the gun at her and gestured that she move towards him. But then she saw that, behind him, as though loitering in the shadows, there was a figure who was somehow familiar. He carried no weapon, yet he was unmistakeably in command. He lingered, held back, as though to suggest his involvement here was coincidental, and she knew that she knew him. She found the courage to gaze upwards at his face and she saw a pockmarked skin, a lowering eye, a pouting, bulbous mouth and, with a moment's understanding of fate and horror, she recognised the Liwali's brother.

They looked at each other, eye to eye. The others did not matter. The preacher had vanished from their consciousness. He reached for the other man's gun – who sprang aside with alacrity – and took it, but he did not point it at her. Instead, he gestured that she approach him. After a long moment, she did that. She had forgotten the creatures in the pit. He was looking at her – hair to heel – as though he were examining a heifer in a market, and she caught herself thinking that she was unkempt, smeared with dust, not her best. She said to herself, they will have to kill me, I have found their secret, and she was terrified, near to fainting, but somehow, in her deepest intuition, she was not yet convinced that her death was inevitable.... He was still glaring at her, his mouth heavy as a rotting peach; she struggled to find the courage to return his gaze, unblinking. Her body was still full of the memory of Tom, she might still have been dripping with him. She looked again at this man, and deliberately held his eyes, and perhaps out of her instinct she held herself straighter, pushed back her tangled hair with a grubby arm. Then she brushed the sweat from off her brow, and when she looked at the man again she recognised it. And at that moment, in the utter extremity of her encounter with death, she forgot Tom Fallon, as she forgot all the others. She would live on, and so she chose.

She took the great decision of her life, and she knelt in the dust and bent her head.

*

Lamu

Sisters!

As I feared, we are now in deepest crisis, and I send this note with tonight's steamer to alert you, lest the situation deteriorate even more...

202

Louise Sasse has vanished, and we fear she has been murdered or at best abducted. Tom Fallon – who we can all now admit has been her lover for weeks past – is like a crazy man, and I fear for him. Sadly, Major Rogers is still on the mainland, putting down some native uprising at Witu. Captain Dugmore has therefore taken his authority – and, as Dekker agreed with me last night, it must now be assumed that the good Captain has all along been closer to the British authorities than any of us, in our innocence, guessed when he meekly requested 'provisional membership' of the Freeland Association. So the Captain is now supervising the search for dear Louise, and making a great noise about it, with Goddfrey and Bosanquet and Salner and Stokkebye and some of the others, all very active, but the French apparently not too concerned (which is scandalous since she comes from Alsace!), while some of the Germans have scarcely been seen for several days.

Julius is so overwhelmed I hardly see him. He and Salner are in eternal conference, though Dugmore is very much the man in charge. There is also a crazy black missionary who arrived at Free House today and makes speeches about slavery and adultery and every other sin you can think of, and Dugmore seems to tolerate him, though I protested.

Ma Fatima has become my friend. She talks to me of important things. Dekker is my other friend.

I have the sense that great events are very close. Believe me, I do not forget you, and I shall try to write again –

   M

                                *

The *umagwata* of Lamu – the superior classes – lived in the stone houses at the heart of the town. Every Swahili mansion of any stature had its *nyumba ya kati* on the ground floor. The household dead were laid out there and washed, so there had to be drainage. It was bad luck to take a body through the main entrance of the house, so the *nyumba ya kati* had to have its own doorway leading out onto a back alley. That door was only ever used for that purpose.

The room was narrow – since all rooms in Lamu have to be narrow – and whitewashed and almost entirely empty. It had one small window, high as in a prison. Scavenius had been given a mat to lay on the plaster slab where the corpse was placed (Martha did not know whether he understood the function of this strange room), and a *kanga* and a cushion and a bowl of water. There was no sign of food, but Martha assumed that Ma Fatima had seen to that.

She said, 'My dear, I have brought somebody – No! I promise you, don't be alarmed...'

The Danish boy said, 'You swore to me that you wouldn't tell.'

She said, 'Something terrible has happened. I know you will want to help.'

Dekker came into the room, and Martha closed the door behind him. He said 'Pier, don't alarm yourself. I have come in confidence, believe me, you have my word. Mrs Wilhelm has told no-one else that you are here, no-one at all.'

'Then why has she told you?'

'Because the situation has changed...'

'You will say that I cannot go away? You will explain that she cannot now keep her word?'

Dekker said, 'There is a dhow – a big *boom* – in the harbour, which leaves for Mombasa and Zanzibar on the morning tide. We have arranged for you to leave the island on that dhow, and only I and Mrs Wilhelm will know. The others are afraid that you are already dead – when you are safe, you may want to reassure your friends. But I repeat – the situation has changed.'

'There have been more slaves?'

'Louise Sasse has disappeared. From Shela beach.'

Scavenius, for the first time for days, was jerked out of his self-pity. He stared at them in consternation. '*Louise*? Good God! From that part of the beach? You're sure she's not just hiding, or having a fling with someone – you know what Louise is like.'

'We've been searching for her for two days. Frankly, my only hope is to find her body. Martha disagrees, she thinks she's alive.'

'So does Tom Fallon,' said Martha. 'He was close to her. He's certain she hasn't been murdered but is – somewhere here...'

'A prisoner?'

'You might call her a sort of slave, Pier. That's why we want your help. Before you leave.'

'I told Mrs Wilhelm what I know. The things I told her would get me killed if I left this awful room for five minutes. She promised me I'd be sent home.' The man-boy was on the verge of tears, he thumped at the wall and glared furiously at Martha.

'You're much safer than you think. Don't you realise that the Freelanders think that you've been killed like Robert Schmidt. They're not even looking for you any more.'

'The Freelanders don't matter. It's the others I'm afraid of...'

Dekker said, 'I promise you, Pier, that dhow will leave without you if you don't help us find Louise Sasse. That's a new promise for you. From me.'

The trouble was that Pier Scavenius did not have much else to tell. He had struck up an acquaintance with Wilhelm Selling on the *Reichstag*, and had attached himself to the older man. He respected him, he kept saying, he was a *serious* man, unlike most of the Freelanders. In Free House he had been appalled by the antics of Stokkebye and Ducoffre and the others. When he – a Dane, and embarrassed by Stokkebye – was invited by Selling to join him and the other Germans one evening at the Denhardts', he found the atmosphere immediately more comforting. He was made welcome and yet allowed to sit back quietly as a junior member of the company. There were the two Denhardt brothers always, and Toeppen of the Witu Company, and sometimes a more dramatic figure from the mainland whom they jokingly addressed as 'Bwana Pembe' because, they explained, *pembe* means elephant, and this gentleman used to be a great hunter. This was a different scale of character – even Selling spoke to him with respect. Bwana Pembe used to hold forth about the English, and the others would listen to his tales of the expropriation of German estates, the burning of go-downs, the murder of honest German traders, the overthrow of local chiefs with instantly forgettable names. Selling used to ask Bwana Pembe about Carl Peters, who was his particular hero, and Bwana Pembe would reminisce about his days in the saddle with Peters and tell of how the two of them had dealt out firm justice to the scoundrels of the region. All this over schnapps and beer on the crenellated roof terrace, peering out at the distant lamps burning on Major Rogers's headquarters building.

'So when the *Eden* arrived and Selling was appointed captain, he asked me if I would like to join him and Buschel as a regular crew. I used to be in the Royal Danish Navy, as he knew, and he said it would keep me out of the way of the goddamn English. I didn't hesitate. Anyhow, it was interesting. Everyone else was wasting time in Free House – except you, Mr Dekker.'

'When did the slaves appear?'

'A couple of weeks later. I remember an evening at Imperial House when the Germans were complaining about the difficulty of sending what they called "private" messages to their friends on the mainland, and Selling said, quite naturally, "Oh, we're going to and fro all the time. Everyone is used to seeing the *Eden*. Can we help?" And Pembe said, in a thoughtful tone of voice, "Perhaps you can." '

'You're saying – Pier! think of that dhow in the harbour outside – that Bwana Pembe took that up as an idea which led to the slave ferry.'

Scavenius gazed at Martha as though pleading for her to give him back her suppport. '*No*! I see what you're getting at. But if you really want the truth, the slaves were never discussed in Imperial House.'

'In your presence.'

'I wasn't there all that often. They never talked in front of me about things that might be confidential. Nor Buschel. I'm not sure about Selling, he spent much more time there than we did.'

'Then how did you start taking on passengers?'

'One day Selling said to me, "I've made a friend on this island who wants to transfer a few of his kaffirs across to Kau. We'll pick them up in Shela, if that's all right with you." He wouldn't normally ask my agreement, so I guessed there was something behind this. Then he explained that we must keep quiet, but it would be one in the eye for the English, because the people behind this were great enemies of the English and were hoping for the Germans to come back like in the old days. But I must keep quiet about it – did I understand?

'I said fine, it sounded a bit of a joke to be doing it behind the backs of the English, and we took the launch into Shela beach at the point where there was a signal above the dune. When I saw the state of the kaffirs we were loading I got a bit upset, and Selling must have seen it because he took me aside and said, "Look, these miserable animals are just being transferred from one *shamba* on this island to another on the mainland. Have you seen how they live just like this, they're all the same, just a kilometre from the Lamu mosques? We're doing a simple dhow job, and the only people to suffer will be Major Rogers and the high and mighty English.''

'I asked him then or on the next trip whether we were doing this as a favour for Pembe, and he said of course not, it was a couple of big local landowners, and we'd be well paid for it at the end of the day, though of course, he said, I might be deciding to put my cut into the Free House account, but please not to mention where it came from.'

Dekker asked, 'You were doing this day after day?'

'No, every three or four days, I guess. We had a terrible problem with the stink on board. Frans and I had to sluice down the whole cabin, until Dr Wilhelm complained the boat smelt of carbolic.'

'So who told Mr Selling when there was a cargo?'

'I don't know,' said Scavenius, and Martha and Dekker knew he was telling the truth. 'Selling would have a message, and we would look for the signal.'

'You dropped them where?'

'Always this side of Mkunumbi. We had to keep them out of sight when we went past Kipungani, but once we were into the Mwa Hidio there was no-one to see us. We used to anchor in the shallows in the channel and wait for another signal – the same system, it was very simple – and the *askaris* would be waiting for us. We never saw where they took them once they went into the mangroves.'

'Then they killed your friend Robert Schmidt.'

'Well, we don't exactly know...'

'For Christ's sake, Pier, you know damn well why Robert is dead. He wasn't strangled for his gold sovereigns, was he? He must have been rooting around in the dunes looking for his precious bones, and he stumbled on your next consignment.'

Scavenius looked him in the eye. 'I agree that that is probably what happened,' he said. 'I have had plenty of time to think about it. That is why I am here.'

'And then they killed Louise Sasse? No?'

'Oh no! They wouldn't do that...'

'*They*? Your German friends might think twice, the lady is half-German after all, but your *local* friends wouldn't give it a second thought. She's just a woman after all. You know what they think of women in this part of the world.'

Martha said, quietly, 'That isn't quite true, Dekker. At least, they might not kill her...'

She said to Scavenius, 'I think you are saying that you cannot help us find Louise.'

'Believe me, Mrs Wilhelm, I thought Louise was wonderful. They used to pull my leg about her in Free House. I suppose you can try Clemens Denhardt – but what could he know? Ask Selling – or you have already. Perhaps Louise saw something, like Robert. You see why I want to get away. *All* of us must get away, yes, you Martha, and you, Dekker, we should never have come here, we don't belong here. I promise you I can't take much more of this place, this awful room – yes, of course I know what it is, Martha, Robert told me about these great houses, it's the room of the dead, isn't it?'

'You'll be on the dhow at first light,' said Dekker. And he added, idiotically, 'Try to forget Lamu.'

As they walked back down the waterfront, always a discreet pace apart, Martha asked him, 'Dekker, when you said at the beginning that the dhow would leave without him – did you mean it?'

'What do you think?'

*

'Mr Thomas! You look as if you've been to hell and back.'

'I'm a bloody hero, sir. Begging your pardon, Captain.'

The Welshman looked dishevelled, exhausted and unbelievably dirty, and somewhere on the way he had been caught in a shower. It was a Rainy-Season day. After a bright beginning, the clouds had piled up again, and the wind got up too and threatened a storm. Palm trees were bending and creaking, the creek whipped up choppy, and a black mist blotted out Manda Island. But somehow Lamu Town was in the middle and escaped it again, the grey cloudbank veered aside, and the breeze delivered only a few drops which did nothing to relieve the humidity.

Dugmore was no stickler for convention. 'You look fagged out, my lad. You'd better sit down – for Christ's sake, never mind Rogers's cushions. Next, you need a drink. Will brandy suit you?'

'I signed the pledge, sir, when I was fourteen. A cup of tea would be nice, thank you.'

'Bloody nonsense! No-one works for me who's TT unless he's a Mohammedan, which you're certainly not. You can have your tea with a dash in it – look at you, man, you're shaking like a leaf. Iqbal Ali!'

Captain Dugmore occupied Rogers's office as to the manner born. It was considerably less tidy, there was a bulldog farting in the corner, and the evening *muezzin* no longer controlled the drinks cabinet, as Iqbal Ali had quickly discovered. But there was also a new aspect to Dugmore, which Felix had wit enough to recognise. The amateur sportsman, the semi-retired gentleman, had given way to the professional soldier, the man who – if he were not still playing at being a Freelander – would be wearing medals from the Afghan campaign. Felix was relieved to be overridden, and only hoped that the Indian would have the sense to put a double tot in the hot tea. Yes, he was fagged out. He reckoned he was lucky to be alive. And that was the last time he was going to go into those fucking dunes.

'So?'

'Captain, I'm awful sorry to be a bit shaky, I just ran all the way from Shela.'

'Then you'd better tell me why.'

'Because I found it, sir.'

'You mean Louise? – Madame Sasse?'

'Oh no, sir. She won't be around any longer, sir. You and I both know that, don't we? No – I found more of those poor bastards. They're back again. They're chained together in the sort of place we used to keep the cows, and they're standing in their own – you know, sir.'

The brandy arrived, and Felix Thomas summoned the strength to explain how he had bumped into the missionary.

'I was back on Shela beach like you told me, sir. Because I know it pretty well by now, like you said. You told me to go back up to my tree, where I used to keep watch, and to see if anything had changed, like, so I did just that, you see, and really, there was nothing different.' Except, he thought, no naked bodies in contortion beneath him, nor ever would be again. 'So I decided to go back down to the sea, so as to do a check on the signal tree – the one they used to give the go-ahead last time – you're with me, Captain? – and when I got there I saw the mad missionary. Fundi George, they call him – you know, sir, the darkie who buried Jimmy Dunn. He's a real loony, but nothing dangerous about him, the locals aren't worried about him, and he likes to have a chat with a white man seeing as he used to preach the word with some poor Scottish minister up on the mainland before they got chopped by the Somalis. I've been told that Fundi George only escaped because those heathen *shifta* didn't believe this black guy was also a man of God. He hid in the bushes, and when they went away he went back to the mission, and when he saw what they'd done to his friends, the minister and his wife, he sort of turned.... Yes sir, beg pardon, sir, I was saying that Fundi George is a harmless bloke, and I shook him by the hand, but this time he wasn't having any social chat, he was in a great state. He didn't even give me a sermon or a hymn like he usually does, he grabbed my arm and said something about Satan on the beach – well, that's his normal subject – and how I must come with him, *"Now now now*, for the sake of Jesus Christ." Frankly, Captain, I didn't have much choice, he had me in a grip like a blacksmith, so I said, "Fair do's, Fundi, I'm coming, just let go of me," and he dragged me into those bloody dunes again. Beg pardon, sir.

'You know, sir, when you go in off that thick white sand, first you're in that ugly weed stuff, a bit like the hyacinth in my auntie's back yard, all green, very bright green, and then you get to the cactus – that's dangerous stuff, it rips a shirt in minutes. Then there's a special sort of bushes, with silver leaves, before you get to those little thorn trees. By that time he had me lying on my tummy, wriggling along like we were worms. I said, "Hey, what's all this then?" and he turned on me and put his big black finger on his big pink lips and said, "Bwana, we're near dead if you don't follow me" – so I shut up and wriggled along, though my elbows were getting cut up in the thorns.

'We went on like that for at least ten minutes, Captain, and he had to keep stopping for me, I was sweating like a pig and beginning to think he was so crazy he was bringing me back to Lamu the long way round. When we got to those baby palm trees, he made me go underneath them, so I was all scratched and torn on top as well as underneath. But by now he was going awful slow, stopping every few yards to listen for something.

'We'd come to a ridge of sand, which was a bit easier, but after a hundred yards he made me stop behind an anthill and then he pointed to a big clump of grass. He kept pointing, sir, like I was dumb stupid, and I kept shaking my head – and then all of a sudden I saw it. You see, sir, the grass wasn't real grass, it was a roof, and *underneath* – that's where the loony was trying to show me – there was a pit dug quite deep. That was when I smelt it. He wouldn't

210

let me go any closer, he whispered there were *askaris*. So I only saw them from twenty paces – but I reckon, sir, there were at least fifteen poor bastards inside that pit. No, they didn't see us, they weren't looking for anyone. I guess they'd long since given up on their lives. Their real lives, I mean. Captain, it was *disgusting*, sir. That's not human. I'd like to top the lot of them responsible for what I just seen.... So we turned ourselves around, very careful-like, and wriggled back the way we came. Then I shook the hand of Fundi George and ran all the way back here – and now, beg pardon, sir, I do admit I've got those shakes again.'

'Another brandy, Mr Thomas,' advised Dugmore, and shouted for the servant.

It was true that Felix Thomas was shaken. He lay in rags on Major Rogers's day bed – a masterpiece of late-eighteenth-century Pate craftsmanship – and had to struggle to hold the cup when it was handed to him by the disapproving Indian.

Dugmore had been deep in cogitation. 'Mr Thomas, I'm proud of you. My judgment of your qualities has been vindicated. I dare say you will go far.'

'Thank you kindly, sir.'

'But only if you stop your perpetual arse-licking, hear me?'

'I hear you, Captain.'

'Then let's get cracking. You're certain you can pinpoint the exact spot?'

'Yes sir, I took a couple of bearings. A tree trunk and a clump of reed and an outcrop of red sand. We'll be able to hoist them out of that cesspit before sunset.'

'Hold your horses, Felix. They can surely wait a little longer.'

'What d'you mean, sir? It's our Christian duty to put in the *askaris* and rescue them. Isn't it?'

'Use your brains, Mr Thomas, I know you have more than your share of them. This is our chance. If there are ten – or twenty – waiting for collection, then arrangements will be under way at this moment to pick them up. The *Eden* is in port – I can see it down there as I speak. It's too late for them to make a return trip this afternoon, so I'll wager they'll be aiming for tomorrow morning.'

'You're planning an ambush, Captain?'

'I am, Mr Thomas. We'll let the poor bastards sit it out for one more night. You and I and a few of our dependable friends – just a few, mind, because I wouldn't want to depend on most of them

211

– will set up a reception committee. We'll be there at first light, and we'll see what happens.'

'We can't be sitting on the beach, Captain, they'll spot us a mile away.'

'So what's wrong with your famous spy-tree? The acacia that you promised me covered the entire beach? Where you lost my telescope, dammit?'

Felix Thomas, who had at last stopped shaking, said, 'It's a fine view we'll have. But if the boat arrives, it'll take five minutes at least to get down the dunes, which will give them time to get away.'

'Good point, Felix. But I, and a friend or two, will have our rifles. We won't need to do any scrambling down sand dunes. Too undignified.'

Felix took the point. They would be shooting to kill, and at four hundred yards these professionals would not miss. It was to be an ambush. He didn't think of it until years later, but neither of them considered what would happen to the slaves.

*

The spy-tree was as perfect as Felix Thomas had promised. It now accommodated Captain Dugmore, Felix, Dekker, Goddfrey, Bosanquet and Stokkebye. 'I trust no-one else,' Dugmore had insisted. 'I'd have welcomed Tom Fallon, but he left word that he's gone off somewhere. I insist that no-one breathes a word of this in Free House, not even to Wilhelm or Salner, do you all hear that? There's no-one else I can absolutely rely on, except yourselves – but we'll be enough, and I've got a dozen *askaris* hidden in Shela village and another dhow load lying low at Ras Takwa. The one essential – you'll take my point – is that no-one on the launch, and no-one at the pen, gets the faintest idea that we're waiting for the bastards.'

That had been his briefing at Charter House the previous evening. He repeated it, almost word for word, as the sun came up over Manda and they drank Iqbal Ali's coffee under the parasol branches of the great acacia tree. Then the Captain issued rifles. Dekker declined – 'I wouldn't know what to do with it.' That wasn't strictly true, but he refused to go along with this. Felix secretly agreed, but took one and fingered it nervously. Goddfrey and Bosanquet were having a cheerful discussion with Stokkebye about range, velocity, the misleading early light, that sort of thing. Dekker was annoyed with himself. Although it was cool, and although he had been exercising himself every day, the climb up the dune cliff through sand that slipped away beneath his feet had been far steeper than he had bargained for. His heart was pumping like the blows of a fist, trying to break out from under his ribs, and when he reached the top his muscles were slack with the effort so that the full weight of his belly, the fat and the gut within, seemed to him to sag out disgustingly. The others, including Dugmore, appeared untroubled. I am older than I thought, said Dekker to himself, I have even less time than I imagined. And no, I shall not take a rifle to shoot down helpless men; I can guess what Dugmore has in mind for those idiot colleagues of mine. He was irritated with himself because he felt trapped in a moral dilemma: he had agreed, without demur, to join Dugmore's plan, but in the perspective of morning he could see it leading to disaster. Shouldn't he have tipped off Wilhelm so that these foolish, misguided Freelanders could have been warned to change their ways? Surely we can deal with the Selling chap ourselves.... Or can we? Perhaps I'm too soft-hearted, perhaps I haven't been thinking about those wretched slaves. I know that Dugmore has his blood up, he'll like as not take a potshot at them: is that what Selling really deserves – a bullet between the shoulders, with all of us looking on from the grandstand?

They had been fortunate in that the moon had been free of cloud for much of the night, and Felix had been able to lead them up the dune without problem. The dogs had barked in Shela village, but no doubt they barked every night. The first thing Felix saw was the familiar tuft flying from a palm tree on the horizon in front of them. 'Captain, there's the signal. It must have been hoisted last night.' 'Is it in the same place as last time?' 'No, sir, it's a hundred yards nearer to us.' 'Excellent.'

'You have my permission to rest, gentlemen,' added Dugmore, *sotto voce*, and grinned at his own expense. Felix had a glimpse of the young subaltern in the Indian hill passes, and warmed to his employer.

Dekker sat down next to Felix. 'I really don't know what I'm doing here. I'm no use to anyone.'

'But you're here to be a witness, sir. You surely see that. With your reputation, sir, you'll be able to tell the world what happened.'

'Hold your tongue, Mr Thomas,' said Dugmore.

They waited for two hours. The protection of Felix's acacia, complete with his sand ramparts, was so perfect that they were able to relax and move around. Felix produced a *kiboko* of Iqbal Ali's provisions, and they breakfasted off chapatis and hard-boiled eggs and sweet Swahili buns and more coffee. Stokkebye produced a hipflask, looked at it, and put it away again. Felix, staring down on the palm trees at their feet, asked himself just once where Louise Sasse might be, and hastily banished all images from his mind.

The tide was going out, and from their vantage point they could see the yellow shadow of the great sandbank arising out of Mataoni Bay. The *Eden*, for all its shallow draught, would have to be careful to swing out to the south and double back inshore in a deliberate and incriminating dogleg if it was to come in to the beach. Then it would be planning to cut right out to sea again, towards the white line of breakers on the ocean reef on the far horizon, and back again, north-west, past Kipungani and down the channel to Mto Mkunumbi, where it would presumably expect to dump its cargo as quickly as possible in the cloudy mangrove shallows.

It was Felix, who was used to the place, who first heard the chug of the *Eden*. He knew to look not forwards but behind him, where Lamu Town and its jetty were only just hidden from sight. 'There she comes, sir. Keeping in the middle of the channel. It'll be at least twenty minutes before we see her again.'

He decided that Mr Dekker was right: he wouldn't use the gun either. This was his first taste of the military life, and it was all too easy, like potting china pigs in a fairground. The Captain had said this morning that he wanted Selling and Buschel alive, but Felix didn't believe him – Selling would be bound to make a break for it while they stumbled down the dune and through the scrub to the shore. Yesterday, when he saw his fellow beings sitting in their own filth in that pit, he would happily have done his best with the rifle. But this morning he had changed his mind. Unless the Captain was a good enough shot to put a slug in Selling's leg or something. And how on earth would the Freelanders survive the scandal? No-one would believe that they hadn't all been involved in slave-running, Felix hadn't before seen it as clearly as this. No wonder the Captain was so cheerful. Talk about disgrace, there'd been nothing like it since the Reverend Gwilym Roberts down at

Haverfordwest, the most powerful preacher in South Wales, put Miss James the organist in the family way.

Dugmore said very quietly 'No more talking now, please. I want no-one to move before I do. I have a whistle for when we call up the *askaris*. Those with rifles to hold the launch in their sights. Mr Bosanquet, please, to take a bead on the kaffir guard who leads them out, Mr Goddfrey to take the chap at the rear.'

The tide was still going out, leaving a smooth, shining field of wet sand. It looked firm, but Dekker knew from experience that it would be soft and unstable, difficult to walk – or run – on. At the water's edge, he saw through Stokkebye's glass that the sand was pitted with craters the size of children's toy buckets, where the crabs had burrowed to safety but where the sand was too wet and too thick to fall back and cover their retreat as they intended.

Suddenly, the *Eden* had slipped into view around Shela's promontory, past the rock which was occupied by the ruins of a tiny Portuguese chapel. It appeared to be setting out for the ocean, but in a minute it had rounded the sandbank and swung almost directly towards them. Instinctively they cowered down behind the embrasure which Felix had built to keep boredom at bay. Felix borrowed the glass and focused it, and could see Wilhelm Selling, stripped to the waist, sitting at the wheel; the breeze was ruffling his grey-blond hair. He thought he caught a glimpse of Frans Buschel midships. 'Put it down, you fool,' muttered Dugmore. 'They'll see the reflection.' Not with the sun where it is, replied Felix, I'm not that daft, but he said it to himself.

The *Eden* was only a hundred yards from shore. Then it changed course and began to beat up the line of beach, quite slowly, parallel to the dunes. Felix risked the Captain's wrath and focused on the palm tree beyond them; the signal was flying, clear and high. He trained it on the thicket of dwarf palm above the high-water mark. Now was the time for the passengers to emerge. Here we go, he told himself...

Nothing happened. The *Eden* ambled away from them, puffing a thin filigree of smoke into the glaring sky. It held its course, that careful hundred yards offshore, and Felix could see that Selling was still sitting at the wheel, a picture of early morning innocence. The familiar, comforting, utterly European sound of a steam engine at an easy half-throttle began to fade.

'Shit!' said Captain Dugmore.

'What happened, sir?'

'Shut up, Mr Thomas. We'd better get down to that hide-out at once – lead the way, at the double.'

'Do we call up the *askaris*?' asked someone.

'No, that will give the game away.'

Someone, thought Felix, has given the game away already.

When they reached the slave pit, it was empty. There was a stench, as Felix had promised, and enough evidence of recent human habitation, but nothing more.

When they were back in Lamu, Felix said, 'Beg pardon for interrupting, sir.'

'What is it, Mr Thomas?'

'Captain, you do believe me – you do believe that they were there?'

Dugmore said, 'Yes, Felix, I believe you. Just as I believe that some bastard got to hear of it. We've been fucked up...'

*

Buschel asked, 'Why did you take us in so close to the shore? I thought you said we weren't planning to stop this time.' The breeze was blowing from the south, whipping up the water so that, for once, the waves showed white curls of foam and the *Eden* began to roll; the dhows beating southward were having to tack far out and then back again, and soon the launch had left them behind. Selling waited until he had taken the boat away from shore and steadied it onto its new course.

'No harm in having a last look at Shela,' he said. 'Say goodbye to Lamu. We shan't be back for many a year.'

'Not until we kick out the English,' retorted Buschel, whose political instincts were passionate and simple.

That may not be as quick as you imagine, thought Selling. And why did I come in so close to shore? To provoke them, that's why. They were there somewhere: I didn't spot them, but my instinct tells me that my friends were right, they were waiting to blast us out of the water. I was tempted to give them a wave, but that would have shown them that I knew.

And how did I know? Because they'd been fools to humiliate that wretched man Rabinek. Why were they such hypocrites to pursue the man? I worked with him on the first shipments to Kipini,

216

and he was going to be one of the best of us. But that idiot Julius Wilhelm had to fall for an English slander which ought to have been thrown back in their faces. We should have said, right! You're snooping into each and every one of us to find a moment in our lives when we were less than holy. You don't do it to your own people, I notice. How many times have Goddfrey and Bosanquet sidled past the law, I wonder. Why did Captain Dugmore leave *his* regiment, I ask myself. So decent fellows like Gustav Rabinek are lumped in with common crooks like Felix Thomas. They'll never know of Rabinek's unwitting revenge – not even he knows of it! But I was saved by Gleisering, too, whom I couldn't stand from the moment I first set eyes on him, and even by that mincing little fool Ducoffre, who bored the pants off all of us with his tales of his conquests – who cares if he used to screw some Belgian tart, I always said. There's a joke I'll be able to tell one day: how my neck was saved by the dregs of Freeland.

'You're very quiet,' Buschel was saying. 'Having second thoughts about quitting Lamu?'

'Never so relieved in my life,' Selling grunted. 'What a bunch of shits.'

So why did I come, he asked himself? What did I expect? What sort of fool am I? Back home, he had been a Freelander out of conviction. He had studied the texts and attended the meetings, and he had explained to his wife that this was where their lives would lead. He had the craftsman's skills which the Association valued. He had neither social standing nor higher education but that, they said, did not matter. He would commit himself to the venture, and he had promised he would send for his beloved family as soon as he was established. And that he was still going to do.

What an idiot I was, thought Selling, bitterly, for the thousandth time. He had quickly discovered that his fellow-members were either fools or rogues. Their leaders were incompetent, and their plans for an assault on the mainland were a farce. He prided himself that he was not a man to waste time lamenting a mistake: he looked for alternatives while he kept his counsel. In his solitary, serious, methodical way, he rethought his family's future. 'Freeland', he realised almost at once, was fated to shatter into smithereens, but he refused to go back to obscurity in Europe. Africa he liked at once – he enjoyed the heat and the exotic atmosphere and the sense that this was a place where a man could

217

make something of himself. He looked around and saw that he might make an impact on this place (he knew his own qualities, though he was rather less aware of his limits, like many unintelligent men). There were no social barriers, he discovered: he – and his family – would be accepted here. Then he met the German community in Lamu, all four of them, and was made welcome by them and saw that it was here, in what the English buggers mockingly called the '*schloss*', that he belonged, not in the squalor and freethinking of Free House. He was deeply gratified to be accepted by them, notwithstanding his poverty and his lowly background (he did not understand that this was nothing more than the instinctive African hospitality of Europeans for other Europeans), and one day he realised that he might be able to repay their hospitality in ways that contributed not just to their own interests but also to his own patriotic sense of the German cause. His understanding of that cause was scarcely worked out as yet, but he had been reading Carl Peters and was always moved, even incensed, when he thought of what the English had done those few years ago to wipe out Peters's brave achievements. At Imperial House, when they discovered this, they applauded him and introduced him to the man who had been Peters's right arm – Bwana Pembe, as he was universally known. Whenever Pembe was in town (for he came and went mysteriously), Selling sat at his feet and devoured his tales of imperial adventure and, in the end, British betrayal.

His disaffection from the rest of the Freelanders may have become too obvious. Julius Wilhelm asked him, apprehensively, if he would take command of the steam-launch – 'You are an engineer, and you could have Pier Scavenius, who did a spell at sea, and perhaps Frans Buschel, who's very keen. I'll rely on you to get the *Eden* into proper condition, and that will keep you away from Free House, which you'd probably prefer...'

He agreed, and soon his tiny crew were in thrall to him. He realised at once that the *Eden* gave him his freedom of Freeland; he was the first of his colleagues to be liberated. It was the *Eden* which sealed his deal with the local Germans. He knew from almost the beginning that the Freeland notion was a nonsense when applied to Africa; he knew, as a proud realist, that he had been deceiving himself out of ignorance and inexperience, that Africa demanded a vigour and boldness and ruthlessness which European ideologists and intellectuals like Wilhelm and Salner would never be capable of; he particularly detested Europeans like Dekker, whose every word, every amicable greeting, every raised eyebrow, made him feel uneducated and doltish. He looked around him, prepared to be open-minded, and concluded very quickly that the local inhabitants – natives, kaffirs, whatever you called them – were undeserving of the slightest respect, and, as a self-proclaimed realist, he drew all necessary conclusions and never raised the issue again.

The boat was to be his escape – as indeed it was, quite literally, on this very day. The Denhardts were kind and hospitable, and he spent more and more time with them, away from the childish scene at Free House, with the English so superior, the French so fancy, the Scandinavians so drunk, and the Austrians so spiritual under that prize idiot Wilhelm and his constipated sidekick Salner. As for the rest, their main concern was who would be next in bed with Louise Sasse. He had no time for that. He had to make his plans. He made them in Imperial House.

Yes, he remembered, I did that first job for Pembe after I had had an exchange of words with Dugmore, who had been extremely offensive about Carl Peters – I almost told him I knew what he was up to. I saw no harm in Pembe's proposal for helping transfer a few kaffir labourers from the island to the mainland. Easy enough so long as the beach was empty. No need for anyone to know.... It's not for us, said Pembe, no profit in it for me, I promise you, but we Germans need to make friends on the island if we are to plan our return. Every favour we do for the mainland makes an enemy for Major Rogers and the English. And every time a landlord on the island loses labour from his *shambas*, he becomes a critic of the English rule. Look at it this way, Pembe had said in the course of one of their long, interesting chin-wags late into the evening, 'Our hosts are splendid fellows and good patriots, but they have to live on this island, so I don't embarrass them by talking practicalities. But you and I, my dear Selling, are men of action, and before you move south – which I recommend you to do, and I will give you an introduction to the General in Tanga – we shall have our little fun at the expense of Major Rogers.'

Selling hadn't understood him at first. He knew that Toeppen would never forgive the destruction and confiscation of his mainland properties ('with not one pfennig compensation!'), and

219

Pembe's plight was apparently even more heartbreaking. 'Do you think that Carl Peters would have sat on his backside so that Rogers could leave the island to its own devices while he was crushing our allies on the mainland and burning their villages?' demanded Pembe one evening, to the alarm of Clemens Denhardt, who was convinced that Rogers had his spies everywhere. One night Selling heard Clemens saying, 'Your dealings with that rogue are your own business, my dear Pembe. If you can control him, good luck to you. But don't call on me to bail you out of the Fort. And for your own sake never tell me anything, so I won't be able to squeal when Rogers gets out the thumbscrews.'

And so Selling was recruited to the cause, but the detail was never spelled out, and he was grateful for both. Some things he did not want, nor need, to know. There were, he gathered, friends in high places on this island who were happy that the English be shown to be weak and ineffectual; some of them were said to be personally bitter about British actions in the past. In the Forest, there was hinted to be a particular friend who hated the English, and Rogers in particular, with a passion which Pembe confessed far exceeded his own (they had both lost their estates, he said; they understood each other). The friend in the Forest was interested in the escaping slaves; perhaps they were to be resettled in the *watoro* Forest villages – Pembe was vague about that. And by the way, there would be a modest compensation. But let's be careful not to talk about these things in front of our hosts – they really have no interest in such things.

It made sense to me, Selling thought, and I knew I'd have no trouble persuading the other two that it was innocent enough. Sometimes our passengers were in such a wretched condition that I wondered who was doing whom a favour, but Pembe urged me not to worry, after a few more trips there would be enough for a pleasant little house in Dar or a down-payment on that farm near Tabora. He kept on saying not to involve the Denhardts. 'They don't want to know,' he would say, chortling in his particularly amiable way. 'They're terrified of Bwana Rajees. I really don't know why...'

The charm of the scheme was that the *Eden* had become well-known for its daily excursions; it was crewed by *wazungu* and had a good reason to travel to and fro between the island and the mainland, so no-one would imagine that its cargo was anything other than stores for the Freeland base camp at Kipini. Mind you, Selling would have agreed, I always knew it couldn't go on. Didn't intend it to either, I had my sights on Dar-es-Salaam after the inevitable bust-up at Free House. Wilhelm was a disaster and Salner no better, Dugmore was certainly an English spy. It was a pity about Robert Schmidt – I hadn't wanted that, and I said so to Pembe, and he pretty well wept and said the *askaris* had lost their heads when they surprised him at the pens. At least he didn't deny it. But I admit I was rattled when Scavenius vanished; I had assumed he was dead, and mourned him. And then Louise Sasse to make a third. Well, she's not on my conscience. 'I'll tell you this,' I said to Pembe last night. 'I'll take one more cargo for you because Rogers is safely out of the way – fine, tomorrow morning, if you say it's ready – but I don't want to find any white females in the party.' Pembe had replied, 'What makes you think the Israelite woman is alive?' 'I'm asking you. I'd like to know. Is she alive?' 'I do not want to know,' said Pembe. 'Haven't you asked?' 'All I am told is that she was foolish. She was alone, and she was found.' 'This is folly,' said Selling. 'When the Major returns, he will tear this island in shreds to find her. And if he finds a body, he'll have every one of us in the Fort, the Denhardts included.'

'He will not find a body. There are other vessels that travel to the mainland. The damage had been done by the time I heard. Believe me, there was nothing I could do, she had already been handled.' (Selling didn't like that.) 'It is better for her if she is on the mainland.'

It made sense, and Selling did not want to dwell on it. There was nothing to be done. If she was alive, certainly she would never be seen again. Pembe said, 'We must try to remember that it is good for us to have local friends who are grateful to us, even if they sometimes make mistakes.'

'That won't help us when Major Rogers hangs your Forest friend and deposes the Liwali,' answered Selling, more prophetically than he can have intended.

I'm here on the open seas and not in the Fort, thought Selling, thanks to that pernicious little criminal Gleisering. I never thought I'd owe him a favour, or Ducoffre either. He was surprised that Gleisering had had the nerve. The man had come to the conclusion, or so he said, that their dear colleague Pier Scavenius must be well and truly and tragically *dead* by now, and since he was a *particular* friend of his he thought he should go to his room in Free House and sort out his possessions so that they could be sent home to his family, no doubt with a letter of commiseration from Julius Wilhelm and, in due course, another letter from Dr Hertzka. That was his story, anyway. I reckon he wanted first crack at the pickings. Imagine his surprise, poor fellow, when he found the room had already been emptied, and imagine his reaction when he was accosted by Bakari and felt obliged to explain himself. Bakari told him that Mrs Wilhelm had already sent her servant Saidi to collect everything. So when Julius Wilhelm happened to arrive at that moment in Free House, Gleisering, no doubt to bolster his story, mentioned his wife's efficiency, and Wilhelm looked baffled and said that that was the first he'd heard of it and that Scavenius's things certainly weren't in his house, Bakari must have misunderstood. Bakari stuck to his guns: Saidi had collected the clothes yesterday.

'Never mind,' said Wilhelm, 'I came to tell you all that at last we have some good news' – and he waved a scrap of paper. 'At least, friends, it's good news in the most important respect. Our colleague Pier Scavenius has written to me to say that he is alive, and to apologise to us all for causing such alarm – and to tell us that he has resigned from the Association and has already left the island to return to Europe.'

There was quite a commotion, reported Rabinek – who had been there – to Selling, who had not. 'Cheers and laughter, as you would expect, and quite a bit of bewilderment. Even irritation. They passed round the letter, which was from him all right, and very brief, and it only referred to "personal reasons".'

'Then I'm very relieved,' Selling had managed to say. 'He was a good lad. I wonder what came over him.'

'Well, one theory – ' said Rabinek, who had made a point of seeking out Selling, ' – or at least, an explanation offered us by Emil Ducoffre, who went into a long fantasy about it in Mabrukki's just now – is that he and Martha Wilhelm had been having a great liaison, and it was the only way to resolve it. Glorious self-sacrifice, said the little monkey, he understood perfectly...'

'That's balls,' said Selling.

'I agree. Most of us told him the same – everyone likes Martha.'

But it was Gleisering who hammered the nail home: why, he

asked, had Martha collected Pier's things without her husband knowing? And where had the young man been? She must have been hiding him after he disappeared. God knows where. That got them gossiping again...

So Martha, for whatever reason, must have been hiding Scavenius. And he would have told her everything, Selling suddenly knew it, in a moment of horrified comprehension, because he understood in his bones how a terrified young man would wish to unburden himself to a woman like Martha. And she would have told her husband – and even Julius Wilhelm would then have no option but to act. Why hadn't they come for him? So this was the end, never mind waiting for the explanations, he'd grab his bags from Free House, warn Buschel and they could borrow the *Eden* for one last time, and with a spot of luck they'd both be on their way to the mainland before anyone noticed. Thank God Wilhelm was an idiot who couldn't take a decision to save his life. What was he delaying for? Surely he wouldn't be waiting for Rogers to get back from Witu?

Rabinek had looked at him curiously. I must put a better face on it, thought Selling: he can't know what this bit of gossip means to me.

'Are you all right?' asked the other man. 'That's not why I was trying to find you. I'm not interested in tittle-tattle about Martha, it disgusts me.'

'What else is there?'

'I wanted to say that I'm getting very fed up with the way our English comrades are ganging up on us, know what I mean?'

'Are they?' He could understand Rabinek having his own grievances against the English, but he ought to be feeling a lot stronger about the shameful way his own comrades had abandoned him.

'I've been keeping an eye.... Nothing much else to do, you see.'

'So?'

'Did you know that Dugmore has taken to visiting Charter House several times a day since Rogers left?'

'Doesn't surprise me. I always thought he was too good to be true.'

'But now he's holding meetings there. English sub-committee, I suppose. Tea-parties.'

Selling, his mind still struggling against panic, said, 'Gustav, what are you talking about?'

Shorn of the evasion, it came down to an afternoon of simple eavesdropping. Rabinek – 'nothing else to do' – had established himself in the alley that ran down the side of the Friday Mosque and came out opposite the company building. He realised he could be overseen from Rogers's roof terrace, but calculated that the sun was still too high for that to be a danger. He could sit on the outer steps of the mosque, hidden in deep shadow, and keep watch on the Charter House entrance door through a trellis against which Rogers had once had a wild hope of training a rose. In the next hour he watched as Dekker, Felix Thomas, Goddfrey and Bosanquet and – 'the non-English guest of honour' – Martha Wilhelm arrived, to be let in by the same Indian servant. They were there for an hour; they left in ones and twos, discreetly.

'So what?' demanded Selling, suddenly impatient to lose himself in action. It had just occurred to him that if he risked delaying his departure until the morning, he could combine it with Pembe's last assignment – and collect his earnings while he was about it.

'I was alarmed by some of the things I heard. The English boys went straight to Mabrukki's, so I joined them – not that they knew, of course, I was also being discreet and, and if they saw me inside, well, I'm not exactly a stranger there. The place was half-empty, not the usual din, so I could hear them. They were talking about having a party, for some special reason. A party tomorrow night, they were clear about that – and then the pretty one said, "By then we'll have fixed those German bastards..." – something like that. Selling, I really don't like it. It's got to stop. This is not what we came to Africa for. We're all supposed to be comrades, it's not right that we go round in these little national groups as if we were still back home. What shall we do, Selling? Will you come with me to talk to Julius Wilhelm about it?'

'Anything else said?'

'I couldn't really hear. Something about Shela, I think, but they were probably talking about Louise, they were crazy about her, in their own way.'

Selling said, 'Let me sleep on it.' Then he went to find Bwana Pembe, to warn him and to be paid off.

Eleven

Against vices and their dangerous results to the community, we did not exercise any right of *punishment*, but only a right of *protection*; and we esteemed *reformation* the best and most effectual means of protection. Since men with a normal mental and moral character, in a community in which all the just interests of every member are equally recognised, cannot possibly come into violent collision with the rights of others, we considered casual criminals as mentally or morally diseased persons, whose treatment it was the business of the community to provide for...

Theodor Hertzka: *Freeland: A Social Anticipation*

You can imagine, Dugmore would later tell his audience at the Mombasa Club, what poor Rogers said to me when he got back from his military triumphs in Witu. When he had got an inkling of what he had missed – and I blame that shifty Indian bearer of his for putting a negative slant on it – he was absolutely livid, not just with yours truly but with the whole flaming universe. I had, he said, made a total balls-up – which of course was true, as I hastened to admit. All his long-laid plans to nail this slave business on our German neighbours, he declared, had been blown sky-high – and again, I had to be honest and agree. 'On top of all that,' he screamed – yes, positively *screamed*, at *me*! – 'I find the Freelanders are still on my doorstep when I expressly told you to get rid of them...' (that was entirely unfair, he had said nothing of the sort) 'and to make things *even* worse you tell me Madame Sasse has vanished. Which can only mean she's been murdered, and no doubt raped in the process.'

There I protested: nothing to do with me, I said, if that particular lady – yes, a lovely lady, I agree – chooses to go off to Shela beach with a Freelander boyfriend and then wanders off by herself, *I* can't be responsible for what happens to her. I thought it diplomatic not to add that if I had been left with more than a handful of *askaris*, we might have had a better chance of finding her – yes, dead or alive. 'And *worst of all*,' declared Rogers, who hadn't even offered me a drink, I now remember, he had come back to find not merely an empty slave pen and a missing white woman, but not a single witness left who could connect the Germans with the slave racket. 'The Danish boy, Scavenius, I'm told has disappeared – gone home to Denmark, for the love of God! The two Germans on the launch – Selling and whatever-his-name – delivered the boat to their colleague in Kipini and told him they had resigned and were setting off for German East, so we'll never see *them* again. Mrs Wilhelm can tell me what Scavenius told her about the operation, and may even be happy to do so, but that's only hearsay. The Germans will deny it and say it's the fantasy of an unstable boy – and it's not beyond them to make hints about his friendship with Mrs Wilhelm, you mark my words!'

Now Rogers is a bright chap, and I couldn't disagree with any of this, said Dugmore. I'd already worked out that the only 'evidence' we had was the absolutely copper-plated eyewitness confirmation of Felix Thomas that he had seen the *Eden* collecting a dozen wretches and setting off for the mainland – and no-one is going to believe that they were being taken home to their own villages. Felix might not possess a spotless character, but he would be able to testify to that, and he had the detail to make it convincing. But even Felix – as Rogers explained, not that it was necessary – couldn't say anything about the Germans. The more Rogers thought about it, up on that solitary rooftop of his, the clearer he must have relished the irony: that the spanking new steamboat of these noble Freeland idealists had been operating as a slave dhow under his very eyes.

I suggested, very diffidently, that he might want to interview our German neighbours, in which case I would be happy to abandon my membership of Freeland and attend the meeting. There was no need for so great a sacrifice, I was told – such sarcasm! He had already summoned the Denhardt brothers and been given the obvious crap that they had no idea what he was talking about, they were so sad to hear of Mr Schmidt and Madame Sasse, etc., etc. And as for our fellow-countryman whom you refer to as Bwana Pembe, it was most unfortunate, but he had left for the mainland only the previous day.

So Rogers sent for Julius Wilhelm. Now – I have to digress for a moment, said Captain Dugmore. (The more perceptive among his audience at this point sometimes remarked to themselves how, although the Captain was so insistent that he was the villain of the tale, he showed few signs of remorse, let alone guilt. Indeed, it sometimes sounded rather good fun – sport and adventure – the way Dugmore told it, though admittedly the years might have added to the drama, softened the anguish.)

There was another complication here, and this one, gentlemen, was yet another tragedy, at least for one of my cast of characters. You have heard me tell how prominently the Englishman Dekker figures – indeed, with distinction. He was the best of the Freelanders, I've always thought, and I always had a lot of time for him. You also remember how we all admired the lady wife of Dr Wilhelm – no sir, *not* Louise, I am speaking of Martha: she was a person of great quality – splendid woman as well. Well, when Rogers summoned Wilhelm to Company House to give him the bollocking of all time – second only, I correct myself, to the one he had just given me – he found that the fellow was in a frightful state. Naturally, Rogers assumed that he'd heard of the private activities of his sailors and was taken with guilt. But not a word of it, he didn't seem to care about what had been going on. No, he was in this terrible state because his wife – yes, Martha – had just informed him that she was giving him the heave-ho. For Dekker, if you can believe it!

Now at this point Rogers has always been a bit vague. Discreet, you will say, but I have my reasons for thinking that it was more than that. Dekker and Rogers had been pretty close in those previous weeks, though only I and Iqbal Ali knew it. He was the only one of the Freelanders Rogers had any respect for. I've always believed that Rogers *guessed* that something was going on between his new best friend and Frau Wilhelm. But of course he'll deny it...

That's by-the-by. I mention it only because Wilhelm was in no state to argue back, not that it would have done him any good if he'd tried. Rogers told him that the Freeland fun and games were over, *kaput*, finished. Free House was closed down. The Freelanders were required to leave the Coast within ten days. That sort of thing. And I imagine he added the detail – that Hardinge was informed, that permission to travel up-country was revoked, that London had been told of the circumstances. Etcetera, etcetera.

But Rogers was always a decent chap. He was probably feeling sorry for Wilhelm on account of the wife – who wouldn't? He offered Wilhelm a deal. Call an emergency meeting and announce the immediate disbanding of your Association, he was told, and I shan't publish the proven facts of your Freelanders' involvement in the slave trade. That was Rogers's promise, and I've always said it was a generous one because, as Wilhelm must have realised, Rogers had it in his power to disgrace him – and not just him personally, but the entire blasted Association, all across Europe. After all, slave-running these days is even less respectable than putting your daughter in a whorehouse...

Wilhelm, as I say, had no fight in him. All he wanted was to go away and howl at the moon. As for defying Rogers and leading his troops to Mount Kenya – forget it! Rogers later told me that Wilhelm actually thanked him while the tears poured down his face.

Then we had a ridiculous meeting at Free House. I was feeling a bit irresponsible – disaffected, you might say – so I didn't excel in the arts of diplomacy that afternoon. Wilhelm stood up and announced, with regret and so on, that he had been informed by the English authorities that permission for the expedition had been withdrawn, that the Association was therefore to disband, that they were required to make arrangements to leave...

Uproar, yes, but remember that this was a meeting notable for its absentees – Martha Wilhelm. Tom Fallon, Louise Sasse, Wilhelm Selling, Pier Scavenius, Frans Buschel, Sasse himself (because old Hassemer died that same night), Jimmy Dunn, Robert Schmidt. I had a bit of a run-in with Salner. He called me a British spy. I replied that he was a fool, words to that effect, and I had the beast on a tight leash between my legs so I had the courage of my convictions. When he tried to persist, I looked Wilhelm in the eye and said, 'I counsel you both to say no more, or I shall have to speak again,' and Wilhelm took my point and pulled Salner back into his chair. Dekker tried to get some sense into things, and Salner, when he had cooled down, was rather impressive, I admit it, but when Dekker said, 'Mr Chairman, in view of what amounts to our expulsion from this island, I move that the Freeland Association moves forthwith to the mainland,' only Goddfrey and Bosanquet said Hear, hear!, and Wilhelm (who was looking like death, especially when he had to listen to Dekker) simply said no question of it, river conditions impossible, the *Eden* out of commission, impossible heat – and so he went on and on, and we all understood that he was determined on an end to it. I was tempted, I promise, to suggest that we set up the barricades on the jetty, but I thought that would be a provocation.

Which is pretty well the end of the story. No, not quite. Did I mention that Selling and Buschel had done a bunk? And we all know that Martha Wilhelm smuggled young Scavenius onto a dhow to Mombasa – all we ever knew about that was that she produced his letter of resignation, which proved that he was alive after all, and said she had sent him home for his own good. She was utterly unrepentant about it, even when Rogers protested to her in person. Perhaps she didn't see that she had denied him his only witness. 'Oh, I've no idea where you can find him,' I heard her say, as though butter wouldn't melt in her mouth. 'I never had his address in Denmark. Perhaps you could write to the Freeland Association in Vienna.' I promise you it was as much as Rogers could do to keep a civil tongue in his head, but Dekker was in the room at the time and, as I say, I always believed those two men had a sympathy for each other. Totally different types, of course, they can't have had a thing in common, but they were friends. It sometimes happens like that on the Coast...

What happened next? I was out of it, believe me. I'd had to shift my things out of Free House for obvious reasons, and I was *very* non grata in Rogers's establishment. So I moved in with Goddfrey and Bosanquet, and began to make plans to go back up-country. Time for a spot of sport, I reckoned. But I hung on for a bit – partly out of curiosity, and also I was bloody angry with Rogers at the time, he'd said some very rough things to me – so I sat on the sidelines, kept my head down, and listened to the rows going on at Free House as they packed their bags. Think of the mess they were in! – Half of them probably didn't *dare* return to Europe, and the other half didn't want to.

Then, one morning, I bumped into Dekker outside the Fort. He was amiable, and we exchanged a few notes – catching up on who and where, that sort of thing – and then he came clean with me. He said, 'Martha and I,' which I thought rather sweet, no more 'Frau Wilhelm' nonsense 'have decided that, despite everything, we still want to go to the mainland. That's why we both came to Lamu. That's what we want to do, together.' He said it defiantly, as though I was going to object.

I said, 'Good luck to you both.' I know that that's what I said, but I honestly don't remember my tone of voice at the time – whether I was pulling his leg in a friendly way.

He said, 'Major Rogers is being difficult. He is insisting that we leave, like everyone else, on the next steamer. He tells me that he "regrets" he can make no exceptions.'

'Sod that,' I said. 'Where do you want to go?'

Yes, I was still not amused with Rogers. But it was more than that. I've never regretted it. Despite everything.

'We have decided to start at Golbanti, and move inland from there.'

'I'll take you myself,' I said, and I did.

I dropped them off at the old mission station at Golbanti two days later – you know, the Methodist place that was raided by Masai *moran* in '87. Fundi George escaped by the skin of his teeth but the Hogarth couple were butchered, with their children. No-one had tried to open it up again.

The two of them were very confident. I tried to warn them, but they said they knew what they were doing. I've never forgotten how they were that day. You know something? They were happy. As simple as that...

Thanks! Just a *chota peg* – the boy knows how...

*

Lamu Island

My dearest Sisters,

I have so little, and so much, to say. We did not find dear Louise. We must conclude that she is either dead or abducted. I loved her, and I shall always mourn her.

Our Freeland members failed in their pursuit of her. Perhaps because they were divided amongst themselves. I absolve the English boys and Lieutenant Stokkebye, who were wonderful. Also Tom Fallon, who has become obsessed with his search for Louise. He has departed for the mainland, and Dekker fears for his life. Captain Dugmore, who was this week reunited with Major Rogers for what I hear was a stormy meeting, tells me he too is deeply worried. As a result of these and other dramas, our expedition has been cancelled. The English have decided to expel us from the island. Julius has therefore disbanded our group, which is instructed to return to Europe. So desperately sad! Dr Hertzka will be devastated.

But – my dears – I am putting off the true point of this letter. You have been told by me before of my friend Dekker. He and I have despaired of the inability of our Freeland comrades to quit this seductive island and make for the mainland, so we are going to do it – precisely that! – together. I have told Julius that I must leave him. Ma Fatima will help, and gives her blessing. Captain Dugmore will be our agent.

There! I have told you. You will understand the import of what we are doing. Do not be distressed, it is what we want, both of us. I have not spoken of love, but if in Hamburg in years to come you sometimes talk amongst yourselves of the mad folly of your elder sister who went into Africa – ask yourselves that simplest of all questions: why did she do it?

The Captain tells us he will escort us to Golbanti tomorrow. Ma Fatima promises me that Louise is lost to us 'for ever ' – those were her words – and that it is time for me to set off.

I embrace that destiny, and send you my dearest love.

Farewell.

M

(Remember always, that I am so happy!)

*

Personal

Free House
Lamu
11 June 1894

Dear Dr Hertzka,

I have reproached myself in the past for appearing to send you an unvarying stream of bad news from your own African Expedition, but now I can hardly bring myself to report on the sequence of disasters – for that is the only word – that have overwhelmed us since my last letter. My only satisfaction is that on this occasion it is possible that I can offer you a clearer and possibly more comprehensive recital than you will be receiving from our official leader. On that supposition, then I must ask you to brace yourself...

In a word, the Freeland expedition is ended. At an emergency

231

(and badly attended) meeting in Free House yesterday, Dr Wilhelm informed us that the English had ordered the cancellation of our project and required us to leave the territory forthwith. Wilhelm announced that, 'therefore' the African branch of the Association was disbanded, with immediate effect.

As you can imagine, the news caused consternation – not least, I admit, to myself, who had been given no hint of what was to come. In the absence of several of our more eloquent members, I took it upon myself to ask for what reason the authorities had revoked our permissions to travel inland. Dr Wilhelm, who I must add looked shattered, even ill, answered that he had been given no explanation. When I pressed him he said, without appearing to share my anger, that Major Rogers (the local *gauleiter*) had arrived back from a difficult military mission on the mainland and, discovering that we were still here, had declared that he was 'fed up' with us and had won the agreement of his superiors to cancel our permits. Apparently he had added various slanderous and unjustified remarks about the townspeople objecting to our presence and to our behaviour.

I was of a mind to argue that we should take a stronger position – perhaps a delegation to Sir Arthur Hardinge in Zanzibar, or an urgent diplomatic *démarche* in Vienna and London – but I must in candour report that I did not seem to command the adequate support of the meeting. Dekker and Dugmore were unusually silent; Goddfrey and Bosanquet seemed to find it amusing; Selling and Buschel were nowhere to be seen, and I since gather that they have taken it into their heads, heaven knows why, to set off for the mainland with the *Eden*. The French suggested that there was no 'significance' to the disbanding of the Association, if you please. Rabinek and Thomas were both there, at the back, but of course have no vote. The Scandinavians were with me in terms of honest indignation, but I did not think they were in a condition to join me in a march on Rogers's headquarters.

This reminds me that I should perhaps have warned you first of the private tragedies that have littered these last weeks. The first was the shocking murder of Robert Schmidt, who was a lovable and enthusiastic colleague: his body was found – in a sad state – on Shela beach, two miles from where I write. His assassins have not been found as yet. There was to be worse to come. The next day we realised that his friend Pier Scavenius had vanished. I greatly feared that he too had been murdered, but we have since received a brief note, signed by him, announcing that he has resigned from the Association and has already left the island. Thirdly, and most horrible of all, dear Louise Sasse, the darling of the expedition, has disappeared. We have all been searching for her for days but with no success, and I confess that I am terrified we shall only find her body. Tom Fallon has been particularly active in the search, and went off – I don't know where – to follow her trail, so he too was an absentee yesterday. Finally, and I report this almost as an afterthought because the poor man had been seriously ill for weeks, Hassemer passed away peacefully a few days ago. He was a great admirer of Madame Sasse, so at least he did not suffer, as does her husband, the agony of her loss.

You see, then, how your party of brave and optimistic Utopians has been decimated by a cruel destiny. On reflection, I realise that it may not be so surprising that my friends and colleagues failed to give me their support at yesterday's meeting in *refusing* our fate. I am tempted to share Wilhelm's dejection...

In that context, I must in strictest confidence tell you something which may influence your attitude towards him when you meet. I reliably understand that his beloved wife Martha has informed him that she intends a separation. There is gossip in Free House of a friendship with Dekker, but I wish to know nothing of that. Let us merely remember that Julius has suffered a double tragedy in these last days.

He and I and you will, I very much hope, be meeting in Vienna in the not-too-distant future. That is a strange, almost unreal – but welcome – thought as I sit here in an equatorial deluge at a temperature which would test your patience and, indeed, your endurance, if I may be so bold. I shall take that opportunity to describe in fuller detail the sad history of our expedition. Let me promise you that I, for one – and no doubt Julius will join me – will earnestly and urgently be planning a second venture to Freeland. We are sadder, but surely wiser, men...

Salner paused for a long moment before he added his signature. He wondered whether he would ever know the full story. So how could he promise Dr Hertzka the truth? Sadder, yes, but how could he be wiser if he did not know the truth? Who was it said, 'the truth shall make us free'?

He scrawled a postscript – 'We shall send you our steamer details' – and signed.

*

Private and Confidential

As from Witu
12 June

To: Sir A Hardinge
    Government House
    Zanzibar

Dear Arthur,

A private note, please, not for the files – I'll write formally when I'm back in Lamu. I can send you this scrawl in the meantime because by good fortune the Navy sent a lighter in to Kipini to get water, and my fellows had the sense to tell me. So this travels by hand of Captain Macaulay.

As you will observe – no doubt with increasing irritation – I am back in Witu yet again, having had to turn around and set sail again almost as soon as I had got back to Lamu. I lose track of the number of my visits this year to these miserable creeks. My present visit is required not only by the latest activities of our friend Suleiman Kimenya – whom, I have formally reported, I missed by a whisker last time – but by the exploits of the d——d Freelanders.

When I got back to Lamu on the 7th, I found the place in chaos. Dugmore, to my utter and unrepentant fury, had set up a cock-and-bull plan to link the Germans with the slave business, and of course the outcome was a disaster. I suspect he had been conceal-ing important evidence from me even before my departure. I'm still not sure about the detail, but it is clear that:

Item: a big pick-up of slaves on Shela beach by the Freeland vessel, which Dugmore had decided to 'ambush', was betrayed and aborted;

Item: the two Freelanders who were running the network have departed in a hurry, no doubt for German East. Their third col-league has vanished – I believe he has left the island for points unknown, which means I do not have a single witness of what I am convinced is German complicity;

Item: I do, however, have evidence of Freeland involvement, and I have therefore ordered their director to close down 'Free

House' and take his members off this territory within ten days. I have taken the liberty of telling him that you have seen fit to withdraw their permissions to travel inland. (*Arthur* – I can't believe you wouldn't want to do that, but I didn't have time to double-check with you.)

Item: most tragically, one of the two Freeland ladies has vanished – she is either dead or abducted. I have inadequate reports from the mainland that she has been sighted in Suleiman's retinue. The seizure of a European lady is manifestly so outrageous a development that this, in itself, would demand my presence on the mainland. To complicate matters further, another Freelander – one of their more sympathetic characters, called Fallon – has taken it upon himself to pursue her supposed trail, and I fear that he can be no match for Suleiman, if and when they meet.

You will therefore see why I write in haste, having left at dawn only yesterday. Dugmore is *not* in charge in my absence. Your friend the Liwali will have to cope. I have instructed my residual staff in Lamu that none of the Freelanders is to move an inch unless it is onto a steamer. I have sent a note to Wilhelm to say that by the time I return to Lamu I will expect to find Free House *empty*.

It will be good to see you when I next get down to Zanzibar. Perhaps we can resume our search for the elusive marlin? But when?

Yours very sincerely,

Rogers

*

Tom Fallon had once been assured by a sermonising lay preacher that we become adults at the moment when we first confront the prospect of our own death. That experience may come in war or in sickness, out of wisdom or meditation, with the assistance of philosophy or religion (the preacher was favouring the latter), but it is the prospect – possibility – probability – and, when we think on it, the inevitability of our very own demise that takes us through a fatal gateway; we can never go back. Jimmy Dunn and Robert Schmidt had not been granted time to see and understand the reality of their own death. Fallon was to be allowed to contemplate, in full measure, not just its prospect but also its imminence.

When he knew for certain that he was about to die, his first reaction, as he lay in the hut where they had thrown him, was a simple, heaving, bowel-loosening horror. He struggled to control his sphincter and himself, and swung to the other extreme. I do not care so very much to survive today, in order to die in agony of a cancer in twenty years' time. That held him, for a while. He remembered he had once been tempted to boast to Dekker that he was half-dead. That was before he knew Louise, but let the point stand because he wished to polish an apophthegm: 'If I am already half-dead, as I know – then death in this Forest can only be half a death.' He tried it out, and was unconvinced. So he switched to another theme, as his brain whirled and swooped in the unconsoling night: 'If I die in this Forest, then my death – here – will have been pre-ordained. So let me sleep, O Lord, in that comfort.' He used to say to his friends, you can lose your faith in God, but you never lose your belief in the theology. That would have to mean the crude Calvinism of his childhood. I do not believe in the eternal life, he would continue, nor in the salvation of grace, nor in the Resurrection and all that, but I can certainly believe that my life – and my death – have been predestined by an omniscient Being.

Yes, he would agree that Calvinism is a self-regarding theology, since it focuses on our personal salvation. Loving your neighbour somehow comes second. Not that he had any difficulty in loving his neighbour, so long as she was agreeable. Meg once said to him that he was a cold-hearted monster, and selfish to boot. She was cross with him at the time. She was often cross with him, so he left her and the children. He now saw that she was right – but it was a bit late to do anything about it. Thank God he had thought to write to the children last week. Perhaps Dekker would have the kindness to make contact with Meg, since he knew he wouldn't be doing it himself.

He found himself wondering whether, when, how, Major Rogers would hear of his death. He allowed himself a moment's satisfaction that Rogers, assuredly and in the not too distant future, would get to know of the event that was about to happen. He did not doubt that Rogers would avenge him. Rogers was not the enemy, he knew now. We needed him, but we did not know it. The admission had come earlier. After he had met Fundi George again, and had not known where to turn, he had realised that this was

236

beyond his powers and the man he needed was not Dekker, but Rogers.

He had gone back to Shela, into the village. He had a fancy that she had been dragged into one of these shacks and ravished – or whatever, it did not particularly matter, because what was more important was that he knew she was not dead. He stormed from house to house, dragging back the curtains, ignoring the proprieties and the screams of the womenfolk, satisfying himself with a quick, cruel glance that she was not there, defying the flurry of stones and curses that followed his progress. The men were old and did not dare to challenge him, he must have had the invincibility of desperation, even madness, about him. When a mongrel dog dared to attack him, brave enough to try to drive him away, he kicked the creature in the neck, seized it by the hindlegs and hurled it against a wall, where it lay paralysed, whimpering like a beaten child.

She was not there. He came down onto the narrow beach beyond the pillar minaret, where the rocks led out to the ruined chapel. Fundi George was sitting on the Portuguese islet, crooning a hymn which, this time, Fallon did not recognise. The minister had discarded his dog-collar and acquired a topee to rival Rogers's. He wore only a wet and threadbare *kanga*, knotted at the waist. They stood and gazed at each other across the waves.

'Brother! Be of good heart,' called Fundi George in his Yankee accent, and waved a benedictory greeting.

'You must be fucking joking,' replied Fallon, though not loud enough for the missionary to hear.

The sand fell away steeply at his feet – he had seen the smaller dhows run confidently between the spot where he was standing and the Chapel Rock, at low tide as well as high; he could not wade out to the other man, and he was not disposed to swim.

He shouted, 'Fundi George! For the love of Christ our Lord – I am seeking my woman.'

'Is she a lamb that has strayed?' came the answer.

That's true enough, thought Fallon and, guessing how he might find access to this crazed soul, he raised the voice that had been praised in many a choir and sang, without preamble or apology, 'From Greenland's icy mountains,/ From India's coral strand,/ Where Afric's sunny fountains,/ Roll down their golden sand...' That's rather appropriate, he thought; the melody came back to

237

him as though he were still a lad, and his voice rang out across the Indian Ocean with an authentic mission-station fervour that must have touched the tortured heart of Henry During (aka Fundi George), because the preacher beamed with delight and responded with a different mission hymn in a different key: 'Lands of the East, awake!/ Soon shall be your sons be free...' Fallon was onto it at once, and added the harmony: 'The sleep of ages break,/ And rise to liberty!' – and so they continued for minutes more.

'Where is my woman?' shouted Fallon, after they had shared a particularly devout 'Amen'.

'She has been taken away.'

'By whom?'

'By Satan's engineers.'

Fallon decided to take the initiative again. 'We shall sing another hymn,' he pronounced across the waves, 'What a Friend We Have in Jesus!' Fundi George clapped his hands in approbation, and set off at once into a robust first verse: 'Have we trials and temptations?/ Is there trouble anywhere?/ We should never be discouraged:/ Take it to the Lord in prayer...' Fallon was listening to the words as if for the first time. They may be very true, he thought, no harm in any of it. But is the fucking Reverend going to tell me where and how to find Louise?

Fundi George was saying, 'Brother, let us now sing my favourite hymn...'

'Which is?'

'Jesus Loves Me! This I Know...'

He set off, in a key higher than Fallon favoured, and the Englishman gave up. He shouted, 'Listen, you silly bugger, what happened to my woman?'

Fundi George heard him and paused and rolled his eyes, whether in terror or madness, and replied, 'She was taken like the whore of Babylon!' and straightway resumed, 'Yes! Jesus loves me,/ Yes! Jesus loves me/ The Bible tells me so...'

Fallon had the wisdom to allow a long silence after the last reprise. Then he said, 'Please, Fundi George, my friend. For the love of God – do you know where she is?'

And in a moment of rare lucidity, Fundi George said, 'She was taken outside the stockade. To my shame, I was frail and so I escaped. But I saw what he did to her afterwards. I was ashamed. Then they took her away.'

238

He had a new hymn to offer, and he insisted on assuring Fallon, 'What a friend we have in Jesus,/ All our sins and griefs to bear!/ What a privilege to carry,/ Everything to God in prayer...'

Tom Fallon did not join in.

'I'm getting out of here,' he said to Dekker. 'I thought I'd let you know. I can't take it any longer.' That was true, he realised, but only a small part of the story. 'I'm fed up to the back teeth with the heat, the sweat, the dirt, the squalor, the smell, the duplicity, the indolence, the arrogance, the complacency, the vice, the slaves, even the poor fucking donkeys. Do I make my point?'

They were standing in front of the post office, where he had been sending letters to his children. It was even hotter than before; the cloud was sparse and the light bounced back off the water. The town was desperately in need of the breeze, which blew too gently from the direction of Shela. Does the creek funnel the air up to this town, he wondered: are Manda and the other islands high enough to act as a crude wind tunnel?

'You do indeed. But that's a sudden decision. Are you going home?'

'On the contrary, I'm going after Louise. I'm going to the mainland.'

Dekker looked at him quizzically and seemed about to say something, then evidently changed his mind.

'I know she's alive,' said Fallon. 'Dugmore and the rest of you have given up.'

Dekker said, 'Believe me, if there was the slightest clue...'

'Do *you* think she's alive?'

Dekker hesitated. 'Yes – I think I do. I agree with you. But that may not be enough.'

'How do you mean?'

'Martha has a friend – a Swahili friend, a lady, a member of one of the highest families. I haven't met her, of course. She is very wise, and seems to know everything. Martha asked her about Louise, and she told Martha that Louise was alive...'

'So!'

'No, wait! She said that Louise is – in her words – "dead to us".'

'What did she mean?'

'Martha and I think she meant that Louise is probably no longer on this island, and that we shall not see her again.'

239

'So you see, I'm right to cross to the mainland.'

Dekker laid a hand on the younger man's arm, as though to force caution upon him. 'But what can you do? Where will you start? Forgive me, Tom – I'd do the same – I'd even come with you if I thought there was a realistic chance of picking up the trail. But this will be like looking for a pearl in a cargo of oysters. None of us knows the mainland, we'll be lost before we start.'

'Then it's a lesson to us all, we ought to have explored the mainland weeks ago. I'm not a fool, Dekker, I realise that I can't find her by wandering from village to village shouting her name like whoever-it-was looking for Richard Lionheart. I'll go to Rogers. We need him. He'll know what to do.'

Dekker was thinking, we are all the victims of our indolence and our self-indulgence. If we had pressed on into Africa, this would not have happened. Louise has paid the price for our irresolution.

'Forgive me, but if you need funds for your *safari*, you have only to say the word...'

Fallon made his purchases in the Indian shops and tipped a boy to carry them back to Free House. In the narrow streets in the shadows of mid-morning it didn't seem so hot, but when he went out into the full sunlight the sweat burst out immediately, staining his blue shirt dark wet within minutes.

Dugmore, alone and at ease in a long chair in Free House, asked, 'And how do you plan to find the Major? I haven't the faintest idea where he is right now, and I doubt if his sergeant at Charter House does either. My guess is that he'll be charging around the Forest, spreading death and destruction – that's his job, you know.'

'I'll go to Witu.'

'Witu is pacified, he won't be there. He'll be somewhere up north, in the Forest villages and the *watoro* stockades around Safareh. He'll be pursuing his old enemy, Suleiman Kimenya.'

'All the better. Perhaps Suleiman will lead me to Louise. If she's alive – and I *know* she's alive – then she's on her way north, and from what I hear, Suleiman's the man I need to find. And Rogers will want to know that a white woman has been grabbed by a slave gang. I'm pretty sure I can guess what he'll think about that.'

'No doubt of it,' agreed Dugmore thoughtfully. 'But you won't find him at Witu, even if you get that far.'

'Someone in Witu will know where Rogers is. We surely haven't left Witu without a garrison.'

Dugmore gestured abruptly for discretion as Ducoffre tripped past them, making convivial gestures. He waved a large hand at the Frenchman so as to greet and dismiss at the same time, and leaned forward to Fallon and muttered, confidentially, man to man, 'Look, I understand how you feel. She was a wonderful lady. But I can't allow this...'

'Shit! What d'you mean, *you* can't allow it? I haven't come to ask permission, I came to ask for advice – practical advice, as a friend, as an Englishman.'

'That's perfectly true, old boy, but you can surely take a spot of advice, very strong advice, from an old hand in these parts. Even if I grant you that it's possible the lady has been spirited off this island – and, since you force me to be brutally frank, my own conviction is that she was murdered by some Arab bastards and thrown down a well – then listen to me when I tell you that a white man travelling without a force of *askaris* at very least in company strength will be extremely fortunate to survive more than a dozen miles on the mainland at the moment. We don't spread this around, but security over there is pretty damn thin just now.'

'I'll take that risk. And I'm not impressed by what you say. *Civis Romanus sum*, if you take my meaning.'

'Ah – yes,' said Dugmore, groping after his Classics. 'Remember that this is the very edge of our particular empire. Hadrian's Wall, that sort of thing, and you're proposing to cross it.'

How to stop him, he wondered? True enough, he probably didn't have the authority. Rogers had left him with no formal powers, so he would have to recruit the Liwali. That would not be a good idea, in the light of his suspicions about the Liwali's brother. What if the woman, by some miracle, was alive? Fallon was only guessing that she had been captured and exported. If by some miracle he was right, that would mean she was in process of being shipped off to some distant *harem* across the ocean. His blood ought to be boiling with outrage, he knew, but he recognised in himself a curious reluctance to draw distinctions in these things: the whole slave business was so outrageous, Dugmore passionately believed, that what could be *more* outrageous in this single case? When he saw her the other day, she had been burned as dark as – darker than – a Somali girl, and she'd bring one hell of a price in Aden.

241

Which was good – they'd be reluctant to slit her throat. That meant there was a chance – a one in a thousand chance – that she might be found when Rogers broke Suleiman's chain. That in turn meant that Rogers would have to operate with delicate fingers if she wasn't to be damaged in the process. Of course, she would have been damaged already, but no point in dwelling on that.... Jesus! Rogers was going to hit the ceiling when he got back to Lamu.

Dugmore said, 'I'll find you a dhow, with someone we trust, to leave at dawn tomorrow. Be at the jetty below Charter House, and for God's sake don't tell anyone what you're up to. You'll need a *kiroboto* to look after you, and a couple of porters. I can't spare you any *askaris*.'

'I don't need anyone.'

'Don't be a bloody fool. You're as innocent as a baby in this world. You're a *mzungu*, for Christ's sake. Do you plan to carry your Hamburg bag in a temperature of 110? You need a guide – a *kiroboto* – to interpret for you – do you speak the lingo? Of course you don't. He'll fix things like baksheesh for the headman and make sure you don't get lost, and explain to everyone that you're not German. No, I'm not joking. Then you need a couple of men to carry your kit and your guns. I agree you don't need to take the full caboodle of tents and so on, if you can make Mpuyani to Witu in a day's march – it's about twenty-two miles, and you look fairly fit. They'll find you a hut in Witu – look out for Harry Singh, mention my name and make it clear you have urgent despatches for Rogers. And keep on telling them you're not a German, do you understand me? I can't promise Rogers will be pleased to see you, but you can convince him he had to know about Madame Sasse. I hope he doesn't ask why I didn't send a runner instead.'

That evening, Fallon was summoned to Charter House by Iqbal Ali. Dugmore was standing in Rogers's study with a bundle of keys in his hand. He had the grace to look faintly sheepish as he experimented with the padlocks on the gun cabinet. 'I ask no questions,' said Fallon, with all the sarcasm he could muster in the circumstances. 'It gratifies me to see that a fellow Freelander has this access to the inner armoury on this island.' Dugmore replied, 'One day we'll have it out over a bottle, and I'll tell you the whole story. I'm very fond of the Club in Mombasa – I'll look forward to being your host, Mr Fallon. Now, to business. You'll have Juma to escort you.

He's a good man, or at least he's as good as any we'll find on this Coast. The dhow captain is called Chui, and he'll deliver you both to Mkunumbi, as close to dry land as he can get – he warns me that the rains have been so heavy that the whole coast is underwater. You may get wet. Now – here's a .500 Express – do you know about these things?'

'Never fired one in my life. I'm a town boy, and I declined to join Lieutenant Stokkebye's shooting lessons. He was looking for a reason to put a bullet in me. You can guess why.'

The two men looked at each other cautiously and then they both laughed, at which point they became conspirators.

'Well, just hold it as though you know what you're doing. Don't point it at anyone, they have a nasty habit of going off. Your *kiroboto* will have his own gun, and when you get to a village and he fires it, don't be alarmed, it's the way we signal that we're here, we're letting everyone know we're not enemies – yes, I know, that sounds a bit of a contradiction. Then they're supposed to bring your food, which you pay for, but leave the detail to the *kiroboto*. By the way, he and the porters get half their wages now and the other half when they deliver you back here in one piece. I've paid them for the first chunk, so don't let them screw any more out of you.'

'That's very kind of you. Let me reimburse you...'

'Oh, for Christ's sake!' interrupted Dugmore. 'Don't be a bore.' It was his gesture to Louise.

Fallon made one last protest: 'I'm only planning to travel the equivalent of London to Beaconsfield. I'm not pretending to be Henry Stanley.'

'You're going into the Valley of Death, my friend, and you won't let me persuade you to think again.'

'To stay in Eden? I call it Lotus Land.'

*

Juma, the guide-interpreter, was a fat and jolly Swahili-Indian half-caste, so fat that he wobbled from chins to knees when he laughed. Fallon wondered whether he was fit for twenty miles and more in the Forest. He projected the character of an amiable rogue: he explained that for years he had been 'Naval Interpreter First Class' – 'that signifies, sir, that I am not loved by the Arab slave traders. That is why Major Rogers pays me so many rupees, and permits me to carry a gun' – and he shook with delighted and helpless mirth. He was not, he explained, a professional *kiroboto*, but he was free for a few days and had an interest in events on the mainland, so he had agreed to Captain Dugmore's suggestion that he accompany Fallon to Witu. There he would leave him. Remember, please, he added, that I report to the Major, not to the Liwali. He may have been hinting 'unlike some of my colleagues', but Fallon was unequipped to catch the subtext.

The dhow captain took the northern route, past Mokowe and down the inshore creek. Fallon remembered how Wilhelm Selling had explained one evening in Free House that he preferred to take the steam-launch around the island by the outer route, through the bay and out past Shela: he had said something about it being faster, so long as the sea wasn't rough. No-one had suspected another argument: that he had business which sometimes required him to stop on Shela beach. Today the dhow seemed to keep up a perfectly adequate speed as it scudded north and then north-west past Mokowe, which was the site of a mainland jetty, and into the dark creek, scarcely four hundred yards wide at one point, that was all that separated Lamu from the continent. There was nothing but mangrove, two grey-green walls of tangled, impenetrable vegetation. Juma was dozing under the awning; the porters, skinny, shifty fellows, squatted midships and chatted with the captain, who held the tiller in his horny toes and shouted commands at a small boy who spent most of the journey bailing out the bilges with a gourd. Fallon sat high above the bows, relishing the breeze on his face, the cool early sun on his back. Twice he saw clumps of palm trees high above the line of mangrove, rising from distant *shambas*. They slipped easily past Matandoni, and the dhow carpenters at the water's edge paused in their endless hammering and shouted taunts and jests at the captain. There was a pelican, flying clumsy and slow a foot above the water, and then a great stork, balancing like a ballet dancer on the top of a solitary kapok tree which was stuffed with puffs of white wool like the hedges around a sheep enclosure. On the western bank he could see the beginning of the deep creeks that penetrated the mainland and would in due course lead him to the Forest. He noticed that there were dugouts, precarious and primitive, emerging from these mysterious black cavities.

The second village was Kipungani: Fallon had heard its name

244

from Dekker, who had walked to it down Shela beach and round the headland, and afterwards admitted to exhaustion. Behind and beyond the village, which appeared to boast only an orchard of tamarinds and a narrow coastal line of drooping *dafu* palms, was a jagged line of white sand dunes; he worked out that they must be the extension of the Shela dunes. Suddenly, the mangroves on their left yielded to a fine steep beach strewn with cactus and bundles of extravagant driftwood. Beyond, out in Mataoni Bay, he could see – four miles distant? – a crackled, silver line of breakers where the ocean destroyed itself on the coral reef. The dhow had begun to pitch and roll in the swell, and with a hurried flurry of activity – thumping sail and swinging beam – they turned due west into the yellow sandbanks; the mangroves which confronted them were emerald-green in the diamond light of the morning sun. Juma stirred himself and said, 'This is Mto Mkunumbi. We must be careful not to run aground. It would be very, very hot sitting here all day and waiting for the tide to turn.'

It has taken me ten weeks to get from Lamu to the mainland, thought Fallon. What fools we all have been.

'Now let us walk, *bwana*. It is best not to be slow if we must arrive at Witu for sunset,' said Juma, and set off at a ferocious pace. Louise and Fallon used to laugh at the extraordinary speed with which the men of Lamu invariably walked when outside the town. Fallon had a theory that they were so accustomed to forcing their way through soft sand, with the extra muscular effort that that required, that on firmer ground their legs declined to accept the easier option and simply sped them ever faster in compensation. Now here was Juma, his *kikoi* knotted loosely beneath a bulging belly – staying up heaven knew how – his enormous, splayed feet jammed into crude sandals, his legs pounding away like pistons. It would be too humiliating to beg a slower pace, thought Fallon, especially after he had made a fool of himself disembarking from the dhow, when he had pompously declined the porters' attempt to carry him to dry land according to local custom and had instead plunged into the mangrove branches, shuddering at the sensation of warm and murky dirt, suddenly terrified of snakes, with the result that his trousers were soaked to the crotch and the natives gazed at the white man in astonishment.

They found the main track – Rogers would know it well, he

observed to Juma, who contradicted him and replied that the Major normally came in to Kipini, thirty miles down the Coast – which was fortunately built up an all-important foot or two above sea level, because the Rains had been heavy and the *shambas* were flooded for miles around. As they moved inland, and the sun moved higher and his trousers dried, the open farmland and the floodwater slowly yielded to bush or low scrub, and the occasional run-down mango orchard. They saw no game except for a family of warthogs, and no slaves in the fields, nor did they meet any travellers on the road, which was now deteriorating into frequent patches of soft sand in which with every stride they slipped back an inch, so that Fallon's calf muscles began to protest and the soles of his feet threatened to blister.

Juma said, 'It will be easier in the Forest. Easier for your feet, but not so safe,' and shook with his infuriating laughter. Fallon suggested that beyond the Forest there were the plains and then the mountains – Africa gets easier all the time, he protested, once you have managed to make your first landing. 'But *bwana*, we are not going beyond the Forest.'

The march became a monotony as well as an ordeal. Why am I so sure that she is alive, he wondered? Is it because Louise was – is! – so committed to life, so much the opposite of death, more triumphantly so than anyone I have ever known? He remembered how Martha last night had repeated to him the words of her mysterious old lady: 'You must consider that dear Louise is "dead to us", Tom. My friend is very wise.' Had Martha been telling him to let her go? No, she had encouraged him, embraced him, given him her blessing. For the first time, it occurred to him that if he failed to find her – and as he surveyed the glittering empty landscape he felt that he was being entangled in tentacles of despair that were like water snakes in the mud of the mangrove swamp – that would not be the worst of all ends. So long as she was alive, wherever, in whatever circumstances, however foul and degrading, she would somehow rise above them. He understood now that his first grief and distress had been selfish: he had been mourning his own loss. There was wonder enough in that, he granted. He had never before felt such a deprivation, just as he had never known the astonishment and exultation of discovering that his need for, and joy in, this woman did not terminate in the drab aftermath of the sexual act. Now it was she who had, so to speak,

246

got up and dressed and slipped away, and he was the one left to weep alone, as his wife used to, and all the others.

He remembered how Dugmore, in one of those ridiculous Free House meetings, had warned them of the up-country peril of the flash flood. They come down on you without warning, he had said: there is no reason to fear them – that's the point, there's no sign of a storm, there's not a cloud in the sky, the bed of the *donga* you're crossing is dry sand that hasn't seen a trickle for years – and the next thing you know is that there's a wall of water charging down on you, coming from God knows how many miles away, and you haven't got a hope of getting across in time. 'So what's to do?' Goddfrey had asked. 'Stay away from a *donga*,' came Dugmore's laconic reply, and he had added, 'but you can't always do that.' Louise had brought him his flash flood, the dry river valley was in flood at last, but they had both been swept away.

Juma called a halt under a fever tree, and they waited for three hours until the hammer of the sun had faltered. The others slept. Fallon eased his muscles and tended his feet. This is not so difficult after all, he thought. Why didn't Dekker and I insist on Wilhelm departing that damned island weeks ago? Fine, we could have left the useless ones behind in Free House and sent out a pioneer group along this route, rather than wait until we could get onto the Tana. We could have taken Salner and the English boys and Scavenius and Stokkebye and Dekker and me and Louise.... Well, that wouldn't have worked. Louise hadn't shared Martha's passion to get moving, she never denied she rather enjoyed life in Lamu, and especially, she used to say, her life on Shela beach. '*Here* is your Freeland...' – he remembered his fatuous line and groaned out loud, and one of the porters looked across at him and muttered a contemptuous phrase to his companions about the stamina of the *mzungu*. I should have resisted her, thought Fallon. I knew that Dekker and Martha were right, and I allowed her to tempt me aside. She seduced me in this as well, and it brought us to – to this. (At that moment he acknowledged to himself that he would fail to find her, but he did not even think of turning back.)

Witu, which had featured so recently amongst the concerns of Europe's diplomatists, turned out to be a scruffy village surrounded by dense forest. Juma became nervous when they entered the Forest, and insisted that Fallon carry his gun and bring up the rear of the tiny column. Fallon was more sanguine, now that they had patches of shade to give them respite from the sun as it began to drift downwards and beam into their eyes. The village seemed half-deserted. He could see at once the smithereens of the famous stockade of Simba, blasted down by General Fremantle's seven-pounders, just as he could see the line of half-built go-downs and huts that were rising, at the reluctant pace of the Tropics, on Rogers's orders. No, said a clerk, summoned by Juma, Major Rogers is in the Forest with his *askaris*, and the *sharif* is visiting the Sultan in Zanzibar. 'Keeping out of Rogers's prison,' thought Fallon. 'He say you can use the *sharif*'s hut next door to the prison,' said Juma. 'Very comfortable! It has a net.' 'Where is Harry Singh?' asked Fallon, remembering Dugmore's brief. 'He is also in the Forest.'

So what the hell do I do next, wondered Tom Fallon as he lit a pipe to deter the mosquitoes after a miserable supper, most of which had been consumed by Juma. He knew that his exhaustion was feeding his indecision and his depression. What shall I do if I cannot find Rogers? If only I had not wasted all those weeks in that place – I could have been preparing myself, like Dekker. He said to Juma, 'So this is the famous Witu, the paradise of all escaped slaves?' 'The *watoro*, *bwana*. They came here for many years, since Sultan Simba.' 'Why? Were they safe here?' '*Bwana*, because there were so many of them, Simba made an army. And afterwards, the Germans pretended to give them protection. Until General Mathews arrived and kicked them out – Simba too!' He cackled.

'Were the *watoro* happy here?'

Juma looked dubious. 'They were the subjects of Simba. They obeyed him when he said, "Work on this *shamba*", or "March in my army". If they were slow, he sold them to the Somalis.'

'So they were really free?'

'Freer than before, I think, *bwana*. Just a little. Not very much.'

'And now, Juma?'

'It is better for some. But many *shambas* are empty. And Suleiman Kimenya is seizing many, many people to be slaves.'

'That's why Major Rogers is here?'

'That is true. But the Forest is very big, and Suleiman is moving all the time. Major Rogers has ordered there must be no more stockades. But in the Forest it is easy to make a stockade, and now that the Somalis are here so often the people prefer to build one, even if it is forbidden, because the *askaris* do not stay.'

In Free House one night Dugmore had said, 'They're not free, you must remember, they're simply a miserable gathering of individuals and eccentrics and villains hiding behind wooden fences – runaways like yourselves! Ha!'

'What the hell do you mean by that?'

'No offence, I'm sure. Now sit down, old man, no offence! Just pulling your leg...'

The Witu mosquitoes were not impressed by the pipe. He went to huddle under the net that was suspended over the simple reed mat.

In the early morning, he told Juma that they would go on to Safareh – 'or perhaps I mean New Safareh. Captain Dugmore said the Major would probably be there, and he seems to know what's going on.'

'That is very dangerous, sir. The Forest is very thick, and the sergeant will not give us any more *askaris*.'

'I have to find the Major. I have important information to give him about the slave route.'

Juma shook his head apprehensively. 'I shall ask.'

There was a child hovering twenty yards from the hut, terrified to approach closer yet unable to retreat from the sight of the remnants of their breakfast laid out on a stool. It was a little girl, no more than five, and she was hollow with starvation under the rag which was her only decency.

'Who is she?'

'She is a slave child. She has lost her mother – her mother has been taken north. No-one knows who she is.'

'But what is to be done for her?'

'Sir, Major Rogers has seen her. He is sending her to Lamu.'

It was a day of frustration, but of course he had known it would be like that. They set out, under the shadow of Juma's undisguised disapproval, on a rough track that struck vaguely north through a belt of thick bush. They saw impala and a buck, and there were birds whose names Juma did not know, perhaps because he was scanning the path ahead with such apprehension, his Martini held tightly in his great paws. There were pools of water on the track, and the sand-soil was damp and difficult for walking. Once there was a sudden storm which soaked them, even though they were half-sheltered under a baobab, and the thunder sounded ten seconds' distance from the lightning flash. The second storm hit them in mid-afternoon: this time the lightning was overhead, the thunder threatened their eardrums, and there was a clatter and crash of branches wrenched from the trees around them by the violence of the tempest. This is dangerous, thought Fallon, and heard a porter shouting, pointing across a clearing at a low roof sunk almost to ground level. The four of them scampered through the flailing grass and leapt inside. There was a stench, and a litter of timbers, but it was a refuge from the storm.

After a minute or two, when they had recovered their breath, Juma said, 'Do you know what you are sitting on, *bwana*?'

It was a rough log – no, it was two logs, or rather, it was one log slit in two and fitted together again. He looked – it was a long bough – and saw that circular holes had been gouged out of the heart of the joint-log, the diameter of – what? – a leg? an ankle? He worked it out in his head, and saw that at each extremity of the log there was a large staple and a hasp, no padlock visible. The circular holes were spaced symmetrically so that a dozen human beings would be able to lie side-by-side, as in a great communal bed, firmly secured by their legs while they awaited their passage to points north. Juma read his mind. 'The Royal Navy, which I am greatly honoured to serve – and well rewarded for my pains! – has made it very dangerous for the dhow captains to convey the slaves up the Coast. But the Royal Navy, *bwana*, cannot come into the Forest. That is the job of Major Rogers and his *askaris*.'

When he woke in the morning (the storm had not lifted so they had pitched camp, insofar as they could do so, in the slave go-down), he discovered that the porters had disappeared. They had not taken the guns and the modest supplies, which Juma declared to be astonishing good fortune. 'These fellows are rubbish, always rubbish! They take their rupees and *skidaddle* at first opportunity. Now we go back to Witu before Suleiman discovers us ...' He mimed the flat of the hand across his enormous throat.

'Like hell we do. We're going to Safareh.'

'No, sir, it is too dangerous. Captain Dugmore told me not to let you do foolish things. Now we go back, please.'

'You want me to put a bullet in your yellow head?'

'Please, *bwana*, be sensible. I am Navy Interpreter First Class, and Suleiman has sworn to crucify me. It is too dangerous!'

They argued for half an hour. In the end Fallon gave up. He said, 'How far is Safareh?'

'Ten miles or so.'

'Then I'll go there myself. Will I find *askaris* there?'

'How can I say, sir? I do not know if Major Rogers has been there this time.'

Fallon would never know that Rogers was at that moment marching back to Kau, in order to canoe down the Tana to rejoin his steamer at Kipini, and thence return to Lamu.

Tom Fallon wandered northwards along the thin and sandy track. He carried Dugmore's gun as a cosmetic device, and a couple of water bottles. The rest he had left with the querulous and apprehensive Juma. *Ego te absolvo*, he had declared to the man, and wondered if he was getting lightheaded. He had lost all sense of urgency. He would find Rogers or he would not. He knew that he would not find Louise Sasse. Soon, he would be lost in Africa as surely as she was. To the north, deep in the Forest, he heard a rattle of firecrackers, and slowly worked out that it must be the sound of gunfire.

There was an irony in this, and he smiled smugly to spot it. She and he – the two who had been the happiest on the island – had turned out to be the first to venture into the interior. Would the others follow him? He no longer cared, he had more important things to work out. He was striving to understand. That the woman had led him here. That he had arrived here too late. That – notwithstanding – he had come here for a purpose. That he had journeyed here out of some guidance that he did not comprehend. 'Grant, O God, Thy protection, And in protection, strength; And in strength understanding, And in understanding knowledge...' began the Gorsedd prayer his grandmother had taught him, and his preacher's brain took it up automatically...

Well, no need of that. It was obscurely satisfying to him that he, and in her way Louise, had turned away from the island, as if they had understood its dangers. He regretted nothing. He wished he might have found her, but they had both left it too late. He knew what he had lost, and that was understanding enough, and therefore strength, and perhaps the rest of it.

He had come out of the Forest into a clearing, a great glade of yellow grain, and in the middle of the glade there was a structure.

At first he thought it was a copse of close-growing high trees, then he saw that it was a species of village, a dense fence of timber protecting something that was hidden within. I have come to one of the stockades, he realised; these will be the runaway slaves in their own Freeland. He remembered Dugmore's instruction and pointed the heavy gun at the sky, hauled back the metal lever which was evidently the safety catch, and pulled the trigger.

They took away the gun. More accurately, it was he who laid it on the ground when a dozen of them surrounded him and held him in the sights of their motley arsenal. He walked, as of his own decision, through the gap they had opened in the stockade. No-one touched him or abused him. He tried a few *Salaams*, but no-one would respond, which surprised him, because it is a part of the world where the courtesies are observed in every circumstance. He had wit enough to understand that they were all very frightened.

They took him to a hut, and allowed him to rest and drink water and compose himself, and then they took him to a man of whom, without a doubt, they were all utterly terrified. Fallon noticed this and was irritated by it: for some reason hidden in his past, he had always hated to see his fellow creatures cringe before the master, the owner, the headmaster, the bishop, the policeman, whoever. Especially when there was no reason, and he reckoned that usually there wasn't. And here he saw a little runt of a man – a Somali, he guessed, from the high cheekbones, the thin nose, the pock-marked complexion, above all the innate, inbred, inextinguishable arrogance of that race. The man was reclining on a string bed in the shadow of a thatched hut, playing with a long string of amber beads and drinking from a handle-less cup in the Arab style. He made no move to offer the Englishman coffee from the great brass pot, as convention surely required. His head was covered in a tangled turban of red and white cotton; he had a wispy beard and wore in his belt a broad Omani dagger with a carved rhino-horn handle; his rifle was propped, within his reach, against the door jamb of the hut. A young Swahili appeared, dropped to his knees in the dust: he was, he quavered, the interpreter.

Fallon said, 'Please make my excuses for my inability to make the proper greetings. I do not have the Somali tongue, nor even Swahili.' That will be my last apology, he promised himself.

The boy gabbled away, and the man did not even bother to look at him, nor reply.

Fallon, seized in that moment with understanding, said to the interpreter, 'Am I addressing Suleiman Kimenya?'

The Swahili could hardly put that as a question. He gazed at Fallon as though dumbstruck and, after a long interval, he nodded as though he could not understand the Englishman's insouciance.

'Then tell him,' said Fallon, who realised that somewhere on the voyage from Lamu he had ceased to esteem his life, 'that I have been looking for him. Tell him that I am in search of a European lady. A colleague of mine from Lamu. I have reason to believe that she is in this Forest, in which case Suleiman Kimenya will certainly know of it.'

The Swahili muttered busily.

'Tell him,' said Fallon, 'that I know that Bwana Rajees is also seeking her. It will be better if I recover the lady. Otherwise much blood will be shed. Assure him that that can still be averted, if he is wise. It is still possible for Suleiman to return to his own country before Bwana Rajees brings his *askaris*. But we must have the woman back.'

He paused while this was translated; he wondered whether he should say it. He added, 'I am here to pay her price.'

He knew at once that he had made a fatal mistake, and he shuddered to discover it. He had joined their game. He had accepted their rules. He could not win.

Suleiman Kimenya looked across at him for the first time, and the invariable arrogance towards the Unbeliever had become contempt and dismissal. He uttered – what? – one sentence, perhaps two. Fallon was seized by two giant guards and hauled back as Kimenya strode from the circle without another glance. The Swahili said, 'Beg pardon, sir, but he says you come from Bwana Rajees, so we cut your head. Very soon.'

Fallon lay in the dust of the hut, and this time his arms were strapped behind his back. He was thinking, Dear God, the man did not deny it, is it possible that I saw an expression on his face which could have acknowledged that he knew of her? If she has not been here, why don't they tell me? If Rogers has been nearby and she has been killed as a result, Kimenya would surely have told me so in order to hurt me, because he is a man who exists in order to give pain.

He took some consolation in that line of deduction. A little. Then he added as an afterthought, But I don't think she can still be here – in fact, I'm sure of it. That must mean she has been passed on already. To the north. Where they will value her, after their fashion. And, he went on, in his frantic, terminal thinking, So she is safe from Kimenya. Then let Rogers come and destroy him – please, Lord! – and it became the irresistible prayer of the agnostic in desperate crisis: Dear God, if you exist, please help me now...

Tom Fallon did not go as far as that. Dear God, he might have said, please save Louise. As for himself, he knew that he was beyond salvation, and he accepted that as a just exchange. He was remembering again his grandmother's Gorsedd prayer – how did it go on? 'Grant, O God, the love of all existences, the love of God, God and all Goodness...' That went too far for him. The love of all existences, yes indeed. God and all Goodness? That he would never understand. Perhaps if he had been granted the fullness of his years he might have learned to return to – well, to some of these things, because they were his inheritance, and an inheritance cannot ever be denied, however you may reject it. For the moment – and that was apparently going to be the final moment – he could only say, Dear God, if you exist, please save Louise. Which was a peculiarly limited and banal conclusion for a man's philosophy. He'd have liked to tell Dekker about that. And one more thing: he hoped that Rogers would understand, in his limited soldier's way, that he – and Louise too – must be avenged. He had not got to the point where he was interested in forgiving his enemies. Leave that for the next time round.

He did not attempt to struggle when they came for him. They half-carried him as though they did not have faith in the courage of his legs. Someone unlashed his hands. He was propelled out into the softening, dusty sunlight into a circle of unknowable black faces; he heard a hum, a murmur of voices, and who knows whether they were voicing bitterness or sympathy. Suleiman Kimenya was sitting on a rough stool and this time he was gazing at him, grinning, as though he was testing the European fear of death. Next to him was a big buck nigger who held a long, silver blade.

Tom Fallon looked up at the sky, the drifting Rainy-Season cloud, just once. His strong heart beat the blood through his veins as he paused for this moment to know and to accept this African destiny. The blood pulsed, his every sinew tightened, his cock stiffened, he felt a terrible strength, he shook off his guards like puppy dogs and raced straight into the embrace of the astonished, panicking executioner, and as the startled sword plunged under his breastbone his arms splayed wide, his seed spilled out, and his heart's blood spurted in a mighty stream onto the dust, so that Kimenya was startled, drew back instinctively, and looked around to make sure no-one had seen his fright.

'Into Thy hands...' said Fallon, but the blackness enfolded him even as his body hit the ground.

*

Dugmore used to say, 'I gather that Rogers went back to the mainland in the blindest of furies – he seemed to have lost all sight of restraint. Funny business! He's always been such a cautious bugger. Stickler for regulations, don't fire till you're dead, set your sights low – look at him today, for Christ's sake! – but when he went back to Witu in August '94 he was on some sort of private crusade. I used to wonder what had come over him. Of course, his patience had been severely tested, not least by yours truly, and the Dekker affair on top of all the rest must have pushed him over the edge. Truth to tell, I reckon he was lucky to get away with it. I made a point of asking his NCOs about that particular operation whenever I bumped into them in the next year or two, and they used to roll their eyes – yes, I promise you, they used to roll their eyes like this! – and clam up very tight. No-one ever did a body count, that's clear. Which is why I say it's funny – old Rogers never had a thirst for blood, everyone agrees he used to lean over backwards, still does today, so what went wrong in '94 to put him into this terrible anger? Of course, he was a pal of Arthur Hardinge, one of Hardinge's blue-eyed boys, so I suppose they hushed it up. What's that? Yes of course he did a "good job", as you put it. We haven't had a squeak out of Witu ever since. Don't get me wrong, I'm not *criticising* Rogers. I'm simply *commenting* that it was a funny business...

'You remember – no, you don't, but I do – that he'd managed to shove the Freelanders off the island, all but poor old Sasse, who lost his marbles. They were supposed to be sent packing back to Europe, though I know for a fact that quite a few of them – those that were left alive, I should say – went south. They probably knew that the *gendarmerie* was waiting for them back home! Then, after the Dekker business, Rogers made it clear that Felix and I must take our *congé*, so to speak, and I did a spot of shooting down towards Kilimanjaro and – well, here I am, a reformed character, and Uganda calls again. But I kept my ear to the ground, and I know that as soon as we were out of the way he rounded up every *askari* he could muster, leaving the island *dangerously* unpoliced, and set off again for Witu. He said he was looking for Tom Fallon, it was his duty. I reckon he was also looking for Louise Sasse. And, most of all, he was looking for Suleiman Kimenya. Why? Because he'd got it into his head that Suleiman was at the other end of the slave chain I was talking about just now. I don't know what evidence he had, but this was the time, remember, when Rogers refused to speak to the *Wa-Germani* on his patch for twelve whole months – in the end they protested to Zanzibar that he wouldn't even accept their mail, and Hardinge had to intervene. But by that time Bwana Pembe was dying of sleeping sickness and Rogers probably felt his prayers were being answered one by one.

'Rogers's problem all along (just as it was mine when I briefly filled his shoes) was that he was short of *proof* where the Germans were concerned. We never had a slave who could point a finger at the Germans, let alone anyone more substantial. He found a couple of women in New Safareh who said a large party had gone through a month before, travelling from Lamu with *wazungu*, but they couldn't begin to distinguish one white man – or woman – from another. I used to think that it all went to prove my own strategy at Shela, which was to catch them red-handed: that's why I left the poor bloody slaves in the pit for one more night so as to ambush whoever turned up to collect them. If we'd freed them that afternoon, as Rogers said I should have, we'd have blown the gaffe and left the culprits free to start again another day. The brilliance of the *Eden* operation was that it had *white* men to run the boat. The German plan – if my suspicions are correct and, gentlemen, I can't prove a word of this, so please don't quote me – was superb because their involvement was so minimal, it was simply to pass messages between Suleiman and Selling.

'No, Rogers didn't find Fallon, nor even, for that matter, Fallon's body. Nor did he find Madame Sasse, nor *her* delightful body. I'm told he drew a blank on the lady – he discovered just enough to conclude that she *might* be alive, but was at best adorning some *harem* across in the Gulf – whereas he managed to find witnesses

256

to Fallon's death. Awful story, I don't like to dwell on it – of course, the chap was just the slightest bit crazy, we all knew he was her boyfriend, it had been an open secret in Lamu that season, but when she disappeared he lost all proportion, charged around the island – all of us trying to help, of course – and then set off for the mainland on a hunch. Fair enough: if what we later heard is true, his hunch was spot-on. She'd been grabbed at Shela, and shipped pretty quick (no, not in the launch, must have been a dhow) over the other side and into Suleiman's network. I still don't believe our German friends had anything to do with it, but Suleiman would have had one look at her and *known* that she spelled big shekels a few miles to the north. A splendid woman, I assure you. But she was a commodity too dangerous for Suleiman.

'He learned his lesson. Rogers came in – how do they say? – like a wolf on the fold. He pounded those village stockades until the poor bloody slaves (because that was what they were) were begging for mercy and the chiefs were running away so fast there was a pile-up on the track to Somalia. I once asked Gopal Singh, his Subedar-Major – there's a splendid soldier for you! – whether it was true that Rogers and Co had taught those chaps a lesson they'd never forget, and he got very coy with me and would only say, "Everywhere we went, Captain, my Major was asking for news of two *wazungu* – a man and a lady." Apparently Rogers went straight for New Safareh, rushed it without worrying about his own casualties, and found only a couple of ancient slaves left there to wait for the Somalis. He also found a fellow called Haji who, as he knew from Hardinge, had for years been an important figure in the slave trade between Kenya and the Somalis. Let's not ask what happened next! Suffice it to say that Rogers got what he needed and went off into the Forest without a pause, except to destroy all the crops he set his eyes on. Haji wasn't seen again, that's for sure. Rogers was using Boni guides, and he sent off a dozen separate parties down the Forest paths, and within three days, thanks to Haji squealing, Suleiman was in the bag – dressed as a woman, it was said at the time, and hiding in a cow byre.

'Well, we'll never know the detail of what happened in Witu Province in August. There's been a conspiracy to keep it quiet, and I don't blame them. I'd have done the same myself. Rogers found his witnesses to Fallon's death – nothing to do with Madame Sasse's fate. He had them travelling with him, so he didn't feel

257

obliged to take the prisoner back to Lamu. Had the trial in the morning – all perfectly proper, I'm sure. Murder of Englishman T. Fallon, that sort of thing, how d'you plead? Sentenced to death. "So let's get it over," said Rogers, who was very cool (or so I was told by Gopal Singh).

'He told me Suleiman had all the dignity of his race – and you can't deny that they have guts, those Somalis. He saw his time was up, though he was apparently a bit rattled when he discovered he wasn't even getting another night to meditate on his sins. Still, he looked Rogers in the eye, and drank a little water, and washed himself and made his prayers.

'Rogers – I know this as a fact, he told me so himself years ago – used to hate executions; he never attended them. But this time, said Gopal Singh, he marched out into the dust and chose a whopping big mango tree and said, "Subedar-Major, the rope over that branch, I suggest," and he stood there, waiting.

'Poor old Suleiman – no, I jest, he was a murdering swine who deserved to end this way – was brought out and still managed to keep some dignity, heaven knows how. Then – and this is where the story turns rough – Rogers said, "Not too high a drop, Subedar-Major," and Gopal Singh must have given him a leery look but did what he was told and ordered the *askaris* to lower the step. That was the moment where Suleiman's nerve apparently cracked. He realised what was going on and began to shout in his own lingo, but they had a couple of big corporals to hold onto him. Still, he managed to wriggle half-free, and he actually spat at poor Rogers, which annoyed Gopal Singh, who hit him a tremendous crack on the mouth and Suleiman's turban fell off, and they all realised for the first time that he was bald as a coot. The fellow suddenly looked twenty years older as well as pretty pathetic, what with the blood dripping into his beard. I gather they didn't bother to give him back his turban; he didn't need it where he was going, Gopal Singh said to me. Rogers was apparently as cool as an iceberg. "You may proceed, Subedar-Major," was all he said, and he gazed Suleiman in the eye like a boy outstares a dog. He didn't even bother to wipe the spittle off his shirt. It's not a pretty image, that scene – not the sort of thing we came to Africa to do, I sometimes think – until you remember Fallon and Louise. When Suleiman was dangling under the mango tree, still very much alive and only just starting to do the St Vitus's dance, Gopal Singh went up to him, pretty carefully to avoid the shit, so as to hang his weight onto the man's legs and speed a decent end, as we always try to do.

'Rogers said, "Stand back, Subedar-Major. Let the man die without your aid." And – I'm told – he stood there and watched the bugger strangle. Slowly. Gopal Singh admitted to me that Rogers couldn't take the whole performance and left before the end. So the Sikh – good chap! – cut his throat with a bayonet, the way those fellows kill their animals, and told the *askaris* to bury the body at once so Rogers wouldn't know.

'I wouldn't ever mention this to him if I were you. He's probably trying to forget it. The whole damn story, I mean...'

Twelve

For man is by nature a monogamous and monandrous being; polygamy and polyandry are inconsistent with the fundamental characteristics of his nature; they are diseases of civilisation which would vanish spontaneously with a return to the healthy conditions of existence.... In Freeland conjugal fidelity is without exception the rule, and unfaithfulness is regarded as a kind of mental aberration.... The sympathy between husband and wife is the strongest, the most varied and the most comprehensive of all. The woman possesses those very excellences of heart and intellect which most charm the man, and the excellences of the man are just those which the woman most highly prizes. Nature, which has physically adapted the sexes to each other, has also psychically formed them as complementary halves...

Theodor Hertzka: *Freeland: A Social Anticipation*

They left Lamu discreetly at first light. Felix Thomas was the only Freelander to stand on the quay and wave goodbye to their dhow, and he seemed to do so without enthusiasm; he was subdued as well as deferential, and when he walked slowly back to Free House as the sun rose between Manda's two baobab trees his face was slack with apprehension, as though burdened with some Celtic intuition. Julius Wilhelm did not appear that morning. The talk at breakfast was of plans for departure, interspersed with bold promises of defiance.

Dugmore said, 'We have to go in over the sand bar. That's the only tricky bit. We can't take it slowly, as I'd prefer, because the waves will sweep us inshore, but our stout friend here assures me he did it two days ago and the Tana is still rising...'

The sea had suddenly lost its sapphire transparency and was thick with rust, stained red and clouded with the silt swept down by the Big Rains of the African interior. The helmsman called out in Swahili to Dugmore, and cackled cheerfully. 'He says the silt is good luck – it keeps the sharks away.' 'Sharks?' 'Yes, there are always thousands of hammerheads at the mouth of the Tana. Be warned, by the way: Kipini always stinks of drying shark meat, but it makes a change after the pong in Lamu.'

Martha was holding Dekker's hand as the three of them huddled low in the dhow, sheltering from the shower of spray; once, she turned to Dugmore and spontaneously pressed his hand, silent, her eyes shining with her gratitude to him. He never forgot that image. She didn't even notice it when they swept over the spit of sand which had held them away from the mainland for so many weeks. The sail came clattering down and the last wave floated them into the approaches to Kipini; they were only yards from a tousled white beach, and she saw that it was littered with thousand upon thousand of the vicious and beautiful jawbones of giant swordfish. She could hear curlew and plovers; an oystercatcher danced over-head. The dhow captain beamed at her, gap-toothed, and she thanked him in Swahili, which surprised and delighted him. She leapt onto the beach and crunched across the coarse sand.

'Now we transfer,' said Dugmore. 'There should be three canoes – the big dugouts. I specifically instructed that they must be big enough to sit steady in the water. One for us, the others for your stores. Then we'll see whether it's going to be easy sailing. But first we prepare ourselves for the curse of the Tana River...' and he produced a raffia bag stuffed with a weird assortment of muslin, butterfly nets, shrouds, yards of elastic and a large medicinal jar. 'Carbonic ointment and paraffin,' he explained. 'It's not foolproof, but everything helps. Now we must button ourselves up, trousers into boots, and – Madame – you must secure your skirts.... The best advice I can give you for Golbanti is to defy the heat and try to wear two layers of clothing wherever possible. The wretched fly will get through the outer garment, but is usually defeated by the second.'

He demonstrated how to put on the face nets, and if Martha had still been writing to Hamburg she would have explained what a 'hilarious' sight they presented when the Captain led them to their waiting oarsmen. She would also have told her sisters that he was entirely right about the mosquitoes. They lived on the river in countless millions. Every leaf, every blade of grass, was coated with them, and – as she was about to discover – their attentions in full daylight were nothing compared with their onslaught at sundown, when they woke anew and coated themselves, like the sand blowing on Shela beach, on every item of human anatomy. She watched in horror as the oarsmen, naked above their loin cloths, would every minute brush a hand down an arm or chest to leave dozens of the beasts crushed and the skin wet with blood.

The better discovery was that Dugmore had been right, the Rains had been so heavy that the river was in high flood and for miles around them the land was underwater. This was great good news, he told them, because the Tana is the most convoluted river in Africa, it twists and turns upon itself so that you have to row five miles of river-length to cover one mile as the crow flies, but at this time of year – 'and I wonder, Dekker, why the Freeland Association did not discover it' – you can hope to cut every corner and sail over the open *shambas*, thus reducing the journey time considerably. 'But I regret,' said their mentor, who was manifestly in high good humour to be off the island, 'that first we must traverse the Belazoni Canal. That is a pretty name for a very narrow ditch which was dug years ago to connect this river – which is technically called the Ozi – to the Tana River proper. I mention it because it is so narrow we shall have to walk while they pole the dugouts through the Canal. That will be about two hours, and the path is likely to be wet.'

Martha said, 'Captain Dugmore, if I am going to settle in this continent I can certainly manage a few miles on foot, if that's what concerns you.'

'Jolly good! That's the settler spirit. So – first, we have about ten miles drifting down this bit of the river. There'll be mangrove on either side, it's a bit spooky but we're quite close to the sea – just over those dunes, we'll be able to hear the waves – and we'd better watch out for hippo. Then we get to Kau, which usually has a couple of Rogers's *askaris* based there. It's a miserable place, I always think – just a collection of huts and a strong whiff of the slave route. Lots of crocodile when I was last here. Then we have our constitutional along the Belazoni, and after that it should be a straight course, straighter than I bargained for, to Charra and Golbanti. We'll be going through patches of forest – lots of syca-more, always a bit of a surprise to find it in Africa, I always feel. That bit of it can be pretty dark and the men will have their work cut out to control the boats against the eddies, but they're good, I can tell, so just sit tight – God knows how an unwieldy steam-

262

launch like the *Eden* would manage in this current – maybe Selling was right, what?

'Keep an eye out for snakes on that last stage. They hang in the bushes, and if we're going cross-country we might disturb them. Leave them to the kaffirs, they're very quick at killing them with a blow of a paddle, no need to waste my cartridges!' He looked at them nervously, conscious that he was going on like the vicar showing the squire's guests around his church. 'You observe what I'm saying, I hope – it's the first miles inland which are the difficult ones.'

As usual, Dugmore was accurate. The walk along the side of the Belazoni Canal was slow and boring and hot and slippery – slow because the men had trouble with the heavy canoes, which were wider-beamed than the norm. After an hour they stopped at a tiny village to wait for the dugouts to catch up with them. It was a wretched place, and Dugmore would not allow Martha to go into the huts, so the crones and the children brought out stools for them to squat on and an idiot boy proffered *dafu*, which Dugmore permitted because, he explained, the milk of the coconut is pure and wholesome. The boy was taken with Martha's hair: he gazed at it and said something in the local dialect to the old women, who giggled nervously, and then, to Dugmore's fury, he went up to her – bearing another *dafu* as excuse – and attempted to stroke her yellow plaits. She saw that he was innocent and smiled at the boy, but Dugmore was suddenly furious and smote at him with a flurry of obscene Swahili, and even Dekker was distressed and rose from his stool to remonstrate. The boy ran off into the bush, keening, and the old women fell silent.

After the Canal the Forest was wonderfully cool, but full of fly and a mysterious stench, and there were creepers and even flowers which groped at them, but they saw no snakes. The current seemed to be very fierce on this stretch of the river, and the oarsmen struggled and cursed, which Dugmore ignored.

He left them the next day in the near-derelict Methodist mission at Golbanti. It worried him that the place was in a rougher condition than he had expected, but Dekker was very insistent and embarrassingly grateful. The main house was infected with bats, and the stench was alarming. Apart from the constant frantic flutter of the things, every wall was coated with thousands of tiny insects, built like miniature scorpions, which appeared to feed off

263

the inch-deep bat droppings. That's no great problem, thought Dugmore, any team of servants can get rid of the bats and all that goes with them, but how will they ever be able to forget the ghosts of Houghton and his wife and the eleven members of the Mission who were murdered inside this very stockade in '87?

Martha must have read his mind. 'Cheer up, Captain,' she said. 'We have mosquitoes, we have crocodile, we have bats, but promise me the Masai haven't been spotted here for years and years.'

'They must have travelled 300 miles without water to get here. That was more than seven years ago. They won't do it again.' He was thinking, the real danger these days comes from the Somalis, but he said nothing.

He had managed to persuade the local chief to send up a dozen men to start putting things in order. They were Pokomo, and he had always had his doubts about the Pokomo. He said, 'You've got stores for three months. You've got plenty of beads and things for trading. The headman is a decent type. I'll try to get back in – let's say six weeks – and I'll bring more stores with me.' Martha embraced him. His boatmen had lashed their unballasted canoes together; from the ever-increasing speed of the river, it was clear that they were going to have a dangerous and headlong ride to the ocean.

*

Dekker had hesitated only once. They had been walking on the beach path to Shela, and had stopped to rest on the old stone bench on the foreshore which is lapped by the high tide. He had been cursing the feathery casuarina trees, whose maidenhair fronds are never thick enough to be effective shade and whose cobs lodged in his sandals and made him limp like a war veteran.

Martha said, 'Major Rogers is right. He said to me last night, when he was so cross with me about Pier Scavenius, "Don't you understand that Lamu turns its back on Africa? Isn't there a warning for you in that?" I didn't understand what he was getting at – but here we are, enjoying this beautiful place, looking at this wonderful view, and he's right, we are sitting with our backs to Africa!'

'You are telling me that it is time we turned our backs on Lamu?'

'Dekker, my dear, you know it as well as I. We must reject Lamu.

264

We must turn inland. And you know that also. That is what you have been preparing for.'

He weakened and allowed himself to remember that preparation was only a rehearsal, it did not commit him to the act; there was a terrible finality in what she proposed. The coward dies a thousand deaths, he acknowledged; to cross that narrow strip of water would mean that he would never turn back, there was no second chance, no evading the absolute reality of the deed. His head swam with the intoxication of the choice.

'Look at me!' she said. 'You are not looking at me.'

He made himself return her gaze. He loved the flecked blue of her eyes. She said, 'This morning I went to see Ma Fatima. She has offered us her wisdom.'

She has her own interests in mind, Dekker thought, traitorously; the Liwali's mother will be relieved to see us gone, just as she helped Martha send away the young man who knew the secrets of the slave ring. But he knew that this was an unworthy thought, and he said nothing.

'She tells us not to stay here. She tells us to go to the mainland, the two of us, but not to go to the Forest, and to avoid Witu, which she says is dangerous for us. She says that we must find the river and follow it inland, as far as we can and as quickly as we can. She says to get away from this coast and from the lowlands and the people here. She wishes us happiness. I have said my farewells to her, and yours too, although you never met her.'

'She is right. I will talk to Dugmore.'

He dreamed he had come upon an enormous baobab tree which grew in the back garden of his Cotswolds house. He had not realised before that there were baobabs in Gloucestershire. He called Carrie and picked one of the dry, white fruit on the baobab tree and made her nibble at it, and she laughed with joy when she tasted the familiar flavour of cream of tartar. They tell me, he explained to her, that the natives use it to keep thirst away. 'That will be useful to you,' she said, and suddenly she wept, silently. His workmen had been redirecting the stream that flowed past the side of his house, and he saw that there was a danger because – as only he had noticed – the roots of the baobab had been deeply exposed by the erosion of the water over the years. Then, at that very moment of his dream, he watched the great tree topple and fall, with a crash that shook the whole building – though it missed

265

his neighbour's place and caused no damage. He tasted the bitter flavour of disaster averted.

*

After a week, the Golbanti Mission had thrown off its cobwebs, though the smell of bat droppings still lingered in the high corridors. The headman from the tattered village on the river's edge turned out to speak a little Swahili, and Martha charmed him shamelessly, so that they had men and women queueing at the gates every morning, fighting for the chance to work for these crazy *wazungu*. The older ones expected to be required to sing a hymn to gain admittance. Dekker protested, 'I have not come to Africa to play the missionary.' She said, 'We must decide if we rebuild the stockade around the station.' 'I'd prefer not to. I want them to trust us.' 'You mean you have not come to Africa to hide behind a wooden fence.' He embraced her. 'That's Freeland talk.' 'It already seems so far away.'

They selected one house from the dozen and sealed every aperture with netting; they paid particular attention to the *stoep*, so that they could sit out in the evening breeze and defy the mosquitoes which thundered against the thin wall of muslin. The house was soon filled with geometrically-patterned grass mats and heavy unglazed pots from the village, and Martha had taken to wearing a heavy necklace of primitive discs and beads, a gift to her from the headman. They had also taken to heart Dugmore's lesson about double-dressing, and they overcame their sense of the ridiculous and took care to wear face nets whenever possible. Nevertheless, they both went down with fever in the second week, and nursed each other, and even drank a noxious draught offered shyly by their housemaids, and seemed to recover surprisingly fast.

Dekker was studying the Pokomo village system. He saw that they grew rice and maize and a particular large banana down here near the river; from what he could discover through the headman, they also planted beans and millet, sugar cane and pumpkin, in small patches of tilled ground set back from the river, and a rank tobacco which they smoked incessantly.

The headman became a friend. He invited them to visit his hut in the early evening, and they sat outside on heavy carved stools, and the wives brought them dishes of curious and unidentifiable morsels and gourds of their maize beer, which Martha did not like but pretended to enjoy. Then they were visited by a sequence of very old men, with whom they held protracted and tedious conversations through the stumbling Swahili of Martha and the headman. 'We are being vetted,' said Dekker to Martha with delight. 'This is precisely what happened to me when I moved to the Cotswolds. This is the equivalent of the English tea-party.'

She said, 'It is much more serious than that. No-one could refuse to have you in the Cotswolds, but here they are deciding whether we will be allowed to stay.'

'Do we want to?'

'I think so. But I'm nervous. I'm not sure I like this river. It disturbs me. I wish we were in the interior.'

Dekker paced the abandoned land at the Mission's perimeters and calculated that he might concentrate on maize and sugar. He wondered about cattle, and looked out for tsetse fly because he realised that ranching might be impossible. But he was secretly tempted by the crocodiles. It touched a chord from his past – he knew there would be a market among his former customers for well-cured skins – for handbags, shoes, belts, luggage, toys for rich Europeans. He would need to talk to the headman. The villagers, he had observed, were almost amphibious, they lived on the river, they were never away from their dugouts, they all swam like ducks, and their delight was to take their spears with foolhardy bravery to hunt the giant Tana crocodile, not for the skins but for the musty reptile flesh – Martha gagged on it. Then there were the *mamba* catfish, which they gathered in great numbers in the shallows by spearing them with long, hardwood tridents: no, there was no European market for smoked catfish, the very sight of the things was repellent, and they tasted almost as bad as they looked. Women were not permitted to fish: there was a strict taboo.

For the first time in years, his commercial instincts revived. He said to Martha, if we stayed here for a while – and I know that we both want to press on inland – we could salt the croc skins and send them down to Lamu and on to Europe. I could ship them to Robert in Bond Street and Lorenzo in Rome.

'We'd need the agreement of the *ngadzi*.'

'Not the headman?'

'No, the *ngadzi* are the elders. I think they are a sort of secret society who keep the tribe's sacred objects somewhere in the Forest – drums and sticks and magic necklaces. They will tell the headman what he is allowed to do. They are the old men we met the other day.'

Dekker was permitted to attend a meeting of the *ngadzi*. Martha was excluded, which made for a serious language problem. He had much recourse to mime, as he struggled to explain his plans for the crocodile skins, and the old men squealed with affectionate laughter. He didn't really understand whether or not they understood him, or were interested. They were all smoking a strange leaf and insisted he join them: he would have declined but feared it would insult them, so he joined them, reluctantly. Late that night Martha said, 'What's happened to you?' – but she was laughing.

Then they fell ill again. This time it was much worse, and the noxious drink did not help. Martha was delirious for four days and the servants vanished: perhaps her illness frightened them, he reasoned. When the fever broke, she was very weak and he noticed how her complexion had lost its bloom, but by then it was his turn to collapse, and from the days that followed he retained only fragmented memories of her worried, thin face as he suffered the physical humiliations of sickness in Africa. The headman came to visit him, though Dekker scarcely preserved a memory of it. Martha had not been decently dressed at the time, and the chief was evidently embarrassed: he sent his senior wife later that day, who was a large and cheerful woman who, to their surprise, cheered them and left a girl to clean the house; later she sent food, and Dekker, in a moment of rationality, acknowledged his gratitude to these people on whom they had imposed themselves. He tried to ask Martha 'by what right' they were here, but the fever came down on him again and he was unable to make his point.

It was after his still-frail recovery that they both realised, separately, that Golbanti was wrong for them. At first they did not admit it to the other, she because she was encouraging his plan for a crocodile project, he because he admired the way she had become accepted by the village. But it was their principal, unspoken law that they would conceal nothing from each other, and soon they were able to agree that this place frightened them – why deny it? It was haunted by their slaughtered predecessors; how can you *settle* in a place which is, at a profound level, so *unsettling*?

We shall have to move up-river, they agreed; we always knew that we must penetrate deeper into the interior, we are still only on the fringes of Africa. Inland, it will be easier. And they agreed, as the mosquitoes screamed at them in the clotted moonlight, that they must strike away from this river. The Tana was not the answer. We must aim for higher ground, and eventually for the Highlands. They held each other, and knew that lessons were for the learning, the future was theirs to command.

How life simplifies itself, thought Dekker, as time goes by. How the opportunities fall aside with every new experience. It used to amuse me, as the years drifted away, to watch the list lengthening of the things I would never do – I shall never play the violin, I shall never score a century for my village cricket team, I shall never read Greats at Oxford, I shall never be an opera singer, I shall never understand Aquinas, I shall never visit America, I shall never marry, I shall never write a worthwhile poem, I shall never plant an orchard, I shall never be Prime Minister.... It's a fast-rising curve from the end of our childhood, and now the alternatives are ended, Africa has become my only destination, Martha my only woman. And this I shall never regret. I did not come all this way in order to become a beachcomber on Lamu Island. He had said to her on that ancient stone bench on the path to Shela, 'So we risk all. We risk the great death in order to refuse the little deaths.'

She had understood him at once. 'Do you tell me that there is any choice?'

'I am not old enough to relish the prospect of my old age.'

'And I am not young enough to regret the end of my youth.'

'We are not young, not old. We are in our prime.'

'My dear, when are we in our prime?'

'When we are happy.'

But they fell ill again.

The Pokomo servants had not returned, despite the kindness of the headman and his senior wife, and when Dekker tried to stagger to the village to seek help from the wife he collapsed before he reached the main gate and had to crawl back to the homestead on his hands and knees. Neither of them had much memory of the week that followed. One or other would struggle to the kitchen to stir the embers in the stove and boil water for tea, and sometimes one of them would find the strength to wash the other. One day she saw that the bats had returned, but she may have been hallucinating.

Some of the young girls eventually turned up from the village.

They tried to help, but they were timid and shy and did not know what to do. An old woman brought kaffir beer in a filthy gourd, but Martha was conscious at the time and sent her away. She afterwards thought she remembered a visit by the chief and his wife, both of whom hovered about them in an evident state of distress, and she managed to compose herself and thank them for their courtesy and send them on their way. Dekker was babbling of Hammersmith that afternoon.

There came a morning when they woke on their stained mattress and declared that they were both very much better. 'I shall bring you tea, my dear,' she said, 'and an egg.'

'And I shall bathe myself,' he replied, 'and we shall make a plan.'

She said, 'We must leave this place.'

'That is exactly what I had decided.'

'We shall go inland, away from this deadly river, and find a village. Then we shall send for our things. We'll be better on the high ground.'

Dekker dreamed that he was visiting Greece with Martha Wilhelm and her husband. They were visiting an archaeological site on a mound where ancient kings were buried. Other people were looking at the tombs, with their stonework and trenches and a few battered pillars, but Dekker discovered that there was another tomb being excavated which was going to be even older and more important. He called to Martha to come away from Julius. There was some surface water, and then he saw a deep fissure leading down into the rock, and he glimpsed still, pure water at the bottom. Then they were travelling on a train, still in Greece; he was diffident and timid, assuming that it would be full, but Martha pushed through and found plenty of seats. They came to a Greek village, and Dr Wilhelm had disappeared. The streets were so steep that everyone had to use ladders to go up and down. It seemed to be a cul-de-sac – but no, they managed to squeeze through and they came to a stall selling primitive crafts and a strange, ancient food. An old man was cooking the food on a fire of twigs and cow dung; it smelt so delicious that they stopped with delight and asked if they might buy some, but the old man shook his head and scattered sand on the flames and made gestures to tell them that they were too late.

They left the next day. They carried only one small bag, and Dekker felt obliged to bring a gun because this was leopard country. They

270

also had a small quantity of water and food. They closed the gates but did not bother to look back, and they were too weary to make their farewells to the headman and his village.

The Mission stood on the west bank of the river and was set back half a mile or so, on the first slopes above the village. There was another Pokomo village a few miles to the west, the headman had said, where the tobacco came from, and he had pointed to a narrow track. Dekker and Martha Wilhelm took that path.

It was strange, they agreed, how slowly they seemed to walk. He took her arm, but he, too, was struggling in the soft sand. He did not say to her that his fever was rising again, and she did not tell him that the sky was swinging above her head and the blood roaring in her temples. They agreed that they were both short of breath, and neither admitted to the other that the sweat was bursting in heavy gobbets from their skin. It came into his mind that they were both extremely ill.

After another hundred yards he said, 'My dear, there is an acacia tree over there which will give good shade. We can sit down and rest for a moment.'

The tree was a perfect parasol, its leaves trimmed by the breeze into a perfect specimen of topiary. There was an outcrop of granite fifty yards away, and a scattering of scrub-bush on the biscuit earth. There had been goats there, but not recently. The tree cast a heavy, blessed shadow.

She said, 'Yes, it will be good to rest. I already feel the breeze is doing me good. When it is cooler, we shall go up to the high ground.'

They sank onto the sand and lay back to rest. He drifted, descended, into dream. She took his hand in hers. He held her hand in his.

*

When he woke, Dekker knew at once that the fever had lifted and that he would soon recover his strength. Martha was sleeping next to him and he leaned on his elbow, not to wake her but to gaze at her face. She was breathing evenly, and he guessed that she too was restored.

An instinct told him that they were not alone.

He looked up and discovered that they had come to a small and perfectly proportioned natural amphitheatre of sand and shrub

271

and, he now saw for the first time, ancient stonework. A small group of natives was looking at them. He guessed that they had been there for some time and had been waiting for them to wake. They were shorter and slimmer than the Pokomo, and carried long spears with broad blades, and beautiful deep-arched bows that were taller then they were; they had quivers of frail arrows slung on their backs, and Dekker guessed that they might be Boni. He struggled to find the strength to rise, but a young man who appeared to be their chief gestured at him to stay seated and walked across the sand and greeted him and put his small hand on his forehead, as though he understood there had been a fever. Then he beckoned to the others, who quickly lashed together pairs of spears so as to make stretchers, and lifted him and Martha onto their shoulders. She was still sleeping, and soon Dekker slept too, lulled by the swinging rhythm as the bearers trotted across the sand-bush, away from the river.

When he woke again, he was in a hut of simplest grass thatch supported on four tall poles. He had been placed on a woven reed mat on the plain earth, and by his head there was a gourd of milk. Martha lay next to him, on her own mat; she was breathing steadily, sleeping still, and the fever had gone from her face. Her head was supported on a tall pillow of delicately carved wood.

A slim girl, naked to the waist and with heavy bead and amber necklaces dangling around her breasts, came across to them. She smiled, said nothing, held his head and fed him milk from the gourd, giggling shyly when he splashed it onto his shirt. No, he seemed to be wearing a *kikoi*, they had taken his filthy clothes, and Martha, he now saw, was swathed in white cotton. He guessed there was a medicine in the milk because he sank back into sleep, unprotesting.

When he next emerged into consciousness, he found that he was sitting outside the hut – had he been carried there? – on a wide chair made of thongs and skins and a cradle of rough wooden branches. He knew at once that he must have eaten again, because he felt the strength returning to his limbs. He gripped the arms of the chair, straining at the muscles of his arms and thighs to test them, and breathed deep of the cool air. They had placed the chair on a low belvedere which caught the afternoon breeze and looked westward – away from the river, as he remembered it – across a cluster of valleys.

The main stream, which could only be a tributary of the Tana, flowed brown and strong a mile or so below him, and on the other side of the valley the hills rose again in a pattern that, though parched and studded with bush, reminded him at once of another geography. The hills were divided by a second valley, dark in the afternoon shadow, and at the confluence of the two streams he saw a settlement of beehive huts with dense woodsmoke rising in overhead plumes, where he somehow expected to see a church tower, a cluster of stone-tiled roofs and, in winter, the darker smoke of wet coal. He could hear the peal of goat bells, the trilling of doves, the distant chatter of children at play, a squawl of maternal anger, and where he would have expected to see cattle and sheep grazing in the valley he saw a herd of wildebeest and a pair of noble antelope.

He gazed at all this for many minutes until he realised that the young man who had found them was standing patiently behind him, looking at him with a filial concern. You must rest, he understood him to say, and when Dekker asked him, 'Where is Martha?' the man also understood, and pointed to the hut and gave Dekker his arm to support him. He joined Martha on the yellow-brown mats, and slept again.

It took them a month to recover, on the high ground of the Boni village. Some days, when their blood seemed to thicken again with the poisons of the river, the chief sent old men who prescribed foul drinks which brought a tormented sleep. Afterwards the girls would bring milk and shredded chicken meat and porridge and a thick, sweet beer. Once they brought them heavy steaks of a charred, bloody meat, and there were sounds of celebration down in the village. When they were both strong enough to sit on their chairs at sunset and look out over the game-strewn bush, they wondered about the Mission and the Pokomo and the mosquitoes, and of course they had no regrets. They agreed that the river was not their proper entry point into Africa: it was too easy, and therefore too dangerous. They had learned that they must stick to the high ground, but they were no longer in a hurry.

When he was better, Dekker announced to the chief that he wished to help the villagers. He asked them to send for their effects from Golbanti – and the chief laughed and took him to the next hut and, to his astonishment, it was filled with their stores and supplies from the mission. Martha said, in her new, quiet voice, 'You can help them to hunt. You have the gun, they only have their poisoned arrows and their spears, and last week they managed to kill an elephant. Do you remember we ate some of it?'

'How could they possibly kill an elephant?'

'My dear, here is surely where we shall settle.'

He became their hunter. That was their tradition, he understood, but they were trapped between the Pokomo and the Galla and the Somalis; they had been forced to cultivate these tiny gardens of maize and beans outside their huts, but their passion was for the hunt. He allowed them to teach him, to lead him through the bush, to demonstrate the spoor, and then, after they had hurled their spears and their tiny arrows against the hippo or the buffalo, he would despatch it with a single shot. Dugmore would have been proud of him; he had never used a gun before, and it turned out to be so easy. But never an elephant. He did not believe that he could take on an elephant, and he did not wish it.

Martha's health had returned, and she quickly learned to speak the Boni language. They taught her to cook in the small clay pots which they plunged into the glowing coals, to pound millet in the deep wooden buckets, to brew the beer in their great, misshapen gourds. There was no longer any distinction between master and servant. At dusk they would all sit together on low stools hacked from dead trees, and plait corn dolls or carve long combs out of sycamore wood. The women were slim and beautiful, as were the children; the men were proud and nervous. Dekker knew that they feared catastrophe. He tried to reassure them, but it was not easy because they did not explain to him what they feared.

Many months later – they had chosen to make no effort to observe a calendar – they heard the blast of a distant hooter. They ignored it because they knew that occasionally a government launch attempted to zigzag up-river to Garsen, but no-one ever needed to stop at Golbanti. The steamer was very insistent, for a space of twenty minutes, and they continued to ignore it; they were busy, in their new ways. Dekker said to Martha, 'I don't want to know. Don't you see, someone is trying to call us back?'

After another hour, the chief arrived, and – to Dekker's immediate fury – he was shaking with apprehension. With him was Major Rogers, in starched and pressed tropicals, his topee planted on the bald head. A platoon of his *askaris* had arranged itself around the village, and there was keening in the huts.

Rogers said, 'My dear chap!', or something of the kind, and when Martha came out of the hut he blinked and said, 'Mrs Wilhelm!' and flushed, as though he had made a faux pas, and removed the helmet from the naked head and shook their hands, nervous as a cadet.

Dekker said, 'What the hell are the *askaris* up to?' and Rogers looked at him as though he scarcely recognised him and said, 'Oh, forgive me – that's their normal procedure in a strange village,' and shouted at the NCO to take them away.

They drank tea together, and the villagers came out of the huts and stared at them across the valley. Rogers said, 'Don't misunderstand me, I have not come to take you back. I have come merely to satisfy myself that you have done the right thing. Forgive me, but I imagine that's what you want me to say. You've done the right thing, haven't you?'

'We have done the right thing, Major,' answered Martha.

'Do you need anything?'

'We need nothing.'

'Then I shall leave you to your happy fate. I shall report to London that Freeland exists after all.'

He allowed himself a smile. They all shook hands, and Dekker introduced Rogers to the chief and commended them, each to the other. The face of the chief reminded him of Harold, the best of his Cotswolds foremen.

The seasons passed. Once a Swahili trader came by with a couple of mules and a boy with a gun and proposed, with menaces, to purchase a girl or two. Dekker took his rifle and strolled across, and the Swahili took one look at this wild-haired *mzungu* and left. The next year a caravan arrived – twenty donkeys and an Arab on a fine horse with a dozen rogues brandishing muzzle-loaders. The Boni had seen him coming. The chief suggested to Dekker that he retire to a distance, and Martha with him.

Dekker said, 'Is that your wish?' and the chief said it was.

They went a short distance up the hill where there was a clump of trees. Martha said, 'You know what you will do, if it is necessary?' and he nodded his head. The Arab and his party rode into the village; the women ran into their huts and the menfolk gathered, trembling, in the clearing. Most of them were old because the young men had to go down to the river to find work, and some of them had already vanished into slavery. The Arab, who manifestly took a pride in his flowing robes, rode like a great man into the simple village. He shouted for attention, and the chief, who was a brave man, walked towards him and asked his business. Martha murmured to Dekker, 'This cannot be,' and he said, 'My dear! Shut up...' The Arab produced a whip and addressed his demands to the chief. The elders heard them and groaned and protested, and were silenced by a crack of the rawhide. The chief replied – Dekker could not hear what he said. The Arab shouted at him, and lashed at him with the whip. The chief, holding his bleeding cheek, replied again, and the Arab reached for his rifle.

Dekker shot him between the shoulders. As he did so, he clearly remembered his early-morning objection of principle when he had stood with Dugmore under the spy-tree above Shela beach. I have changed, he thought. The rabble panicked, their horses rearing, the men screaming, and Martha said, 'Best to take one more, for a lesson' and Dekker shot a black NCO between the eyes, and the survivors set off on a mad gallop. The chief held up his open palm in salutation and greeting. When he and Dekker embraced, they were both trembling.

After the Rains that year, the village gave them a new hut and a new *shamba*, which Martha dug and planted. She grew good crops, and Dekker praised her and explained that it would not be fitting, in a Boni village, for him to be seen to help with the tilling and the weeding; she threw a corncob at him, but seemed to accept. He was hunting still, but he now had a private ambition, which was to use his European gun less and less. He studied the skills of the trappers; he learned to mix the dangerous herbs which they smeared on their arrow heads; he practised the thrust of the long-handled spear. In these first years he carried a gun and sometimes he used it, but after a time it was a matter of honour with him to kill with his friends and in their traditional style.

One year the young chief, who was no longer so young, invited Dekker to join the Council of Elders. Dekker said to Martha, 'This is a great honour, but I'd have to go through the initiation – I can't!'

She said, laughing at him,' My dearest, why not?'

'But I *can't* go through an initiation ceremony at my age...'

'Why not?'

'Because – oh, you must know why not!'

'Maybe we could skip that bit of it. We can explain to the chief that you're too old for it to matter.'

'*Too old*?'

She said, 'Let's forget it. No-one is going to take a knife to you, if that makes you feel better. I shall forbid it.'

'No knife, no Council of Elders.'

'So be it.'

One day there was a hubbub below them, and a group of villagers climbed the slope towards their hut with a waving of spears and an unusual air of aggression. Martha ran out and said, 'Oh, let them free. They are friends!' and the Boni released two perspiring and terrified Swahilis. They were Bakari and Saidi.

'Come and rest!' said Martha, and sent for tea; Dekker embraced them and tried to console them and reassure their fears.

After they had relaxed, Martha said, '*Karibu!* But why have you come?' And Bakari said, 'Memsahib, we have come at risk to our lives to invite you to return to us.'

Saidi added, 'Madame, you do not belong here with these kaffirs. You belong with us and with your own people.'

Dekker said, 'You are wrong. We belong here. Tell the world of that. Go in peace. We thank you for your *safari* to visit us.'

So Bakari and Saidi went back to their dugout and returned to Lamu, where no doubt they told everyone that Dekker and Martha were lost to the world.

Dekker grew to love the hunt, and as the years fell away he was honoured by the tribe for his skill. The young men were sent to him to be taught how to mix the roots and berries with the secret parts of animals and the venom of snakes, so as to make the poisons that were smeared on their arrow heads, and then he would accompany them to the daily battle with the kudu and the antelope, the wildebeest and the buffalo, though he knew that he no longer had the agility to race into the herd to hurl a spear or launch another arrow. He carried a gun still, but it had become his pride not to use it. And he understood, with a profound joy, that they killed only

for food: they did not need to challenge the lion, he told them –
wiser to let the lion make the kill and then appropriate the carcass,
as he several times demonstrated – nor the rhino, which he loved
as greatly as they feared, nor even the giraffe, except when they
persuaded him of the irresistible delight of the marrow of its
neck-bones (when Martha turned her back on him after he had
joined the sucking and the slurping around the village fire).

He tried but failed to learn their skill with the snare. They had
a hundred varieties of trap and noose, and the men demonstrated
them to him again and again in return for his own skills, but his
fingers were clumsy with the springs and the grass ropes and the
tension in the saplings. He also knew that he would never learn
their knowledge of the spoor. Nor did he enjoy this style of
hunting, as Martha always reminded him. There was a justice, a
clean necessity, in the sting of the fast-acting poison of the arrow,
the spear to the heart, but the noose around the neck or leg, the
thrashing hours of darkness and terror before the butchers arrived,
disturbed him. As a child he had fantasised that an execution
should be clean and abrupt: how else our fascination with the block
on Tower Hill, the guillotine in the Place Vendôme? His father had
once explained to him that, before his escape from Dresden, he
had dreaded the hangman and would have pleaded for the firing
squad, but, said his father, the jailers had laughed at his protests.

For a similar reason, Dekker used to protest (they used to cackle
with laughter, and a curious affection, as he struggled to find their
words) against their preference for disabling the quarry by slicing
through the hamstring and then dealing with the shrieking animal
at their leisure. Some of the young men were especially trained in
this skill, and it was true that it called for the highest courage and
speed, but Dekker would turn aside and leave them, or else he
would have been too tempted to despatch the desperate creature
with the gun, rather than leave it to its slower torture. He had
once looked into the eyes of a young elephant, its rear limbs
useless, thrashing and trumpeting as it saw its kinsfolk flee and the
men close in for the kill with their spears, and he would take no
more of that.

So he would have sickened of the killing if he had not understood that it was necessary to feed all of them. They had eggs, of
course, and maize flour and greenstuff from Martha's tiny *shamba*;
there were coarse and greasy barbel from the river, and sometimes

the chief sent his young men down to the Tana to trade with the Pokomo and bring back dried fish and strips of crocodile biltong (which Martha refused). She learned from the women how to gather fruit and seeds and roots from the bush. They drank the thick mealie beer, and grew to like it. Once, after an epic hunt, the chief presented Dekker with a bottle of Dutch gin; it would have been an insult to refuse. Martha kept a goat and made a rough cheese from its milk, but knew that the villagers disapproved. At night they held each other, lay together, slept together, fitted, matched – would one day be found together.

In the end, they became hunters of honey. Dekker was fascinated by the small, wild African bees. He had read – or perhaps Dugmore had told him one night in Free House – of the extraordinary and deadly ferocity of the species, and he had seen a swarm descending on the village cause a panic exceeded only by the arrival of the Arab slave train. But then he discovered that there were families in the clan whose function was to gather honey from the bees' nests; their young men were excused from the hunt so long as they supplied the village with the precious sweetness. He approached them and persuaded them that he would not betray their secret skills, and discovered that they worked with – relied upon – the honey bird. They had an extraordinary rapport with these tiny birds: they would summon them from their nests with an uncanny imitation of their chirruping call, and somehow despatch them on the search, racing behind them through the bush. There, almost without fail, the bird would be signalling a swarm. Then the dangerous part would begin, with climbing of trees or scrambling up cliffs, and always the intimidating thunder of the buzzing of a million crea-tures who had it in their power to kill a man in minutes. It was done, always, with great caution, and uttering of ancient prayers, and entirely without protection, and when the smoke made from secret herbs had been puffed into the tree and there was a sudden deafening silence, the hunter would extract no more than was permitted to him (by some traditional understanding) from the amber comb, and he would always, without exception, leave a chunk of the dripping wax conspicuously on the bough or ledge, as necessary reward for the bird who had made it possible.

Dekker studied this operation with the help of his anti-mosquito face net from Golbanti and at the cost of a dozen painful stings, and decided that the area was so richly gifted in bees that the village might be brought to benefit. He talked to the chief, who summoned the honey clan, and for weeks they explored the hillsides together, tasting and testing the different honeys, deciding between the flavours and the consistencies, which varied quite dramatically between one area of bush and another. The villagers preferred the darker nectars, but Dekker persuaded the chief that they should concentrate on the subtler, more fragrant combs on the higher *kopjes*. It was more difficult and more dangerous to reach them, but Dekker had his way, and over the next two years they amassed a great vintage of the finest, most exquisite honeys. They sent them down to the Pokomo village at Golbanti, where the dugouts took them to Kipini and Lamu, where the Denhardt brothers turned out to be efficient agents, not for their export to Europe but for their distribution through the length of the Coast, such was the quality. And the Boni honey became a delicacy of the region for many years to come.

Hunting remained, as it had to be, the central preoccupation of a tribe which had neither space nor inclination to cultivate larger crops. Dekker, having renounced the rifle but failed to master the snare, was attracted by the Boni skills of disguise and subterfuge. He learned to smear his body in a rancid grease made only by an old woman who lived on the outskirts of the village, which prom- ised to allow him to wander, unchallenged, through the herds of game. He experimented over several years. At first he found that the lesser buck would accept him but the antelope and kudu would move away – though without any infectious panic – as soon as they had his wind. So he went back to the old woman, and she adapted her recipes, and one day he found he could walk among zebra and wildebeest, and they moved away only so as to grant him passage. He still carried his gun, but he had forgotten when he had last used it. Martha had observed all this and approved; she cautioned him only against the lion and the rhino, and he promised he would think of her and be prudent for her sake. (They had no child. It was their sorrow, and they knew it was the subject of comment in the village, but they were nonetheless happy in their lives.)

He said, 'I want to pass among the animals and be accepted by them, without fear or flight. When a zebra joins the buck at the waterhole, and the giraffe comes down to drink with the hippo, they do not fear each other. Why can't they learn to accept us on those same terms?'

'When the lion and the leopard come to the waterhole, the others move away.'

'We are not lions, leopards. We simply collect the honey.'

'You are their enemy because you help the village in the killing.'

'That is necessary. The animals also kill each other.'

'The giraffe and the buck do not kill each other.'

'You know that I hardly ever kill these days.'

'I know that. But the animals understand what you do, never mind that filthy stuff you've been smearing on your body.'

Dekker told the chief that he wished to withdraw from the hunting for a while, and the chief (no longer young, but increasingly wise) agreed. Dekker wandered every day amongst the game, coated in every variety of unguent. He was – he told Martha, triumphantly – accepted. There was scarcely a species that moved away from him any more. But she insisted he still carry his gun: 'If you don't,' she said cunningly, 'they will notice the difference and be frightened.'

He was accepted by the buffalo and the wildebeest and the water buck and the giraffe and the rhino and the elephant and the zebra and the eland and the hippo and the gazelle and even by the warthog, but he was rejected by the ostrich, which is the grandest and also the most stupid of birds.

Dekker was angered by this. He wished the ostrich no ill. The villagers did not ask him to shoot it for its mangy flesh, and they did not even try to snare it; they had no difficulty in collecting its eggs, with which they made gigantic and over-rich varieties of Europe's omelettes and sauces, and this tribe had no interest in wearing ostrich plumes.

One day he said to Martha, 'Here, cook it if you wish, I've no idea how, I have shot an ostrich.' She protested. He said, 'I need the skin, the feathers. Just this once, I'm sorry...'

So the next day she saw him go out into the veld in a very approximate and stinking disguise of an ostrich. He had draped the skin and the feathers over his shoulders, though no-one would ever have confused him with the bird. She watched him wander, haphazard, in the direction of a flock of the idiot birds, and she saw that they accepted him, and she was happy for him. She feared at first that they would be frightened by this newcomer and kick him, and she knew they were able to run so fast that he would not be able to escape; also, because of the feathers, he had left his gun at home, but she soon understood that they ignored him, which is after all a form of acceptance. Afterwards, he often brought back ostrich eggs, but he never allowed her to break them open in the European way: he would pierce them carefully, and drain the contents, and then he would hang the shells on a string, suspended from the ceiling rafter at the corner of their hut. He never had more than seven. He searched for the biggest, and the most perfect, and when he found a larger one the smallest was smashed and rejected. Martha had never been to Matandoni, and she did not understand.

It took years before the old woman perfected her ointments for the higher animals. First she found a confection which gave him immunity against – with – the buffalo. Martha had protested, but he showed her that it worked: the buffalo shifted and sidled and even sniffed at him as though he were an English farmhand working amongst the year's new heifers, and although the buffalo is the most dangerous of creatures, he knew at once that he was safe. But with the buffalo, Martha always insisted that he carry the gun.

Now, he said to the old woman, I want to go with the lion, and she nodded and agreed, and after months of experiment she gave him a precious gourd. He said to Martha, 'I go to meet the lion,' and she said, 'So be it.' He walked out of the village, down the slope towards his valley. The afternoon sky was as pale and perfect as the backcloth to a *quattrocento* portrait. When he looked back, a thin column of woodsmoke was rising, vertical in the still air, and he realised with a pang of delight that it came from his own hut.

He walked among the buck and the zebra and the buffalo, and they did not even bother to move to let him through. He saw the elephant, grazing on the trees a mere hundred yards across the *vlei*, and the giraffe next to them, nibbling on the higher branches, and they looked at him and somehow acknowledged him, and resumed their eternal grazing. Then he saw the lions – three of them, two male, one female – who looked up at him and snarled, though not as though to promise attack. Dekker walked towards them, and they held their ground. When he was three yards short of them, he stopped and waited. He gazed on their beauty, and they returned his stare with their golden eyes. Their tails were

282

lashing automatically because the flies were angry overhead. They stretched themselves, and rose, gigantic, on their four legs. He was not frightened. They strolled across to him. He stood still, and then he sank to his knees, and the gun fell, useless, to the ground. The first lion embraced him. Which means that it set its two great paws around his shoulders. Those paws caressed him. They scratched – tore – inevitably, although it was trying to be gentle, through the cotton of his shirt, so that he felt the blood spout from his wounds, but there was no pain in it, just as there was no aggression. He put up his arms and returned the lion's embrace.

Later, when Martha dressed his wounds, and did not reprimand him, she said, 'Ma Fatima has brought me a message.'
'Brought you? Sent you?'
'She has been here to visit me this afternoon. She came by canoe, she could not stay.'
He said, 'What did she tell you?'
'She said that she is old. She came to say goodbye.'
Martha suddenly was weeping heavy, salt tears, not so much of grief as of farewell.
'That was all?'
'She said that she saluted us. I gave her our love.'

The wounds of a lion's claws do not heal easily, and Dekker lay under a fever for many months. Martha had also sickened. They lay for day upon day on their mats, side by side, his right hand invariably clenched in her left. The chief, who was now very old, visited them every day, and the girls of the village looked to their every need. There was one moment when Dekker rallied and said, whether she heard it or not, 'My dear, we are dying...' And she said, though he could hardly distinguish her words, whether it was his weakness or hers, 'Rather this than any other...' And he said, 'Then we have arrived.'
She said, 'Why has that young man been breaking a hole in the back wall of our hut?'
He said, 'My dearest love, you remember that they cannot take the dead through the front door...'
Or he may have thought better of it, and did not say it.
She said, 'I am not so strong as I was.'
He said, 'Perhaps we are at the end.'

283

She said, 'There is no end. You know it. You said yourself that we have arrived. I have always believed you.'

He discovered that he was a young man again, hanging onto a rope, a swing, a giant pendulum, suspended over earth and sea. The rope went up into the sky and – somehow, but there was no doubt of it – it was held firm there. He did not need to worry whether his grip was strong enough, nor whether the rope might fray. So he began to swing to and fro, up and down, daring as a trapeze artist, whooshing from side to side, and in his arms he held – oh, so carefully! – the biggest ostrich egg the world has ever seen.

Thirteen

All that I have described as really happening *might* happen if men were found who, convinced as I am of the untenability of existing conditions, determined to act instead of merely complaining.... The intrinsic practicability of my book extends beyond the economic and ethical principles and motives underlying it, to the actual stage upon which its scenes are placed. The highlands in Equatorial Africa exactly correspond to the picture drawn in the book. In order that 'Freeland' might be realised, nothing more is required than a sufficient number of vigorous men. Shall I be privileged to live until these men are found?

Theodor Hertzka: *Freeland: A Social Anticipation*

The old man was dying, the doctor had told her so when she met him in the lobby – dying, he said, but babbling of Africa. She drew the shades to shut out the dusk that was coming down over Central Park, and busied herself with the routines of her trade. Her patient would last the night but not the week, they had promised her that at the agency; he was very old. That was the sort of job she preferred. After the end, she would take a vacation, perhaps go to visit with her sister up in Maine – she'd call her tonight to tell them to expect her by Monday latest. And there'd be no problem with the overtime, to judge by the size of this apartment. She'd just check there was another TV in the kitchen – she didn't intend to miss the news now that Jack was in Saigon, there'd been footage last night of the Marines going into Da Nang. Milk in the icebox, yes, eggs, half a loaf, still fresh, and she'd brought a nice piece of liver for her supper. Plus coffee. She needed coffee these days. Later, she'd take one of those pills Madge had slipped her – keep you awake and not leave you with a hangover, she'd promised, and she was right as usual.

Is there family on the premises, she'd asked the agency, and they said no, no sign of kin. A housekeeper – Haitian – who comes in at nine every morning, been there for years but can't cope with the nursing side. So why isn't he in hospital? To judge from the address, he'd have no problem with the fees. Insists on dying at home, they told her – 'I've always had a preference for my own bed,' Mr Thomas had said while he was still lucid. 'Especially when it's a matter of *death*, you see.' He was a character, they said, no doubt of it, a cheerful old man despite the circumstances. But definitely mysterious. There was a background in property, they didn't know the detail, and apparently he'd had quite a reputation in this town after Prohibition, but who remembered that now? He was very old.

The doctors were being sensible and not trying to keep him going for the sake of the money. So it would be simple nursing, the caring kind – medication, injection, an oxygen cylinder if we need it, and, most important of all, a hand to hold if he gets lonesome in the night. Not too much pain, thank God, those were the jobs that switched her off. She began to wash him, combed his thin white hair; tomorrow she'd shave him. The day nurse had changed the bed-linen, and it would do for the next few hours. His face was frail as ancient parchment. That was the way it always was.

When she turned back to the bed, his eyes were open and he was gazing at her. She did not believe that he could see her, register her, but she said, 'Good evening, Mr Thomas, how are you today?' in her professional voice, and he said, in a clear tenor and in an accent that was mysterious to her, 'I've always remembered there were the clouds, you know. When I looked back at the sea, the sky was full of them – big fluffy clouds, that's all you can say about them really, big and fluffy...'

'Gee, that's a nice memory for you, isn't it?'

'They always used to say that in Africa the skies are the highest in the world, and I suppose, my dear, that that's right, but for me it was the clouds that counted...'

He paused, as if relishing the last images of a failing brain.

'I remember how Captain Dugmore – he will have passed on by now of course, especially if he stayed out in that climate – how he said to me one morning, "Mr Thomas" – he was always very *courteous* to me – "Mr Thomas, we can't leave them in Golbanti without at least checking that they are alive, can we now?" '

She thought, so this is going to be one of the talkers. Well, my girl, that's what you're paid for, and I only hope someone does the

286

same for you and Jack one day. So she sat down on the chair next to the bed.

'Now I knew, though I didn't say so, what was on the Captain's mind. I usually knew. He'd taken them off to Golbanti because he was real mad with Major Rogers. What we had here, I said to myself, was an old-fashioned case of guilty conscience.

'So off we went in a dhow. (Funny, I never liked those boats – I suppose I never felt absolutely *safe* in them.) The mosquitoes were something terrible, I remember. "We'll just pay a social call," said the Captain, to make a joke of it. He was always joking, the Captain was. Even when Major Rogers came up in conversation, though I was always very careful not to mention him.

'Golbanti, my dear, was a *mission* station...' – she suddenly realised that the old man was entirely aware that she was there, and was tailoring the story for her benefit as well as his – 'I forget whether they were Methodists or Baptists or Calvinistic Methodists – it doesn't really matter any more, does it? – but they'd all died a terrible death when those Muslims came down from the North. Or was it the Masai from the West? – I'm not as young as I was, I forget these things. That's why we had taken them there. To start a new life.

'Captain Dugmore got more and more impatient with the journey, I remember – he was shouting at his men, and telling me to put a good foot forward, and I could see that, although it was only a month or two since we'd dropped them off, he was worried.... Maybe he had an instinct, somewhere deep down in his soldier's soul. Me? Oh, *my* instinct had told me long ago what was going to happen, and I didn't tell anybody. What's the point, I ask you? They wouldn't have thanked me, and they wouldn't have had it any other way. I remember how the island hadn't wanted to know about our problems, there was a marriage going wrong – the weddings were so important in those days, and they weren't really interested in outsiders. I can remember it all to this day, how helpless we were.

'Well, I don't want to bore you, love, you've got better things to do than listen to the ramblings of a silly old man. To cut a long story short, we got to Golbanti in double-quick time and – nothing! The place was empty as a chapel on a weekday. The Captain gave a great shout, and rushed around in a state, and said to me, "They were here until recently," which I could see for myself, but they

287

weren't there any more. I didn't see it as my duty to point out that there was illness all over the house. If he couldn't see it, then why bother?

'What I did say – trying to be helpful, like, about the things that matter – was that they had left a trail. Even I could see it, through the river mud and into the bush, aiming inland, always west, and one of our boys was a genius at tracking, so all we had to do was follow and catch up with them, and then we could have our "social call". All of which I told the Captain, who said, "Well done, Felix!" – he only called me that when I was in his good books – and we charged off to the rescue like your US Cavalry...

'Now I don't want to delay you, and I've been over this in my head so many times that I don't relish this bit any more. But I promise you we found them within the hour. They can't have been there for long, because they were *undamaged*. By which I mean – no, you know how Africa is – they were lying in a sort of depression in the sand, under an enormous thorn tree and pretty close to an outcrop of rocks. It gave them a lovely patch of shade, though it wasn't as big as my tree at Shela. There was a breeze, so the flies weren't too bad. They were lying on their backs, like a happy married couple in a big wide bed, I remember thinking, because their hands were locked together. Captain Dugmore tried to separate their fingers, but they were – well, as I say, they were locked.... That's right. The Captain tried to separate their hands, but they were fastened so tight together that he gave up.

'The two of them were thin and pale, but they didn't *look* dead, if you see what I mean. Not yet. They didn't even look particularly sick. Just pale and thin and sleeping. The Captain had gone off for a little walk, I reckon he needed to *compose* himself. Then he came back and said something very gruff and strict about the boys going back to get spades.

'We buried them, my dear, as the sun was going down over Africa. I managed to remember some of the prayers from my chapel days, and the Captain asked me, very kindly, to speak them. I've always remembered that. We all stood, looking at the setting sun, and the boys had dug the grave facing the same direction, all westward, you see, and the African sky was the palest, purest blue over in the west, and it was the *quietest* moment of my life. You know, my dear, the point about Africa is that the skies are so

288

wonderful. But behind us – I never forgot it – when I looked back towards the ocean, towards the island in the east, towards that place called Lamu, those clouds were just like enormous mountains in the sky, piling higher and higher and higher from the sea...'

Postscript

Today, one hundred years on, the Freelanders are not remembered in Lamu. It is possible to make a confident guess at the location of 'Free House', and Major Rogers's IBEA Company building, after long service as the headquarters of the colonial administration, has become a handsome and excellent museum overlooking the main jetty. The Denhardts' house still has its battlements and is next door but one to the Post Office, just beyond the Fort. The mosques and the *muezzins* haven't changed much, except that some of them have benefited from Saudi money and have electrified the call to prayer. There is still vague talk of opening a route into Africa up the Tana River, and UN experts sometimes float the idea of a petrochemical plant on Manda Island.

Today, as the *muezzin* still sounds from the island's twenty-two mosques five times a day, the dhows still line the jetty and the *boriti* poles still lie soaking in the seawater where Jimmy Dunn drowned. The flag of Kenya is still lowered in a daily ceremony at sunset, but few of Major Rogers's successors follow his example and abstain from alcoholic liquor until the call to the evening prayer.

Major Rogers is also forgotten. His successors are Kenyan DCs, usually Kikuyu, who drive the island's only vehicle (because there is still no motor transport, no proper road: the donkeys and the dhows are still the only means of transport). The island – its beaches, its *shambas*, its unique Swahili architecture – is still very beautiful.

It therefore attracts tourists, in manageable numbers thanks to its remoteness. So in one sense European 'dropouts' still arrive, but Mabrukki's has vanished and now they drink Tusker beer in Petley's Bar on the waterfront. Shela beach is still one of the finest in Africa.

There is a good hotel in Shela, not far from Felix Thomas's thorn tree, and these days you can also have water-skiing and deep-sea fishing and chilled South African wines. The human bones from the battle of 1813 have vanished deep into the sand dunes by now, but the crabs still scuttle in and out of the tide. The beach is very long and empty, and visitors have been known to make love in the shaded privacy of the palm trees that fringe the high-water line. And every few years, you will read in the newspapers that a white man has been murdered on that same idyllic beach.

*

Of the historic characters who appear in this fiction:

Captain A. S. Rogers (I have promoted him) stayed on in Lamu until 1902; he became Sub-Commissioner of the Province of Tanaland on its formation in 1896, and eventually moved to Zanzibar as First Minister and also Regent for the Sultan. He retired in 1908.

Captain Dugmore became a District Commissioner in Uganda, where he fought with distinction in the 1897 Uprising. He died of fever in Mombasa in 1900.

Dr Theodor Hertzka candidly admitted the failure of his Utopian proposals, and died in Vienna in 1924. It is not clear whether Julius Wilhelm rejoined him. William Morris died in 1896, Edward Carpenter in 1929, Charles Ashbee in 1942, Eleanor Marx committed suicide in 1898.

Hans Salner, Emil Ducoffre and Reinhold Gleisering returned to Europe in July 1894 and vanished from sight.

Wilhelm Selling went south to Tanganyika and joined the German Colonial Service. Gustav Rabinek was last heard of in Tanga, where he had joined the German East Africa Rifles.

Goddfrey and Bosanquet applied for 500 acres of land in the Tana Valley. After winning a court dispute with Julius Wilhelm about the disposal of the funds obtained from selling the Freeland supplies, they eventually settled in Mashonaland (in today's Zimbabwe).

Herr Sasse stayed on in Lamu, where he became progressively deranged. At the last sighting he was reported to be living, with his grief, on board the *Eden*.

291

Buschel went to Rwanda, Riekh to Portuguese East Africa, Kaufman to the Transvaal.

Pier Scavenius, having returned to Denmark, later wrote a book about the expedition – *Frilands expeditionen dens tilblivelse* (1897). Not surprisingly, this description of the expedition is less than candid about certain aspects of the history of the Association, and is anti-British in tone. Alexander Stokkebye returned to his estates in Denmark.

Sheikh Sud bin Hamed continued as Liwali of Lamu until 1904, when he became insane and was deposed. His brother Sheikh Abdullah ruled again as Liwali.

The Denhardt brothers continued to live in Lamu. Some of their collection of Swahili textiles and artefacts may today be tracked down in various German museums.

Suleiman Kimenya, as we have seen, was hanged (by Rogers) in Witu in August 1894.

Of Martha and Dekker, Tom and Louise, and Felix? There is no record...

*

Two months after these events, between October and November 1894, the Somalis were repulsed and the Forest pacified. Fumo Bakari was exiled to Zanzibar, and a new administration was set up for Witu and district under the Sultanate of Zanzibar. Lamu became the capital of Tana Province.

In 1895, the British Government bought out the IBEA Company charter for £250,000, and declared an East African Protectorate (the Uganda Protectorate had been established in June 1894). Sir Arthur Hardinge, previously HM Consul in Zanzibar, became Commissioner for the British East Africa Protectorate.

In December 1895, the Sultan of Zanzibar agreed that the coastal strip be entrusted to British officers, appointed by London, who would have full powers of executive, judicial and fiscal administration; the Liwalis were to be accommodated within the British system.

In early 1895, Germany demanded the restoration of its Witu Sultanate. Hardinge in response appointed a Liwali to be the

292

'Sovereign Sultan of Witu', but Rogers, Sub-Commissioner for Tanaland, was additionally designated 'Resident' when dealing with Witu, which ensured his authority on the mainland.

In 1907, the status of slavery was abolished in Tanaland Province and compensation paid to slave owners; in the same year, the sovereign powers of the Witu Sultanate were significantly curtailed. After being governed as a separate part of British East Africa, the Sultanate of Witu was incorporated in 1921.

In 1963, Kenya became independent, and President Jomo Kenyatta, visiting Lamu Island, urged the women to unveil and to take their own freedom. His suggestion, made in a public speech in the 'stadium' on the edge of the mango *shambas*, was not appreciated by the older generation. It is said – I do not know if it is true – that even today there are still a few elderly retainers in Lamu's family mansions who are effectively slaves. But, on reflection, I'm sure that cannot be so.